All the Colours Above

All the Colours Above
Copyright © Amelia Grace 2021
Published in Australia, 2021
by Lilly Pilly Publishing
lillypillypublishing@outlook.com

All the Colours Above is the sequel to *The Colour of Broken* © Amelia Grace 2018

This is a work of fiction. Names, characters, places and incidents are products of the author's imagination or are used fictionally. Any resemblance to actual events, locales or persons, living or dead, is entirely coincidental.

https://www.nla.gov.au/trove
ISBN: 978-0-9923557-2-2 (print book)
ISBN: 978-0-9946205-8-3 (eBook)

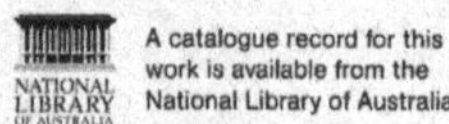

This book contains storylines with neuroscience, memory deletion and a cure for Meniere's disease. While the subjects have been heavily researched, the storyline is a product of the author's imagination.

This fictional book is sold with the understanding that the publisher and the author are not engaged to render any type of psychological, legal, or any other kind of professional advice. Neither the publisher nor the individual author shall be liable for any physical, psychological, emotional, damages. Our views and rights are the same: You are responsible for your own choices, actions, and results.

Content warning: physical assault (minimal)

The medical information in this book is not advice and should not be treated as such. Do not substitute this information for the medical advice of physicians. Always consult your doctor for your individual needs. Consult a physician for matters relating to your health and any symptoms that may require diagnosis or medical attention.

Cover design by Lilly Pilly Publishing
Cover image art: Shutterstock Image ID: 1929356861 Romolo Tavani
Jacaranda flower art: Creative Market: DioFlow
Moon art and dandelion wishes: © Julieann Wallace
Nanobot: Shutterstock Image ID: 023491761 Volodymyr Horbovyy
Starry Night: *Vincent van Gogh* - paying homage to *van Gogh* as a fellow Meniere's sufferer.

Dedicated to *Judy McNamara Tripp*
- Creator of *The Meniere's Awareness Project* -
Your dedication to raising awareness about
Meniere's disease is truly inspiring.
Thank you for the gift you sent me in 2018.
Opening it ignited the spark that started *All the Colours Above.*

To those with *Meniere's Disease* - this is my walk in life too.
I understand your daily struggle.
I understand how desperately you miss your life before Meniere's,
and I know how much energy and courage it takes to fake being well.

And to those who suffer from trauma -
physical, emotional, psychological, verbal, religious, cultural, social ...
Enough is enough!

Amelia Grace is the pen name of Julieann Wallace, a bestselling multi-published author whose *#8wordstory* was chosen by the Queensland Writers Centre to be featured on the back of their business cards in 2018.

Julieann resides in Australia, and was diagnosed with the incurable (for now) Meniere's disease in 1995. In her quest to defeat the disease (violent unpredictable vertigo, profound hearing loss, and relentless, impossibly loud tinnitus), she chose to have her balance cells destroyed in 2004 to stop the vertigo, relearning to walk again. In 2020, Julieann regained her hearing with the gift of a cochlear implant.

Prior to her career as a writer, Julieann was an educator with Education Queensland (Australia) for 25 years, and was nominated twice for the National Excellence in Teaching Awards. She now teaches in the Arts Faculty at a Secondary School, encouraging students to use the Arts to be change-makers and a voice for others through use of the power of written words and visual art.

Julieann is a self-confessed tea ninja, chocoholic, and papercut survivor, and tries not to scare her cat, Claude Monet, with her terrible cello playing.

All the Colours Above

Amelia Grace

Lilly Pilly
PUBLISHING

Chapter 1

Three words would have changed everything. From *him*. Tobiah. On that day that can't be *undone*. On that day of the wish that can't be *unwished* …

Just. Three. Words.

Chapter 2

I pushed my hand into the breast pocket of my white cotton dress. My love letter to Tobiah was still there, along with my wedding vows, even after climbing the lofty Jacaranda tree under the glittering sea of stars of the nightdom of the full moon. The *nightdom*. I had called it that since I was six, after I had fallen in love with the word "kingdom" during my beloved fairy tale phase.

I brushed my fingers over the textured, handmade paper in my pocket. I had written the letters the night he asked me to marry him, compelled to express how I felt so I would never forget the feeling of the saturation of his love potion; my heart blooming like a thousand red roses with the scent of old rose, with warm and heady notes, softened with a dash of sweetness, and surrounded by a meandering, dreamy, exhilarating love melody in my internal consciousness. I never wanted to forget how I felt on that day that couldn't be undone.

I inhaled deeply to quell the electric anxiety that skirted my skin. Tonight was the night. The full moon would be the witness to the sealing of our passion. Our love. That inexplicable emotion that could only be explained by chemistry. My *first* love. My first *lover*, soon to be. I loved him so deeply it thrilled and scared me in a complex elixir.

I sighed, then ran my hand over the rough trunk of my Jacaranda tree. *My* Jacaranda tree. The tree of my youth. As a neuroscientist, I was *everything* about measurable data. Yet, love was so elusive. It could not be measured, and the neural "signatures" of love could not give us a correct, or even a complete picture. Findings could not even be replicated.

Love. It could only be felt.

I blew out my anxiety through my pursed lips. Was Tobiah my happily ever after, if that even existed? And what if, love hurts like they say? If we … Tobiah and I … made love … would our relationship change? Would we fall out of love because the most intimate physical connection of love had been achieved and conquered? And if we fell out of love, or if *he* falls out of love, where does that leave me?

Anxiety rumbled through me like an elephant stampede. I closed my eyes and shook my head. Maybe tonight wasn't the night. Maybe it would be better for us to wait for marriage like I always intended to do; to give my husband my purity as a gift, instead of it being something he took with him as a single man, if he left me. I would feel like a used woman then. Tarnished. Physically and emotionally. I didn't want to have to deal with the aftermath of that regrettable emotional baggage.

And I didn't want to be that girl who had slept with a hundred men in her search for "the one". Her supposed "soulmate". I didn't want to be that girl who carried memories and mistakes and heart-scars of regret that felt like daggers twisting in flesh, like an emptiness trying to be filled with physical love without heart and mind love. Desperation and lust. Destruction of the soul. It would be for my soul. I know we are all different with what we allow and don't allow. What we want and don't want. I had to stay true to me.

Uuggh! Why are relationships so complicated? Why did the first time I fell in love leave me in such turmoil? What if our love is to death do us part? What if he is my "soulmate", if that really and truly exists?

Was I overthinking, again? Of course I was overthinking. I always did it. There was no such thing as a "soulmate". The concept came from an ancient tale of Aristophanes, and the word first recorded in 1822 by English poet, *Samuel Taylor Coleridge*, in a letter. It was all so mythical and fantastical. It was all desires and longings of the heart for acceptance, to be loved by another. I preferred the term of "well-suited partner".

I lifted my face to catch the magical moonbeams and smiled. The full moon was the sign for our secret rendezvous at the Jacaranda tree. Ever since we reconnected at the park of our youth a year ago, we met once a month, on the full moon. Every twenty-nine and half days to be exact. It was light enough to see, but dark enough to cloak our presence. No one could possibly know we were here once a month. Together. Alone.

'Hey.'

I smiled at the sound of Tobi's voice, warm like liquid chocolate on this Midsummer's Eve. Something fluttered in my stomach, and an echo of desire filled, me making me wish we were already naked. I looked down to the base of the tree.

There was the love of my life. My husband to be. Dressed in his fitting white t-shirt, accentuating his wide shoulders and broad chest, and his casual blue shorts that reminded me of lazy beach Sundays relaxing under endless blue skies with the sound of the crooning ocean. Yes. I was ready for the most physically intimate act two people could share.

Our eyes connected, dark in this early night hour of the nightdom, but light enough to see. A dimple on his cheek grew deeper, and my cheeks warmed.

'Hey,' I said, my heart accelerating. He was standing in the very place I planned to get naked with him. Where I planned to give my body to him. Sex. Would it be as mind blowing as the movies made it out to be?

'Hello!' A high voice clambered up the tree trunk like a weed.

My heart stopped. It was a girl. A woman. Wearing a loosely buttoned white blouse and short white denim shorts. My smile slid off my face like melting wax. *He* had brought a woman to *our* tree! He had broken Rule Number 6!

She moved closer to him and put her hand on his shoulder, like he was hers.

'Hi,' I squeaked, anxiety scorching my skin.

Tobi started to climb *our* tree, looking down as the woman climbed after him. Halfway up, as she struggled to navigate the dorky limbs of the Jacaranda tree, he offered his hand to her. And she took it. Like they had done this a million times before. My chest burned and nausea gathered like a lead ball in my stomach.

Tobi sat on a branch opposite me. I looked at him with a quiver of anxiety and fear of the unknown, of confusion about what was going on, and tried to soak in the image of his dark wavy hair parted on the side, his broad forehead, strong cheekbones and angular jaw, in case my future hopes and dreams were stolen from me like an attack from a fire breathing dragon.

I waited in anticipation for his sweet kiss, like he always gave me, but instead of gazing tenderly at me, he focussed on the woman, who sat precariously beside him. His eyes were on her like a protective lover, and when she found her steadiness on the branch, she looked at Tobi and smiled, her eyes twinkling, trying to pull him closer to her. Tobi smiled back, and jealousy hit me like a poisoned arrow flying through the nightdom in a hail of chaotic music notes full of rage and negative energy ready to fight.

He turned his face to me. 'Indi, this is Willow,' he said with caution, scratching the stubble on his face. Was he expecting me to be all friendly and lovely about a new person in *our* tree; a tree for two; a tree that was officially declared as our tree seven months ago? And a woman? He had just broken our rule of *exclusiveness*. What was he doing?

'Willow,' I said, looking at her, leaving the final "w" lingering in the air like an annoying echo. 'What brings you scaling the limbs of an innocent Jacaranda tree in the moonshine at this hour of nightdom?' I grinned at her and raised an eyebrow, wondering where those smoothly delivered, uncharacteristic words had come from, inherently knowing it was from me trying to suffocate the panic inside of me.

'Tobiah.' She smiled at me and placed her hand on his thigh.

Tobi looked down at her hand, but didn't remove it.

I cleared my throat as my skin burned. 'That was nice of … *Tobiah*. Is it the first time you have climbed a tree?' *Nobody called him Tobiah out loud. Ever. People knew him as Tobi.*

'No. I was a tree climber when I was young.'

'So, you feel safe up here?' I wanted her to take her hand off Tobi's thigh. Now.

'Absolutely.' Her hand was still there, claiming a stake on something that was mine.

'Good. So back to the original question—what brings you scaling the limbs of an innocent Jacaranda tree in the moonshine at this hour of nightdom, besides *Tobiah* making you tag along?'

Her beautiful face hardened, and she narrowed her eyes at me, ugliness seeping through her mask of perfection. 'He didn't *make* me tag along. He said he wanted to show me an amazing tree on its own island. I didn't know *you* would be here.' She raised an eyebrow at me.

I smiled to myself at her barb, then looked at Tobi and swallowed the lump in my throat. The fire of deception flushed through every cell of my body. I took a slow, deep breath, while a thousand questions flicked through my mind, and a thousand more captured a scene of the two of them together, as lovers. My body tensed, fight or flight possessing me like a raging inferno. There was only one thing I could do. 'Then, I shall go and leave you to enjoy the tree together, just the two of you.' I connected my eyes to Tobi's, reached into my breast pocket, pulled out my two treasured letters of love and devotion and threw them at him. As they floated to the ground like the side-to-side motion of a conductor's baton, I placed my hands on the branch on either side of me, and shuffled towards the trunk of the Jacaranda tree to escape. *My* Jacaranda tree.

My heart was aching. Breaking. Darkness seeped into it and blanketed its light of trust and love for Tobiah.

Betrayal.

My Tobiah. *Our* tree. Just *us.* There was now an ugly memory imprinted onto the tree that I did not want, blemishing its composition, based on love. *Our* love.

'Stop, Indi!' Tobi's firm voice cracked. 'It's not what you think.'

It's not what you think, bounced around in my mind in a melody of out of tune black piano notes. I snapped my head towards him. He ran a hand over his contorted face. 'I wanted Willow to meet you, and this is the only place where I thought it was safe.'

'Ah—the story starts to unfold,' I said with bitter sarcasm. I laughed. Loudly. 'You thought it would be safe, this high up in a tree?' *Bizarre.* 'How?'

'There's no one here to see you … meeting … talking.'

'But *Tobiah*, not a skerrick of that makes any sense … why did you not tell her I would be here?'

'Because … I thought she wouldn't come.'

Willow looked at Tobi and raised an eyebrow at him. The shimmering blueness of her eyes glowed, caught in the beams of the full moon. Her long, dark, wavy hair fell over her shoulders and her full breasts making her look like she was a goddess, dressed in her white clothing of pureness. She gathered some strands of hair in her hand and twisted them around her finger while still holding onto Tobi's thigh with the other hand, keeping her balance. She dropped the twisted hair and narrowed her eyes at him. 'I'm perfectly capable of making my own decisions. And you're right. If I had known that *she* was going to be here, I wouldn't have come.' Willow's words spat letters of anger.

I raised my eyebrows at Tobi, waiting for his next comment. He was in deep, insufferable trouble with not one woman, but two.

'Look … I want you to be friends.' His voice calmed; his brows furrowed. 'Willow knows this amazing stuff about the stuff you know about and I thought, I thought …' Tobi looked down and shook his head, defeated. 'And … Willow is new to Tarrin.'

My body tensed as anger built inside me. 'Tobi, firstly, you know nothing about the depth, the width, nor the breadth of my knowledge of my job, and don't ever think you do. Secondly, how can introducing us in a treetop be safe?' I raised my eyebrows at him.

Tobi's jaw flexed as he clenched his teeth.

I poised my next my question at Willow. 'How … did you meet?'

Willow face softened and she smiled at me, her eyes becoming daytime dreamy, like she had the most wonderful life. 'At the bar. Tobiah saved me from some men.'

Tobi flicked his head toward her. His eyes were wide.

'And how did he do that?'

'He pretended he was my boyfriend.' She connected her eyes to his and smiled at him. 'There's not many men who are courageous enough to stand up for a woman,' she added. 'I am so thankful. He's one of a kind. A keeper.' She moved her hand higher up on Tobi's thigh.

I smiled at her despite the painful tightness in my throat. I looked at Tobi. His face was flushed. In my mind, he saved a damsel in distress, then brought her along as his prize. Is he trying to hurt me? If he is, he's succeeding.

I tried to speak, but the words queued up in my throat and were sucked into the void as I struggled to breath. The second time I opened my mouth, they floated out with a sharp, cutting intent at Tobi. I wanted to hear his version of the story. 'Tell me how you met, *Tob*—no don't bother. I've heard enough.' I dragged my hand over my face wanting this entire moment to vanish. I needed to jump out of the tree and run.

'Do you want to know the best part of our meeting, Indi?' Willow said, like adding kindling to the fire that was raging inside me.

'Somehow, I know you're going to tell me whether I want to hear it or not.' I kept my watery eyes connected to Tobi's.

'He has the most beautiful lips.'

Tobi blinked and shook his head slightly.

'And I *wished* that he would place them against mine, and he did, and then he—'

'You know what. I'm done.' My words flew from my mouth in forte. 'Tobi, we're do—'

'She's lying!' Tobi said, his voice low. He pressed his lips together and swallowed.

'Is she?' I asked, my voice becoming softer, like a musical diminuendo.

Willow ran her hand along her neck and over her chest. 'You know how Tobiah's hands feel when he—'

'Stop, Willow!' Tobi growled under his breath.

'Tobiah brought me here to tell you he doesn't wa—'

I covered my ears. Her words were like red, raw agony, like someone had reached inside to my heart and ripped it in two.

'I wish … I wish you'd fall out of the tree and die!' The shouted words exploded from my lips with malice, and within the next breath, she'd disappeared from the branch of the tree.

The thud of her body hitting the ground below made me wince, and at once, my veins filled with the burning of panic, like acid, my blood pounding in my ears.

I held my breath and looked at Tobi; his eyes were wide. Like mine. He had stopped breathing. Like me. I didn't want to look down to where I had heard the sickening thud, and a sigh, like a final breath.

I started to tremble. I watched Tobi's Adam's apple rise up, then down. I swallowed in the same manner as he did, with a gulp of disbelief. His arms and legs jerked as he started to move to descend the tree. Our beloved Jacaranda tree. I held a hand over my mouth, waiting. Waiting for a sound. Waiting for something. Anything.

A bluebird chirped. Once. Twice.

'Indi. Come.' Two simple whispered words came from Tobi's mouth that were about the change everything. Forever. Like the entire landscape would be sucked into a hole and blanketed in darkness. Like music ceased to exist and we were left with the ugliness of angry human voices.

I swallowed, and willed my body to move. Then I hugged our tree of secrets, branch by branch, trying to lock away this one event forever. If I wished for something to happen, could I unwish the wish and reverse time? Could I unwish the fact that I had met Tobi in the first place?

I continued my slow, regrettable descent to the place I never wanted to be. I wished myself in a different place. A different time.

But that wish didn't happen.

Tobi knelt by Willow's side. 'Look—but don't touch!' His voice blew into the air like it was an imposition to be there, like he didn't have permission to speak. 'No fingerprints.'

My heart raced. A thousand thoughts passed through my mind in a nanosecond—a thousand "what-ifs". I felt blood drain from my face.

'She looks—' Nausea threatened to materialize. I pursed my lips and blew a long, controlled breath between them, 'Dead.' I spluttered over the word. Bile rose in my throat and I started to sweat. Panic warmed my blood until it felt like fire was running through my veins. 'Tob—'

Tobi placed his finger over my trembling lips to stop my words. 'Stay with her. I'll get help.'

I flicked a tear from my face and sucked in a deep breath while my bones gave an interior rattle. I gave a quick nod.

Tobi stood. Even in this light I could see the look of hatred in his eyes as his looked down at me; his pupils piercing, boring through to my core, dipped in the poison of revulsion. I was a despicable human being.

The earth shuddered beneath me as he walked away. I just lost the person I loved the most in the entire world. The friend I held dearest and closest. The one who I wanted to spend the rest of my life with.

I lowered my head and winced in pain at every crunch of stone under Tobi's footfall as he walked to the water's edge. I jumped at the touch of a splash of cold water after Tobi had stepped into the water then jumped into the rowboat; like acid had spilled onto my skin.

I held my breath until I could no longer hear the oars entering the water with each stroke, and rocked myself back and forth with silent sobs that shook my body.

'I'm sorry,' I whispered after a while. 'This was never meant to happen.' I tugged Willow's hair in the hope she would wake from the sleep of death. But she didn't stir.

I walked over to the safety of the Jacaranda tree, *my* Jacaranda tree, wanting it to wrap its branches around me so I could dissolve into it.

'I wish … I wish you were undead,' I said, pushing the words to Willow, imagining my voice entering her ears and weaving their way to her mind to wake her up as if she were Sleeping Beauty, then travelling to her heart to give it a defibrillator shock to restart her heart.

If I could wish her dead, could I wish her undead?

I wrapped my shaking arms around myself, desperate for some sort of comfort. Then darkness fell as clouds clothed the full moon. I was glad. Hiding in the darkness. Unseen.

The clouds departed and the moon beamed, sending a sharp glint of light from beside her body to my eye. I walked over and crouched beside her. Just beyond the reach of her hand was a diamond-studded, gold object. A pocket-watch perhaps? I picked it up and pressed on the knob. It flipped open and it shot me a bright moonbeam, blinding me, highlighting me as if to say: *"Here is the murderer!"*. I stopped the light with my trembling hand and inspected the object, expecting to see miniature clock hands stopped at the time of her death, but discovered two mirrors instead. It was a compact. I closed it with a faint click and placed it back to where I found it.

I turned my head to the side and squeezed my eyes shut, then cursed under my breath. *Fingerprints*. Now my fingerprints were all over it. The police would know I was involved. I would be held accountable. And I should be, shouldn't I? I did set the wish free into the darkness of night.

'I'm sorry,' I whispered again, reached out and picked up the compact and dropped it into my breast pocket where the love letters had been, and buttoned it up. Evidence taken care of.

I stood and looked around, feeling like I was being watched. But I was alone. With Willow. Or her body, I should say. I covered my face and shook my head. This couldn't be happening.

This shouldn't be happening. It should be just Tobi and me, here, naked and wrapped in each other with declarations of undying love, joined as one.

I let out a silent scream then escaped to the other side of Jacaranda Island. It had been over an hour since Tobi had left to get help. I dived into the water and swam, my arms in a flurry of movement like a thrashing fish trying to escape its deadly end.

I stopped. My boat. I swam back to the island, ran past Willow's body and to the dark blue, borrowed gentleman's rowboat, pushed it from the shallows, jumped in and rowed, aiming to make the strokes of the oars as silent as possible.

The moment I hit the stony shore of the mainland, I jumped out and ran across the stones with the intent to disappear into the night. I would be home soon. Safe. But I stopped. *The boat. Fingerprints. Evidence.* My heartbeat thumped. I retraced my steps and stopped before the boat. I had to get rid of it.

I pushed it off the shore, leaped in and just floated on the lake, numb to my core. Where was Tobi? He should have been back by now.

I grabbed the oars and rowed, the water barely registering the entry and exit of each stroke. I had to make sure I didn't attract any attention. I steered away from Jacaranda Island and stopped at about the length of a football field away, so I could still see the mainland and Jacaranda Island.

And there I sat. Waiting. Watching. Praying for the return of Tobi. He said he had gone to get help. I trusted him.

But he didn't return, even after two and a half hours. I swallowed my internal tears filled with gut wrenching screams of panic. I needed to look after me now. But first, I had to make the boat disappear.

'I'm sorry,' I whispered, hoping the words would somehow enter the dreams of the boat owner who lived across the way. I grabbed an oar and thumped it into the side plank until it cracked and opened, then focussed on a bottom board and stabbed the oar into it until water seeped in and the boat started to fill with water and sink.

I abandoned the boat. *The evidence.* And side stroked my way back to the stony shore of my childhood, surrounded by a heralding calmness I hoped didn't precede the worst storm of my life.

When I reached the shoreline, I stood and faced the Jacaranda tree. The purple blooms still glowed in the moonshine at this hour of the nightdom as a gentle breeze blew like nothing had ever happened. I focussed my gaze for any movement. I didn't want Willow to be dead.

I captured my breath and stared at the tree where my love for Tobi blossomed, fertilised by his essence. It swayed with an ominous rebuke. 'Til death do us part. But whose death? Of a person, or of love?

I picked up a white stone and pegged it as hard as I could, hoping to hit Willow, lying motionless on the other side of the island under the tree, the shock of the impact waking her from unconsciousness. I didn't want her to be dead. I didn't mean the wish of death that had escaped my thoughts and materialised as words in my mouth and expelled, then seized by the grim reaper.

I turned and ran to my car, unbuttoned my lower dress pocket, pulled out my keys and disappeared into my safe escape from the scene. I drove the roads of Tarrin to my apartment, meticulously obeying every road rule ever invented so as to not draw attention to myself, lest I be pulled over by the cops. I drove, wishing that in the morning when I woke, I would discover that none of this had ever happened.

That was my wish. *My only wish …*

Chapter 3

Tobi stood at the fire pit in the park of our youth on the nightdom after the incident, clothed in the colours of death, hiding his presence. His hands were tucked into his pockets, and his shoulders looked as though they were in a permanent shrug. He turned his hooded head toward me as I approached. I stopped at the fire pit opposite him, fuming—he didn't return to help me with the body. He didn't call. He didn't answer any of my texts. But he *must* have read them, because he was here. On time.

'Where were you? I waited for you, and you didn't come back!' I spat.

'I … I couldn't get away.'

I scowled. 'There was something more important than returning for a body?' My voice was almost an octave higher than I intended it to be.

'Yes.' His low voice lingered on the "s".

'Yes?'

'Work. I—'

'That was more important?'

'In this case, yes. Willow was already dead. I can't change that. But at work, I could save a life. It had priority.'

I looked over at the Jacaranda tree resigned to the fact that he was right. 'We'd better go and retrie—' I hunched over with the urge to vomit. I worked with bodiless living brains, yet the thought of a dead body sent me into a vertiginous tailspin. By the time I centred myself, Tobi was walking to the water's edge. I stood taller and followed.

He turned to me, 'Where's your boat?'

I stopped before him. 'I got rid of it. You know. Evidence.'

Tobi pushed the hood off his head and ran a hand through his dark hair and frowned at me. He closed his eyes and nodded. 'Right. Time to borrow another boat, then.' He looked downstream and started walking, stopping fifty metres away, jumped in a boat and paddled towards me.

He held his hand out to me as he came closer. I placed my hand into his, and my other hand onto the side of the boat and clambered aboard, and kneeled on the other side of Tobi. I leaned over the side and pushed my hand through the water, like he did.

The bottom of the boat scraped the shallows of Jacaranda Island within ten minutes. I got out and followed Tobi to where Willow lay.

Except, there was no body.

My heart thumped and panic ran through my veins like hot poison. 'She's gone!' I whispered, and looked at Tobi.

He lowered his head, brushed a hand over his mouth then rubbed the back of his neck.

'She was dead, right?'

'Absolutely! No doubt.' Tobi let out an exasperated breath and paced. 'We pretend it never happened. We deny all knowledge of the event.' His words were fast. He stopped pacing and looked out over the water, and then back to the place where we last saw the body.

Agitated, I looked around in the muted light of the night after the full moon. There was no evidence of movement on the grass. No footsteps, nor dragging marks in the sand before the water. How does a dead person—a lifeless body—disappear like that? Without a trace?

Tobi grabbed my arm and I winced as he pulled me towards the lake. 'Get in the boat!' His words were rough.

I climbed in, as Tobi did the same, and we left Jacaranda Island—the island that never used to be. I looked over my shoulder at it while I paddled in time with Tobi. What was once a beautiful island full of light and love was now stained with bitter darkness and death. And now, a secret.

When the bottom of the boat scraped the shallows of the mainland, Tobi jumped out and pulled the hood over his head. I followed him back to the fire pit of our youth.

'Deny ever seeing Willow. Get an alibi together. You don't know me, and I don't know you.' He closed his eyes and lowered his head, turning it slightly to the right. After a moment he raised his head. 'I have to go.' He ran into the darkness.

The township bell of Tarrin sounded a minute later. Followed by shrieking sirens that swallowed the presence of the one I loved.

A moment later, a notification sounded on my phone:

The kissing forest. On the night of the new moon.
9pm

Chapter 4

I sat at the park beside the fire pit where I met Tobi last night, leaving in a state of intense panic and confusion. I fixed my gaze on Jacaranda Island. Where did Willow's body go? I sucked in a deep breath, and brushed a strand of my golden-honey wavy hair from my face, my hand with an uncontrollable tremor. I watched all the sunset colours of above shift, as the second sky—the nightdom—descended to kiss the horizon of the earth, like nothing important had happened.

With an increasing need to hide my guilt, I scrambled down to the kissing forest of my youth and sat amongst the trees that offered their canopy of invisibility. With my fingers still shaking, I pushed the button on the classic, diamond-studded, gold compact. Not mine. Stolen. By me. On the night of Midsummer's Eve when time stood still and all the colours above vanished, vacuumed into a witness jar and sealed and marked to be released on the day of truth.

The compact flipped open.

There were two mirrors. *Mirror, mirror.*

I gazed into the left mirror. My reflection was smaller, like a distant me of the past. I frowned, then looked into the right mirror. My reflection was magnified, like the me, now. In the present. A tingle ran down my spine. The me of the past, and the me now.

I turned my attention back to the left mirror. The me of the past, when, once upon a time I wasn't in the habit of falling in love. When, once upon a time I wasn't one of those girls who gushed and swooned and hyperventilated at the sight of a man. No matter how beautiful he was. Or how talented he was. Or how soulful his singing was. Or how athletic he was. Or how intellectually gifted he was. But maybe, just maybe, the male species reading a book does make him kind of look … interesting.

A bluebird chirped—once, twice—and I looked up, searching for it, without success. Was it the same bird that had chirped at the time of Willow's death? Like an announcement. Did it know of the secret of the full moon and the Jacaranda tree on Midsummer's Eve, never to be forgotten?

Disappointed, I returned my gaze to the Jacaranda tree, isolated from the world, trapped by a lake that never used to be, then looked back into the mirror at the reflection of the me of the past. Once upon a time, I wasn't one of those women who were in love with being in love, leaving a trail of boyfriends behind in the pursuit of that hypnotic, transcendent, euphoric feeling of love.

Once upon a time, I was happy. By myself. Alone. Living a life with a melody of hope and optimism and peace. No one else to please. No one to disappoint. The *quintessential* life.

I inhaled shakily and shook my head. Once upon a time, I thought love was overrated. Too complicated. I had watched too many friends keep the peace with the one they loved, at their expense, running to me with mascara running down their faces like a creation of emo art with a melody of grief and restlessness trailing after them.

Once upon a time, I absolutely did not want that crippling, disorderly distraction of being in love with someone, added onto the complexities of my life-changing research. Ever.

And the thought of locking lips with another—creating a gentle suction and exchanging saliva and the 700 species of deadly micro-organisms, microbes including germs, billions of bacteria, fungus, and other unknowns in an intimate act, didn't interest me.

No. Once upon a time, I most definitely was not in the habit of falling in love. Nor did my heart have the room to fill every space with a saturation of the love potion, clouding my mind, my thoughts, changing my behaviour and interfering with my important, classified research.

I lifted my eyes to all the colours of above, and then lower, to the Jacaranda tree. The moon threw its misty light beams through the canopy, the purple hues glowing with moonshine so they were the colour of blue, like blueberries in the magical, almost time of nightdom.

The colour of indigo.

The colour of me. Indigo Feather Danube.

I closed my eyes and placed my hand over my breaking heart. I wasn't in the habit of falling in love until, love's spell had undone me. Me—Indigo Feather Danube—a neuroscientist, studying the most complex object in the universe, mapping regions of the brain that stored memories and researching how to access them, digitally. Yet, once upon a time, just the thought of *him* made my heart race and skip a beat—it made me feel all kinds of warm and soft and—it made me feel … like I was intoxicated.

I looked back at the compact. *Mirror, mirror.* Two mirrors. The me of the past, and the me now. I felt like I was in a state of suspended animation. Eternally confused. Inconceivably betrayed. Guilty. My life was in a clash of psychedelic colour on steroids colliding with a cosmic boom inside of me trying to make sense of the catastrophic chaos. Of the event. Of the mess. Of the … what on earth had happened?

And furthermore … where did my relationship with Tobi stand? Was it still an *us*, or just a *me*? Was this just a complication we had to work through?

Somehow, it felt like we were broken.

When the long shadows of the trees faded with the last rays of the sun of the daydom, replaced by the intermingling darkness of trunks and branches filled with soul crying laments of my deep sorrow and lostness, I left. There were two weeks until the darkness of the new moon to meet Tobi again. And those two weeks would be filled with intense research at the Brain and Mind Institute where I could dissolve into my world of research and experiments and data analysis, and the event of Midsummer's Eve would be obliterated.

Out of sight. Out of mind.

Chapter 5

Tobi paced to and fro. The rhythmic crushing of dry leaves and branches underfoot created a sharp crack like the sound of bones being snapped. I shivered. Goose bumps formed on my skin, but not from the coolness of the first month of fall—the autumndom.

A bluebird chirped. Once. Twice.

I hesitated before I stepped out from the shadows of the kissing forest of our youth, and pulled the black hood off my head. 'Your paranoia is unsettling.'

He removed his hands from the pockets of his black jeans, placed them behind his neck and winced. 'You're late.'

'I'm late?' I said, my voice rising with annoyance. 'I arrived at the exact time you appointed, 9pm on the new moon! Then watched you pace like a person with psychomotor agitation for one minute, wondering whether it was safe for me to be here.'

He stilled and ran a hand over his face, his stylish stubble now a grumpy beard. 'What happened to us?' His voice cracked.

'I gave up on us when you were no longer here.'

'I was always here,' he whispered.

'In body, yes. But not in mind. It's been three months since you spoke to me at the fire pit. THREE MONTHS! Delaying our meeting since—'

'I wish—' he said, lingering on the "sh".

'Don't say it—' I swallowed the thought of the word wish. It left a sour taste in my mouth after the night of the incident.

'I wish you had never—'

'I wish you had never invited *her* to our tree!' I cut in with aggression. 'It was *our* tree! For us only, not to be shared with anyone else. Rule Number 6! Look what *you* did?'

'Look what *I* did? Seriously?' He shook his head, disappointment dripped from his words like melting candle wax. '*You* … made her fall out of the tree!"

'I didn't touch her!'

'It was your words. What is said, cannot be unsaid!' His voice was painted with the colours of disgust, leaving a screech of vile tinnitus in my ears. He turned away from me.

My body tensed and I held my head higher. 'I. Didn't. Touch. Her!'

'But it was enough!' His words were sharp, enunciated with perfection to cut into my heart.

'I didn't touch her …' I whispered and tried to stop the tear. I failed. 'What if it was *you*? After all, she looked at *you* before she—' I couldn't say anymore. Nausea rose and swirled at the visualisation of the incident that night. I cut out of my mind vision before the sound of the sickening thud occurred.

He turned his head away and cursed. I stepped closer to him so I could see his eyes. Those ocean-blue eyes I used to love. His scent of sweetness and spice flowed around me, trying to heal my "you-broke-my-heart" scars. I placed my hand over his heart. The heart I used to love.

He looked down and covered my hand with his. His hand

that used to send a tingle down my spine at his touch, now absent.

We were broken, like a deeply distressing sound belted out on an out-of-tune piano. My heart twisted.

He let out a slow, breathy sigh and connected his eyes to mine—the eyes that I knew with fine detail, dark at this time of the nightdom.

'I can't see you anymore,' I said, my heart starting to ache.

He blinked at me. Once. Then closed his eyes. 'We could move. We could start again. We could leave the past behind.' His heart thumped hard. I could feel it against his chest.

I shook my head. 'You can't leave memories behind. You can't forget—' I stopped talking and sucked in a sharp breath. Of course we could leave memories behind—my research—at the Brain and Mind Institute. But … in our case, was it lying?

We didn't choose for the incident to happen, but it had.

Could we reinvent ourselves?

Could I fall in love with him all over again, without the weight of guilt of the scene that had happened, pressing down on me so hard it was asphyxiating?

I sucked in a silent calming breath as I filled with the spark of hope, thinking of the possibility of a future with the only man I once loved, and still loved, if I was honest with myself. 'There's this research I've been working on.' My speech was fast.

He placed a warm hand on my cheek and his face softened.

'We could do a reset … you and me … we could—'

'We could what? What are you implying?' he said.

'There's this brain.' I shook my head. I couldn't tell him any of the details. 'Well, there's many brains, but, we …' I couldn't say anymore. I had already told him too much. I paused and placed a hand on his shoulder. 'I have the knowledge. I have the skill. We can start over. We just need to keep *one* shared memory of us that will be the same—' I stopped talking and watched for his reaction.

He lifted his eyes to the tree canopy and brushed his fingers over his beautiful face. I dropped my hand from his shoulder as he started walking to the left of the tree.

Was he leaving? Was this it? The end?

Had I told him too much and it scared him?

He disappeared, then re-appeared on the other side of the tree and stopped in front of me. 'Let's choose our last memory together … the one to keep,' he said, his voice low, laced with the quiver of anxiety.

He looked down to my hand and threaded his fingers through mine like he was locking us together, forever. 'The one that will bind us for earth time. The one that will become our light in the darkness. The one that drives us back to each other, no matter what happens, no matter where we are … until we meet again, and our fates are sealed as they were meant to be.' His words were more confident now, whispered and warm, each syllable singing its way inside my ear and to my core, blooming in my chest. Heat rushed to my cheeks.

Thunder rumbled in the distance, pulling me from the moment and from his intoxicating presence.

The scent of petrichor blew in on the breeze. I shivered. But not from the cold. From what we were about to do.

Totally illegal.

Totally unethical.

He removed his fingers from mine, tucked his hands into his pockets and paced to and fro, leaves crunching underfoot once more. I watched him with patience, wondering how the revelation that I could reset him would affect him. Anxiety burned a path over my skin.

He stopped before me. 'How do you do a reset?'

I should have expected this question. I paused, trying to find the right words without too much detail of my classified research. 'It's … specific memory removal.' In the darkness, I could see a frown blemish his beautiful face.

I stretched my fingers out, then relaxed them, trying to rid the profusion of unease from my body. I looked up at the tree, at all the monochromatic gray colours of above, then down to the lowest charcoal coloured branch, took a step forward, and climbed to a sturdy limb to sit on.

I breathed in the distance between us, relieved to be away from his intensity as he considered my proposal.

I looked down. Tobi shuffled from foot to foot, and the harsh staccato sound of crunching dead leaves bounced up the tree trunk, became caught in the canopy of living leaves, then fell back to the ground where it had come from, rejected. I watched as Tobi hugged the tree, then placed a foot on a small branch before he climbed upward at the speed of a sloth. I shook my head.

He settled beside me, taking an excruciatingly painful amount of time to find his balance on the tree limb. I turned on my phone light so he could find his bearings more quickly, and at once, our surroundings exploded in a symphony of colour in shades of browns and greys and greens.

When he settled, he looked up at me and connected his eyes to mine. And there they were, in full colour from the phone light—the eyes that I loved. Ocean-blue. Almost luminous.

His lips parted like he was searching for the right words, and after a moment he said, 'Is it painful? Will I still know who I am once you have removed the memories, once you have done the reset? Will I still feel like me? Will I be confused, like a part of me is missing, you know, like when people have amnesia after a brain trauma. Will I know that some memory is gone … and if I do, will I continue searching for it, discontent with my life until I find the missing piece?' His eyes darted around in a panic, then slowed and transfixed on mine, his pupils large, trying to steal light from my knowledge to find answers deep within me.

Answers he had no permission to access.

I blew a slow breath between my pursed lips. The truth was, I didn't know all the answers to his questions. The research wasn't definitive yet. We were still in investigation and trial mode.

'It's not painful, and yes, you will still know who you are. It's just a small memory in the timeline of your life, like a blink,' I lied. Thunder rumbled, resembling the restlessness of my state of mind.

He gazed deeply into my eyes, lighting up a part of my heart, trying to ignite that once eternal flame. I wanted to disconnect and look away, but I didn't. My mind was exploding in a multitude of "what ifs", and "would he go through with it?" If he did, then I would also have to delete my memory of that fateful night.

Could I do it?

He looked away from our intimate light and to the beyond, into the inky nothingness that surrounded us. The darkness of the new moon never disappointed with its cloak of secrecy.

'Let's make a new last memory,' he said. He connected his eyes to mine once again. 'One not associated with anything that has happened … and, we should create new names for our new identities so we can't be found.' His voice was scratchy, laced with the gnarly roots of nervousness.

I looked over at the Jacaranda tree, sitting on its own little island. I could just see its silhouette from where we sat. It was shrouded in the sombre greys and eerie charcoals of the nightdom. *My* Jacaranda tree. My once beautiful Jacaranda tree.

A car horn sounded and I turned off my phone light. Headlights beamed towards my Jacaranda tree illuminating it like it was in a police line-up, revealing its browns and greens and jacaranda blues, ready to be identified as a suspect for a witness to a crime. My heart saddened. The Jacaranda tree wasn't to blame for the unpredictable, terrifying incident. I pushed heartfelt healing vibes towards it, watching as the last blooms fell, gently like snow, creating a magical illuminated lavender-coloured carpet at its base. In an instant, it reminded me of the taste of strawberries and cream of spring, when life was uncomplicated. Carefree. Happy. I wished we could sit on that magic carpet. I wished we could command it to lift us into the nightdom and take us away. Far, far away.

I *wish* ...

Dread filled me like a dark, heavy cloud, threatening to release a bolt of electricity with the intent to kill. My Jacaranda tree was filled with childhood memories, mischief as a teenager, and love as an adult. How could I erase even the most minuscule part my Jacaranda tree and its blooms of memories from my life?

Thunder sounded. Louder this time. I took a courageous breath. 'Yes ... we should create new names,' I said. A tear dropped from my face like a bomb of betrayal.

The car lights turned off, and the magical show of the Jacaranda tree disappeared into thin air, just like the body had on that night of the full moon on Midsummer's Eve.

Here one minute. Gone the next.

'When you delete my memories of the incident, will I still be me?' he said again, pulling me back to the moment.

I pressed my lips together, keeping my eyes on the silhouette of the Jacaranda tree. I didn't know the absolute truthful answer to his question. We weren't up to Phase 3 with the research trials in human subjects, yet. 'Yes. It's just a small moment of time in your life. Like a blink. Like one small breath,' I said, presuming my prediction based on research and analysis, would be the truth. I hoped he believed me.

I turned my face toward him when I felt the tree quiver. His head was lowered, his eyes closed, and his chin turned toward his right shoulder. 'I have to go. We need to discuss this further ... make plans ... as soon as possible.'

I gulped down the knot of anxiety that was lodged in my

throat. 'Understand that you are sworn to secrecy about what I have told you.'

He nodded, then manoeuvred his body and descended the tree faster than I could tell him to be careful. After a moment, I followed, landing on the ground ten seconds after him. I adjusted my black hood over my head and turned to say goodbye, but he had vanished.

My muscles tensed. I was now alone in the dark kissing forest of our youth. Being a woman alone in any setting was never a good choice. Ever.

The stillness of the trees became heavy and the silence unnerving. I fingered the diamond-studded, gold compact in my pocket, my fingers now familiar with the rise and fall of the artwork that decorated it.

A wind picked up, and with it, lightning lit up the forest with the colours of daydom, followed by the crack of thunder.

And I ran.

I feel like I've been running since that moment in time. From that nightdom of the incident that had no answers. I feel like people look at me, knowing about my wish. My only wish now is that I wish it had never happened.

What is a wish anyway? Does it have enchantment encrypted in the words? Is it released from your mind, carried with your breath until something captures it, good or bad? Does a wish really have a magical quality that can make your dreams come true? Or is it just your heart's desire, fanciful thoughts filled with extravagant wants, a bliss-bomb of a dream that can never be achieved, or a wish for a result that you never put in the effort for: the unattainable, blown on the wind in silence, and destined to return to the earth, unfulfilled?

Chapter 6

Dear Finn,

Hey. I hope you remember me. I met you at Kingdom Adventure Park during the spring of the most amazing flowering season ever.

You—

I squeezed the blue pen between my fingers then stabbed it into the off-white handmade paper, ripping it. I screwed it up and threw it at the bin, hitting the rim before it fell to the floor, joining my seven other writing attempts. Why was this letter so hard to write? It's what Tobi and I were planning to do. It was our chance to escape from the situation that had unfolded before our eyes on Midsummer's Eve. The situation that should *never* have happened.

If only Tobi had said … *if only*—my throat tightened. Three words from him would have changed everything. *Just three words.* From his perfect lips. Straight from his heart. His once beautiful heart.

I kicked the leg of the study desk in frustration, and my mind filled with a tragic melody of grief and despair. I succumbed to the music in my mind and lost myself in the involuntary perception that crossed over between my senses. My emotions were connected to music. Different feelings triggered different musical keys, notes or melodies, not only in myself, but when I perceived emotion in others.

I choked back my tears, closed my eyes and lifted my head toward the ceiling in a prayer of complete confusion. I was lost in the darkness, blacker than *Vantablack*, or even *Black 3.0*, between what was right and wrong, and I didn't know which was which.

Should we be entering the realm of my forbidden neuroscience research?

Should I listen to my heart, or should I listen to my mind?

What had he done? What had *we* done?

A silent scream scratched my throat. I opened my eyes and looked out the window of my apartment and into the nightdom.

The nightdom.

I sighed. My childhood name for the night. It was part of who I was.

I moved my face closer to the window and squinted. The stars from the nightdom had vanished. Had I done that? Did *I* wish for the clouds, the deepest colour of depression, of chaos and anger to roll in? Did I wish for the lightning to scatter the nightdom with blinding whites, highlighting the sage greens and cobalt blues of the cloud cover?

Incandescent. Luminous. Powerful.

Greens and blues. Blue. Ocean-blue. Tobi's eye colour.

Every story has a beginning.

This beginning started thirty years ago when, our parents, as a group of teenagers, first met at the Introverts Dance—

even as they tried to melt into the walls, avoiding eye contact, hiding behind books in the corners, shy, yet seeking connection with another compatible introvert. Somehow it worked. Hearts collided and friendships formed, and the introverts weren't so introverted anymore.

And this story continued when the thought of babies were still a twinkle in their eyes. A thought that we may exist, someday. There was never any way that my life could not become entwined, complicated, and filled with an inconceivable, heartbreaking tragedy, with the other offspring.

I reached into the pocket of my jeans and pulled out the classic diamond-studded, gold compact. Not mine. *Stolen.* On that day that can't be *undone*. The wish that can't be *unwished.*

Mirror. Mirror. I pushed the button on the compact, and it flipped open.

Two mirrors. Two of me.

The one before the event. The one after.

I gazed into the left mirror. The reflection of me before the event. Distant. It held me like the swinging fob watch of hypnosis, like the flickering flames of a ravenous fire … like the fire pit we had sat at as children, teenagers, and young adults, and shared our lives, our stories and our secrets, hungry for details to fill our curious minds and out-of-control imaginations.

My mind released the memory of the second fire pit we had installed: the new, burnt sienna fire pit that held the oxygen-hungry, fatal flames of orange destruction, of trance-like stares and mellow moods, but not of laughter like the first fire pit did.

The old fire pit had split in two after one of us had an ugly, anger-fuelled loss of control, filled with the deep grief of death. A love lost. Never to return. To remain as a memory. A painful memory, now an embedded scar burned into every cell of our being.

I slipped further into the reminiscence, and I could have

sworn the rich oaky smell of burning timber was real. I remember looking over at the Olds. There were back to their hippy-happy-selves after we, the offspring, had all passed over into adulthood, and after the long grieving period when one of us had gone, never to walk the earth again.

I shook my head. My mother had insisted that I attend that day, to attempt to reunite the childhood friends back to some sort of normalcy. But she didn't understand, we could never have normalcy again. Not after the death of one of our own.

And so, there we sat, at the new burnt sienna fire pit of perceived perfection in the park of our youth, away from the Olds, like we always did. The new fire pit was like a cosmetic procedure concealing our collective scars of pain and grief and devastation of the past. There were eleven of us twenty-something-year-olds with nervous smiles and hesitant conversation starters. Four were missing. One of them dead.

I pressed my lips together. I wished for the old broken fire pit back. At least it still held the perfect memories of all fifteen of us, unlike this one that held the new, orchestrated, and tense memories of thirteen, tainted with heartache and carefully chosen words.

I looked around at my childhood friends in their grown-up bodies. Each stared into the fire pit, hypnotised by the belly-dancing flames. I wondered if they were fighting the uncomfortable urge to leave, needing to escape the painful memories. Like me. I watched Lachlan lift the fourth beer to his lips, misery painted over his face like a firestorm, ready to devour anything and everything that came his way, with an abhorrent rage.

There was an ache in my chest, and I shuffled to my left a little. I wanted to save a space for Mia, next to me, with Yolande on the other side of her like we always did. The three of us together.

I inhaled deeply, pushing the feeling of heartache back into its place of "forget", and locked it deep inside me. I gazed over at the Jacaranda tree, the water lapping at its own personal shoreline that never used to be. Once, it had sat in a large meadow where we would run and play. But not now. Not after my wish.

I looked beyond the tree to where all the colours above were; hues of the sunset singing with harmonies of blended perfection in azure blue, amethyst, flamingo pink and dandelion yellow before it faded to a hint of arctic blue, heralding the beginning of nightdom.

Yolande squatted on the shore and gathered stones. The white flat ones I knew from memory. She stood, cutting a lean figure in her loose fitting dark blue cargo shorts and long-sleeve, white, hooded T-shirt, and skimmed the stones across the surface of the water, one at a time. All of them, except the last one, which she pegged with all her might. It landed before the Jacaranda tree, bouncing, until it rested next to the thick, pale grey trunk.

My lips curled up. That was my Yolande. My forever childhood friend. Active. Smart. Pushing the boundaries between male and female. Always challenging the boys and beating them. Like me. A kindred spirit.

She placed her hands on her hips, let them fall, then turned and strode towards our fire pit with determined steps. She stopped beside me, locked eyes, then wriggled her way beside me, smelling like pink roses after a summer storm. Our hands connected, warm and filled with past stories, and of grief shared, our anxiety as one. She squeezed my hand and gave me a courageous smile. I offered one back, breathing out my sadness so I wouldn't burst into uncontrollable sobbing.

I twisted my hair around my finger and redirected my attention. 'Hey. Nice boots,' I said. They were brown leather safety boots. Worn to inflict maximum damage.

'Thanks,' she said, looked at them and tapped them together, twice, like something magical would happen next. I held my breath, wishing they were magical, and Mia would suddenly appear in the place I had kept for her, squeezing between Yolande and me with a giggle that made our hearts bloom like sunflowers in the summertime.

A cacophony of laughter rang out from the Olds. I looked over my shoulder at them sitting around the large wooden table like they always did. It was good to see the fifty-something-year-olds laughing together. Mia's death had charred their friendship web, and at first, I wasn't sure it would mend. But maybe their shared wisdom and tightly knit history pulled them through.

I squinted to focus my eyes a little better. There was movement behind them. A tallish guy walked past them. He wore faded, blue skinny-fit jeans, and a round neck, white T-shirt. He didn't belong to us. He ran his hand through his dark hair and scanned our group of misfits, bound together by our parental friendships. As he came closer, his eyes searched faces, then remained on one.

The corner of his mouth quirked up and my insides melted. I couldn't stop my eyes from widening, shocked by an unexplainable physical reaction to his smile lighting up his face like he was some sort of angel. What was he doing here?

Yolande pulled her hand from mine, and its weight fell onto my shoulder as she jumped up with more energy than a green monster juice drink mixed with an energy drink. She skipped over to him and dived into his arms. He lifted her up and spun her around like she was a lightweight ballerina, then turned her away and kissed her, her hand sliding behind his neck and into his dark hair. *Intimate*. When they released from their embrace, she took his hand and pulled him over to our group, beaming more brightly than the midday sun.

'Everyone, this is Xander,' Yolande said and looked at him, her eyes twinkling like stars, in all the colours of above in the nightdom. 'Xander … this … is everyone.' She waved her hand over our group like a magician, and gave Xander a shy smile, like her gesture was some sort of a private joke.

My lips curled up on one side and my heart warmed.

Xander grinned, held up his hand in greeting and nodded. Then Yolande sat, pulling him down beside her. I watched him fold his athletic body into a sitting down position in one smooth movement. Our once close-knit group watched him with caution. Yolande was on the top of our unspoken protection list. We would go to the ends of the earth to keep her safe.

I glanced around at our circle of friends. Their eyes were glued to Xander. A judgement had already been made, and it wasn't pretty. They say that people make their mind up about you in the first seven seconds of meeting you, or worse, in the blink of an eye. Had that judgement been made just now, or when Yolande ran to him and he caught her and kissed her?

My gaze wandered over his sculptured face and his dark manicured hair. He was attractive. Possibly too much. He was the type usually seen in social circles with a beautiful model latched onto him, with her knowing that within a moment, he would ditch her for the next beautiful thing that came along. What was he doing in Tarrin? What was he doing with Yolande? Our Yolande. *My* Yolande?

I leaned forward and extended my hand to him to break the tension that weaved through our circle like a sinister venomous snake, flicking its forked tongue out to taste its victim. 'Hi. I'm Indigo.'

He took my hand with a firm grip. 'Nice to meet you.' His azure blue eyes met mine. They were filled with sincerity and intelligence.

A weight lifted from my shoulders. 'So … how did you meet *my* Yolande?' I asked, staking my claim on her, and my inferred allegiance. If he hurt her, he would have to deal with me. The hideous me.

Yolande looked up at him, her eyes bright and filled with the ooey-gooey love potion.

Xander looked away from me and down at Yolande, raising an eyebrow as he grinned at her. 'At her grandmother's flower shop. She laughed at me when I complimented her.'

I burst out laughing. That was my Yolande. She hated being complimented on her physical attributes, and often sent men running, scared. But he didn't? I must hand it to him, he had broken through her protective wall and survived her steel-capped work boots! It was obvious that he made her happy. And that was everything, considering what Yolande had been through. In that instant, my opinion of him changed. I liked him. A lot.

I gazed around at our group. Their eyes were still on him. Assessing him. If he broke her heart, he would have to deal with them as a pack. A savage pack. And that would be so beyond ugly it's unmentionable.

His eyes reconnected with Yolande's. He adored her. He leaned in close to her and I heard him whisper, 'What's with the boots, Yolande? You know you don't have to wear them when I'm with you.' He furrowed his eyebrows.

Yolande looked up at him. 'I know ... but—' A sadness swept over her face that made the sunset less beautiful. It tugged at my heart. Hard.

Xander pulled her hand to his lips and kissed it.

A heavy quietness settled over our gang. It was too quiet with their judgemental gazes locked on Xander. Twenty questions would be coming soon. I could see it rising on their faces. Will he pass their test? In *5, 4, 3, 2, 1 ...*

'Xander, have you been in Tarrin long?' Dean said. *Question 1.*

He nodded. 'I grew up here. I was the geeky kid nobody liked.'

'I think I remember you. At football. You sat on the bench for the entire season!'

Xander laughed. 'That was me. And that was my intention. I joined to keep my dad happy.'

'Oh man … sorry about that,' Ethan said.

'Don't be. It kept him off my back.'

'Why did he want you there?' Emily asked. *Question 2.*

'I did ballet and he worried that it might make me gay. Soccer was the antidote, apparently.' Xander's mouth quirked at the corners.

Well answered, Xander, I thought.

'Did you dance for long?' *Question 3.*

'Yes. I stopped just a year ago to continue with my medical research.'

I watched as eyebrows raised. But I frowned at him, wondering how he could dance and study a medical degree at the same time.

'What are you researching?' Liam asked. *Question 4.*

'Incurable diseases, specifically Meniere's disease.'

'Never heard of it, but nice,' he said.

'Who is your father?' *Question 5.* All eyes peered at Aidan. His tone suggested disdain.

'Dr. Parker.'

'*The* Dr. Parker?' *Question 6.*

'Yes.' Xander's jaw flexed as he clenched his teeth.

'So, you have grown-up with privilege?' Aidan was bitter. *A nasty Question 7.*

'Materially, yes, until I chose to leave home and my father's wealth, but emotionally, no. Everything I have, I've worked hard for. Nothing was handed to me on a silver platter.' Xander narrowed his eyes and looked down. He had made an enemy. Was it because of his relationship with Yolande? Or was it because he threatened the person's perceived hierarchical order within the group? Maybe it was both.

'I hope you achieve what you want to achieve with your research, Xander,' I piped in to douse the words that had erupted in flames. There were two types of privilege: those who born into it and flaunted it, and those who worked hard to achieve it.

'Do you have Meniere's disease?' Sophie asked. *Question 8.*

Xander looked up. 'No.'

'Then why choose to research it?' *Question 9.*

'Vertigo is the most debilitating condition anyone can experience, feared by doctors who never wish to have it. And, it's an interesting symptom. One that seemingly can't be controlled in the vestibular system. However, in ballet, when we perform pirouettes, we use a technique to avoid vertigo, called spotting—we rapidly move our head to fix our gaze on the same spot as much as possible. Interestingly, brain scans reveal the cerebellum is smaller in dancers because we don't use our vestibular system, but rely on highly co-ordinated pre-programmed movements. Apparently, our brains adjust over years of training to suppress the feedback of feeling dizzy or off balance. In my research, I'm wanting to monitor that area in patients with chronic dizziness. And beyond that, I want to find a cure for vertigo, and for Meniere's disease.' Xander looked down and frowned, then looked into the fire. 'I can't help to think that, what if what I discover in my research, unlocks the common factor to cure other incurable diseases. It's fascinating, and a challenge I have accepted to take on. It's my Physician's Pledge …'

Well explained. Kudos to you, Xander.

'Xxxannder … a ballllet quessstion fffor youu,' said Lachlan, his words slurring. He winced, 'Why do mmale balllet danncers wwear that … ththtat—'

Question 10. Sigh. *Grow-up, Lachie. If you were sober, you would never have asked that question.*

'Dance belt … they're specialized athletic supports designed specifically for dance. They are essential to protect our junk from moves that can otherwise result in pain or even injury. When I was still dancing, we would often have footballers attending classes. It helped them to become stronger and more co-ordinated, as well as improving their core strength and balance—and ultimately, improving their game.'

Good deflection, Xander.

'How did you meet Yolande when she is hardly ever in Tarrin?' Chloe said. *Question 11.*

'I was trying to get permission to use the old Cruiser bicycle that sits outside Flowers for Fleur, for my mother's birthday. I left letters in the flowers in the basket asking for permission, and Andi would leave me barbed responses back that I couldn't have it.' Xander looked into Yolande's eyes and grinned.

'Did you get to use Fleur's famous bicycle?' Bella said. *Question 12.*

'Yes. Yolande's grandmother's kindness overrode Yolande's crankiness.' Yolande kissed him on the cheek and there was silence. Eyes left Xander and focussed on the flames of the fire. The questioning had finished.

I looked up at Xander and Yolande. Their lips met in a brief caress. If it was nightdom, when the stars twinkled, instead of the time of colourful sunsets, I'm sure we would have seen electricity spark between them.

The sound of running steps came closer, then stopped. I looked up at a six-foot something guy, who then sat next to me in Mia's spot. I pressed my lips together in a hard line of disapproval, then watched as he threw bags of marshmallows around our circle with cheers echoing around the fire pit. Which parents did he belong to? I frowned as no memory of him came.

'Remember those giant marshmallows we use to have at your house? The ones that we put together to make a marshmallow man?' Aidan said. There was laughter. I raised an eyebrow. I never went to his house and made giant marshmallows. Was it a guy thing?

'And when we put an entire sealed bag of marshmallows in the microwave to melt to make our S'mores?' Liam added.

'Man, I was in so much trouble. I was grounded for a month!

And my mother never bought marshmallows again!'

'And remember when Mia—' Dean started. There was a loud, rough cough, cutting Dean off.

I looked at Yolande, as did Xander. He rubbed his thumb over the back of her hand and narrowed his eyes. Did he know what happened to Mia? Did he know Yolande was there on that terrible day?

Yolande took a visible, deep breath, and cleared her throat. 'It's okay. You can talk about her.' But there was an uncomfortable, profound silence.

'Remember when Mia broke into Dean's room and recreated his bedroom on his front lawn?' Chloe said.

I inhaled at the thought of how much courage it took her to talk about Mia.

'Yeah—she was the best. I miss her,' Bella said.

A flush crept up Yolande's face and she lowered her head. I watched as a tear, reflecting the orange light of the fire pit, rolled down her cheek.

Xander laid back on the grass and pulled Yolande to his side, and tenderly kissed the top of her head. My heart broke then, and I struggled to breathe, like all the air from my lungs had been sucked out by darkness trying to pull me below the ground to where rotting corpses lay.

Xander stood, tagged Yolande and said, 'You're it!', then ran.

I drew in a breath at his distraction and his choice of a childish game for us mid-twenty-year-olds, wondering if it would help pull Yolande from her sadness that was spreading like contagion. Yolande shook her head, sat up, stood, and gave chase, leaving her sadness behind grovelling in the dirt like a sulking child.

Xander was faraway, so Yolande returned to the fire pit and tagged the guy who sat beside me. 'You're it!' she said, then ran, steel-capped safety boots imprinting the ground like the steps of a giant.

Game on. Chaos. Friends running everywhere, except me. My plan was to stay put.

I waited for him to run but there was no movement from beside me.

He looked down and smiled, a dimple revealing itself on his cheek. 'Remember when we use to play hide 'n' seek at these gatherings … and you won. Every single time,' he said, his voice somehow, intimate.

Who was he? I had no recollection of him.

'Where did you hide?' he asked, and looked up at me. He raised an eyebrow.

A million images from my childhood memories visualised before me as I tried to put a name to his face, and, as I tried to remember his face, even. He had a sort of rectangular type of face shape, with a square jaw, dark wavy hair, full lips and a straight nose. I couldn't remember him. Nothing. But I smiled anyway, pretending I remembered him. Childhood memories of fun were the best. Of mischief were even better.

I raised my eyebrows and looked to the tree covered in purple blooms in the centre of the island, still visible at this time of lingering light. 'See that Jacaranda tree? I climbed it. I was out of sight to everyone, but I could see everyone and knew exactly what was going on.'

'Hmmm. Clever.'

I pulled my eyebrows together. 'Where did you hide?'

He looked down with a crooked smile and my body felt like it had been switched on. I breathed out the feeling that came without invitation. I still couldn't remember him.

'I would run as fast as I could, trying to keep up with you. But I never did. When I ran out of breath, I would just lie in the long grass in the meadow and hope for the best!'

I grinned, our eyes connecting: his bluey-green to my greeny-blue. His, reminding my of the colour of the ocean. Ocean-blue.

And that symphonic burst of desire hit me again. I breathed it out like it was a noxious gas from inside me. 'You should have headed for the parked cars. That way, you could move around there as the seeker looked for victims.'

He looked out over at the Jacaranda tree, the afternoon light illuminating his eyes. They were pretty. Eyes you could fall in love with.

'How did the tree end up with water around it like that? There was nothing but land before,' he said, frowning.

'I wished it to,' I said with a grin. 'It's true. Once, while I sat high up in the Jacaranda tree, hiding, I wished for it to be surrounded by water so I wouldn't have to re-join the hide 'n' seek game after we had played it four times already. And then, one day, we returned to our picnic place, and there it was—Jacaranda Island.'

He smirked and shook his head at me. 'Wishes don't come true. Making a wish doesn't make it happen.'

'Of course not. How absurd!' I said. But I wasn't convinced. There was something dodgy about making a wish. Something out of your control.

An uncomfortable pause floated between us. I still couldn't remember this athletic looking man beside me, who was once a boy I played hide 'n' seek with. Apparently.

'Indi,' he said, like he had known me forever, and a wave of guilt washed over me. 'I dare you to climb the Jacaranda tree, now.'

I looked at him, then grinned in a lopsided kind of way. Did he know that I could never resist a dare? If someone told me not to do something, I would go out of my way to do it. I liked pushing the boundaries. I liked proving people wrong.

I gazed over at the Jacaranda tree overloaded with lavender-coloured blooms on its own little island like nothing else in the world existed, and like there was nothing more important in the world than this moment, right here, right now.

Could I walk there, wading through the water? Was it deep? Could I find something to float on? Was it still too cool for a swim?

I pressed my lips together and looked back at him and nodded. 'Challenge accepted,' I said, irritated that I still didn't know his name. His ocean-blue eyes widened, the colour of his irises becoming impossibly more beautiful and my heart melted. 'But only if you come with me,' I added.

He swallowed, then looked back at our parents. Loud laughter erupted. 'I'll take a rain check. The Olds will be doing the cake soon.'

I frowned. 'Are you too scared to climb the tree?' Time stopped in that moment as I waited for his answer.

He looked back at me with pinched eyebrows. 'No!' His voice was curt and stabbed at me like a sharp pencil.

'Tobi. You're it!' Aidan shouted.

Tobi? Ah … Tobi! I remember now. The tag-along. The annoying, unremarkable kid who was a little older than me. He was most certainly remarkable now.

'I reverse the tag!' he yelled.

'You can't do that!' a voice called back.

'I just did!' he yelled, adding a staccato to the "d".

My face froze. He was either still annoying, or possibly, clever. I narrowed my eyes at him, a wave of caution flowing through my veins.

'I had surgery on my knee a few months ago. I don't want to run like a lunatic yet,' he said. He pulled up the leg of his jeans and showed me three scars around his right knee.

I raised my eyebrows. 'How's the rehab going? Or the physio?'

'Good, so far. I'll be back skiing in no time.' He pushed the leg of his jeans down then tapped me on the shoulder. 'You're it!' he said, raised an eyebrow at me and smirked.

I lifted an unimpressed eyebrow back at him. 'You know those messages you get on social media, where people ask you to pass it on. They always stop with me. The end. Like your tag. Game over,' I said.

He tilted his head to the side a little and closed his eyes, then opened them. 'Are you always a killjoy?'

I clenched my teeth together to stop a piercing rebuke from exiting my mouth. I took a half-breath. 'It's my second name,' I said, and pushed him. 'You're it.'

He fell to the side, putting his hand down to stop himself from falling further. He looked into the dancing flames of the fire and narrowed his eyes, the air around us becoming thick, laced with a bitter taste.

'Checkmate,' he said, his voice low with a dusting of failure. He produced a long stick from beside him and shoved a marshmallow onto it, then placed it above the flames. He toasted the marshmallow to perfection, and let it ooze with an uncomfortable silence.

One by one, our group returned to the fire pit. I looked at each person. Good people. Genuinely nice people. *Chosen friends.* We had known each other forever, and I was thankful. For a moment I wondered if our friendship would last for our lifetimes, until, one by one we vanished from the earth. And if it did, who would be the last one standing?

'Hey, Indigo.' Dean's voice pulled me from my dark thoughts. 'Do you still work at the … the—'

'Brain Lab?' I asked, stopping myself from rolling my eyes. The general population called it the Brain Lab. But it's official title was in fact *Brain. Mind. Memory.* It was a secure, highly confidential medical facility of experimental research. There were other divisions there as well, such as ears and eyes. I let friends and family use the term "Brain Lab" without showing a physical reaction in any way, shape, or form. The less fuss the better.

'That's it,' he said.

'Yes,' I said, and pulled a toasted marshmallow off Tobi's stick and placed it into my mouth. He raised an icy eyebrow at me. Was that because I took his marshmallow, or because I worked at the Brain Lab?

'*The* Brain Lab at the Brain and Mind Institute?' Bella added.

I let out a sharp breath. 'Yes.' *Here we go.*

'Are the rumours true?' Aidan said.

'Which ones?'

'Keeping brains alive without a body?' Ethan widened his eyes, straightened his arms and wiggled his fingers at me.

I laughed. Pretend laughed. 'We have brains, but no,' I lied, and wrinkled my nose, feigning disgust. I couldn't tell them about our research with disembodied brains. I couldn't tell them about the "Reset Project". If people knew, we would become victims of hatred. We had brains that had been donated, with the consent from people who had stepped into eternity, or had chosen physician-assisted suicide to escape their earthly prison of PTSD, trauma or memory torture of what had happened to them in the past. Before they died, they knew in detail about the research we were conducting, and they had volunteered to help others so no one would have to suffer, like them.

'Come on ... tell us more,' Dean said.

'Sorry ... gag order. Confidentiality. An oath. Much like Yolande when she does her research for the Defence Force.' I looked at Yolande and she fist bumped me, followed by our squiddily-fish hand gesture from when we were young. We laughed, until I caught Xander's eyes piercing me. Did he not approve of our handshake, or did he not approve of the Brain Lab? Did he know of it? Had he heard the rumours? Being a doctor and a researcher, did he know a bit more than anyone else?

Squeals of laughter rang out from the Olds. I looked over. Their reunion seemed so much less intense than ours. How did they do it?

'Kids!' a voice yelled. 'Come over!' *Birthday cake time.*

The sound of groaning performed the Mexican wave around the fire pit. The Olds had an oath to embarrass their offspring, I'm sure.

We walked up the hill and gathered around the large timber table decorated with wine glasses and platters of fruit and cheese.

The cake sat in the middle like a prettied-up announcement decorated with tragedy. I stared into the flames of the million and one candles, my stomach rolling and my heart heavy, then tuned out to everything except Yolande, beside me.

I felt her hand slip into mine as the birthday song began with reluctant voices. I knew what was coming. A speech about those present and the one who had left us. The impossibly heavy weight of the mention of Mia's name and her memory would smother Yolande.

I held her hand tighter, but it wasn't enough.

She ran, with a heart wrenching melody of grief, despair and self-punishment chasing after her.

Xander placed a hand on his forehead before brushing it over his face, then went after her.

My heart broke. The loss we felt for Mia was heavy, but for Yolande, it was impossibly worse. She lived Mia's death. And I don't think she will ever heal from it—

Memories. They shape us. They define us. They impact our personalities. They control our behaviour. And if you let them … they'll destroy you.

My tear dropped onto the desk. It was late. I needed to get some sleep. I had an important day of research tomorrow at the "Brain Lab", as my friends and the general population called it.

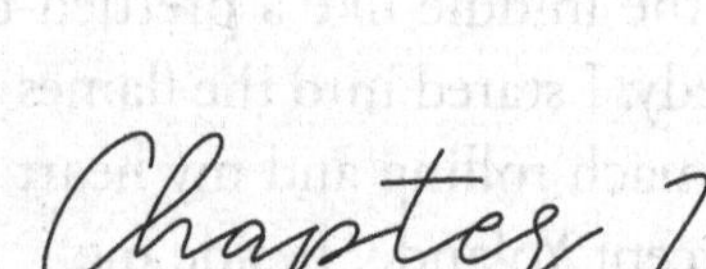

Chapter 7

'You're late! Where were you?' Scarlett signed.

'I stopped to grab a coffee,' I said to my work colleague, who also happened to be a best friend. I pulled on my lab coat.

'Liar,' Scarlet signed and frowned at me, her brown eyes boring into me.

'How do you know?' I said, wondering why Scarlett was signing to me like when she was deaf, before she received a cochlear implant in one ear, and was regrowing her hearing cells in the other ear under experimental hearing research.

Scarlet widened her eyes and glared at me. She shook her head, her straight red hair moving in sync. 'I'm deaf. I have a built-in lie-detector. It's in your non-verbal language. It's in your eyes,' she signed.

I raised an eyebrow at her as an undertone of guilt flowed through me in a melody that sounded like the gnashing of teeth.

'So, spill the beans. Where were you?' she signed.

I grimaced, buttoned up my white lab coat and kept my eyes

focussed on the floor, my hair covering my face. 'Just late. No interesting stories to add.' I looked up at her to see if she heard my words clearly and believed my lie. I fastened the last button on my coat and slipped my hand into my pocket, then looked up at her.

'Careful. Your pants will catch on fire!' she signed, then turned her back on me.

I took a deep breath and caressed the jewels that covered the gold compact in my pocket. Not mine. Stolen. Truthfulness was my default, and telling an untruth never sat well with me. I couldn't tell her I had been to the park of my youth this morning, at the lake of secrets, the tree of memories, the island of death. Or was it? Even I was unsure. All I knew was that the body was missing, and Tobi was running scared. Like me.

I tapped Scarlett on the shoulder. She turned to face me, her shoulders sagging. I stepped closer and hugged her for a moment, inhaling her fragrance that reminded me of Sunday mornings, white T-shirts, and my favourite pair of jeans.

As I parted from her, I glimpsed her cochlear implant processor sitting on her desk, like it had been exiled from the land of computer-brain interfacing.

'Thank you for putting up with me,' I said without sound, like I always did before I learned sign language to talk to her. What was the use of using voice volume when someone couldn't hear you? Or could she? She was part of a clinical trial with hearing cell regeneration in her right ear.

She pressed her lips together and raised an eyebrow. 'Only because of our pinky promise when we were seven … and the fact that you were my only friend left when I lost my hearing…' she signed.

'What?' I said, and cupped my ear to tease her.

Scarlett bopped me on the upper-arm. 'You'll keep. Don't you have research to complete?' she signed.

I smiled at her then narrowed my eyes. 'I do, but first, what's with your cochlear implant processor decorating your desk?' I signed. I picked it up and held it in front of her, swinging it like a hypnotic pocket watch.

She lifted her tear-stained eyes to mine, her face suddenly the colour of gloom. She raised her hands and let them fall.

I placed my arm around her and walked her to the lunchroom where I sat her down, then fussed about, making her a cup of tea. I placed it in front of her and sat on her left side. 'You okay?' I said in a quiet voice. There was no answer.

Scarlett sipped on her tea, her eyes downcast.

'What's going on?' I said. Still no answer. I left my chair and sat opposite her, leaned forward and tapped her hand. She looked up at me. 'Sissy-boo,' I signed with gentleness. She narrowed her eyes. 'Are you okay?' I signed.

She shook her head in a disjointed movement then ran a hand down her face, and back over the tattoo on her left cheek, tracing it to behind her left ear.

I widened my eyes at her, waiting for more information.

'The world of sound is ugly—so ugly!' she signed at speed. 'I'm not wearing my cochlear processor anymore. I can't do sound anymore!'

'What?' I mouthed.

'I heard shouting. People shouting at each other in anger! And unkind words … and screaming … and people being nasty to each other … I don't want to hear those things. I don't want to hear ugly. And the city … it's so noisy … nothing but a blur of incessant noise … why is the world so noisy?' she signed.

'Oh, Scarlett.' I paused, trying to find an answer for her question. 'I guess I'm just used to all the noise and filter out sounds. What does your audiologist say?' I signed.

'She says it's my brain absorbing all the sounds at the moment. She said it would take a little while for me to get used to hearing sound again. She told me I was like a baby learning to hear for the first time. It's so tiring … I'm so tired … I'm mentally exhausted. I want to get off the merry-go-round for a while,' Scarlett signed. Her lips turned down and a tear rolled down her cheek.

'Nobody said learning to hear again was going to be easy,' I signed. 'You've come so far and I'm so, so proud of you!'

Scarlett twisted a tissue around her finger then dropped it onto the table. 'I keep see-sawing between I love my cochlear implant and I hate it,' she signed, then sighed. 'Today is just a bad day.'

'Remember when ... you were thinking of hearing again, and I said that if you had a cochlear implant, you could choose whether to wear it or not?' I signed.

Scarlett nodded.

'Well … today could be a day not to wear it. Let you mind relax and recharge,' I signed.

Scarlett frowned then nodded.

'Today will be a better day,' I signed. 'Take time to centre yourself.' I sipped my tea and grimaced, wondering why people even drank the weird tasting brew. 'How's your right ear with the hearing cell regeneration … do you think it's working?' I said, my voice in a conversational tone.

'Classified information,' Scarlett signed.

'So … if you're replying to my spoken words, I do believe your hearing is returning, dear Scarlett,' I said.

'Maybe. Or is it just that I am exceptional at reading lips?' she signed.

I covered my mouth and spoke, 'Careful. Your pants will catch on fire!'

Scarlett raised her eyebrow at me, picked up the external processor for her cochlear implant and positioned it on her head, and looked up at me with a fake smile. 'I'm putting my processor back on, for the researchers, not me,' she signed, then gulped down the rest of her tea. 'Don't you have research to do before my pants catch on fire?'

I followed Scarlett to her desk with an uncontrollable grin, and positioned myself on her cochlear implant side. If I was her partner in crime in helping her to relearn to hear, I wasn't going to make it easy for her. There was only one way to learn to hear with a cochlear implant, and that was to use it. 'I need to see the traces from all of our brains, please.'

Scarlett lifted her head and stared straight ahead. After a beat she turned her head to me and beamed. 'How soon do you need them?' she signed, then wrapped her arms around me in a tight squeeze.

'As soon as you can,' I said.

Scarlett nodded. 'And thank you for forcing me to listen with my CI,' she signed.

I laughed. 'Well … if you're going to be a spy …'

Scarlett raised an eyebrow. 'Maybe I am ... now go back to work so I can retrieve the traces for you.'

I saluted, then signed back. 'Later, Sissy-Boo!'

I walked to the iris scanner for entry to the Memory Lab, hidden in the depths of the Mind and Brain Research Centre. I looked about the room of clear glass boxes; coffins for the brains in the state of between worlds. Living bodiless brains, implanted with wireless electrodes.

The anosmic laboratory scent reminded me of the unearthly, intrusive research I was involved in, and I was hit by a feeling of guilt—I was involved in unethical research, something we should never tamper with. My chest tightened and I took a deep breath, reminding myself that the ultimate outcome of this research was to help people trapped inside their minds and their memories, unable to escape, where their lives were filled with an endless deep depression, or where they saw death as the only option after their traumatic event.

'Morning, Indigo,' Biran said. 'There's no neural activity to report in any of the specimens according to the intracranial electrocorticography.'

I gazed over the computer recorded analysis. 'Did you perform any functional magnetic resonance imaging?'

'Not today.' I looked up at Biran. He pressed his lips together, shook his head and adjusted his glasses. 'I was hoping that we would have some sort of recorded activity at this point of the research.' His voice was dispirited.

I put on my virtual reality headset. 'Maybe we need to do the reset, or reboot?' I winced at the noise coming from the neural signals of the brain. A shiver ran down my spine as music like existential angst played in my mind. I shook my head to exit from the music in my mind, in the key of the dark night of the soul.

'No. You know I don't like ECT. We have no control over whether it will erase memories permanently or temporarily.'

'What about Transcranial Magnetic Stimulation—you know it doesn't affect memories?'

Biran walked around each of the glass boxes filled with our subjects' brains, suspended in fluid. He ran his hand over the last box and leaned in closer to it, studying it. 'I can't do that yet.'

'Can't or won't?'

'Can't … what if the specimen feels pain in the meninges, and we haven't given it anything to make the procedure humane?'

I shook my head. 'Then more time is what we need. And patience.' I projected the hologram of the functional magnetic resonance imaging (fMRI) of 100B-1's brain. 'Or … we give one of the brains a re-engineered "Sleeping Beauty Pill", the Zolpidem sleeping medication, as we had discussed. It won't erase their memories. It won't alter anything physical in the brain.'

Biran looked into my eyes for a moment, then gave me one short nod. He left the room. I watched as he walked away, running a hand over his bald head, then raised his head to the ceiling.

I frowned. What were we doing wrong? What had we missed?

I walked up to the first encased brain and pressed my hand to the glass. 'Good morning, 100B-1.' I looked at the electrocorticography. It showed coma patterns. *Unconsciousness.* 'Sleep well.'

I moved on to the next brain and pressed my hand to the glass. 'Good morning, 100B-2.'

No new electrical activity response. *Unconsciousness.*

Next. 'Good morning, 100B-3.'

No new electrical activity response. *Unconsciousness.*

'Good morning, 100B-4.'

No new electrical activity response. *Unconsciousness.*

'Good morning, 100B-5.'

No new electrical activity response. *Unconsciousness.*

'Good morning, 100B-6.'

No new electrical activity response. *Unconsciousness.*

'100B-6, I've decided to give you some medication to help you sleep better. It's called the Sleeping Beauty Pill. But unlike the fairy tale, Sleeping Beauty, you won't have to wait for a prince to kiss you to wake up. Huh … those poor women of the 15th century. Those insufferable men who were so scared of women they had to suppress them!' I released a suitable dose of Zolpidem into 100B-6's nutrient tube. 'Talk to you soon.' I moved on to the next research subjects. 'Good morning 100B-7, Good morning 100B-8, Good morning 100B-9. 100B-1 and 100B-2 aren't talking. They must have some juicy secrets to keep. What are you up to today?'

No different electrical activity response. *Unconsciousness.*

I let out a sigh. Every morning I greeted my brainy friends. Every morning they responded the same. Living but unconscious, as if they were in an eternal sleep. Perhaps it was better that way.

'Good morning, 100B-10,' I said with an extra chirpiness.

No response. *Unconsciousness.*

I stretched my fingers then relaxed them, then went to fetch the book I had been reading to them as if they were children, *How the Brain Works*. I sat on the red leather chair in the corner of the room and flipped through the pages, and stopped at the dog-eared page, Chapter 46. If I had to read another chapter of this book, it would surely put me into a coma! I snapped it shut and reached for a novel from my childhood.

The corners of my mouth quirked up as I ran my fingers over the hardcover of the exclusive collector's edition of *Alice in Wonderland*, cleared my throat, and began to read, 'Alice was beginning to get very tired of sitting by her sister on the bank, and of having nothing to do: once or twice she had peeped into the book her sister was reading, but it had no pictures or conversations in it, *and what is the use of a book*, thought Alice, *without pictures or conversation?*'

I stopped, looked up and burst out laughing, then changed the words. Surely, I was going insane. 'Indigo was beginning to get very tired of sitting by the ten brains encased in glass, pumped with artificial blood, and of having nothing to do: once or twice she had peeped over at the brains, but there was no electrical activity response, and what is the use of waiting, thought Indigo, without any response or conversation?'

Scarlett burst through the door, eyes wide, panting. Alerted, I jumped up from the chair, my heart rate increasing. Was there an emergency?

'Keep reading!' she signed at speed. 'Don't ask why, just keep reading!' She grinned and ran from the room.

I looked back to the words and continued to read, my body fuelled by adrenaline. Tears rolled down my cheeks. I couldn't look up to see the brainwave traces, but I knew enough to know there was a change, otherwise Scarlett would not have iris scanned to enter the lab. I desperately wanted to look up at the electrocorticography trace. I desperately wanted to gear up with the virtual reality headset. Not knowing or seeing the response was killing me. I needed evidence. I needed data. Now!

I detected movement at the door in my peripheral vision, and looked up.

'Stop reading,' Scarlett signed.

I frowned, closed the book and put it down. 'What happened?' I signed.

'We have an awakening!' Scarlett said out loud, and in that moment, her eyes sparkled with delight.

I squealed, then looked up at the brain monitors, one by one, looking for the change. I narrowed my eyes, then felt a heaviness descend over me. They were unconscious. All of them. I looked at Scarlett with my palms facing upwards. I shrugged and raised an eyebrow.

'It was 100B-6. I think it responded to your humour. I've printed out the recording of the electrocorticography, plus the recording of the fMRI. Come and see for yourself,' she said.

Before I left the room, I stopped at 100B-6 and placed my hand on the glass. 'Thank you for waking up, Sleeping Beauty. 100B-6, I love you.' I blew the brain a kiss, then followed Scarlett to the analysis area.

She spread the trace along a lengthy desk, and I studied it with fervour to see which part of the brain had responded. This was a significant breakthrough. We had been waiting for this awakening for months.

Within moments, four neuroscientists arrived and congregated around the table. And within moments, the electrocorticography was gone, taken to be analysed. I wanted to follow them to the conference room and participate in their conversations, analysis and findings. I wanted to be there when they collectively put on their virtual reality headsets and interacted with the hologram. I was part of the neuroscience team. I was the reason we had an awakening, but I was instructed to return to the Memory Lab.

I connected my gaze to the iris scanner and re-entered the lab. This is what we had been waiting for. An awakening.

Warmth radiated throughout my body. I felt like doing a victory lap around the disembodied brains. Instead, I chose to do the dance of joy. I had dreamed of this day and had rehearsed my dance a thousand times in my head. But in real life, it was a sight to be seen.

I smiled as the feeling of success settled inside of me. Phase 1 of the "Reset Project" was accomplished. We just needed to connect to the other brains to awaken them to fully complete Phase 1, and then Phase 2 could begin, accessing memories. *Digitally*.

Chapter 8

The calming colours of the sunset had disappeared in a blink, replaced by dense, towering vertical clouds—thunderhead clouds. The study room in my apartment had the best view of all the colours of above, at any time.

I ran my hand over the off-white handmade paper that sat on my desk, picked up calligraphy pen, dipped it into the blue ink and began to write—

Dear Finn,

Hey. I hope you remember me. I met you at Kingdom Adventure Park during the spring of the most amazing flowering season. Ever.

You started talking to me in the queue to the Marvellous Super Rollercoaster, then you sat next to me in the car and held my hand as I screamed my lungs out in the darkest, scariest tunnel where I think we were inverted, holding on for dear life.

When the ride ended ——————

Annoyed, I dragged my pen across the handmade paper, creating an arty contour line, breaking the nib as anger engulfed me. Anger at *him*. Tobi. He blamed *me* for the incident on Midsummer's Eve that was never meant to happen.

I watched as blue ink pooled on the paper like a psychology test, then screwed up the letter and threw it into the wastepaper basket, this time landing it in the bin instead of the floor.

I grabbed the compact—the one belonging to another—and my car keys, then left my apartment slamming the door behind me so hard the walls rattled.

I ran down the steps trying to outrun the feeling of entrapment; my body tensing, a scream trying to erupt from deep within. That's what secrets do. They snare you. They eat away at you. They cast you into a prison. I needed to escape from that prison. From the trap. From my past. Somehow. Did *he* feel the same way?

Three words would have changed everything. Just. Three. Words. From *him*.

Lightning lit the nightdom as I drove, highlighting all the colours of above, the clouds painted with hues of purples and greys, and sometimes green. The wipers swiped double time, fighting the battle of the heavy raindrops.

I turned into *his* street. I needed to know—did *he* feel the same way? Did *he* feel trapped and angry?

In that moment, I realised I hated him. I hated how he made it feel like the accident was my fault. I wanted him to say those three words to release me. *Just three words …*

I slowed my speed as I passed his house: a white bay-and-gable two storey house built onto a slender plot of land. The house I had never been to because he said we could never meet on the mainland. I blasted my horn at his residence in aggressive disapproval, and unease and discontentment. Would he know it was me? Would he even bother to look out the window?

I kept driving. In a trance.

When I stopped the car, I found myself at a familiar place; the headlights shining on the beautifully landscaped park of my past where the fire pit was, and still is, where we had sat at as children, teenagers, and young adults, and shared our funniest stories and deepest secrets ... where I had reconnected, with *him*.

The rain stopped. I grabbed the compact and slipped it into my pocket and left the car. In the darkness I wandered down to the lake of secrets.

The lake that had never once been.

The lake that had appeared after I made a wish in my youth.

I stood on the white pebbled shoreline and looked over at the Jacaranda tree. *My* Jacaranda tree. It was silhouetted in the darkness of the storm like a troubled soul. It was trapped, like me. I wanted it to disappear and take away all of my memories of that fateful evening of the full moon, on that night of Midsummer's Eve—that tragic nightdom that changed everything.

I breathed in the scent of earthiness and freshness—petrichor—and pulled the compact from my pocket. I ran a finger over the diamonds. They sparkled when the sky lit up with sheet lightning. I pushed the button on the side. Click.

Mirror. Mirror.

I gazed into the left side. The distant me. The me of the past, and the memory of fifteen months ago, when I met Tobi at the shoreline in the late afternoon of the Springdom to complete the dare, came—

'Where did you get the boat from?' Tobi's voice was deep and rich in its tones, winding through me.

'I borrowed it from there,' I said after a beat, breathing out the acoustic addiction of his voice and my visual attraction to his presence. I cast my gaze over his stone-coloured chino shorts, and fitting black T-shirt, showcasing his athletic build. I pointed to the white house with the neglected jetty jutting out from the overgrown backyard, grown wild with crabgrass, tangles of pigweed, white clover, and huge nettles.

He followed my line of view, his eyes revealing their stunning ocean-blue colour in the late afternoon sun, and my stomach fluttered.

He looked back at me and connected his eyes to mine. 'You mean, you stole it!' he said, raising an eyebrow.

I shook my head. 'No. I borrowed it. Stealing means you take it and never return it. However, I'm putting it back to where it was … so …. technically, I borrowed it.' The corners of my mouth rose.

'Semantics,' he huffed. He pressed his lips into a hard line. 'I don't know whether it's a good idea to meet you here?'

'Your dare, your rain check … remember? To meet before sundown.' I spread my arms out like introducing him to the horizon. 'And here we are,' I said, and raised my eyebrows at him. I hoped he wasn't the non-adventurous kind, the type who needed three weeks' notice before he could decide on a plan, ruining everything about adventure with the adrenaline rush. 'Jump in the boat and I'll show you where I used to hide in the Jacaranda tree!' I held my breath.

'Jump in the stolen boat?' He frowned.

'Borrowed … remember?' I let out my breath, exasperated. Whatever fascination I held for him before had now evaporated.

'A boat taken without permission—stolen!' He narrowed his eyes at me.

'Whatever—jump in,' I said, not caring whether he would or not. I was over him already.

He cast his gaze over the dark blue boat and inhaled deeply, then bent over and unlaced his shoes, tucking the laces inside the shoes, and placed them on the pebble shoreline, left shoe next to right shoe, in perfect alignment. I smoothed down my white T-shirt and denim shorts then folded my arms while I waited for him. He placed one foot into the boat, and paused, followed by the other, holding on to the side for dear life.

I grinned, grabbed the side of the boat and wobbled it. A little. He froze like a statue, eyes wide.

'Are you sure you want to do this? You look kinda nervous.' I tilted my head to the side and tried to keep a straight face.

He narrowed his eyes at me and lifted his chin, 'Get in before I go without you!'

I smirked. 'As you wish.' I placed my hand over my heart and dipped my head, picked up his shoes and threw them into the boat haphazardly, and climbed in, gently.

I looked at Tobi. His lips parted and a look of relief settled over him like a blanket, so I bounced up and down in the boat, rocking it to and fro. A little. He grabbed onto the sides of the boat; his eyes wide. It was an odd reaction. I stopped, deciding to save him from whatever he was scared of.

'Sit,' he said, his voice assertive.

Hmmm. This is not the Tobi from the fire pit. When did he get so bossy? 'No, please?' I asked as I sat.

He pressed his lips together, parted them, then let out a sharp breath. 'Please,' he added.

I looked into his ocean-blue eyes and gave him a small nod, then took hold of the oars and used one to push off from the bank before I started to row.

'Shouldn't I be rowing, while you're sitting?' Tobi said after a few strokes.

'Why? Are you going to propose to me?' My mouth quirked up at the corners.

He frowned at me before looking across at the lake full of blue. 'No.' He pressed his lips together again.

'Then, I'm pushing the water with the oars—it's completely safe.' After a moment, I released the oars and held the edge of the boat and rocked it from side to side, a couple of times.

Tobi's arms flew out. He grabbed the sides of the boat, his knuckles white. When the boat stilled, he looked up into my eyes and his mouth twitched.

I lowered my head with a grin, picked up the oars and resumed rowing, our eyes connected, greenish-blue to ocean-blue.

'You should look at where you're rowing to,' he said. His forehead creased.

'Tobi, here's the thing about rowing … you can't see where you're going … you are now my eyes … the coxswain.' I watched his Adam's apple move up and down. He ran his hand through his dark hair. 'To the Jacaranda tree … in case you had forgotten where we are going.'

He gave me a half smile and looked out over the glistening water of the lake full of blue, then back to me. 'There's no rudder, so you'll have to follow my directions. Can you do that?' he asked, lifting a brow.

I didn't reply. Instead, I gave a half smile and tilted my head to the side a little.

His lips parted, and he inhaled, his shoulders lifting. 'Continue on your current path.' His eyes glinted.

I kept rowing. 'Do I need to correct my stroke, at all, coxswain?' I asked and raised an eyebrow.

'Turn the boat to your left,' he replied, his cheeks colouring.

'Aye, aye,' I replied, my face deadpan.

He lifted his chin a little. 'To your right, somewhat.'

I stopped moving the right oar to allow the rowboat to turn to the right.

'Keep going with an even, but firm stroke,' he said, and raised an eyebrow at me.

I smiled and rowed a little harder.

'Right again, then even strokes,' he added. He rubbed the back of his neck.

I kept my eyes connected to his. 'Tell me when to stop. After all, I am following your orders … sir.'

After a moment's silence, Tobi placed his hand on the side of the boat and jumped overboard, landing in knee-high water. He walked to the front of the touring boat, once called a gentleman's rowboat, and pulled it to shore.

I felt the lurch of the boat as it found the ground on Jacaranda Island, as I had aptly named it. Tobi stood beside the boat, and held his hand out to help me step onto the ground. But instead, I jumped out of the boat and kicked water at him.

His shoulders lowered. 'My hand was offered in kindness,' he said, his voice soft. 'The least you could have done is placed your hand in mine.'

'Why? Are you trying to impress me?' I asked, my eyebrows raised.

He looked down and shook his head, then pulled the boat further up onto the ground so it was secure. He turned and started to walk toward the Jacaranda tree.

I caught up to him. 'I'm sorry. I will play nice from now.' I placed my hands behind my back and gave him a gentle smile.

He looked down at me. 'I don't believe you can, Indigo,' he said, and looked ahead. 'I can't trust you.'

'What—so I have to *earn* your trust now?' My body tensed.

'Well, so far, you have scored zero out of four, for moments that you could have shown me that you weren't going to be completely unpredictable—'

'You're keeping score?' I clenched my teeth together.

'No—it's just—'

'It's okay. I can read you like a book. I will wait for you to turn the pages first from now.' Energy was sucked from the air around us.

He frowned at me.

I grabbed his hand and pulled him to the Jacaranda tree. I stopped before the wide, rough, grey trunk and looked up at all the colours above. 'Do you see that, Tobi?'

I watched him as he raised his head. He squinted. 'See what?'

'Lavender-coloured blooms creating an umbrella of magic. Each bloom filled with stories, thoughts, whispers, dreams, love, hope … and the unknown.' I took a deep, enchanted breath.

Tobi lowered his head and looked at me with a raised eyebrow. 'You work at the Brain and Mind Institute doing research, right?'

I nodded. 'Correct.'

'You spent years studying Neuroscience at University, didn't you?'

I nodded again. 'Why do you ask?'

He waited a skip in time before he answered. 'I didn't think you would be into … imagination.'

'Do I take that as a compliment, or an insult?' I frowned at him.

'Or,' he pointed a finger at me, 'are you trialling some mind-altering psychedelic drugs?' He raised his eyebrows.

I let out a sigh. 'I think your understanding of an academic is out of whack. We do have an imagination, and we do like to have fun … albeit, sometimes in a different way to the general population, but nevertheless.'

He arched an eyebrow. 'Good to know … all work and no play—'

'Do you—' I reached forward and ran my fingers over the rough tree trunk, '—like to have fun?' I asked, thinking of his panic in the boat.

'It depends on—'

'If it is precisely calculated, checked four times and thought through and deemed safe?' I finished for him.

He faced his body towards me. 'Well—'

'It's okay, Tobi. We all have our limits of comfort. It's just that I like to jump outside mine. I don't expect you to follow me when I do that.' I picked a piece of bark off the tree.

'Why would I follow you?'

'Oh. I'm sorry. I was projecting ahead in time. I shouldn't,' I said. I flicked the bark onto the ground.

He frowned at me. 'So, you can see into the future as well?' He gave me a sardonic smile.

'But of course. Can't all girls?' I punched him on the arm, then started to climb my Jacaranda tree.

'I'm not answering that,' he mumbled.

I kept climbing, as high as I could go. Higher than I did when we played hide 'n' seek when we were young, and as high as I could, to be certain that Tobi would never attempt to follow.

Satisfied, I sat on a strong branch and looked down, then battled to contain my laughter as I watched his clumsy attempts at keeping his balance as he ascended the tree.

When he finally arrived at the height of the branch I was on, I patted the space beside me. He stared at it and blinked. Once.

'It's perfectly safe,' I said, suddenly aware that he smelled of sweetness and spice. I watched as he took a deep breath. 'Trust me. This time,' I added.

He pressed his lips together before he worked out where to put his arms and legs to balance beside me.

I placed my hand on his shoulder once he settled. 'Well done.' I watched as he lowered his head and the corners of his mouth turned up. 'I didn't think you had it in you to climb this high.'

He gripped the branch, his knuckles white. 'Well … I … I must admit … I've never climbed a tree before, so it was a challenge.'

I took my hand off his shoulder. 'What? You. Have. Never.

Climbed. A. Tree. Before?'

He shook his head.

'Brave! I am impressed. I will now call you, Tobi, *the Brave*.' I moved my hand in the air like I was making a public announcement, then dubbed him.

'Thanks. I think,' he said. A dimple graced his cheek with his shy smile.

'What do you think of the view? Can you see how I could watch everyone while we played hide 'n' seek?'

Tobi nodded. 'If only I could keep up with your speed back then, this could have been our Jacaranda tree.'

'It could've been. But you didn't. And those are the facts, Tobi, *the Brave*,' I said.

Tobi held my eyes in his, drinking me in.

'What?' I asked, trying to ignore the sensation of warmth flooding through me, as I felt the pull of his ocean-blue eyes, dragging me to the bottom of the deep blue sea.

'Can we—' he started, then lowered his head before he looked back at me. 'Never mind,' he finished.

'That's easy,' I said.

'What's easy?' he asked.

'Never minding what I am supposed to mind that I never knew that I was minding.'

Tobi smiled at me. A smile that reached into my heart and grew a rose garden around it, filled will sensual, decadent scents, that emitted a joyful and satisfying melody in my mind. And at that moment I knew, this Jacaranda tree was not just *my* Jacaranda tree anymore, it was *our* Jacaranda tree—*our* Jacaranda tree of moments never to be forgotten. Of moments to be created. Of moments that would be etched upon our hearts and minds. Of moments to be shared, just the two of us. We could never go back. It was too late. It had already begun. And it couldn't be stopped—

I snapped the compact shut and flicked the tear away that had rolled down my cheek. How could Tobi and I have become what we are now? In the beginning, it was beautiful. It was, *so* beautiful.

I stared out across the lake of secrets and at all the colours above, so dark on this nightdom, the clouds concealing the light of the muted moon.

Did it know our secret—Tobi's and mine?

Did it watch those events unfold on that fateful Midsummer's Eve, when the full moon shone with its glorious luminosity, lighting up stage where the act played out?

The clouds parted and the moon appeared, reflecting upon the water, perfectly still, like it was holding its breath and waiting to speak. And then, in the next moment it was gone, hidden by the curtain of clouds before the whisper of rain yelled in angry, heavy drops.

I dashed to the shelter of my car and lowered myself into the seat, the windows fogging up and hiding me. I needed answers. But first, I needed the right questions. Time will work its magic. The truth always surfaces in the glory of its ugliness, like the shocking thump of low, out-of-tune keys on a battered piano.

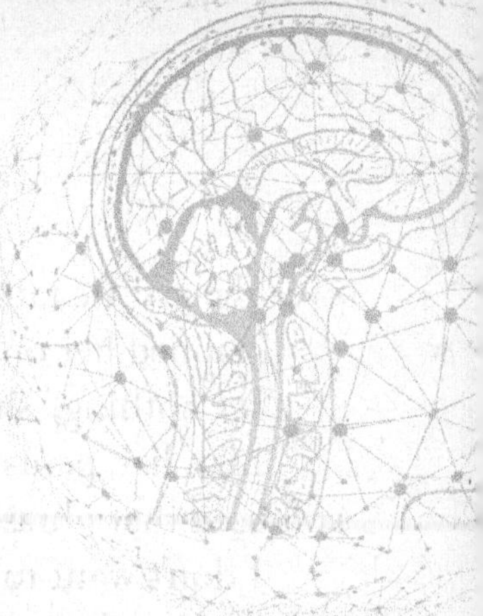

Chapter 9

The sky always seems more crisp and clean the morning after a storm-filled evening. I entered the Brain and Mind Research facility and placed my hand on Scarlett's shoulder. She turned to me. 'Good morning,' I said before glancing down at her desk. Her cochlear implant processor lay there like a decorative element. Again.

'Good morning,' I said, this time without volume.

'Good morning!' she signed aggressively, like shouting. 'You have to stop doing that!'

'Doing what?' I mouthed.

'Saying your words without sound. I can tell there is no volume to your voice when you talk to me like that.' Scarlett pressed her lips together and frowned.

'You can? How?' I said, this time with volume.

'When you talk without your voice, you over-pronounce your words, like I'm deaf.'

'But you are deaf!'

Scarlett looked down and shook her head. Her red hair fell

over the artistic tattoo that adorned the left side of her face.

I tapped her on the shoulder and signed, 'What?'

'It's nothing,' she signed.

'Liar, liar, pants on fire. Tell me,' I signed, wondering why we still used that phrase from our childhood?

'I don't want to talk about it,' she signed and pressed her lips together in a hard line.

'Okay. But I'm all ears when you are ready,' I signed, and instantly regretted my words. I grunted under my breath, berating myself for my insensitivity.

'Great. Can you give me some of yours since you have so many!' Scarlett signed at speed, her eyes reddening.

I deserved her angry words, plus more. I squeezed my eyes shut, then opened them. 'I'm sorry, for being an arse,' I signed.

Scarlett closed her eyes and her shoulders fell.

I wrapped my hand around hers until her eyes opened, then released it. 'Have I told you how much I love your tattoo?' I signed, trying to distract her.

She ran her hand from her left ear and over the right half of her face. Her tattoo was a half-mask of swirls and spirals and meandering vines captured in melody of melancholy. It was beautiful and sad at once. 'I wish …' she signed.

'I wish what?' I signed at a slow speed.

'I wish I'd have waited another second before I was sent to Earth. Then perhaps my life journey would be different.'

'How's that?'

'I wouldn't have been at the fireworks that exploded. And I wouldn't be incurably deaf.'

'Nothing is incurable, the solution just hasn't been found yet. Researchers are making gains all the time—you're a research subject for hearing cell regrowth, and you have a cochlear implant!'

'So it is said,' she signed, then sighed. 'And yes, I can hear with my cochlear implant, and regrowing my hearing cells is totally intriguing. I need to stop feeling sorry for myself and be thankful ... hey, don't you have work to do?'

'Hint taken,' I signed, 'but you know, it's kinda cool talking to you with our own sign language. It's like having a secret conversation. Others can see it, but don't understand it.'

Scarlett pressed her lips in a hard line and shook her head. 'I wish we didn't have to have a secret way to converse.' Scarlett ran a finger down her face from the corner of her eye, like a tear. Sad.

'I'm sorry,' I mouthed and placed my hand over my heart, then walked to the iris scanner for entry to the lab, taking a pause to change my focus to the room I was about to enter.

Neuroscience. Brains. Memories.

The door opened and I wrestled with my olfactory deprivation of the odorless room, centred myself then looked about at the clear glass boxes with suspended brains implanted with wireless electrodes. My skin burned. We had an "awakening" yesterday. It had injected euphoria into me at the time, making me feel invincible. It was what we had been waiting for. But today … I was scared. I had no idea what would happen next.

I paused and let the awakening sink deeply inside me. We had a brain without a body that had reacted to human interaction. I was more than scared. I was absolutely terrified.

I clenched my jaw to fight the anxiety that crept through me.

'Morning, Indigo!' Biran's voice interrupted my mini panic attack. He was one of only four neuroscientists chosen to have direct human connection with the brains. It was a big deal.

I blew a calming breath between my pursed lips. 'Good morning. Have there been more awakenings?' I asked.

'Negative. There's no neural activity to report in any of the specimens according to the electrocorticography. The—'

'Stop, Biran.' I placed my hand on his shoulder and stood in front of him instead of our usual side by side interaction. 'Tell me, how do you feel about the awakening yesterday?' I wanted him to cease from being so analytical. I wanted him to cease from being emotionless, like a robot. I wanted—no—I needed him to show his human side. He was more than a just an intelligent brain in a body used for analysing and reprogramming and technological design of systems to break the barrier of the workings of brains and memories.

He froze and averted his eyes from mine.

'Is there a problem?'

He looked back at me and put his pen down. 'Only one brain awakened, right?' His eyes focused on the brain specimens.

'Yes.'

'I've been racking my brain and going over the electrode placements, searching for why 100B-6 was the only brain that awoke. What is it that the brain responded to?'

'Voice … reading from a book … a particular book—'

'Exactly—voice; sound.' Biran stood before specimen 100B-6, and put his hands on his hips. 'What if the auditory brainstem implant to allow hearing without the auditory system of the human body is placed incorrectly in the other brains, therefore, that is why they did not wake from their perceived coma?' He turned and faced me, then frowned. 'We should verify the positioning of the cochlear implant electrodes to the auditory nerve to rule out any misalignment or mis-connection of the electrodes.'

I shook my head. 'I don't believe that to be the case. The electrodes were positioned precisely at the same location on all of the brains. What if, the reading of the story I chose elicited a memory, which then awakened it? What if, that particular story, was not familiar to the other brains, and there is something else needed to awaken them? I'm thinking we need to look back to the detailed studies of the donors to see what they did and what they liked listening to, and see whether any of those is the catalyst. We also need to attend the debriefing, all four of us—it's important.'

Biran sighed. 'I agree with revisiting the detailed studies of the donors.' He walked around each of the brains, stopping at 100B-6. 'Do you think 100B-6 is female or male?'

'I wish I knew,' I said. 'Would it be of benefit for us to know whether the brains' host bodies were biologically male or female before the encephalectomy?'

Biran walked to the door. 'I believe we have more questions than answers, Indigo. See you at the debrief!'

'See you there.' I turned and walked up to the first encased brain and pressed my hand to the glass. 'Good morning, 100B-1.' I looked at the electrocorticography. *Unconsciousness.*

I moved on to the next brain and pressed my hand to the glass. 'Good morning, 100B-2.' *Unconsciousness.*

Next. 'Good morning, 100B-3.' *Unconsciousness.* As were 100B-4 and 100B-5.

'Good morning, 100B-6. I'm a bit cranky with Biran. He didn't answer my question about how he was feeling. He used the diversion answer technique where you go completely off topic. Anyway, what are you up to today?'

I looked at the electrocorticography. It had registered a spike in activity.

'So, you like talking, I see.'

Spike.

My eyes widened. I wanted to run around the room, but I kept my cool. 'I'll be back. I need to say good morning to our other friends.'

'Good morning, 100B-7.' *Unconsciousness.*

'Good morning, 100B-8.' *Unconsciousness.* As were 100B-9 and 100B-10.

I looked out the viewing glass. Scarlett signed animatedly, 'We have connectivity!'

'I know,' I signed back. Then I mouthed. 'Are there any directives from the neuroscientists, or am I to do what I think needs to be done to keep 100B-6 engaged?'

'You're doing it again,' she signed.

'What?' I signed and frowned at her.

'Over-pronouncing words when you speak without sound.'

'Sorry. It's just that, I don't want 100B-6 to know what is going on,' I mouthed, concentrating on not over-pronouncing.

'Forgiven,' Scarlett signed.

I gave her a wink and went back to 100B-6. I placed my hand on the glass. 'I need your help, 100B-6.' I looked up at the electrocorticography. *Spike.* I couldn't stop my wide grin. 'I want to be able to communicate with you so we both understand each other. But I need you to let me know how to do that.' *Spike.*

I looked to Scarlett. She gave me a double thumbs up as our team of neuroscientists surrounded her to view the brain traces.

'Let's play twenty questions. Your answers are yes or no. I want you only to respond if your answer is yes. Do you understand?'

Spike. *Yes.*

'Does Earth, have three moons?'

No movement.

'Is the sky blue?'

Spike. *Yes.*

'Do fish live in water?'

Spike. *Yes.*

'Do humans have tails?'

No movement. No.

'Do you want to listen to some music?'

Spike. *Yes.*

I turned around and grinned at the team. They gave me a signal to keep going.

'Electronic dance music?'

No movement.

'Jazz music?'

No movement.

'Country music?'

No movement.

'Classical music?'

Spike. *Yes.*

'Pop music?'

No movement.

I wanted to ask, "Are you happy?" but I was too scared to. What happened if 100B-6's answer was no. What then. Does the experiment end?

'Classical music?'

Spike. *Yes.*

'Good. Let's choose a composer.'

Spike. *Yes.*

'Beethoven?'

No movement.

'Mozart?'

No movement.

'Handel?'

No movement.

'Strauss?'

No movement.

'Bach?'

Spike. *Yes.*

'Tchaikovsky?'

No movement.

'Chopin?'

No movement.

'Verdi?'

No movement.

'Bach?'

Movement. Yes.

'Bach it is. Any piece?'

Spike. *Yes.*

'How about Air on the G String?'

Spike. *Yes.*

'Enjoy,' I said.

Bach's *Air on the G String* music filled the room, hugging me like a soft, warm lavender-scented blanket on a cold day. I sat before 100B-6's brain and kept my eye on the electrocorticography. The brain vision recorder appeared to dance. I closed my eyes and immersed myself in the melody, imagining I was lying in a meadow filled with pinkish-purple blossoms filling the air with the orange-like fragrance of wild bergamot, gazing up into the floating white clouds. Bliss.

'INDIGO!' My eyes flew open and I placed my hand over my earpiece at the loud voice. I looked up at the electrocorticography traces. Three more brains were active: 100B-1, 100B-3 and 100B-9. I grabbed a virtual reality headset and pulled up their holograms for a detailed observation.

All of a sudden, I couldn't catch my breath, and I felt light-headed. I placed my hand over my heart and attempted to calm my breathing. Then I smiled. Twice. Once, for the awakened brains. And once, for Scarlett. She had used her voice to yell at me! She had not yelled at me since she went profoundly deaf at the age of seven. My eyes burned and a tear rolled down my cheek. As I wiped it away, three neuroscientists entered the Lab. They fell into their world of observation and data and analysis. I removed my VR headset and took a step back. And another. Then left the room.

I made a beeline for Scarlett and locked my eyes with hers. I slowed my pace, raised an eyebrow at her and smirked. She moved her head from side to side, slowly, her bottom lip trembling. I broke into a run and threw my arms around her and pulled her close.

She let out a quiet cry, then stopped. 'I'm okay now. Thanks,' she whispered, her speech running together and unclear, but enough for me to understand.

I took a step back, taking her hands in mine. I raised my chin and looked at her with narrowed eyes. 'You are courageous,' I said. 'I love you,' I added, my eyes wet.

Scarlett took a deep breath, then blew it out between pursed lips. 'Hey, don't you have work to do?' she said.

I held up her cochlear implant processor. 'I do, once you put this on. I am with you on this hearing journey, remember? The more you use it, the easier and better it gets.'

'Thanks,' she said, connecting the processor to her head.

I smiled, turned, and iris scanned into the Lab. I stood in the corner, gazing at the active brain holograms and the neuroscientists, interacting with them, lost in discussions of hypothesis, observation and analysis.

My body flooded with the feeling of weightlessness as my heart overflowed with happiness. Music is always the key, unlocking the depths of our minds that we are just learning to discover.

Today was a good day.

Chapter 10

Neuroscientists involved in the "Reset Project" had a rule at the research facility. Two hours of hyper-focussed research, followed by a break, long or short, depending on your mental well-being at that moment in time. My first two hours in the Memory Lab were up. I wanted to continue my current course of thought, analysis and observation, but rules were rules, and I knew from experience that even though I had stopped my focussed attention, my brain hadn't. Sometimes during the imposed break, answers or solutions came that we couldn't find before.

I exited the building, accosted by the aroma of freshly roasted coffee, and headed to the café, grabbed a takeaway cappuccino then crossed the main street, strode across the lush lawn, and lowered myself to the ground under the 100-year-old sugar maple tree, an impostor at Tarrin. The vocal tree-purists wanted to remove it, but the townsfolk had saved its life. And rightly so—a tree is a tree. Lungs of the earth. Valuable. Loved. Besides, its display of changing colours of leaves throughout the seasons was a beauty to behold.

I gazed up at all the colours above: the legendary brilliant yellow, orange, and red hues that heralded the Autumndom, *Fall*, and I was filled with an imaginative melody in a simplistic, happy key.

I leaned against the tree trunk and closed my eyes, basking in the nature connection that filled me with a rejuvenated energy, like a magical communication of life forces had taken place.

I opened my eyes and smiled inwardly. Tarrin. My birthplace. Twenty-five years ago. There was a country town feel to it, but it was a hive of activity like you would find in a metropolitan city. There was nothing but locally owned shops—a non-negotiable—plus one tallish building that was fifteen storeys high—a grand hotel. It was always bursting with visitors.

The township was designed in the shape of a square with a splendid, enormous park in the middle, and was central to places that branched out from it—a state-of-the-art hospital, a large university where the *Brain. Mind. Memory. Research Facility* was hidden deep within, two large housing estates—soon to be five, three police stations, two schools—soon to be six, a creative arts precinct with an impressive Performing Arts Theatre, as well as a community hall. Each of the places were fifteen minutes' drive from the town centre.

Tarrin was strange, in an indefinable way. It seemed to be a little bit "more" of everything—*more* sunny, *more* rainy, *more* hot, *more* cold. The sky was *more* blue and the plants were *more* green, the flowers *more* colourful. It was like you had stepped inside a bubble of heightened awareness of the space around you.

I took a sip of my cappuccino, enjoying the creamy, a little bitter, nutty and mildly sweet flavour, and hope blossomed inside me. Milestones in our research made me happy, after the initial hit of anxiety. Step by step. Not always predictable, but still, we were making gains with our research.

As I emptied the last drop of caffeine from my cup, I pulled the compact from my pocket to check that I had no milk froth residing on my face. The diamonds captured a beam of light through the tree and glinted, like a wink. My stomach knotted, and a wave of heat skimmed over my skin. Guilt. The compact wasn't mine. I pushed the button and it flipped open.

Mirror. Mirror. Two of me. One of the present. One of the past.

I gazed into the me, who was close. The me who was now. In the present. I moved my head back and forth, up and down, checking for milk froth. There was none, unlike that day I returned to work with a milk moustache that nobody had the courage to tell me about, and when I returned from two hours in the Lab and looked about, everyone sported a milk moustache and was looking at me, all in on the joke, smiling as my confusion set in and sending me into a panic where I didn't know what was going on and perhaps, just perhaps, my brain had a glitch with memory, and I had lost my sense of time and place, my intelligence.

I wiped my upper lip to make certain no milk was there. I sighed at the memory and the feeling of panic at that moment in time, overriding the laughter of my colleagues and the realisation I had a milk moustache. In hindsight, I know it was meant in good fun. But still, I placed my fingers around the compact ready to snap it closed like a clam shell. But, the image of me in the past held me, and my memory slipped back to the Jacaranda tree with Tobi. In the beginning, when it was beautiful. *So beautiful.* We were still in the tree the first time we had climbed it—

His ocean-blue eyes captured mine, pulling me closer, close enough to fall into his soul as he drank me in. I couldn't stop my left eyebrow from lifting as my blood warmed, filling me with a transcendent feeling of rapture.

I sucked in a deep breath to break his trance and jumped

from the tree. It was safer that way. Once I had stabilized my landing, I gazed out over the water. I frowned. How does that work—looking into someone's eyes, and suddenly you are filled with an unexplained emotion; an extravagant emotion you want to bathe in for a thousand years.

A twig snapped above me. I looked up to see Tobi descending the tree with the slowness of a sloth. I closed my eyes and grinned.

'Welcome to *Zero*,' I said, when he finally stood beside me.

He smiled like the cat that got the cream, then frowned and brushed his hands over his shorts. 'Zero?'

'Yes. Neither *Above*, nor *Below*,' I said, then added, 'then there's *Waaaaaaay Above* and *Waaaaaaaay Below*.'

Tobi looked down and shuffled his feet. His jaw flexed. He looked up at me, raised an eyebrow and said, 'What about … *Within* … the heart dimension that feels like intoxication?'

I placed my hand over his heart, his eyes darkening, and there was that current there, lurking beneath the seemingly light words, almost a shadow beneath his gaze. 'The immeasurable, unexplainable dimension that makes people do crazy things like—' I paused, not wanting to finish my sentence.

'Like what?' he whispered, lingering on the "a", and finishing with a staccato "t". His eyes caressed my lips before slowly returning to my eyes.

'Like …' My gaze wandered down to his lips. Full. Soft. Beautiful.

His lips parted. Then he lowered his head close to mine, an arc of bliss rolling through me. He placed his fingers under my chin and lifted my lips to his, almost touching, silently asking for my permission.

I closed my eyes and whispered, 'I can't … I'm sorry…' I stepped back, my hand falling from his heart.

He drew his eyebrows together, then closed his eyes like he was in pain. The sting of rejection.

I'm sorry. My heart cried. 'It's me, not you.'

He looked towards the horizon and all the colours above that were being swallowed by the nightdom, and ran his hand through his dark hair, the last of the sun's rays illuminating his eyes to the most heavenly ocean-blue colour I had ever seen. My heart skipped a beat.

He turned away from me and took slow steps to the boat. He put one hand on it, looked at me, and held out his other hand, his gaze holding mine.

Like a bee to a flower, I walked toward him and placed my hand in his, a spark of electricity lighting my cells. I felt more alive than if I had lived a hundred lifetimes. I knew all about conductivity and the human body from neuroscience research, but how does one person's touch make you feel all warm and fuzzy, while another's doesn't?

I looked into his eyes. 'I'm—'

'Don't,' he whispered, lingering on the "n" and finishing with a staccato "t".

I clambered into the boat and sat, then Tobi pushed the boat off the shore before jumping in. He sat on the middle seat, facing me, and took control of the oars.

'I—' I started.

'I,' he interrupted. And that was enough. He started rowing, his muscles flexing through his black T-shirt. My eyes wandered to his lips. I wanted to trace my fingers over them and along his jawline, feeling the softness of his stubble. I looked back into his eyes, dark and vulnerable, brooding.

I broke away from the intimate intensity of his gaze and focused on the Jacaranda tree, filled with the lavender blooms of our childhood hide 'n' seek.

'Are you regretting it?' he asked, the timbre of his voice singing to my soul.

I looked back at him. 'I'm in the habit of living my life with no regrets,' I said, 'you?'

He narrowed his eyes at me. 'Nothing ventured. Nothing gained.'

I blinked. Too many times. 'I need to know what you do for a job.' I looked to beyond *Zero*, to the lake full of blue, darkening by the minute.

'Why?' His voice drew me back to him.

I bit my lip and looked away from him, the setting sun blinding me. 'Because it makes the difference between I can't, and I won't.' I looked back at him, 'To … I can, and I will.'

Tobi raised his eyebrows and stopped rowing. He looked down and smiled crookedly, before he looked back at me. 'How does that even fit into the story of boy meets girl?'

'My job.' I closed my eyes. 'I need to know that I can trust you.'

When he didn't say anything, I opened my eyes.

His jaws flexed. 'Do you ask this question to all the guys who make a move on you?'

'No. Just you.'

He looked to beyond *Zero*, the lake full of darkening blue, then back at me, his eyes intense. 'Just me?'

I nodded.

'Why?'

I closed my eyes again. I didn't want to reveal my heart. In a single afternoon he had managed to derail my practised composure of keeping absolute distance from love with simply his presence. 'You climbed the tree when you didn't want to.' I opened my eyes.

'And?'

He was making me work hard. 'And … I appreciated it.'

He nodded, then started to row again.

'So, where do you work?' I asked.

'It doesn't matter where I work, or what I do.' He raised an eyebrow. 'Trust me,' he whispered, his eyes capturing mine. 'Let's meet back here by the light of the full moon when the evening star appears.'

I pressed my lips together and tried to counteract my racing heart. Trust needed to be earned. Trust needed to be tested. And I hoped, if I did trust him, he would never break it—

A bluebird chirped. Once. Twice. I snapped the compact shut and looked about for the feathered creature, without success. I exhaled loudly, looked at my watch, then stood to return to the Memory Lab, slowing as I passed an old man dressed in tattered dusty clothing, lying on a flattened cardboard box with two discarded beer bottles beside him. He was next to the wall near the entrance of the Research Facility. I frowned. Never had there been any homeless people outside the facility, nor on the University Campus.

I entered my workplace, but exited in the next few steps, feeling weighed down by the man's situation. I walked to the café, where I bought a sandwich and a coffee, then headed back to where the homeless man lay. I placed the food on the ground next to him, then stepped back, repulsed by his odour. I pulled some money from my pocket and placed it under the coffee cup. 'Buy some new clothes with the money. It's under the cup.'

He pulled the hood further over his face, grunted, and waved me off like I had annoyed him. I returned to the Research Facility feeling lighter. I had brain and memory investigations to do.

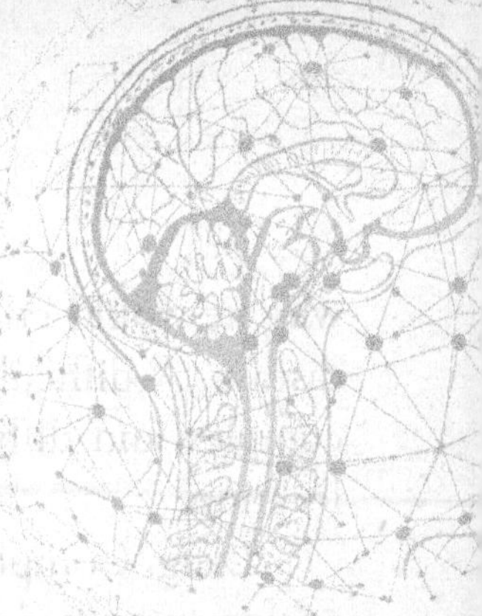

Chapter 11

I saw him before he saw me, wearing navy-coloured skinny stretch business pants, brown leather shoes with a matching belt and a white business shirt rolled up to his elbows. The only thing missing was a tie. He walked through the fellowship of researchers during the lunch break, feet angled in that danseur way. Tall. Lean. Sculptured. Graceful. Oozing with confidence. The type you observe and know there is something deeper about them, something … intriguing, mysterious. Something they have worked hard for to achieve beyond the above average person. The elite in the most polite and respectful way.

'Hi, Xander,' I said as he sat opposite me, lowering himself into the chair in one smooth movement. There was no clumsiness about him.

'Hi. Thanks for meeting me.' He connected his eyes to mine, revealing their dreamy blueness. Eyes that had reached into Yolande's soul, giving her breath. He folded his long-fingered hands together on the table.

'How's your research going?' I asked, still perplexed as to

why he would take on the enormity of researching an incurable disease. A difficult incurable disease at that. The inner ear was complex and difficult to study due to its protected anatomical location.

'Long. Complicated. But I'm not giving up. Yours?' he asked, raising an eyebrow.

'We've had a significant response and will soon enter Phase 2. Just proceeding with caution at the moment.'

'Ah—you're living my dream. I wish I were at your phase with my quest to find a cure for Meniere's disease.'

'Have you got a decent bank of donors from autopsies to use? And living subjects?' I said.

'No and yes.'

'Wouldn't it be a dream come true if the world's Meniere's researchers united at one location, with one vision as a team, sharing knowledge so the same research is not repeated, wasting precious time. One shared purpose. One shared glory of finding the cure. Together.'

'I'm working on it, and gathering a team as we speak. It's not easy going against the grain,' Xander said. He shook his head and a melody in the key of struggle and frustration saturated my mind.

'Tell me about it.' I pressed my lips in a hard line. 'How's Yolande?' I changed our focus. I didn't want to talk any further about going against the grain. That was my job. My research field was in a media blackout for a reason. The global backlash would shut us down.

'That's why I'm here—I want you to remove her memories of the incident.' His gaze was deep and pleading. He was hurting. He was like a song with a melody of grief and despair.

I sucked in a sharp breath. I wanted to ask him how he knew about the classified research I was involved in, but then my love for Yolande overruled it. I let out my breath. 'Did she ask you to come and see me?' My heart was aching for him. There was a difference between the person with Post Traumatic Stress Disorder, or PTSD, asking for help, and someone else asking for help for them. The Yolande I knew before the incident was distinctly different to the Yolande now. It was like her vibrant bold colours had been drained from her until she was nothing but shades of pale pastels with an undertone of darkness, or her colour had been broken even, in a key of sorrow and deep grief. But to be fair, Xander had injected fresh, healing sunshine into her life. But he could never heal her completely. Only Yolande could do that.

'No, and I don't think she ever will. It's just … she says she is coping with Mia's death, but there's the little things that show she isn't, like still wearing safety boots, or when she wipes a tear from her face when she thinks I'm not looking, or when … she just runs, like she is trying to escape from something. I love her, and it kills me to see her suffering. I just—' he winced, '—want her to be happy.' He looked away from me to his right, then took a deep breath and reconnected his eyes to mine. 'With or without me.' Xander ran a hand through his dark hair and the skin around his eyes bunched as a pained stare stole the dreams of blue from the windows of his soul.

I held my breath for a moment and shuddered on the inside. 'You do know what happened to her ... and Mia … what the media released, at least … don't you?' I spoke the words with caution, trying to release the tightness in my throat. I didn't know whether he knew of the incident with Mia or not. If he didn't, I wasn't going to be the person to tell him. I watched his face for a reaction: no change. He didn't know the story. If he knew, he would have frowned, or pressed his lips in a hard line, or nodded his head.

'No. I want Yolande to tell me when she is ready.' His forehead creased.

'Just a roaming thought, Xander … if you live in Tarrin, how can you not know the story?'

He shook his head. 'I was away … my life as a Principal Ballet Dancer, plus studying medicine in the midst of it all. I didn't keep up with anything happening in this part of the world.' He shrugged.

'You could look it up. It would be easy to find. But it would just be the one sentence statement due to the Court Suppression and Non-publication Orders Act. The details of what happened on that day are sealed until after Yolande's death.' I lifted my chin and looked at him. He was super intelligent. I wondered what was stopping him from doing the research about Yolande's past. Was it his love for her?

He looked down at the table and traced a decorative swirl pattern, like the cochlear in the inner ear. 'I have been tempted ... but no. I can't risk betraying her trust. Trust is everything.'

I nodded. He was right. Trust is everything. I placed my flat white coffee on the table and folded my hands under my chin. 'If Yolande chooses to remove her memories, she'll need to wait for Phase 3, when we call for volunteers for the research. I'm not sure how far away that is. It could be next week; it could be five years. How patient are you?'

'Til death do us part.' He raised an eyebrow at me.

I gave him a half smile. 'And what if, once her memories are removed, her personality changes? Behaviourally, there is a possibility that she won't be the person she is now—she won't be the Yolande you fell in love with. If you are staying with her to rescue her, your role will be done. She won't need you anymore.'

Xander rubbed the back of his neck. 'It's a risk I am willing to take. Her happiness is my priority. Like I said, with or without me.'

'You're a good man, Xander. I wish there were more men like you. Do you want to talk to Yolande about it, or do you want me to approach the subject?' I berated myself for using the word "wish", although, if wishes really did come true, more good men like Xander would be a good wish to come true.

His shoulders lifted as he inhaled deeply. Then he exhaled like a heavy weight had just left him. 'You've been friends since you were young. You know the story that changed her life. I think the suggestion would be better coming from you.' Xander lifted his chin and looked down at me, waiting for my reaction, his blue eyes imploring.

I lifted my coffee to my lips and took a slow sip, my eyes connected to his. I placed my cup back onto the saucer, leaned back in the chair and folded my arms. I nodded. Once. 'Okay. I'll see if I can help her.'

Xander's face melted in relief, his tension evaporating like a single white cloud in the blue sky. He placed his hands together in front of him like he was praying, and whispered, 'Thank you.'

'I can't promise anything,' I added.

'I know,' he said.

'If she does have her memories of the incident removed, it could change everything within, and about, your relationship.' My voice floated in the air with a sombre melody. I didn't want to give him false hope.

'That's a risk I'm willing to take. If she can be released from her mind torture, her demons, my soul will rest well, no matter the outcome.'

I stirred my flat white coffee, even though it didn't need stirring, trying to quell the burning anxiety prickling over my skin. Xander had unsettled me with his unconditional love—that intangible, unrecordable emotion that drives human nature. He had triggered too many questions about life and about my research. About human connection. About the state of being human and what we really were and everything existential, and it made me uncomfortable. I had no answers.

I lifted my cup to my mouth and gulped the remainder of my coffee, hoping it would give me courage to take a path with Yolande that could potentially destroy her relationship with Xander. It could break his heart, and I would be the reason for that. Every choice we made affected us, and someone else, somehow, somewhere, touching others with the fallout like a meteor shower of dangerous debris, or of uplifting glitter.

Xander held his hand out to me like we had made a deal. I guess, in a way, we had. I was going to talk to Yolande about deleting her memories. I placed my hand into his. 'I'll keep in touch,' he said as he stood.

I cleared my throat. 'Have you asked her to marry you yet?' The words slipped from my mouth before I had time to sensor it.

He stilled and looked down at me. 'Yes. But she said no.' He winced.

My eyes widened. She said no to the perfect man! He was like the proverbial knight in shining armour. 'Don't give up,' I said. 'You are exactly who she needs.'

He pressed his lips together and nodded, then walked away in that graceful danseur way.

I checked my phone calendar. I had a window of time in a few days when I could visit Yolande at Flowers for Fleur. But tomorrow, I needed to visit Jacaranda Island under the cloak of the darkness, and Sunday was my day as an extraordinary collector of curiosities and peculiar things. It was my mind distraction to retreat from the heaviness of the content of research at the Mind and Brain Lab.

Chapter 12

White pebbles groaned underfoot as I walked along the foreshore of the new inland lake I had wished for, and for a moment, I wondered if I could unwish it. I stopped and scanned the houses to the right for a rowboat. There sat a red one; partially hidden by the reeds. I walked toward it and stopped a couple of metres away, checking that no one was about. Convinced all was safe, I waited for the last rays of the sun to vanish so the new moon would cast its darkness over the land of the nightdom, then placed my hands on the front of the boat, pushed it out of the reeds and jumped into it, quickly moving to the middle seat to pick up the oars and start rowing.

I wasn't stealing it; I was borrowing it.

My arms felt heavy as I moored the boat against the jetty of Jacaranda Island. Built by Tobi. Once upon a time. The heaviness was not from muscle fatigue. It was from the oppressive weight of memories. Anxiety burned a path through my body while I decided whether to disembark or not. I hadn't been here since the incident on that Midsummer's Eve that was meant to be a

Midsummer's Eve dream of first intimacy. And then that dream was gone in a mere moment. By a wish that couldn't be unwished. By words that couldn't be unspoken.

I sucked in a deep breath, grappling to find my inner strength, turned on my torch then alighted from the rowboat. I stood on the jetty, my heart racing while I decided where to go; the Jacaranda tree, *my* Jacaranda tree, or to the deck Tobi had built? I had to remove any evidence that could connect us to the missing body.

I fell forward as if released from a spell, and rushed to the Jacaranda tree of my youth, missing the swing hanging from the thickest branch and avoiding the place that held the incident on that Midsummer's Eve. The incident that only two people had knowledge of. And it had to stay that way.

I wrapped my arms around the Jacaranda tree as tightly as I could before I went to sit on the deck where my story with Tobi unfolded, then bloomed in a beautiful, harmonious, spectacular symphony, and died on the last note of Midsummer's Eve with a sickening thud.

I struggled to lift the leaden weight of the past from my mind and looked out beyond *Zero*, the lake full of darkness under the invisible new moon of the nightdom, like my mood.

A melancholic melody entered my mind, and I turned my head to the right at the Jacaranda tree. Stars and coloured mini-jars, barely visible, hung from branches. I filled with the enchantment of Tobi, until my eyes settled to that place beneath the Jacaranda tree where time had stood still. I pulled the compact from my pocket, remembering the first time I touched it, and wondered why I still had it.

Mirror. Mirror. I pushed the button on the compact and it flipped open.

Two mirrors. Two of me. The one before the event. The one after. I gazed into the mirror on the left, the one before the event, the one distant, and a memory presented itself to me—

'By the light of the full moon,' he said, his voice deep and rich in its tones, creating a melody of heart-string vines growing and surging through my veins, directly to my core in a key full of longing and searching. He lowered himself beside me, smelling of sweetness and spice and my heart skipped a beat.

It was just the two of us on our own little island in the magic of the nightdom, created by me. *My* wish.

'Let's make it a rule,' he said, and leaned against the rough trunk of the Jacaranda tree, one knee bended.

I looked at him, smiled and gave a small nod. 'As planned. And I agree, it is now Rule Number 1—*we shall meet by the light of the full moon, when dark shadows become a whisper of themselves.*' I spent a moment in his eyes, dark at this twilight hour, trying to remember their true colour, then let my gaze fall to his fitting white T-shirt and ripped denim shorts, then looked away and took a deep breath to calm my thumping heart. 'I see you stole a boat,' I said, to change my focus.

He cast his eyes over at the charcoal gentlemen's rowboat. 'Borrowed,' he said with a crooked smile.

'From a lakeside house, like mine?' I lifted an eyebrow at him.

'No … that's stealing. I borrowed mine from a friend.' He lifted his chin and gazed down at me, setting a trail of fire burning through me.

I furrowed my brows. 'What if … the person living at the lakeside house, where my boat comes from, is my friend?' I widened my eyes at him.

'What if … I think you are a not a very convincing liar?' He arched an eyebrow at me.

I couldn't stop the involuntary blink of my right eye. I thought men who considered themselves a suitor were supposed to be nice. His comment was like barbed wire. It was like a cacophony of discordant notes trampled with muddied boots on an out-of-tune piano. I didn't like being called a liar. I did, however, like to bend the truth a little. I liked to implant ideas. I liked to weave tales of untruths to reveal the truth, like a storyteller. But I was not a liar who deceived to get what I wanted.

Anger bubbled inside me. I swallowed it, hard, but not enough to disable it from turning into a horde of callous hot words spewing from my lips, 'What if I think you are keepi—' I stopped myself from finishing the accusatory sentence about him keeping a secret from me. I wanted to question his job that he had said I didn't need to know. I needed to be able to trust him. Withholding information is like keeping a secret. I hated secrets. It was a power play.

Plus, the last time we met, I had hurriedly verbalized my mobile number and substituted some numbers with letters as a test to see what he would do with it before we parted ways. Firstly, he remembered the ten numbers and letters from a mere mention delivered in a speedy manner. Secondly, it would have taken some time to decode my mobile number. I wondered how many people he had texted in his search of mobile numbers before finally reaching me.

'What if you think I am keeping what?' he said, the "t" pronounced with staccato.

'Nothing ...' I murmured.

'It is something, Indigo. Like I said—you are not a very convincing liar.'

I held my eyes open. Wide. To stop the involuntary blink of my right eye. I pulled my knees up to my chest and cupped my hands around them and looked beyond *Zero*, the lake full of darkness, while I thought of way to avoid answering his question about my thoughts on withholding information so it became like a secret. 'So … how did you do it?' I picked at a pretend thread on my off-white shorts.

'How did I do what?' he asked.

'Text me?' I pretended to brush off a leaf from my button-up, mustard-coloured, cotton, sleeveless shirt.

'You gave me your number, remember?'

A wave of anxiety rolled through me. I looked at him. Was he telling an untruth? 'No, I gave you numbers and letters—ten of them. The average person remembers seven or less numbers at a mere mention at best, yet I threw in some letters to increase the difficulty and—'

'And maybe I am more intelligent than the average person?' He tilted his head to the side a little.

'But what you did … decoding the information … is not normal. No other guy has managed to work out my contact number.'

He shrugged. 'The process of elimination,' he said and frowned.

'Plus, more,' I added with accusation.

'Perhaps a little … *more*,' he said, his voice softening, showing "a little" with his thumb and forefinger. 'And maybe,' he connected his eyes to mine, 'they didn't want you as much as I want you.' His words lingered in the air like a symphony of hopes and dreams. I wanted to capture them and pull them inside me. But I didn't. I needed to trust him before I let him seep in through the cracks of my heart.

I hit him on the arm with the back of my hand. 'What if I think you are a not a very convincing liar?' I reused his words to stop his enchanting word-smithing from etching onto my episodic memory in my hippocampus.

His eyebrows furrowed and he looked down at his feet, now crossed over each other, his mood plunging to the uneasy key of worry and discontent.

The air stilled between us, frozen in time. Words stung. My words. I changed my sitting position as an uncomfortable emotion persecuted me. Guilt? Regret? I had hurt him. I closed my eyes and pressed my lips together as I swallowed a cup of virtual bitterness. I had done it again. Pushing someone away instead of pulling them toward me.

I opened my eyes at the sound of his footfall on the ground. He was walking towards his borrowed boat. Was he leaving? I didn't blame him. I clenched my fits in self-disappointment and closed my eyes again. Why did I always do this to guys I liked? Was it to hurt them before they hurt me?

I didn't want to watch as he rowed away. I didn't want that memory embedded into my mind to replay over and over again, always wanting to go back and change my actions, my words. Like an *undoing*. I didn't want to relive that moment, allowing it to steal my sleep, to steal my happiness, to steal my energy. Entertaining that cognitive behaviour and wallowing in sadness was self-destructive.

So, I set my mind to far away, to another time and place to barricade my heart. It would be over soon, and I could get back to my life of research, of helping others, of conducting illegal, unethical research that ultimately would improve the lives of people and save lives. We were on the cusp of a major breakthrough at the Brain and Mind Institute.

There. Done. He was a distant, unconnected memory.

I opened my eyes when a fruity perfume filled the air. Before me was a bouquet of delicate cup-shaped white roses, white daisies, and white peonies, and Tobi kneeling before me, his arms cradling the scrumptious bouquet. 'Do you believe me now?' His eyes, filled with sincerity, gently fell on mine, capturing me.

'Tobi,' I whispered, bottling the need to cry before it erupted from deep within in an embarrassing gaffe. I took the flowers from him and lifted them close to my face and inhaled, allowing the fruity elixir to flow through me filling me with peace, like my worries had been injected into the setting sun, then carried into the depths of the dark void beyond the horizon to be forgotten. 'They're beautiful,' I said.

'Like you.' His voice was tender, sprinkling his bravely chosen words over his symphony of hopes and dreams, tempting me like a bee to a flower.

I stilled. I was anti the word beautiful. It was always so shallow, based on physical attributes one was born into without choice. I preferred the depth and breadth of a person—the essence. 'Outside or inside?' I said, pulling a petal off a daisy to represent the beauty of imperfection, planted into Tobi's subconscious to awaken at another time.

'Outside can only be my answer because I don't know the real you … yet.' His words glowed like a beacon, a guiding light, and at the same time, a warning. Were his words genuine, or chosen to what he thought I wanted to hear?

I dropped the petal, watching it twist and turn in panic until it nestled on the ground, waiting for its life to recede. 'If you could see me inside, you may not like me.' My courageous words escaped on my breath in a mis-happen, unmelodic tune.

'What does it look like?' His eyes pulled mine to them like I was in a trance.

I extracted my gaze from his before I became trapped in his hypnotic allure that threatened to wash over me like a spell. I moved my head from side to side in a minimalistic way and pulled another white petal from the sacrificial daisy bloom. 'Chaotic. Messy. Lost. Sometimes. Filled with too many questions and not enough answers.'

'Good,' he said within a heartbeat, his articulation lingering on the "d". He sat beside me and leaned against the trunk of the Jacaranda tree; one knee bent.

'Good?' I looked at him with wide eyes. Men stuttered and fell over their words when I told them how chaotic, messy, and lost I was. And then they left. Were my words the curse of honesty, or a test of their commitment to me?

He nodded, like he was moving his head in time to a relaxing melody. He raised an eyebrow at me. 'It makes you … more interesting.'

I looked down at the flowers and focussed on a white rose this time, and caressed a petal, as soft as velvet. I made an oath to myself in that moment, an oath not to break—to not to tell him my innermost thoughts. Deep and meaningful conversations would be off the menu for us. Or for me at least. I didn't want him to see inside me in case he discovered my ugliness. He would run from me then.

I ran my finger over the logo of the bouquet paper. 'Flowers for Fleur,' I whispered. My lips curled up.

'The best flower shop, I'm told,' he said with raised brows.

'I have to agree. You know that Yolande's grandmother owns it!'

'Nice,' he said, a dimple showing on his right cheek.

My heart skipped a beat. I was in trouble. I was falling for him and it scared me.

I looked up at the Jacaranda tree to all the colours above, to distract myself from his sweet and spicy scent, the perfume from the flowers, and the warmth rising within me. He was romance personified. I consciously cut off my place of thinking, of feeling and directed my focus to the full moon highlighting all the colours above. The purple hue of the Jacaranda blooms glowed with enchantment. I grinned. 'A new rule to add to the full moon.'

Tobi looked upward. 'And that would be?' His voice cracked. Was he nervous?

'On the nightdom of the full moon, when dark shadows become a whisper of themselves, the Jacaranda Tree of Jacaranda Island must be climbed. Rule Number 2.' I smiled up at the tree, imagining the rule weaving and curling around the trunk and kissing the blooms.

I turned my attention to Tobi. His eyes remained focussed on the canopy of purple magic. Then he lowered his head and looked at me, his eyes narrowed, and his eyebrows squished together like he was in a state of confusion. 'Nightdom?'

'Of course. "Dom" means a state or condition, so nightdom means a state of the night … and then there's daydom. And Springdom. And Winterdom. And cloudom. And raindom. And stardom. My invented words from my genius self at the age of six.' I beamed a smile, then shrugged one shoulder, wondering if it was wise to share my fictional words from my childhood with him.

He arched an eyebrow at me. 'Of course.' He paused. 'It makes total sense, doesn't it?'

I breathed out the feeling that he was poking fun at me. I lifted my hand, palm facing upward to steer him off analysing my choice of words. 'Shall we?'

He looked up and frowned. 'Aren't we too old to be climbing trees?'

'Tobi.' I sighed. 'You can never be too old to climb a tree. Climbing a tree … changes things.'

'Changes things?' He squinted.

'Absolutely. It changes your perspective, literally and mentally. Climbing a tree makes everything better.'

He pressed his lips together and swallowed in an exaggerated way. 'Right. Let's get it over then,' he said.

'Let's get it over?' My voice rose higher on the last syllable, more than I intended.

He looked at me and nodded, then wiped his hands on his jean shorts. I placed the flowers on the ground, stood, then offered him my hand. He took it, sending a warm sparkle through my fingers. When he rose, I released my hand and rubbed my fingertips, while he looked up at the tree again.

'You really don't have to climb the tree if you don't want to, Tobi, *the Brave*.' I raised a brow.

He grinned. 'Well. I have no choice now, do I?'

I frowned, and my excitement fell, forming a stack of jumbled musical notes at my feet from the happy, yet naive melody that had been swirling around me. 'You always have a choice. You are the boss of you.'

He drew his eyebrows together. I could see thoughts turning over in his mind. He had just lost the courage of stepping out of his comfort zone. Hesitate, or think too much, and you are less like to act. You lose the battle.

'See you at *Above*,' I said, then disappeared up into the tree. *My* Jacaranda tree. I settled on a branch that jutted out halfway. It was safe. For someone like him. I closed my eyes and breathed in my happy place of hide 'n' seek from my childhood, where I managed to stay hidden, sometimes for hours at a time, oblivious to my friends.

I heard the ground moan below and looked down to see Tobi moving from foot to foot while he plotted his climbing gig. The ground grumbled again, and then there was silence, like all the music of nature on Jacaranda Island was holding its breath. I watched as Tobi hugged the tree while he climbed at the speed of a sloth. I was tempted to shake the branch a little to tease him, but decided against it. When he was almost at my branch, I moved over for him to sit next to me.

'Brave,' I said with a grin as he manoeuvred onto the tree's limb. I wanted to add "Sloth-man", but didn't. I had already hurt him once tonight.

Tobi's lips curled up at his accomplishment, then he reached into his pocket and pulled out a pocketknife and flicked it open.

I stiffened, my heart pounding. I kept my eyes on the shiny blade, wondering whether he wanted to meet me under the moonlight to kill me. After all, I didn't really know him. Just because his family was associated with mine didn't make him a person of integrity, or morals. My adrenaline spiked and I had an undeniable need to jump from the tree to get away from him. I placed my hands on the branch on either side of me, ready to jump in 3, 2—

'I want to carve our names on our tree,' he said, blinking numerous times.

I looked at him with wide eyes, then relaxed a little.

'Technically, it's my tree,' I said with raised eyebrows as my heart calmed. I blew an undetectable breath of relief between my lips.

'Then … *may* … I carve our names into *your* tree?'

I lifted my eyes to the full moon and all the colours above, and closed them. 'No,' I said, then opened my eyes and looked at him.

He held the pocketknife towards me, the handle facing me. 'You do it, since you believe it's your tree.'

I shook my head. 'I can't. It's a living thing.'

'And it has feelings?' he said in an incredulous voice.

'Well, I would hate for me or you to carve our names into the tree, and it died! Death is so final, for trees …'

'Nah. That won't happen. Think of it this way—it's just like getting a tattoo, like humans?'

The hair on the nape of my neck prickled. 'Here's the thing … humans choose to do it. The tree isn't choosing.'

'So, the tree has rights?'

'It's *my* tree.' My skin burned with anxiety. I wanted this conversation to evaporate, with the pocketknife.

He folded the blade of the pocketknife in and pushed it back into his pocket. 'You're right,' he said.

I frowned. 'About tree rights, or my tree?'

'Tree rights. Technically, it's not your tree. It's not your land and you didn't plant it.'

I nodded. 'It just feels like my tree. I grew up with it, and the wish and all.'

'The wish?' His words were painted with disbelief.

'I wished for it to be surrounded by water, and it happened. So, I kinda feel … *connected* … to the tree,' I said, testing his thoughts on wishes.

He chuckled. 'Wishes don't come true. They're just words of no consequence imbued with a person's conscious dream.'

'I disagree. I believe that wishes are words that—' I stopped and looked through the leaves of the Jacaranda tree to the few stars that were part of all the colours above on the nightdom of a full moon. I didn't want to tell him what I really thought wishes were. He would think I was truly strange. I was an adult after all, with a degree in neuroscience.

'Don't stop,' he whispered, his words tender and hypnotising.

I took an audible breath. 'Okay … I believe that wishes—' I hesitated, wondering if I could trust him with my belief. I narrowed my eyes at him to gauge if it was safe to tell him. His gaze was intense, even in this muted light of the full moon, like the next words uttered from my mouth would save his life. I closed my eyes for a moment before I looked to the full moon again, luminous in all the colours above. 'Wishes … change things.' I nodded. That was enough. For him. For now. Even though it was not the entire truth of what I thought.

He cleared his throat. 'That's it? Wishes change things?' His words were imbued with the sound of laughter embedded into each letter of each word.

'Yes.'

'Hmmm … so, if I wish for something right now, it will change things?'

I raised an eyebrow at him. 'Absolutely. Go ahead.'

'Okay.' His eyes lingered on mine before he lifted them to the nightdom. I could see the reflection of the moon in them, bright and beautiful. Like him. Warmth filled me, melting me, and ignited the feeling of light and love. It was like I had been waiting for this moment in time since the day of my birth, and I was finally awakened, ready to grow and bloom. After a moment he looked back at me, his eyes glinting. 'Wish, wished. How long should I wait?'

'It depends. Did you add a time limit to your wish?'

'Good point. Let me wish again.' He lifted his eyes to the nightdom sky, splattered with the most courageous stars competing with the light of the full moon, giving me time to explore his profile—sculptured with a straight nose, his jawline defined.

I berated myself for judging his physical appearance. It was I who was anti the societal concept and opinion of perfection in beauty, but why did the beauty paradigm enter my consciousness? The media needed to work harder with the paradigm shift, with their social manipulation of what was acceptable with beauty. I aimed for the philosophy of *Wabi-sabi*; imperfection as the basic principle—finding beauty within transience and imperfection; acceptance. It is what it is. I brought myself back to the moment. 'Wait. Is it something that is likely to happen, or something that is impossible?' I said.

He looked back at me. 'Does it make a difference?'

I nodded. 'If it is something that is likely to happen, would it have happened without the wish? If so, that nullifies the wish.'

'So, wishes have rules?'

I nodded. 'Has your wish happened yet?'

'No.'

'Then tell me what your wish is.' I tilted my head to the side and narrowed my eyes at him.

'If I tell you, it won't come true.'

I frowned at him. 'Who said?'

'Cinderella.'

'Cinderella?' I laughed, surprised by his answer.

'Yes.' He looked across the water. 'Let's see … if he tells you, it won't come true. If you cut to it, it won't come true. If you say it out loud, it won't come true—'

'If you wish on a falling star, your wish will come true,' I finished reciting for him.

And at that moment, in all the colours above in the nightdom, a star flashed across the heavens leaving its trail of light like a dusting of magic. A shocked silence sat between us, then Tobi leaned close to me, his scent of sweetness and spice pooling inside me. 'Wish, wished. Now I just have to wait.'

I giggled at the absurdity of everything that had just happened. 'Consider us officially waiting.' I frowned. 'How do I know if your wish comes true if I don't know what it is?'

'That's for me to know, and for you to find out.'

'Aye. The web of lies of a wish. What if I made a wish and it was opposite to your wish? Whose wish would come true?'

'I've never thought about that. Did you make a wish?'

I shook my head. 'It's too dangerous.'

'Dangerous?'

'For me. Always.' I pressed my lips together, remembering that very day I wished for the Jacaranda tree to be surrounded by water, and then the geographical disaster struck: the gentle tectonic movement that created the freshwater lake basin, making Jacaranda Island.

'Well then. That leaves my wish in a strong position to come true then, doesn't it?'

'It depends. Do *you* have to make it come true, or is it something *I* have to do to make it come true?'

Tobi picked a flower from the tree, inhaled its scent, then twisted it round and around. 'I guess,' he paused as he handed the beautiful lavender bloom to me, 'I could tell you that part. It is something I wished for you to do.' He gazed into my eyes and raised an eyebrow at me.

Right then, I wished he had never said those words. I gave him a lazy smile. 'Great. Now I will be second guessing everything I do with you, and for you. I will be wondering if it is it my will, or yours? See … your wish has changed things already.'

Tobi closed his eyes and shook his head slightly. 'You're right.

My wish has changed things already, but is it because I told you part of it?'

'Probably. I think you have to unwish your wish.'

'And how do I do that? Once you wish for something, you can't unwish it, can you?'

'You need to retract it.'

'Do I need a falling star to do that?'

I shook my head, and let out a sigh. 'I don't know.'

He narrowed his eyes at me. 'I don't want to retract my wish. I still wish for it, with all of my heart.'

'Okay,' I whispered. I looked at the luminous full moon, higher in the nightdom of all the colours above. 'Did you know, the moon looks different depending on which hemisphere you live in?' I glanced at Tobi; his eyes moved from the water to the moon.

'No. I didn't. But it makes sense.'

A cool breeze blew off the water and I shivered. Tobi put his arm around me and pulled me close, warming me. I fought my internal battle of whether to allow myself to be physically close to him or not. To trust or not to trust. I didn't want to get hurt. My heart wasn't ready. It would never be ready, would it? I wished for a little courage and a little faith in myself, then placed my head on his shoulder with a torment of anxiety of possible rejection from my action. I held my breath and waited. Would he remove his arm? Would he withdraw his arm, his care?

Something changed in that moment, in the silence that wrapped us in a cocoon of emotional connection, ministering to my emotional vulnerability with the waving of the white flag; a surrendering to a war; my heart war; my impenetrable wall protecting me from love. It felt like his life-force had connected to mine, our two grey paths colliding and joining as one, creating an impossibly bright spark of white light before cascading down in an explosion of colour. My heart bloomed in my chest and I felt like I was floating with a satisfying melody of optimism and declarative notes in a most wonderous key. Did he feel what I had just felt?

The full moon disappeared behind the clouds creating a cloak of darkness, hiding all the colours above, and I returned to the branch of the Jacaranda tree from my epiphany.

'I have a confession,' I said, high on his love potion.

He removed his arm from my shoulders and I adjusted my balance on the tree limb. 'You have a boyfriend?' His voice quivered.

'No.'

'Good,' he said, his voice tender. He placed his arm around me again.

'I turn into a grump at midnight on the nightdom of the full moon. I need to go home.'

I watched as he looked down and smiled. He was beautiful. He looked up, connecting his eyes to mine. 'Now that I would like to see.'

'No, you don't. Start climbing to *Zero*.'

'Zero?'

'Yes. Neither *Above*, nor *Below*, the ground, remember,' I said.

He nodded. I watched as he descended the tree with the slowness of a sloth. I shook my head then jumped from the tree and went to wait for him where the water kissed the shore. I looked out beyond *Zero*, to the lake full of darkness with a hint of dark blue, calm at this time of the nightdom.

'You'll keep.' His breath was warm against my ear as he stood behind me.

I turned to face him. 'Tobi, if you can't navigate tree climbing with confidence by now, I don't think you ever will.'

'Perhaps,' he said. 'But what if I'm just pretending to be a bad climber?' He handed me the flower bouquet I had mindlessly left at the base of the tree, the fruity perfume infusing the air, lingering, and releasing a magic spell I refused to acknowledge.

I narrowed my eyes at him. 'What would you gain from that?'

'Your attention.'

I raised an eyebrow at him. 'A calculated lie. Is that a wise move when you asked me to trust you?'

'What then, if … you know … it's like when people dim their light to fit in with others? Like perhaps, I could scale the tree blindfolded, but I don't want you to feel less capable, and I am choosing to be kind to you?'

'Again, what would you gain from that?'

'Your attention.'

I let out an audible breath of exasperation. 'Any more versions to tell?'

'Okay … what if, I am being terribly careful because of my recent knee surgery, and climbing the tree is off my list of things to do, but I am doing it just for you?'

'Well … that would earn you bonus brownie points. Which of your stories tells the truth?'

He lowered his head and looked up at me. 'The one that makes you like me.'

'You think I don't like you?'

He lifted his head and pushed his fingers through his dark hair. 'I'm having trouble reading you. I keep trying to reach out to you, but four out of five times tonight you rejected my attempts to make a connection.'

'You're counting?' Anxiety bubbled in my stomach. He really had no idea how he affected me.

He looked down and closed his eyes, then pinched the bridge of his nose. His perfect nose. He looked up, opened his eyes, and rubbed his bottom lip with his finger. 'It's how I work out whether it is worth my while to keep trying with you.' He kept his eyes connected to mine.

My throat tightened. 'I told you … I'm chaotic. Mes—'

'Messy. Lost, sometimes. Filled with too many questions and

not enough answers. Let me help you find answers,' he said, his eyes softening.

'And when you do, will you leave me?' I kept my focus on him, trying to suppress the feeling that a road train was about to hit me.

He looked out beyond *Zero*, to the lake full of inky darkness, then back to me. He placed a finger under my chin and lifted my face so our eyes connected closer. 'What if … you leave me?' He held my eyes until I felt like I was falling. Crashing. Melting.

I looked at his lips. I wanted to place mine on his for a taste. Just a little taste. I blinked, releasing me from his spell. 'I need to go.' I turned and placed the flowers into my boat.

'I know you do.' Tobi stepped into the water and placed a hand on the side of the boat to steady it for me.

As I climbed into the boat, he held out his other hand for me to take. The moment our fingers touched, my skin ignited. My breath hitched and I looked up at him through my eyelashes. He nodded with a knowing, then looked over the water and towards the house from where I "borrowed" the boat. 'What's wrong?' I said.

'We need Rule Number 3 for Jacaranda Island,' he said.

'What would that be?'

'One boat allowed on the island at a time.'

'So it doesn't look suspicious?' I said.

'No. So I know you are safe.' He lifted my hand to his lips and pressed a feather soft kiss there, sending a tingle through my veins.

I sat on the middle seat of the boat then looked up at him. 'Has your wish come true yet?' I said.

'No, but there's still time.'

'How much?'

'Until you row into the darkness.'

I picked up the oars. 'And when your wish doesn't come true—'

'It will. I wished upon a shooting star, remember?' He raised his eyebrows and gave me a coy smile.

My lips curled up in a slow smile, suppressing a loud laugh that wanted to decorate the darkness with psychedelic high -pitched notes. 'Good night, Tobi,' I said, and started rowing.

'Good night, Indigo Feather Danube. Until the next full moon,' he said, his voice a little louder.

I stopped rowing, the boat gliding over the smooth water. 'I want to break Rule Number 1,' I yelled.

Tobi stopped pushing his rowboat off the island and looked at me. 'I'm listening,' he called.

'I want to meet under the azure canvas with the sun that casts no shadow.' I waited for him to answer but he just stared at me. Perhaps his wish had just come true? I watched as he jumped into his boat with quick careful movements, executed more like an athlete than a clumsy solenodon moving at the pace of a sloth. He rowed toward me with planned luxurious strokes. Was this the same Tobi that I knew? Maybe his story about being terribly careful because of his recent knee surgery was the true one?

He stopped rowing and his boat glided, stopping gently next to mine. He reached over and held onto the side of my boat, pulling it against his. 'Say it again,' he said, running his other hand through his hair looking like he had been completely undone.

'I want to meet under the azure canvas with the sun that casts no shadow.'

Tobi smiled and looked away from me, beyond *Zero*, to the lake full of dark, inky blueness.

'What? Was that your wish come true?'

He looked back at me. 'No. But each moment it is getting closer, with all my heart.'

My breath stuttered at the melody of his words. 'Really? What did you say the time limit was?'

'Until you row into the—'

'Darkness,' I finished.

He nodded and placed his hand on his chest.

I looked around. Technically it wasn't dark. The full moon guaranteed that. His wish was more complicated than it seemed. 'I think I like your wish,' I said.

'I know I do,' he said, his look dark and brooding.

My heart skipped a beat and my gaze wandered to his lips. They parted. Just a small kiss—

I snapped the compact shut and lifted my finger and ran it over my bottom lip, then breathed out the memory. How did it all go so wrong? My heart fell into a looping melody in the key of worry as I wallowed in lamentations.

Three words would have changed everything. Just. Three. Words. From his lips.

A cool breeze bounced off the water, stinging my eyes. It was time to get off the island, but first I had to retrieve Tobi's Book of Unfinished Stories. I rushed over to the Jacaranda tree and looked upward, but then remembered that he didn't have it on him that fateful last night we were here together. I returned to the deck that Tobi had built, opened the storage hatch and shone my torch down into the cavity. And there it was: the book with the dark blue hard cover, the book of endless possibilities, of mind probing, and inner revelations. The book of once upon a time … and of the dark night.

I reached down and grabbed it, then returned to the Jacaranda tree. I needed the box of connections; the box of *us* we had buried. I looked up at the tree and aligned the branch I had made a mental note of, followed it down to the ground and started to dig. I uncovered the box wrapped in brown paper, and tied with a piece of string just like on that day, stood and brushed the dirt off it, then walked to the jetty and back to the rowboat. I climbed in, connected with the oars and rowed back to the mainland.

Evidence removed. Mission accomplished.

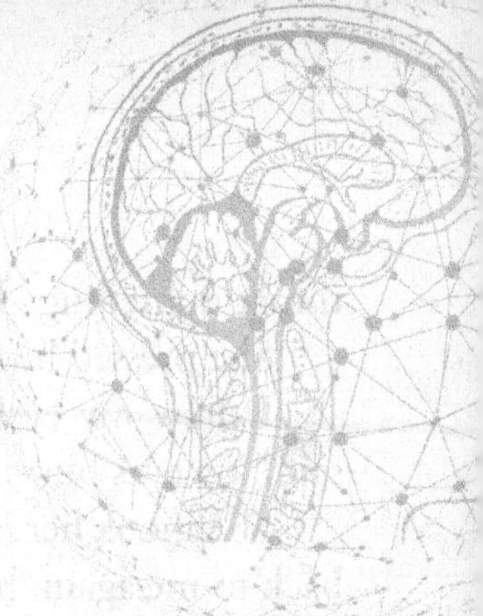

Chapter 13

Scarlett entered the work station of the Memory Lab with sadness clouding her face, stealing her sunshine in a swirling melody of melancholy. I waved at her to catch her attention. She looked at me. 'How are you?' I mouthed.

She smiled with the emptiness of a void. That mask you wear that conceals your truth. 'Well, thanks,' she signed.

She most definitely was not well. I moved closer. 'Hi, Scarlett. How are you today?' I signed with exaggeration. She needed to stop lying to me, her best friend.

She frowned. 'Good, thanks,' she mouthed.

'Letti—are you okay?' I said into the microphone of her cochlear implant processor. I stood in front of her and raised my eyebrows.

'I'm fine!' she signed, over-pronouncing the mouthed words and glaring at me. Her eyes watered and glistened. She looked down and shook her head.

I stepped closer and put my hands on her shoulders. She looked up at me. I raised an eyebrow. 'Tell me?' I whispered, my throat tightening.

She pressed her lips together and shook her head.

I drew my eyebrows together. 'Make … me understand!' I said, my eyes burning.

She shook her head, yet again. She looked away from me, and back to me again, her hands working with speed, 'I have to work a hundred times harder than anyone else because of my hearing loss, and relearning to hear. I can't tell them how hard I have to work because I don't want them to feel sorry for me. I don't want them to look at me with pity in their eyes.' Her eyes reddened and filled with tears, balancing on the edge of her eyelids. 'I feel like an inferior, weak person, like I have done something wrong to deserve this prison sentence there is no release from. It makes me feel incompetent at my job when I struggle … it makes me feel … not good enough. Never good enough.' She flicked her tear away. 'Sometimes I think it would have been better to be born deaf instead of losing my hearing, then I wouldn't know what was taken away from me. This …' she waved her hand around our workspace, 'being deaf, but knowing what it is like to hear, and living in a hearing world makes me what to shatter into a thousand pieces to be blown away with the wind to the uninhabited ends of the earth.'

'Don't say that, Scarlett!' I signed, not wanting to draw any more attention to us. My heart was hurting and I wanted to cry.

'Why not? Because it's the truth?' she signed and covered her face with her hands, then removed them. 'I miss music, Indi. I want to hear music again—the singing, the instruments, the bands. I want to hear songs of love, songs of sadness, songs that make me feel high. I want to hear all the instruments in an orchestra—and all the stupid synthesiser music, no matter how ridiculous the sound is. I want to hear voices, real voices. I want to connect to the sound of voices and understand what is not being said. I was to feel the emotion in sound again.' Her bottom lip trembled and a tear rolled down her cheek. 'I want …' She let out a heavy sigh. 'I want this process of hearing with a cochlear implant, and the hearing cell regeneration to speed up so I can hear like a normal hearing person again.'

I felt an ache in my throat and closed my eyes. I had no response, no words of understanding or encouragement. I did the only thing I could—I pulled her into my arms. 'I'm sorry,' I whispered, knowing my words would be heard through her cochlear implant, but not really sure if my voice sounded like my voice, and wondering how much natural hearing she had regained in her right ear with the experimental hearing cell regrowth program.

I released her from my embrace, put my hands on her shoulders and looked into her eyes. '*You* … are smarter. *You* … are better at reading hearts of people when their true character is blocked by their deceitful words. *You* … can choose not to be exposed to the hate and jealousy in people's word choices, or their disgusting bullying and hate speech. Have you ever thought that you are protected in some way by not hearing the ugliness of this world?' I mouthed.

'I know what you are doing, Indi, and it doesn't help.' She pulled off her cochlear implant processor so she was almost back to the non-hearing Scarlett I grew up with. 'This is me. Deaf. It is the way I am meant to be,' she signed.

'But what if it isn't? What *if* … your place in the hearing cell regrowth research is a huge success, and because of you, other people regain their normal hearing?' I signed.

Scarlett frowned as if she was about to cry, then swiped her fingers across her closed eyelids. She took a deep breath. 'What *if* … the regrowth of hearing cells is working. And what *if* … it makes me scared of entering the normal hearing world again?'

I shook my head. 'We're in this journey together, remember. I'm all ears, apparently, and will help you to readjust to the life of hearing.'

'You would do that?' She signed slowly; her brows drawn together like she was in a state of disbelief.

'Without a second thought. I was there when you lost your hearing, and I'm here as you get your hearing back. I wish for you to be happy, and if hearing again is going to make you happy, then I wish for you to hear again.' I growled inwardly, berating myself for my use of the word wish.

Scarlett blew out a breath between her pursed lips. 'Okay. I'll keep working on it.' She looked down for a moment then back at me. 'It's getting easier to hear with my cochlear implant, you know. And I think … I may be getting addicted to it … to hearing again.'

I smiled at her words. 'Meet me for lunch,' I signed.

Scarlett's eyes sparkled, then she held out her hand showing the sign language for "I love you".

I placed my hand over my heart and nodded at her. I stood beside her on her cochlear implant processor side. 'Back to work now, Miss,' I said after a beat.

'You get back to work, Indigo. Brains await,' Scarlett said and beamed. And suddenly, there was her sunshine dancing to a melody of victory like Scarlett had just won her war.

I grinned and walked to the iris scanner and entered the Memory Lab, hit by the absence of a laboratory scent. I looked about the room of clear glass boxes, coffins for the brains in the state of between worlds. Living brains, implanted with wireless electrodes. My scalp prickled. I touched my thumb to each of my fingers to distract me from my conscience.

'Good morning, Biran.' He turned to me and nodded. I smiled. We were in this together.

'Morning, Indigo,' Biran said. 'I have kept the neural activity neutral as we had decided before naming each of the brains.'

I put on my virtual reality headset. 'Perfect. Thank you.' I walked up to the first encased brain. 'Shall I proceed?'

'Affirmative,' he said.

I gave Biran a nod, then pressed my hand to the first glass brain coffin. 'Good morning, B100-1.' I looked at the electrocorticography. Coma patterns. *Unconsciousness.*

'Good morning, B100-2.'

Unconsciousness.

'Good morning, B100-3, B100-4, B100-5.'

All in the state of unconsciousness.

'Good morning, B100-6. Are you still awake, or has the Sleeping Beauty Pill worn off?'

Unconsciousness.

'Good morning, B100-7, B100-8, B100-9, B100-10.'

Unconsciousness.

Their response was the same for each of the two hundred and sixty-seven days we had been researching them. No change with the morning greeting.

I pulled up the hologram of B100-1. 'Did Scarlett provide the data on each of the lives of the brains before their ... physical death of the body?'

'Affirmative.'

'Great. Put your headset on and let's get started.' A shiver ran down my spine. I had no idea what was about to happen. Awakening a bodiless brain felt ... wrong. It felt like ... we were intruding on something ... sacred.

Anxiety coursed through my blood, burning my skin, and everything in my body was telling me we were entering a forbidden territory. I called the brain the 'G-Factor'. It was still a mystery. We knew multitudes about other body organs, but the brain ... it felt like it was encoded in a way so that we could never discover it's secrets, or that was far beyond our human understanding ever could. The 'G-Factor'. The God Factor. A Genius who made humans look far from intelligent in comparison.

I hesitated before I placed my hand on the glass case of B100-1, and took a deep breath to slow my heartbeat that was battering my ribs. Somehow, I felt like I was keeping a soul hostage. 'Good morning, B100-1. I've learned that your name is Quinn. It's so nice to finally use your name. Thank you for volunteering to be part of this research.'

Spike.

I looked over at Biran. He held the goofiest grin on his face like he had just won the lottery.

'Quinn, we are honoured that you are here. I'm just going to chat to the rest of our friends. Listen in if you like.' I moved on to the next glass encasement. 'Good morning, B100-2. I've learned that your name is Emerson. It's so nice to finally use your name. Thank you for volunteering to be part of this research.'

Spike.

'Emerson, we are honoured that you are here. I'm just going to chat to the rest of our friends. Listen in if you like.' I moved on to the next glass encasement. 'Good morning, B100-3. I've learned that your name is Ardon. It's so nice to finally use your name. Thank you for volunteering to be part of this research.'

Spike.

'Ardon, we are honoured that you are here. I'm just going to chat to the rest of our friends. Listen in if you like.' I moved on to the next glass encasement. 'Good morning, B100-4. I've learned that your name is James. It's so nice to finally use your name. Thank you for volunteering to be part of this research.'

Spike.

'James, we are honoured that you are here. I'm just going to chat to the rest of our friends. Listen in if you like.' I moved on to the next glass encasement. 'Good morning, B100-5. I've learned that your name is Alex. It's so nice to finally use your name. Thank you for volunteering to be part of this research.'

Spike.

'Alex, we are honoured that you are here. I'm just going to chat to the rest of our friends. Listen in if you like.' I moved on to the next glass encasement. 'Good morning, B100-6. I've learned that your name is Mica. It's so nice to finally use your name. Thank you for volunteering to be part of this research, and I love your choice of music!'

Spike.

'Mica, we are honoured that you are here. I'm just going to chat to the rest of our friends. Listen in if you like.' I moved on to the next glass encasement. 'Good morning, B100-7. I've learned that your name is Jordan. It's so nice to finally use your name. Thank you for volunteering to be part of this research.'

Spike.

'Jordan, we are honoured that you are here. I'm just going to chat to the rest of our friends. Listen in if you like.' I moved on to the next glass encasement. 'Good morning, B100-8. I've learned that your name is Hunter. It's so nice to finally use your name. Thank you for volunteering to be part of this research.'

Spike.

'Hunter, we are honoured that you are here. I'm just going to chat to the rest of our friends. Listen in if you like.' I moved on to the next glass encasement. 'Good morning, B100-9. I've learned that your name is Charlie. It's so nice to finally use your name. Thank you for volunteering to be part of this research.'

Spike.

'Charlie, we are honoured that you are here. I'm just going to chat to the rest of our friends. Listen in if you like.' I moved on to the next glass encasement. 'Good morning, B100-10. I've learned that your name is Nic. It's so nice to finally use your name. Thank you for volunteering to be part of this research. We are honoured that you are here.'

Spike.

I stilled. All ten brains had just been awakened. All ten! What had we done? My stomach churned as nausea hit. The sound of applause entered through my hearing connection from the world of neuroscientists outside the Memory Lab. I didn't want to turn around to see them. They would see the tear that had rolled down my face. They would also see the look of terror on my face. Because that is what I felt on the inside. Sheer terror. What had we done?

I looked over a Biran. He was motionless, as if he had been carved from stone, his eyes cast on the ceiling. Was he trying to suppress an emotion? Did he feel the same way as me? Or did he feel the blissfulness of happiness?

'We did it, Biran,' I called over to him, overriding my feeling of doom.

He took a deep breath, removed his focus from the ceiling, looked at me and nodded. His eyes were red. I had never seen him react like that before. He was an intensely private person who kept his heart hidden.

'Shall we move on to the next step of engagement?' I watched him with caution.

He cleared his throat and rubbed the back of his neck. 'Yes.'

I turned to face Scarlett. Her image was scattered with the reflections of lights and holograms and trace readings on the glass that kept us in our own protected bubble. 'Scarlett, please play the selected sounds in a random order,' I signed.

She made her hand into a fist and bobbed it up and down.

I breathed out the uncomfortable anxiety that had made its home in my stomach and turned to face the holograms. According to the living history of the brains, there were sounds they detested and sounds they loved. Both should result in a response from them. This was our procuring of brain numbers to names and memories, then we would attempt to delete their selected traumatic memory as our number one research goal, and Phase 2 would be complete.

The sound of a barking, medium-sized dog filled the Memory Lab. I smiled as memories of the unconditional love of my pup warmed my heart. Nic's hologram activated, glowing red in her hippocampus.

I gave Scarlett a thumbs up, and cello music filled the room. Emerson's hologram activated as expected. Next came "Happy Birthday", and Jordan's hologram engaged. A cat meowed. It was Charlie's turn. The sound of rain reverberated in the Memory Lab and James reacted. Heavy metal music infused the room and I covered my ears at the noise, but Alex liked it, according to his hologram. A canary sang, calling to Quinn, who responded, before the classical music of *The Blue Danube* by Johann Strauss II began, waking Hunter.

Two to go.

Children laughed and Mica responded and finally, the Memory Lab was filled with the calming ambience of waves at the beach. It was Ardon who connected.

I walked around the ten brain holograms. Phase 2, Part 1, was complete. Now for Phase 2, Part 2. It would be like stabbing in the dark as we trialled our hypothesis, trying to access stored memories.

I walked around and touched each of the glass encasements projecting a faux calmness, and thanked each of the brains by name, then left the room. And the building. Almost breaking into a run before I exited the security doors like I had committed a crime. Another crime. I pushed my hand into my pocket and fingered the diamond-studded, gold compact. Not mine. I lowered my head, filled with a suffocating melody of discordant notes, a reflection of my life of dark shadows and regrets.

Sunlight struck me like a slap in the face when I stepped out onto the road to cross over to enter the park. It followed me like a spotlight on stage, scrutinizing my every move and playing truth or lie, trying to extract my inner thoughts and my life's narrative to hang them out for everyone to see.

I made my way with haste to the tree invader, the 100-year-old sugar maple tree, and sat under its protective limbs wanting them to move to the ground, wrap around me and lift me up in into the highest branches, hidden from the world, hidden from what I had done. But it didn't.

I lowered myself to the ground and leaned against its trunk and closed my eyes, and watched a kaleidoscope of life events cavort with deeply hidden secrets filled with regrets and failures. I sighed. My mind was sending me red flagged signals to stop the dangerous game I was playing as a neuroscientist. And that was it in its entirety. Living brains used as an experiment, playing with the final destinies of those courageous, or passionate enough. Playing with trying to help other people from having to go through the day in, day out pain that resulted from a traumatic event committed against them without their consent.

Was it unethical if we were just carrying out the wishes of the owners of the brains?

Wishes. There it was again. Wishes are dangerous. The owners of the brains wished to help, but ultimately, we were the keeper of their wish, and the final destiny of the wish.

'Wishes made on Midsummer's Eve are most likely to come true,' I whispered, reciting a well-known, but suppressed verse from my childhood. My eyes widened and I inhaled sharply and held my breath for a moment, then pulled out the gold compact from my pocket. I ran my fingers over the diamonds, too many to count, that adorned the cover like a hypnotizing piece of artwork, and shoved the compact back into my pocket. It was my forever reminder of the incident of the wish I had made on Midsummer's Eve. Evidence that tied me to the tragedy. But I couldn't get rid of it. Yet.

My watch vibrated, reminding me of my lunch date. I didn't want to be late.

I placed a bouquet of yellow daffodils across the table, the strong vanilla scent reminding me of baking cupcakes with my father, of dad jokes, and of licking cake batter spoons and flour fights while cleaning up. Scarlett would be here soon. I needed her to know how much I loved her and would support her on her journey to hearing again.

I leaned back in my seat and looked about. To my right was the baldest man I had ever seen. Bald was bald, but his head was just so … shiny. At once, my mind vision started drawing the brain onto his skin; the four lobes, the small grooves, larger grooves and bulges. I squeezed my eyes shut to stop the obsessive-compulsive anatomical illustrating of his brain, then opened them and focussed on his other features—a dark beard, dark glasses, a geeky brown bow tie, and an old man's cardigan the colour of caramel sauce. He was probably an intellectual. Like me. I tilted my head and looked at his left hand for a wedding ring, wondering whether he was married, or had devoted his entire life to academic pursuits, or research for the good of humanity. I hoped he wouldn't be lonely into his old age. But perhaps … he preferred his own company, and that was okay too.

I squinted. The fourth finger on his left hand had a scar on it similar to Tobi's. Odd. I watched him turn a page in his book and bury his nose deeper into it, seeming to be devouring it. Intellectual nutrients.

My line of sight was obstructed as Scarlett arrived, breaking my inappropriate study of Bald Guy. She sat opposite me and smirked.

'How was your last mapping of your cochlear implant, and how does it compare to the regrowth your hearing cells?' I said, then inwardly chastised myself for *1)* not using a greeting first—sometimes I forgot to do that, just diving into the conversation that was foremost in my mind, and *2)* talking out loud about the classified research with the hearing cell regeneration.

'What?' she mouthed.

'How was your last mapping for your cochlear implant, the fine tuning, and how—' I started to sign before Scarlett lifted her shoulders and put them back down. I stopped signing.

Scarlett's eyes were so wide I thought they might pop out of her head. She relaxed them then started to sign. 'Firstly, hi Scarlett! Glad you made it to lunch after negotiating with three neurotic neuroscientists who wanted me to gather five million and one files for them.' Her signing was painted with sarcasm, as were her facial expressions. 'And then … what? As in I heard you word for word, but can't believe you didn't start with hello.'

I lowered my head and winced, then signed, 'Hi, Scarlett. Thanks for making it to lunch after negotiating with three neurotic neuroscientists who wanted you to gather five million and one files for them … and … we are such good friends that when I am with you it is like we were never apart. I talk to the brains about us all the time and what you are doing with your hearing to make small talk to keep them engaged and stimulated, and we make plans and sort through the necessary and unnecessary. We also talk about the exact mechanisms of why and how they can hear.' Employees from the research institute were forbidden to talk about our work outside of our floor in the lab. But Scarlett and I did, using our version of sign language. It was to our advantage.

Scarlett smiled. 'And what did the brains think?' she signed.

I shook my head. 'You were watching the monitors from the outside. No response.' I looked down at the menu, wondering if I should say what I was thinking about how valued she was. I had a compelling need to say the words that were queueing in my throat and bumping into each other. I let out a sharp breath and lifted my hands. 'You are the best person for your job, Scarlett. Other people are distracted by noise around them and miss nuances in the data feed. But you don't. You see everything on the monitors, you never miss a thing. And for that I am thankful,' I signed. 'What we have discovered and achieved couldn't have been possible without you.'

Scarlett looked into my eyes, then placed her hands over her eyes, as though she was holding in her tears. She removed her hands, nodded, then mouthed, 'Thank you.'

'You're welcome,' I said, then added, 'I love you like a sister.'

'And I love you. I think of you as my sister,' she said.

'These flowers are for you,' I said out loud to engage her in relearning to hear with her left cochlear implant and newly growing sensory hearing hair cells in the right inner ear. 'What would you like for lunch?'

Scarlett signed two numbers to me; one for the food item listed on the menu, and the other for the drink. I put my hand up to stop her. We had done this a million times before and had it down to a fine art, but she needed to use her voice to reintegrate into the hearing world. 'Tell me,' I said.

She sighed. 'Ah … three and eight,' she said, her speech intelligibility a little rough, almost monotone.

'Perfect. I'll go order.' I left the table and spoke to the waitress, and returned with our drinks.

I sat and took a sip of my purplish juice, and winced. 'I think I have your drink. It tastes awful!' I said.

Scarlett put her straw into the drink and took a sip. 'No,' she said. 'That's definitely not the strawberry, banana, mango, ice-cream smoothie I ordered.'

'I'm pretty sure it is!' I said, hoping to convince her of a drink swap. There was no way I could drink this concoction of beet, carrot, lemon, ginger and apple juice. It was exactly what I had ordered. Why did people choose to drink "health" drinks? It tasted awful. So it must be good for the body, right?

Scarlett raised an eyebrow. 'You always do this, Indi. You go on a health bender, where you dive right into the deep end and wipe everything out of your life that you like to eat or drink and choose the extreme health food regimes. Use my motto. Everything in moderation, and eat for pleasure. Be kind to yourself,' she said, her speech becoming clearer with more tone variations.

I narrowed my eyes at her, leaned forward toward my extremely healthy health food drink and took a long, loud slurp through the straw, knowing very well that the sound would be found in her sound memories from when she was young.

'Childish,' Scarlett said.

I frowned at her.

'I can feel the vibration of sound through the table, and hear it in both ears,' she said as our food was placed on the table.

'Really?' I said.

'Indeed,' Scarlett said, and then picked up her cutlery and started to eat the hot chips.

'Did you know,' I signed while having a mouth full of food. Another advantage of sign language—you can talk with your mouth full. 'That birds and amphibians can regenerate hearing cells throughout their lives?'

Scarlett raised an unimpressed eyebrow at me. Of course she knew.

'Do you see anyone who has their sight restored while you go for your hearing observations?' I signed. This was an out of bounds question, but I hoped that Scarlett would answer.

She raised her other eyebrow at me. The gag order.

But I kept going. I was trying to get information from her as to how they were restoring her hearing. 'And,' I signed, 'they are also trialling gene therapy with cochlear implants, where they inject a DNA solution into the cochlear before the implant, and then fire electrical impulses to trigger the DNA transfer once the implant is inserted. It will allow regrowth of auditory nerves to regain hearing. And then there's the optical cochlear implant—using light to apparently give improved pitch resolution, and the single intratympanic injection ...' I cleared my throat. Scarlett was not giving me any sign of which of the hearing trials she was involved in. So, I changed the direction of our one-sided conversation. 'What's the first thing you are going to do when you realise you can hear 100% normally again?' I signed.

Scarlett slow blinked. 'Close my eyes and just listen, then walk everywhere listening to everything. Go to concerts, to the beach, to a park and listen to the laughter of children … go to my parents. I want to hear their voices again.' She stopped talking and looked down. 'I'll probably just cry,' she signed.

'I'll cry,' I signed, my eyes becoming wet. I breathed out my emotion to stop my tears. It would be so much easier if she could hear and talk normally. I had a million things I wanted to tell her but not enough time nor the knowledge of sign language to be able to talk to her the way I wanted to talk to her. I was so clumsy with my signing, and our own sign language created when we were young was terribly limited.

Scarlett smiled. My heart warmed at that smile I had known since we were too young to understand the complicated world, too young to imagine what a grown-up life would be like. I watched her pick up her hamburger, holding it in that weird way she did like on the night that took her hearing, when we were together, before I was whisked away by my parents because my mother had a "funny" feeling. I just wished she could have whisked Scarlett away too, and then she would never have been exposed to the sound of the massive explosion of the fireworks, rupturing her eardrums and stealing her hearing, leaving her in a world of ringing, buzzing, and roaring tinnitus. The loudness of the silence of deafness. It's so catastrophic that some people choose to end their lives because of the incessant tinnitus.

I took a deep breath. Choices. Every choice you made had consequences. Every moment of every day. The path of life. It's not straight. It's more like a tree with limbs for pathways. If you step onto a bad leaf, it falls to the ground with you on it, so you have to start again.

Did you learn your lesson?

Would you choose the same pathway again?

Chapter 14

I placed a deep-red leaf on my desk next to the gold compact. I had pulled the leaf off a maple tree as I walked to my car to drive home after work.

I poured myself a coffee, then returned to the desk, sat, and traced the veins on the leaf, my thoughts swallowed by the memory of Tobi's agitation when we last met under the darkness of the new moon in the kissing forest of our youth. His implication in the incident could be terminal for his career. As is would be for mine. Everything I had studied and worked for. We were so close to our research goal at the Memory Lab. I couldn't let the team down because of a stupid wish I had made. Tobi was right. We needed to remove our memories of the incident that wasn't meant to happen.

I grabbed a new sheet of off-white homemade writing paper, flattened it out with my hand and picked up my calligraphy pen. The letter needed to contain the information for our last memory that we would act out. It was the only memory of us to keep. It was a must have so we would recognise each other when we met again in the future.

Dear Finn,

Hey. I hope you remember me. I met you at Kingdom Adventure Park during the spring of the most amazing flowering season. Ever.

You started talking to me in the queue to the Marvellous Super Roller Coaster, then you sat next to me in the car and held my hand as I screamed my lungs out in the darkest, scariest tunnel where I think we were inverted, holding on for dear life.

When the ride ended, we looked at each other, our smiles wide, our eyes caught in each other's.

Afterward, we ate burgers and I drank Coca-Cola for my nausea, while you laughed at me. I fell into your—

I dropped the pen onto the paper and thumped my fist on the desk in frustration, accidentally clipping my coffee cup, spilling coffee onto the paper and the stolen compact. How could writing a letter be so hard? I picked up the soppy paper and screwed it up before launching it into the air to hurtle to the paper bin. It missed.

I grabbed a tissue to wipe away the excess coffee from the desk, then picked up the compact to dry it.

Mirror. Mirror. I pushed the button on the classic diamond-studded compact and it flipped open. Two mirrors. Two of me. I gazed into the left side, the one distant, and a memory came of Tobi and I—

'What happened to Rule Number 3?' I said. The shiny, new, red gentlemen's boat awaited, its colour a warning of danger.

'One boat? Here it is,' he said, his voice deep and rich in its tones. He held his hands behind his back, emphasising his broad shoulders and pectoral muscles, accentuated through his white T-shirt, reminding me of lazy summer Sundays eating ice-creams by the sea.

I breathed out his alluring visual appeal, breaking his spell. 'No. With your friend's boat here, that makes two boats. And besides, your *borrowed* boat is boring. I prefer the excitement of *my* borrowed boat.' I looked over at the dark blue rowboat by the rock near the house closest to the lake. Walking over to it by stealth was always a challenge, and then rowing away in it without being noticed was exhilarating.

'Your *borrowed* boat is stolen. If I am caught with a stolen boat … I … my …' He lowered his head and shook it. 'I just can't get caught.'

'Because?'

He lifted his head and closed his eyes for a moment. When he opened them, the sunlight highlighted his eyes, the stunning colour of the ocean, clear and captivating. He sighed. 'I could lose my job.'

'Speaking of which, is?'

He shook his head. 'I can't tell you.'

I narrowed my eyes at him. 'Are you a cop or something?'

He laughed then stopped, lowered his head and shot me a dark gaze. 'Get in,' he said, and held out his hand.

I didn't need to take his hand. I wasn't clumsy or incapable. But I placed my hand in his anyway. I wanted, no … I needed, to feel that spark of energy he gave me when we touched. That tingle that shot up my arm from where he had touched me. As a neurologist it fascinated me. As woman, it captured me like an addiction with a feeling of exhilaration.

'Thank you,' he said.

I was lost in a moment of deliriousness. 'For?'

'Taking my hand. I know you don't need help getting into the boat.'

'I was being socially smart, instead of intellectually smart,' I offered as a reason without telling him how he made me feel.

'Is that so, Ms. Danube?' He offered a crooked grin.

'Be thankful, Mr. Brooks. It did cross my mind to pull you over as I stepped into the boat to see if you would fall into the water … but I chose to be nice.' I sat on the middle seat to be the rower.

'And you are worried about trusting me? I think I am the one who should be worried,' he said, the corner of his mouth curling up.

'Get in.' I reused his words and raised an eyebrow at him.

He gave a nod and placed his backpack into the boat before he climbed aboard, watching me with caution.

'You don't trust me, do you?' I said.

'You just … keep me on my toes, that's all,' he said, looking at the seats. He stood in front of me with his hands on his hips, perfectly balanced. My eyes wandered down his body, over his white T-shirt and his mustard-coloured shorts, hugging his athletic legs.

'Is there a problem?'

'I want to row,' he said.

I stood. 'I want to row.' The boat bobbed a little.

Tobi placed his hands on my shoulders. 'My borrowed boat. I get to row.'

I gave him a half smile. 'You don't trust me?'

'If you rock the boat to throw me off balance, I'm taking you with me,' he threatened.

'Ah – Tobi, *the Brave*.' I raised an eyebrow at him.

'What happened to social intelligence instead of intellectual intelligence?'

I couldn't stop the involuntary blink of my right eye. His comment stung. But he was right. I lowered my head and moved to sit away from the seat with the oars. I gazed over beyond *Zero*, to the lake full of blue at this time of the day, focussing on the magical water sparkles, and lost myself in silence.

The boat started to move. I placed my fingers in the cool water and left it there, watching the small wake it made.

'You can't win all the time.' His voice broke my inner silence.

'I know,' I said, keeping my eyes on the water and the ripples created by my fingers. I sighed.

'Do you always do this?'

'Do what?'

'Sulk when you don't get your way?' he said.

I frowned and pulled my fingers out of the water. I looked at him. 'I'm not sulking. I'm just being quiet.'

'I don't like this version of quiet,' he said, lingering on the "i" and finishing with a staccato "t".

'There's different versions?'

'Most definitely,' he said. 'Quiet, when you are happy and enjoying the moment. Quiet, to save your life. Quiet, to agree with something or someone. Quiet, when you disagree. Quiet, when you are angry. Quiet, because you are shutting down. And noisy quiet when you stop yourself from saying something that won't end well.'

I looked beyond *Zero*, toward Jacaranda Island as I absorbed his words. The tree was getting closer. 'None of those. It's an inner-search quiet. Analysing and reflecting.'

His lips quirked up. 'Overthinking, perhaps?'

'Always.'

'Stop overthinking and accept my gift of kindness. You don't have to be the one doing everything. You don't have to be strong, all the time.'

In the heart. That's where his words hit me and infused me with tenderness. My eyes burned and I closed them. 'I know. It's just …' I opened my eyes and looked away from him as a tear fell, then wiped the wetness from my cheek.

'It's okay. You don't have to explain.' His voice was tender.

I looked back at him and pulled my eyebrows together. 'Thank you,' I whispered.

'Tell me when to stop rowing.' His ocean-blue eyes danced. 'Here's the thing about rowing,' he said, 'you can't see where you are going … you are now my eyes … the coxswain—your words when you first terrified me in the stolen boat, remember?'

I looked down and smiled, revisiting the memory, then looked back at him. 'It was the *borrowed* boat, I returned it … stop rowing.'

Tobi held my gaze—his ocean-blue eyes to my greeny-blue—and stopped rowing. I drank in the eye intimacy he offered as the boat glided in the quietness, feeling like time had stood still, just like my breath and my heartbeat in that moment.

'Now,' I said, sucking in a deep breath as I came out of the spell and the closeness of Jacaranda Island dawned on me. Tobi half smiled and climbed out of the boat into the knee-deep water and pulled the boat onto the bank of Jacaranda Island. It tilted to its right side a little and Tobi proffered his hand. I didn't hesitate in placing my hand in his, anticipating the thrill of the spark he gave me, and stepped out of the boat and onto *Zero*: the ground.

I walked halfway between the shoreline and the tree and stopped. The sun warmed the top of my head. I looked up at the sky to all the colours above, a heavenly hue of blue just like the colour of my mother's dress she wore when she was happy, and when she adorned her brown hair with an enormous ribbon the colour of yellow, like the sun. I turned my gaze to the ground and my heart warmed. 'Under the azure canvas with the sun that casts no shadow, before the nightdom of the full moon,' I said with a smile. 'Rule Number 1 has been broken.'

Tobi circled me; his backpack slung over his right shoulder. 'You're right. No shadow. It can only be downhill from this point in time.'

'What? In watching shadows grow, the sky change colour until it captures our attention with sunset palettes infused across the heavens that glorify the Creator. There is no downhill, but only spectacular to look forward to,' I said, my voice incredulous.

Tobi stared at me, his eyes drinking me in. 'Downhill … in that my time with you is ebbing away. I have to return the boat by 7pm.'

'And after that?'

He walked towards the Jacaranda tree, opened his backpack, and pulled out a blanket. He smoothed it out under the tree and sat on it. I followed.

'After that, I have to report to work,' he said.

'Ah … work. On a Saturday? What is it that you do for a job?'

'I'm not at liberty to grant you that information,' he said.

'Well then, is your job noble? Is it grand?'

'I'm using a noisy quiet,' he said.

'So, I won't approve of your job?'

'I didn't say that.'

'But you said that noisy quiet is stopping oneself from saying something that won't end well.'

'Let just say that by not telling you—one; I'm disapproving of your intrusion about it, and two; I'm protecting you.'

'From?'

'The subject is closed. And I need you to not ask me about my job.'

'But Tobi, I can't be with you if your job interferes with my research, or is in contradiction with my research, or—'

'Tell me what you do so we can be clear and know where we stand.'

'I can't tell you exactly what I do. It's in my contract.'

'Touché.' Tobi placed a finger under my chin. I lifted my eyes to his, falling into the ocean-blue of my dreams. 'Because you mean more to me than my job, I will tell you that what I do is not illegal, and it is important.'

He lowered his eyes to my lips and my breath hitched.

'Do your parents know what you do?' I said to change my wayward thoughts.

He raised an eyebrow at me, disconnected his eyes from mine, then leaned forward and pulled a book out of his backpack before lying on the blanket. A male species reading a book. Possibly the only type of male species I could fall in love with.

I rubbed my arms to change my focus. 'Since I didn't get the memo about bringing a book, will you read to me?'

He looked at me and grinned. 'Of course. But I'm not sure if you'll like my type of book.'

'Why is that?'

He ran his hand over the deep blue hard cover like he was lost, in another place and another time. 'It's hard to explain. I'll read a chapter to you, and you can tell me.'

'Okay.' I furrowed my eyebrows then reclined onto the blanket next to him, tugged down my sage coloured, buttoned rib-knit crop top to cover more of my stomach, and closed my eyes. I waited for him to begin, suddenly hyper-aware of his scent of spice and sweetness. I heard him turn the page, once, twice, thrice, four times, and then there was another moment of silence.

'He would have married her all over again for their ten-year anniversary if ...' he said, his voice fruity, like an elegant red wine.

I waited for him to continue reading. When he didn't, I opened my eyes and looked at him.

He connected his eyes to mine. 'Finish the story,' he said, his voice like velvet.

'What?'

'It's what you have to do with this book. It gives you the beginning of a chapter, and you have to finish it.'

I frowned at him. This was the stupidest book I had ever heard of!

'I like to escape into the words and get lost in my imagination. It helps me to relax and stop overthinking life,' he said as a way of explanation.

I inhaled deeply, wondering what would make him overthink, then decided to go along with his little charade and humour him.

'Okay …

> He would have married her all over again for their 10-year anniversary, if she had said yes when he proposed to her, this time, with more forethought and romance, not like eleven years ago when he blurted it out when he thought she was about to die. When she didn't answer him, this time, he walked out the door and fell to his knees, his heart hurting.

There. End of story.'

There was silence. I looked over at Tobi. He was staring upward into all the colours above, at the Jacaranda blooms of purpledom. After a moment he turned his head to look at me.

I frowned and shook my head. 'I'm not good at telling stories,' I said as an explanation.

'I disagree. Why didn't she answer him?'

'She felt she wasn't a good match for him.'

'Hmmmm.' He frowned.

'I want to hear your version,' I said.

He ran his hand through his dark wavy hair. 'Okay.' He placed the open book onto his chest and gazed into my eyes. 'Close your eyes,' he said. 'You'll see the story with more clarity.'

I kept my eyes bathing in his for a little longer than necessary, enjoying the euphoric feeling he gave, but then closed them.

> 'He would have married her all over again for their 10-year anniversary, if he hadn't sent the flowers to the wrong address.'

I smiled.

> 'The flowers,' he continued, 'had the love letter that bared his heart and soul, his past, his present and his future. With her.
>
> He pushed his hand inside his pocket. A woman had sent the letter back to him. Why didn't he reread the address he had given to the florist? If he had, he would have realised the florist had mixed up the numbers.
>
> And now, here he stood, alone, as the super moon rose, pausing like it was balancing on the water, throwing moonbeams into the waves with the baton of a majestic conductor. His wife would never know that she was meant to be here with him, at this moment in time he had chosen, just for them. He took one long last look at the super moon and turned away and started walking, eyes downcast, dragging his heavy heart behind him.
>
> He glanced up as he walked his lonely way along the jetty, then stopped. She stood there before him. His wife. Stunning. How did she find out?
>
> Once he caught his breath, he took a step closer to her, took her hand in his and lowered himself to bended knee. He reached into his pocket and

> pulled out his love letter. She could only ever say yes after he proposed to her. Here. Now. With the super moon as their witness. They had a lifetime to share together. And that would be his hope, his wish, come true.'

My heart pounded. Was he baring his soul through his story? I opened my eyes and looked at him. His eyes were closed, his long lashes almost touching his cheeks.

'That was beautiful,' I whispered.

'Thanks,' he said. He opened his eyes and closed the book. 'It's just a story. Fiction.'

'Mmmm … he loved her with his life. You, Tobi, *the Brave*, are a magnificent storyteller!'

'Not always. When I finally get to sleep, sometimes I fall into a dream loop of the story I have created and can't get out of it.'

'So, do you then consciously finish the dream with a happy ending.'

He beamed me a smile. 'Yes.'

'How many story beginnings are in the book?'

'Three hundred and sixty-five. One for each day, or night … whenever it is that you decide to read it. They have different themes. You can read them in any order or according to your needs at the time.'

I kept my gaze focused on his face, my mind in a whirl about his odd nightly activity. What could possibly keep his mind overthinking three hundred and sixty-five days a year? 'Do you ever revisit any story beginnings?'

He hesitated, tracing the embellishment on the cover of the book. 'Yes.'

'Which ones?'

'The ones set in castles.'

'Ah—princes and princesses and knights in shining armour.'

'Not always.'

'Wait, you're a psychologist, aren't you? You're testing me and analysing my story content.'

'How does that make you feel?' he said, before giving me a crooked smile, his eyes sparkling like the waves glistening under the summer sunbeams and dancing to an innocent, happy melody.

I narrowed my eyes at him. 'You'll keep!' I said, falling deeper into his ocean-blue eyes. I dragged my eyes to his lips, tracing the outline of them with my vision while being engulfed with the urge to place my lips upon his. I blinked, got up and walked to the water's edge to create space between us, and looked out beyond *Zero*, the lake full of blue. It was safer that way.

He stood beside me, his scent of sweetness and spice intoxicating me.

'Do you ever feel trapped?' I said.

'In life? My job? A relationship?'

'With everything. Like … you've taken the wrong path.'

'No. I feel like I am where I need to be at this point in time,' he said.

At that moment, I felt the anger of jealousy. I wanted to be where he was. I wanted to be able to look back on my life and tell myself "well done" instead of looking back at the chaos. The mess. The destruction to get where I was. 'Is that a good place for you?' I asked.

'Very.'

I closed my eyes and frowned. 'Why are we here?'

'On earth?'

'No. Why are you here … with me. Right now?' I opened my eyes and faced him.

His lips parted. 'I like being with you. I like how you are not sugar and spice and all things nice. I like that you are not fake. I like … that you have an untamed side to you, one that doesn't want to be like everyone else.' He paused and lowered his head, then connected his eyes to mine in a depth I didn't want to climb out of. Time seemed to stop. Then it started again. 'I like … your essence,' he said, his voice soft and sensual.

I took a deep breath to break from his intoxication and looked beyond *Zero*, the lake full of blue. He had used my philosophical word: essence. Could he read my mind?

'Why are you here with me. Right now?' he asked.

I should have expected this question. But still, it took me by surprise. My skin burned and my heart started to race. I wanted to tell him that I didn't know. I wanted to tell him that I was no good for him. I wanted to tell him that he would be better off with a girl who would worship the ground that he walked on, because it wouldn't be me. I wanted to tell him that none of my relationships had worked out. I wanted to tell him that I was filled with so much self-doubt that it would fill an ocean on every planet in the universe. I wanted to tell him that my research put me in a very dark place at times, questioning what we are, and whether any of this is reality, or just a perception of it. I wanted to tell him I didn't understand how we could feel so lonely surrounded by people, and that maybe, just maybe, he was looking for a connection with me that I could never reciprocate because maybe, just maybe, there was something wrong with me. I wanted to tell him that I felt like I was always in the wrong place at the wrong time. I wanted to tell him that I wished that make believe was true and we never had to return to the real world ... I wanted to tell him … that I didn't want him to hurt my heart. But maybe he was different. We had known each other since we were young. Maybe—

He placed his finger under my chin and connected his eyes to mine again. And in that moment, I lost my internal war. 'Because I'm scared of how you make me feel and I want to find out why.' There. I said it. Truthful. Raw. Exposed.

His eyes moved to my lips. 'Brave,' he whispered. He released his finger from under my chin and looked out beyond *Zero*, to the lake full of blue, while I stood, frozen in fear from revealing a part of inside of me to him. He looked back to me, looked down and rubbed the back of his neck, then walked toward the tree, grabbed the blanket, and shoved it into his bag with his book, and walked to his borrowed boat. He paused and glanced at me, before he pushed the boat off the shallows, climbed in and rowed away, leaving me on the island without any way to return to the mainland.

I choked up as my eyes burned. I thought he liked me. That is what he had just said, didn't he? He had just done exactly what I didn't want him to do? I couldn't stop the involuntary blink of my right eye. His action was like barbed wire. It was like a cacophony of discordant notes trampled on an out-of-tune piano by an elephant.

I squeezed my eyes closed, trying to dull the ache in my heart. I turned and walked to my tree and climbed to the highest branch that I could. And I cried until my emptiness consumed me and the sun was turned off for the night.

Rejection, my friend. We meet again. Maybe I should delete my memories of Tobi. If I never knew him, it could never hurt, could it?

As the stars of hope for a new tomorrow decorated the inky sky with all the colours above, I descended my beloved childhood tree. I was about to jump from the lowest branch when I stopped. *He* sat there with one knee bended, looking up at me. He stood and held out his hand.

I shook my head. I didn't need his pity.

'Please,' he said. 'Let me explain.'

I closed my eyes and took a deep breath.

'Please,' he whispered. 'I owe you an explanation.'

I looked over at the red rowboat of danger for an escape.

'At least hear me out so you know it's not you, it's me.'

I gave a short nod and jumped from the tree. I stood, facing him, and folded my arms across my chest, over my heart, protecting it.

He looked at my arms, my shutting off from him. 'I deserve that, seventy times seven.' He sat on the ground and leaned against the tree trunk.

I too, sat, but further around from him, listening in a passive aggressive way.

'I have been infatuated with you since I was young. Every time our families gathered together in the park … I would be ecstatic because I knew you would be there. Never in my wildest dreams did I think we would connect. You were too smart, too beautiful, too amazing, way out of my league. And … the guys told me if I pursued you, or we became involved, I would be cursed for life. It was their way of trying to scare me, and I believed it in my teenage years.'

'There was a competition between them, you know,' I said, feeling a little calmer.

'I know ... anyway, when you said you were scared of how I made you feel, the memories from the conversations of the guys came flooding back. I needed to put some space between us. Your words made my heart race and I felt nauseous. Then I thought you would think I was weak, and I wasn't a strong enough person for you. I panicked, so I retreated. I needed to gather my thoughts and regroup my physical being that felt like it was going to crumble into a thousand pieces. I know you are scared, but I have more to lose if we connect, if we are together. Every other girl I have dated has been compared to you, and they never measure up.'

I leaned around from around the tree and looked at him. 'You mean, your conjured version of what I am in your mind. What if the real me disappoints you, and you discover you have already met the one for you but passed them by because of some fantasy about me?'

He shook his head. 'The time you have already given me is so precious that I hate stepping out of our bubble. It physically hurts to part ways with you.'

'Tobi … I worry that you think I am something that I am not.'

He shook his head again. 'Give me your hand.'

I looked down at his hand as I placed mine into his. My skin ignited at his touch, warming my being. I looked up into his dark eyes at this hour and breathed slowly, trying to slow my erratic heart.

'I know you feel what I feel when we touch. It's like time slows down and our eyes must meet to finish the connection of our souls.' He moved his lips to my hand, his eyes lingering in mine at this hour of the nightdom. 'Forgive me.'

My breath hitched. I was mesmerised by his sincerity and the feel of his warm lips against my skin. I moved closer to him. 'Has your wish come true yet?'

He placed my hand on his thigh, and traced over each of my fingers filling me with a heady, giddy rush. 'Are you rowing away into the darkness?' he asked.

I looked up at the full moon and breathed out his love potion. 'No,' I whispered.

'Then, no,' he whispered back.

I cleared my throat. 'I thought you were starting work at 7pm.'

'I was, but I called in sick when I was out in the boat.'

'But, don't you have an important job?'

'I do, but you are more important,' he said, lingering on the "n" then emphasising the "t".

A million butterflies battered my stomach and I felt light-headed and woozy. He had hit all of my happy chemicals at once—the love cocktail of feel-good chemicals—

My phone lit up interrupting my memory. A text.

The lighthouse. 21:00?

It was 8pm.

Yes. I replied. I needed to go.

The chair screeched across the floorboards as I stood. I grabbed my gear and headed out the door.

Chapter 15

It was a stargazer's paradise, each person looking in awe at all the colours above. The moon was absent and the stars projected their brilliance, creating a nightdom blanket of dazzling diamonds. People were scattered everywhere with cameras and tripods and blankets to sit upon with their baskets of celebrations and whispers of plans for the future. It was like walking into an orchestra playing a significant, splendid and dreamy piece of music. The stargazers were waiting for the meteor predicted to enter the earth's atmosphere tonight.

I wondered why I needed to meet *him* here. Tobi. People would see us together. We always met where we were hidden from view. Our relationship undetectable. As requested by him. My stomach clenched. A red flag.

A bluebird chirped. Once. Twice.

I stepped through the people, looking for *him*. It was 9pm. Exactly. He couldn't accuse me of being late. Where was he? His text: the lighthouse. I rolled my eyes and looked down at the lighthouse near the edge of the cliff.

My phone vibrated.

You like climbing. Find the ladder.

He was watching me. Of course. I pulled my hood over my head, my black jacket and jeans almost like an invisibility cloak, and walked towards the lighthouse and disappeared into the darkness, hidden from the view of others. I stopped before the structure. Tall. White. Proud. The scent of salt and seaweed and iodine blew off the ocean.

I ran my hand along the cool curved wall of the lighthouse as I searched for the ladder. I circumnavigated it once without success. I sighed, and started again, looking upward as I trekked around it. And there it was. Higher than I liked. A metal ladder facing the ocean. Out of view.

He was right. I liked climbing. Trees. But a lighthouse was a different story. It was unforgiving. I felt like I was about to scale a cliff face with no protection.

I rubbed my hands together and looked up at the bottom rung, doubtful I would be able to reach it, even with a jump. I bounced on my toes, then bent my knees with my arms back, and launched into a jump, swinging my arms to lift me higher. The fingers on my right hand hit the bottom metal bar, and slipped off.

I needed more boost. I pushed the hood from my head and took five steps back, then ran at the lighthouse, eyes locked on the bottom rung of the ladder and launched myself at it. I smiled when my fingers curled around the cold metal. I held on tight, walked my feet up the wall of the lighthouse, and moved my right hand onto the next rung, then my left hand. Up to the next one, higher and higher, until my feet were also on the ladder rungs.

I climbed up seven crossbars, and stopped. I looked up. The lighthouse was as tall as a 3-storey house. If I fell off at any point, my chances of dying were high. I closed my eyes for a moment. If *he* could do this, then so could I. I clenched my jaw, and continued my ascent, going against every bone and fear alert in my body. My focus was purely on moving my hands and feet, ensuring they connected securely with each movement.

As I neared the top of the ladder, a hand appeared before me.

'Fearless.' His voice was tinted with humour. I placed my right hand into his and he hoisted me over the top rail and onto the galley deck.

I shook my head as my muscles burned with lactic acid. At the realisation that I was now safe, my muscles released their tension. But my heart was still thumping, fuelled by adrenaline.

He wrapped his hand around mine and pulled me to a seat under the revolving light. 'I need more details.'

I inhaled his sweet and spicy scent and lined up my words with succinctness. 'We'll need to have one memory the same that is not removed … so we can identify each other, and reconnect.'

He nodded. 'It makes me nervous.'

'Anything new—the unknown—causes anxiety,' I said.

'I wish we could move forward. If I am associated with what happened … my job … they'll …'

'Let's not wish, for it will never happen. Let's make a plan.'

He placed his hand over his mouth then stroked his chin. 'Our new memory … at a beach?' he said.

'No.'

'By a cosy fire?'

'No.' I shook my head.

'In the snow?'

'No. It's got to be something that injects a large dose of adrenalin. It will create a stronger emotional bond between us.' I couldn't risk our final memory failing. It needed to be strong. Unbreakable. It was for us. For our future. To be together.

'Then it most definitely has to be me making lo—'

I raised my eyebrow at him. 'No.' I paused. 'It needs to be a different type of adrenaline—one involving fear and then the enjoyable resolving of the fear.'

'Like climbing a ladder of a lighthouse?' He smirked at me.

My lips curled up. 'Exactly like that, but less life endangering.'

He ran his hand through his hair, then stood at the rail. I waited a beat, like a syncopated rhythm, then moved behind him. I placed my hands on his shoulders then slid them around him in a hug I never wanted to let go from.

His chest expanded as he drew a deep breath. 'I don't want to lose our memories, of all our time together. Our conversations, our first kiss, our collection of connections, the love I feel for you. I don't want to forget that.' His voice cracked.

I shuddered at the memory of the look of hatred in his eyes on that fateful night. Had he moved beyond that emotion he had burned into me?

'We can make new memories. New conversations. New connections. A new story … a new first kiss … a new us with no backstory, no history,' I whispered.

He placed his hands on mine and pulled them away before turning toward me and connecting his eyes to mine—his eyes almost luminous with each sweep of the lighthouse light. He placed a finger under my chin and lowered his lips close to mine, hesitating, magnifying my heartbeat and the fire that burned beneath my skin.

But then he pulled away and turned his eyes to the heavens, to all the colours above.

I looked upward, following the direction of his gaze and was hit with the harsh feeling of rejection. He chose not to kiss me. My reaction to his choice jumped on the same neurological pathway as physical pain, and I tensed. 'Are you sure you want to do this? I mean … it will be like I never existed.' *Perhaps it would be better that way?*

He placed his hand on the side of my face, looked into my eyes and tenderly moved his thumb over my cheek, reawakening the butterflies in the pit of my stomach. And right there on his face I saw love, and pain. 'We'll find each other. I'll make it work,' he said and frowned, closed his eyes and lowered his head, turning it to the right.

'Are you okay?'

'Yes. I need to go.' He grabbed my hand and pulled me around the galley deck. On the other side of the structure he stopped at a door and opened it, revealing a spiral staircase. Relief flooded me followed by questions. He started walking down the steps. 'You're braver than me,' he said.

'You mean—'

He shook his head. 'I never climbed the ladder.'

I pressed my lips in a hard line to stop the words tumbling out of my mouth that I would regret later. I made a mental note to always look for other options, regardless of where I am or who I'm with.

When we reached the ground floor he stood in the shadows with his hand on the doorknob. 'You go first. We can't be seen together.' His voice was low. Almost unrecognisable.

I pulled my hood over my head. He opened the door in one swift movement, and I disappeared into the night, weaving through the stargazers and back to my car.

Our conversation was not finished.

Chapter 16

A midnight-green coloured Cruiser bicycle leaned against the antique-white storefront of Flowers for Fleur; the signature bicycle that had sat in the exact same location for fifty years, appearing every morning at sunrise. It was the embodiment of Tarrin—historical, uncomplicated, and homely. A bouquet of stunning pink peonies adorned the wicker basket of the bicycle, beaming their colourful happiness at everyone who walked past. I leaned in toward them and inhaled—sweet and spicy with a touch of citrus—reminding me of Tobi's aftershave on nights spent together in the Jacaranda tree gazing at the luminous full moon. For a moment, I wondered what it would be like working in an industry that created smiles and happy hearts with scents that induced memories. And for a moment, just a moment, I felt lighter, like a heavy burden had been lifted from my shoulders. I frowned. I was certain the cruiser bicycle used to be a different colour.

I took one step into the store filled with the psychedelic scent of what smelled like a thousand flowers and saw Yolande.

She stood behind the sales counter in the signature floral skater dress, her wavy dark-brown hair in a messy updo. She looked up and flashed a wide smile the moment she laid eyes on me. I walked towards her and stopped at the counter, returning her contagious grin.

Yolande raised any eyebrow at me. 'Flowers, tea, coffee ... or books?' she asked, grinned and dipped her head before she skipped around from the counter, her safety boots heavy on the timber floor. She stopped before me and wrapped her arms around me, her hug fuelled with fun childhood memories. She released her embrace a little, then hugged me harder before she stepped back from me. 'Indigo Feather Danube, what brings you to Flowers for Fleur?'

I looked down at her footwear and smiled, then looked back at her. 'Oh, you know ... I'd like to buy some safety boots. I hear they look amazing with floral dresses.'

'You mean, you're finally going to become an aeronautical engineer, like me!'

I hooked my arm through Yolande's. 'Sounds tempting. Let's be the first women to grow a flower farm in space!'

'Aaah—Cosmic Blooms—flowers that are out of this world!' Yolande's hand painted the sign in the sky like an artist. 'It has great marketing potential.' She pulled her eyebrows together, then laughed, her happiness weaving its way into my heart.

'Absolutely.' I gave her a wink.

'Are you okay?' she asked.

'Yes. I've had some interesting progress with my research.' I drew in a deep breath to calm the anxiety that bubbled inside. I needed access to her fortified heart to infiltrate her mind. It felt like forbidden territory. 'Hey, Scarlett's got a cochlear implant. I want to give her some flowers as a celebration for smashing the word recognition tests. I'm pretty sure your grandmother will be able to create the most amazing arrangement for her ... do you think?'

She smiled and nodded. 'For certain. Gram has bionic hearing now too. Good old *Cochlear*. It changed her life! It's like she's back to her old self before Meniere's disease, the ugly life-stealer! She's just so … happy!'

'Really? Now I know why I was drawn to come and see you. Do you think you can spare a moment for coffee and give me some tips about how to help Scarlett? I hear Flowers for Fleur has the best barista in town.' I wiggled my eyebrows at her.

The corners of Yolande's mouth turned up. 'We do.' She turned to her grandmother and raised her hand, her pinkie finger straight, while her other fingers where fisted. Grandmother Fleur nodded, then Yolande linked her arm with mine and we walked to the café of the flower shop and sat at a table by the window. The smell of coffee permeated the café, followed by the sweet aroma of baking cakes.

'Tell me about—' we both started.

'You first,' I said.

'No, you.'

'Okay—Scarlett has days where she dislikes her cochlear implant. It was a big decision for her to choose to hear again since losing her hearing when she was seven. She keeps taking the thing she has to wear, off her head, when she thinks the world is too ugly or too noisy. I want to find a way to encourage her to keep it on.'

Yolande nodded. 'Mmm, change is difficult. Especially stepping out your comfort zone. I remember Gram being exhausted, mentally. All the time. I recall her talking about the intense focus she needed. But Gram being Gram, she persevered and hasn't removed her new hearing since the day she was activated … except to sleep. She has wholeheartedly embraced her new hearing technology,' Yolande said.

'So, it's about attitude? I keep telling Scarlett if she hates what she is hearing, she can choose not to wear the thing-a-me-bob that attaches to the—' I waved my hand around the side of my head. I had no idea what I was talking about when it came to a cochlear implant.

'The processor?'

'Processor?'

'The outer part that attaches to the magnet under the skin.'

'Yeah—that bit.'

'Maybe she could drop in and talk to Gram about it?'

'Thanks. I'll talk to her and send her in this direction,' I said. I glanced over at the bike. 'Wasn't Grandmother Fleur's bicycle a different colour?'

Yolande laughed. 'I think we need to write a newspaper article about it so we don't have to keep answering that question.' She smiled. 'The Museum of Tarrin decided it had historical worth and has it displayed in "The Story of Tarrin"—'

'Good morning!' I looked up at the tall, red-bearded man with a deep voice.

Yolande's eyes sparkled. 'Hi, Darcy. I'd like you to meet my friend, Indigo. Indi, this is Darcy, barista extraordinaire!'

'Nice to meet you, Indigo. What can I get for you?' he said, the tenor of his voice strangely comforting.

'Just a cappuccino, please.'

'*Just* a cappuccino? Sure,' Darcy's voice smiled. He looked at Yolande with a raised eyebrow. Yolande nodded, and he left. Hmmm. They had a secret language.

I looked around the flower shop and cafe. It was busy. I wondered if Yolande was happy here. She was super intelligent and my nemesis at school. How could working in amongst the flowers fulfil her?

I cleared my throat. 'Do you miss working for the Defence Force?'

Yolande took a deep breath and looked over her shoulder,

gazing about the store. She looked back at me. 'You mean in a flower shop with either its intoxicating happiness, or miserable allergies … unless the flower is a Titan Arum, which then will have everyone running for the hills to escape the pungent scent that smells like a rotting corpse!' She raised her eyebrows at me and kept her face deadpan.

I grinned. 'That's exactly what I mean.'

Yolande threaded her fingers together and rested her elbows on the table. She closed her eyes. 'I feel safe with family around me. I like the people connection, as long as they don't look at me with pity—for those who remember the incident—and the shop is super busy and keeps my mind from wandering to places … to memories … where it shouldn't.' She opened her eyes and looked at me. 'There. I told you the truth.'

I nodded my understanding as Darcy placed my cappuccino on the table, then Yolande's teacup and teapot. He added two cupcakes to the ensemble.

I looked up at him. 'Thank you,' I said.

'You're welcome. Rest assured, it is not, *just*, a cappuccino. Is there anything else you would like?' he asked.

'No. This is … the … not *just* a cappuccino … is perfect. Thanks,' I said.

He dipped his head and left. I watched as he took a cup of tea to Yolande's grandmother.

Yolande put her hand on the teapot and looked at me before she turned it three times, mouthing the counting of one, two, three, then shrugged her shoulders. She always made me laugh. Academic nemesis, and a good, best friend.

'Y-you know … I can h-help you with your memories,' I stuttered, berating myself for such a clumsy delivery of my offer of help. I watched her face, waiting for any sign of intolerance to my words, to my offer of escape from her past.

Yolande picked up her teacup and squinted at me over the top of it. She took a sip, staring at me. I squirmed as an uncomfortable feeling flowed through me, like the slow burn of hate. I wanted to evaporate on the spot.

She placed her teacup back onto the saucer, picked up a cupcake and took a bite and leisurely chewed, then swallowed. 'I doubt it,' she said with a shrug of one shoulder.

'You do know what my field of research is, don't you?' I asked. My chest heated with the sting of rejection. She didn't even want to know any details. I raised my coffee mug to my lips and took a sip.

'Yes. You interfere with the workings of the brain, the *essence* of a person.'

I choked on my cappuccino, covered my mouth with my hand, and coughed. I shook my head. 'Where did you get that idea from?'

'Well … you remove memories, don't you? Memories create the person you are.'

I frowned. 'Three words. Yes and no.'

'How can it be yes *and* no. It's got to be yes, or no. Black and white.'

'It is black and white, Yolande. We choose the specific memories to be deleted, and leave everything else exactly the way it is—'

Yolande lowered her head, cutting her eyes into mine. 'I *never* ... want to forget her.' Yolande's low, rough words were filled with aggression. She covered her mouth with her hand and let out a quiet sob, then closed her eyes, her eyebrows pinched together.

My heart broke. I inhaled deeply, then swirled my carefully chosen words around my mouth before I released them. 'You won't forget her. I will only remove the memories of the incident that resulted in her death. That's it. You will be freed from that day. You won't have PTSD. You won't have anxiety. You won't have flashbacks. You won't have survivor guilt. You won't feel like you are the reason for her death—' A tear fell from Yolande's eye and I stopped talking and held my breath.

'But—' She stopped as her bottom lip trembled. 'If I have no memory of her death, how do I not expect her to walk into the store to see me, or text me, or call me?'

I lowered my chin to control the wave of intense sadness that swept through me. I wanted Mia back too. She was one of my childhood best friends, like Yolande, and the world was darker with Mia gone. I wished I could unwish her death. Not that I had wished it in the first place. But I wished that she was still alive. I wished there was an *undoing*. 'I … don't know. Do yo—'

The chair squealed as it moved along the wooden floor when Yolande stood abruptly. She looked at me, her chin quivering, pressed her lips in a hard line, then ran. By the time I stood to follow her, she had disappeared out the front door of Flowers for Fleur and was gone.

My throat tightened as I held in my sob. I covered my eyes with my hands, then felt a hand on my shoulder.

'She'll be okay, Indigo.' Darcy's voice was calm, like this had happened a thousand times before. Maybe it had.

I lowered my hands and turned and looked at him. 'I know I can make it better for her, if only she would trust me.'

'What if she doesn't want it to be better?' he asked. 'What if she thinks she deserves to feel the way she does, every single day?'

'No one should feel that way.' I shook my head. I can't help someone who didn't want to be helped. *I'm sorry, Xander.*

'She'll get in touch with you, Indigo. She always has an attack of guilt and regret when she does a runner. It's her way of coping,' Darcy said.

'I know … and thanks,' I said. 'Can I have my *just* a cappuccino in a takeaway cup to go. It's too good to leave unfinished.' I offered Darcy a smile that was meant to be warm, except, it kind of melted off my face with the sadness I felt inside, like a depressive song in a rapture of melancholy.

'I'll make you a fresh one with a dash of sunshine and a sprinkle of problem solving, on the house,' he said with a wink.

I let out a calming breath. 'You are way too nice!'

Darcy gave a short nod, his eyes full of sadness. I sat and gazed out the window and waited.

After five minutes I exited Flowers for Fleur with a cappuccino in one hand and my cell phone in the other, and tripped over the foot of a street cleaner, catching myself just in time to save myself from an embarrassing face plant.

'Apologies, ma'am,' he said and looked at me for a snap in time. His cap was pulled low over his eyebrows and he wore a green surgical mask that covered his mouth and nose. *Odd.* There were no contagious viruses in Tarrin at the moment.

'My fault. I should watch where I'm going. Sorry,' I said, studying him more closely. His voice had the same timbre as Tobi's, without the inflections … and his eye colour … I narrowed my eyes at him. He nodded and turned away at once.

I walked back to the Brain and Mind Institute, my heart heavy. I had failed to help my friend. Was it the delivery of my suggestion? Did I not sound convincing? Was I too clinical? Was I heartless in discussing removing the memories of Mia? Or was it Yolande? Did she have an impenetrable mental barrier? I wished I knew. I looked down and shook my head.

Wishes.

They are nothing.

Wishes should not be wished.

They do nothing.

Absolutely nothing.

I entered the institute, donned my lab coat, iris scanned into the Memory Lab, and slipped back into neuroscientist research mode.

'Good afternoon, everyone,' I said to the brain specimens.

No response.

I walked up to the first encased brain and pressed my hand to the glass. I slowed my breathing and gazed over the gyri and sulci: the peaks and grooves of the cerebral cortex. I frowned. For all we knew about the brain, it was still a mystery.

The more we knew, the more we didn't know.

I had too many questions, and not enough answers. How could … all of this … be us? Our "brainprint", unique like our fingerprint. Our personality. Our identity. Our … *essence* … who we are, held in place by the confines of the skull, perfectly cushioned from harm. The signature of us.

And for those of us who know, who have witnessed it, the brain is a glorious symphony of electrical storms of light. We are made of light, except, we are living, breathing, intelligent, creative, and given the power to change the course of our own lives, others lives, and the future story of the Earth.

A feeling of euphoria swept over me, replaced in an instant by a wave of fear rolling over me and knotting my stomach. We were interfering with the internal light of the brainprint. I clenched my teeth and reminded myself that we were saving lives crushed by trauma. We were removing memories that darkened the light, that erupted in a chemical pool of negative reactions that affected the whole person, from thoughts to actions to the point of the person choosing death to escape their memories.

I pursed my lips and exhaled slowly, then beamed Quinn's hologram above his brain. 'Good afternoon, Quinn.' I looked at the digital representation of his brain constructed from fMRI. The middle and superior frontal cortex and superior temporal cortex of his brain lit up. It is what happens when people hear their name. I touched my finger to the audio folder on the projected screen and opened it, then chose Quinn's favourite music—*Handel's Messiah*. The digitally altered music streamed directly to his auditory nerve via a wireless electrode, through the brainstem and onward to the auditory cortex of his brain. I smiled as his brain erupted in a kaleidoscope of light in many lobes, confirming the research that music affects all parts of the brain, not just the temporal lobe.

I moved on and projected the next brain hologram. 'Good afternoon, Emerson.' We had light in the correct places. *Consciousness.* In his audio folder I opened *Air on G String* by Bach. His brain lit up in a symphony of light.

Next. Hologram projected. 'Good afternoon, Ardon.' *Consciousness.* I smiled and opened the audio folder, found *Bitter Sweet Symphony* by The Verve, and pushed play.

Next hologram. 'Good afternoon, Jamie.' *Consciousness.* Audio open—*Let It Be* by The Beatles. Play.

Next. Hologram. 'Good afternoon, Alex.' *Consciousness.* Audio open—*Behind Blue Eyes* by Limp Bizkit. Play.

Next. Hologram. 'Good afternoon, Mica.' *Consciousness.* Audio open—*Hungarian Dances* by Brahms. Play.

Next. Hologram. 'Good afternoon, Jordan.' *Consciousness.* Audio open—*Saturn* by Sleeping at Last. Play.

Next. Hologram. 'Good afternoon, Emerson.' *Consciousness.* Audio open—*How To Disappear Completely* by Radiohead. Play.

Next. Hologram. 'Good afternoon, Hunter.' *Consciousness.* Audio open—*Riverside* by Agnes Obel. Play.

Next. Hologram. 'Good afternoon, Charlie.' *Consciousness.* Audio open—*Stop Crying Your Heart Out* by Oasis. Play.

Next. Hologram. 'Good afternoon, Nic.' *Consciousness.* Audio open—*Concerto for Piano and Orchestra No. 23 in A major* by Mozart. Play.

I stepped back and watched the brain holograms alight with colour as the music activated multiple lobes, and my heart broke. For all their differences, two things connected them: their terrible traumas, and their choice of sad music. For a moment I wondered what would happen if I played the ten songs out loud at the same time instead of streaming directly to their auditory nerves. Would they all sync and create a harmony of discord that mirrored depression, chaos, and a death wish?

I shuddered, then stretched my fingers to ground me to the present. I inhaled slowly. The next step was to test them with a sound from their traumatic event. But I wasn't ready. I couldn't find the courage to hurt them.

They would have to wait.

The experiment would have to wait.

I placed my hand over my mouth and dry retched.

Chapter 17

Mindless running.

Thump. Thump. Thump.

The rhythmic pounding on the pavement calmed my mind while it followed the pattern.

Thump. Thump. Thump.

Brains love patterns. Pattern recognition is its deep core capability.

Thump. Thump. Thump.

I gravitated to running when my mind was in turmoil. Lately it felt like it was every evening in the time of neither here nor there. *Twilight.* The colours of above in the *in-between.*

Thump. Thump. Thump.

Stop. I was at the park of my youth.

I hunched over and placed my hands on my thighs and tried to catch my breath, then walked closer to the shoreline and lowered myself to the ground. I closed my eyes and shook my head. How could I ever tell Yolande that I was the reason for Mia's death? It was my fault. *All my fault.*

I opened my eyes and stared at the Jacaranda tree beyond *Zero,* a stone's throw from the mainland. There were no identifiable flowers in shades of purple adorning its branches. The Autumndom had stolen them. Now the tree was dressed in leaves of green turning yellow. Some had fallen, unable to hold on to life anymore. A melody of languishing and soul searching floated in the crisp air around me, emphasising the fact that the tree was isolated from the world, trapped by a lake that never used to be.

My wish. *My fault.*

But the tree seemed happiest when it was surrounded by water the colour of purples and blues, from the reflection of the purple blooms, like in Claude Monet's *Water Lilies,* except now, there were no Jacaranda blooms, just shadows of shame and regret and heartbreak. If Claude Monet were here now and knew the secrets of the lake, his brushstrokes would be in a palette expressing the macabre I felt inside. Claude Monet. Words triggered a memory of when I met Tobi on the nightdom of a full moon—

He stood tall with his hands behind his back, his broad shoulders and pectoral muscles accentuated through his light blue T-shirt. I stopped before him on the pebbled shoreline, and he held out his right hand for me to take, his eyes connecting to mine.

'By the light of the setting sun before the nightdom of the full moon,' I said, and placed my hand into Tobi's. My skin warmed at his touch that felt more like a caress of the heart than a steadying hand.

'As planned,' he said, his voice low and deep and rich in its tones, his eyes piercing with a secret seduction.

I raised an eyebrow at him as I rode the wave of euphoria he gave, climbed into the gentlemen's rowboat, sat on the end seat and opened my white lace parasol, even though the sunset was almost upon us.

He clambered onto the rower's seat, grabbed the oars, and started to row. After two strokes, he fell into a smooth rhythm that felt like we were floating on air. He smiled crookedly before he looked beyond *Zero*, to the lake full of blue and the land beyond, the afternoon sun illuminating his ocean-blue eyes. He focussed his gaze back on me, his eyes drinking me in. 'If I were Claude Monet, I'd paint you.'

My breath stopped. He knew of Claude Monet? He knew of art? What was his background that he was so determined not to share? 'Claude Monet? I never imagined you as … cultured,' I said, my voice whimsical.

'Are you saying men can't be cultured?' He frowned.

'Be careful, an appreciation of art opens the mind. It changes the way you look at life. I don't know many men who want to look inside and outside of themselves through art.'

He glanced beyond *Zero*, to the lake full of blue, then back to me. 'You project yourself into art. What you see, tells your story,' he said.

I closed my eyes. 'What you see, tells your story,' I repeated in a whisper. 'Sometimes the story that doesn't want to be told,' I said and opened my eyes. 'Is art for the deep thinkers, the philosophical kind? Or does it invoke that condition?'

'I think … at first, it invokes the condition of deep thinking and philosophy. To me, art appreciation shows a passion for life, a willingness to see something from someone else's point of view and consider its validity. Like reading … it makes you a better person.'

I narrowed my eyes at Tobi. 'Are you trying to tell me something about your job that you can't openly sa—' I stilled. Silent. Like my words had been stolen from me. The far side of Jacaranda Island came into view. But it was different. A candle lit jetty jutted out from the shoreline.

The rowing movement of the boat ceased. We were no longer

floating on air, but rocking to the waltz of the lake.

'Do you like it?' Tobi's voice was quiet, articulated with tenderness.

'Tobi … I … I don't know what to say … it's … perfect,' I said, wanting to add "like you", but didn't. I returned my gaze to Tobi. He lowered his eyes and gave a shy smile. 'Did you build it?'

He looked back up at me. 'Yes,' he said, lingering on the "s".

'When?'

'When you were on silence for research, and uncontactable. Building this stopped me from going insane. I've missed you so much.' Tobi's jaw flexed before he began rowing again. 'I hope you like it.'

The rowboat glided, then slowed with perfect timing to the side of the jetty. Tobi leaned over and tied the boat's rope to the post. He stepped out of the boat and onto the timber boards, then offered me his hand.

I collapsed my parasol and placed my hand in his, bathing in pleasant electricity that ignited my cells, then stood. With my eyes connected to his, I stepped out of the rowboat and onto the jetty. Tobi entwined his fingers through mine and led me along the short stroll to another newly created platform, scattered with colourful cushions. I took a calming breath. He was so … romantic.

'Madame,' he said and gestured for me to sit.

'Monsieur,' I said, sitting as gracefully as I could, trying not to stumble when I was conscious of being watched, like the time when I was sixteen and walking with Yolande and Mia. It was a stinking hot day on summer break, and we were at the Kingdom Adventure Park. There was a group of young men lined up at the Soda Pop Stall waiting for a soda laced with an unadvertised something else. The moment Mia saw them her personality changed. She veered away from us and headed directly towards them. Mia was a party girl. She loved flirting and rode the thrill like it was an addictive drug. She loved to tease, incapable of controlling herself, even at the slight whiff of the male species. She flicked her long hair to the side, changed her walk, swaying her hips as she moved toward them, oozing her availability.

'What colour is she, Yolande?' I said. Yolande had a gift of seeing people in colours. She was a synesthete.

'She was yellow. But now she is red. Sexuality and action—'

I ran after Mia. I had seen this version of her before. She was headed for trouble. I caught up to her, grabbed her elbow and turned her in the opposite direction and fell. Face first into a pile of manure recently deposited by a passing cow headed for the judging ring. It was still warm—

'Excusez-moi,' Tobi said with a dip of his head, interrupting my memory.

'Oui,' I replied. I watched as he walked to the Jacaranda tree, where a wooden box sat. He carried it back to the platform, opened the lid, pulled out a bag, and collected two wine glasses and a bottle of wine. He sat and handed a glass to me, opened the wine bottle and poured red wine into my glass, a third of the way, and finished with a professional twist of the bottle as he stopped the flow. I watched as he did the same with his own glass. He picked up his glass of red with the secret handshake of the wine elite. So, I changed my "wine-glass-girls'-night-out-hold" to match his, holding the wine glass towards the base of the stem, between my thumb and forefinger.

Tobi raised his glass, his eyes simmering, 'To our childhood, where we first met.'

I raised my glass, allowing myself to fall into his eyes, drinking me in, 'To our childhood, and to hiding in Jacaranda trees.' I took a sip of the wine, the fruity notes of cherries, strawberries, and plums dancing on my palate, and as I swallowed, the experience was complete: balanced, harmonious, and complex, with a lingering, satisfying finish. For a moment, I wondered whether this wine mirrored Tobi.

'I have a confession,' I said.

'Go on …'

'I'm feeling guilty.'

'About?'

'All of this. You have done so much, and I have done nothing.'

The corners of his mouth turned up, revealing his dimples. 'It's a gift, to you. As is the swing hanging from the widest branch.'

I looked behind me and there it was. A tree swing made from a wide timber pallet, decorated with a pillow and a blanket. Why didn't I notice it before? My heartbeat quickened. 'But, Tobi, it's too mu—'

He placed his finger over my lips. 'Sssssh,' he whispered. 'Enjoy.' He lifted his chin and looked down at me, connecting with my eyes in a depth that made me feel weak at the knees, filling my body with warmth, my stomach turning somersaults. I wanted to place my lips onto his. But I didn't.

'Thank you,' I whispered, my voice lower than I intended, my eyes falling into his once again, entering the point of no return.

Tobi pulled his eyes from mine and looked beyond *Zero*, to the lake full of blue. 'Indi … the sunset.'

I followed his gaze, and melted into the explosion of colour of the sunset—all the colours above: the sinking sun projecting hues of pinks, purples, yellows, oranges, and reds into the clouds. And as it fell beneath the horizon, gasping for one last breath, one last burst of majesty, it splashed the colour of green for a nanosecond, and then it was gone. There would be no encores. The stage was set for the stars to sing in the all the new colours above.

I focussed on the brightest star in the sky and felt Tobi's fingers slide between mine.

'Star light, star bright, the first star I see tonight; I wish I may, I wish I might, have the wish I wish tonight,' he whispered.

I smiled, then looked at him. 'Are you mocking me, Mr. Brooks!'

He raised an eyebrow at me. 'What if … I am the keeper of wishes?' he said. 'Have any more of your wishes come true?' He leaned close to me, his eyes wandering to my lips, caressing, and then gave a slow blink.

I breathed out the thrill that travelled through me, warming my body as it has never been warmed before. 'As a matter of fact, yes. Once, I wished for a magical island, right out of a fairy tale. And here it is.' I waved my hand over the candlelit jetty and the wooden platform covered with colourful square pillows, and the tree swing.

'Hmmmm … does that mean your wishes have a direct line to my mind and heart?' he said.

'Only if your mind and heart are rebellious, Tobi. You broke a Jacaranda Island rule.'

'I did.'

'Yes. Rule Number 4—*you cannot be on the island alone*.'

'True. But let me add another rule for Jacaranda Island. Rule Number 8. *You may only break Rule Number 4, to add an element of surprise for the significant other*.' Tobi stood and held out his hand to me. 'It's time for Rule Number 5.'

The tips of my fingers connected to Tobi's, and he led me to the Jacaranda tree where the green leaves danced in the breeze. I climbed first, as I always did, and slowed as I reached the usual branch we sat on together; the one that seemed to be safe for Tobi to sit on. I looked down, wondering what was taking him so long. He was even slower than his usual sloth speed. He looked up, then wiped his hands on his dark blue shorts, and let out a controlled breath. Did he hate climbing the tree that much?

'Hey,' I said when he secured his balance on the bottom

branch, hugging the tree trunk like it was his source of life.

He removed a hand and raked his fingers through his hair, a curl falling back over his forehead. 'Hey.'

'Do you hate climbing the tree that much, Tobi, *the Brave*?'

'I'm getting better at it,' he said.

'You know, rules are meant to be broken. We can break Rule Number 5. We don't have to climb the tree every time we are here.'

'I know,' he said. 'But the tree is important to you.' He placed his free hand higher on the trunk of the tree, and started to climb in his uncoordinated, unconfident kind of way. He stopped at my branch and settled himself, then looked into my eyes. 'Perhaps … and don't let this go to your head … perhaps … you are more important to me than the tree?' His eyes moved to my lips and my breath hitched.

'Are you trying to terrify me?'

Tobi shook his head, then looked down with a crooked smile. My heart skipped a beat. He pulled up his light blue T-shirt and pulled out the Book of Unfinished Stories he had secured with his belt. He caressed the dark blue hardcover with his fingers.

'Ah. The book of endless possibilities, of mind probing, and inner revelations. The book … of the dark night,' I said.

Tobi looked up at me through his eyelashes. 'Now I am the one who is terrified.'

'Good,' I said. 'Read to me.'

He opened the book to the dog-eared page and looked at me, his eyes seeming to challenge me to say no. I didn't. 'Close your eyes,' he said, 'and give the story life, with your mind, then speak it with words.'

I held on to the branch to secure my balance, and closed my eyes.

'Are you ready?' His voice fell into a tone and cadence that felt slower, intimate even, and my heart melted. I waited with great expectation for him to begin. And it did, without disappointment.

'He threw open the heavy, wooden doors, but the Great Hall of the castle was empty, except for the breeze that blew the curtains.'

A vision entered my mind. I was in the castle, in the Great Hall, hiding. I moved my hand to Tobi's thigh to anchor myself, to stop me falling out of the tree, or to protect me from where my imagination would lead me to, I wasn't sure.

I drew in a calming breath ...

> 'He threw open the heavy wooden doors, but the Great Hall of the castle was empty, except for the breeze that blew the curtains so they danced to the sound of tragedy. The metallic taste of my own blood turned my stomach as I hid beneath the dining table, too scared to breathe in case I was found. I tucked my dress in around me to make sure none could be seen by the intruder. The king's prophet had told me I was number 7. Six had already died. Now it was my turn. But what if his dreams were incorrect? What if, his dreams could be interpreted differently? What if, I could change his dream? After all, a dream is not reality. I could change the outcome of his dream, couldn't I?
>
> Think, think. What is a man's weakness? I shook my head. Of course. A naked woman. But that would be my last resort for survival.
>
> The floorboards squeaked as he walked; slow and even. The he stopped.
>
> Silence. Deafening.
>
> Anticipation. Incapacitating.
>
> *Sh-ting*! The sound of the unsheathing of his sword bounced off the walls and shattered inside

my ears with a sharp warning.

Footfalls landed on the floorboards again. Closer this time, until I could see he was on my right side. As my heart hammered against my rib cage, I managed to manoeuvre up onto some chairs, lying flat. If he looked under the table, he would be less likely to see me. I held my breath.

'I know you are here. I can smell you!' he said, his voice deep and threatening.

As I released my breath, his dark eyes appeared beneath the table and connected to mine. This was it. I was about to become Number 7. Sliding onto the chairs was a bad move. I should have thought it out more carefully. I was more trapped in this position than on the floor where I could have pushed a chair out to create a space to make a run for it.

His face softened and he smiled. 'It's you! I thought I would never see you again!'

'Altalos, my friend!'

'Yes. It's me. What are you doing under there?' he said, his voice softer and full of heart.

'Isn't it obvious? What are you doing here?'

'I came to fight Ansfrid. But it appears I am too late.'

'Ansfrid? He was never here. It was Jacomus who caused this,' I said.

'Jacomus? Are you sure? Look … come out from under the table so we can talk. I need to know of the events leading up to this … this … unspeakable act. Look at the Great Hall. If it looks like this, what is the damage to the people of the kingdom?' He rubbed at his brow.

I slid off the chairs and onto the floor, fiddled about for a moment, before climbing between the legs of the chair to stand. By the time I was upright, Altalos stood before me.

'The people are safe,' I said.

'But why are you still here?'

'I bought them some time. I chose to be the sacrifice to protect the others.'

'Dear, dear Gabriela, why would you do that?'

'Because the men were fighting another battle in the forest of souls … someone had to do it!'

'And that,' Altalos lifted his sword, 'is why I have come … to take your life.'

I gasped. 'No. NO. You are my friend! What has happened to you? The Altalos I knew would never betray me like this. You don't have to do this. I am a mere woman. What harm can I do to anyone, or anything?'

With my right hand behind my back, I pulled a knife from my belt. I had landed on it when I slid off the chairs and concealed it behind me as I fumbled about.

Altalos ran his hand over his face. I lifted the knife, poised to strike—'

I opened my eyes wide. My heart rate spiked and I was rendered incapable of telling anymore of the words. 'Tobi, I can't continue the story,' I said.

'You have to do it. Change the path of the narrative. Add another character.'

I shook my head, then swallowed and nodded in time to my erratic heartbeat. I closed my eyes and entered the story again.

'I jumped backwards as Altalos lunged forward to strike me with his sword. My knife was short, pitiful and useless, but I slashed through the air anyway, cutting into his forearm, opening his flesh to release his life-sustaining blood.

Fuelled by anger, Altalos raised his sword again, this time closer to me. This was it. The end of my earthly life was upon me. I didn't want it to end like this. I didn't want to die in fear. So, I dropped my knife. The clatter of it echoed around the Great Hall. I let out my breath in a calmness I didn't know I possessed, then closed my eyes and waited for the piercing of the sword.

Thwish. Thump. One sound came from behind me. The other in front.

I opened my eyes to find Altalos on his knees, clutching at an arrow that had pierced his torso. As light faded from his eyes, he looked up at me. 'Forgive me,' he whispered.

I nodded, and he fell backwards. Dead.

I turned to find the archer. He stood, eyes focussed on me, arms by his side, spent, his face contorted in pain.

I ran to him. He pulled me close, his lips meeting mine for a moment in time, then stepped back from me. 'Wife … had I been a second later, you would have been … been …' He ran his hand over his face as a tortured sound escaped his lips.

'But I saved more than a thousand lives. Isn't one life taken better than a thousand?'

'Not when it is you. You are more precious to me than all the stars in the sky. If you die, my internal light will be extinguished.' He placed his hand over my growing stomach, 'And our son … a gift. Please let others take care of you.'

I frowned. Even two lives taken is better than a thousand. 'I love you,' I said, to ease his pain.

'What do I have to do? Lock you high up in the tower to keep you safe?' His lips lifted in a half smile.

'Only if you are there with me,' I whispered.

He smiled. 'Come. Let us seek the safety of the underground.' He took my hand, and we fled.

I opened my eyes, satisfied with the ending of the story. I blew a silent breath between my lips, but still felt unsettled by my story.

'That's better,' Tobi said. 'Are you okay?'

'Now I am,' I lied. I pressed my lips together and made a note to myself to enter our story time with the aim of an uplifting tale.

Tobi looked at me and moved his lips as if he were about to speak. But he didn't.

'Was my story too much?' I said.

'Not at all. I found your storytelling … fascinating.'

'U-huh,' I said and gazed at him longer than intended. He looked so much like the hero archer in my story. 'Your turn.'

He gave me a slight smile. 'Close your eyes, listen and watch.' My hand was still on his thigh. He lifted it to his lips and gave my hand a kiss, then put my hand on the branch. Warmth flowed inside me that calmed and elated. How did he make me feel this way?

'Once upon a time, he threw open the heavy wooden doors, but the Great Hall of the castle was empty, except for the breeze that blew the curtains.

'Juliet,' Quinn called, his heart racing in

anticipation of seeing the love of his life.

He heard her feather light steps before he saw her. And then she appeared in a flowing, white dress, her braided hair, the colour of a cloudy orange and golden sunset, falling over her shoulder. His heart missed a beat as it always did the moment he saw her, then glowed when she gave a little skip and ran to him.

Quinn fell to bended knee before her, took her hand, and kissed it. He wished for his kiss to be on her lips connecting their hearts. But not here in the Great Hall of the castle. It was too dangerous. 'My Love, I would be honoured if you would accompany me to the Grand Ball.' He held his hand over his heart, looking up into her eyes, blue, like the summer sky.

She shook her head, biting down on her bottom lip. 'My father has already promised King Rainard that I will go with Prince Fendrel.'

Quinn's spirit fell. He frowned and looked toward to ground. His heart ached. He should never have let his hopes get so high. He stood. Slowly. He knew what was happening. Prince Fendrel wanted her for his wife. What man wouldn't want her? He stepped back from Juliet and bowed to her. He knew never to dishonour another man or woman. 'It seems then, that I am too late.'

'Quinn. I'm sorry. I did not choose this; it was my father and King Rainard.'

Quinn looked at her, his heart full of sorrow. A tear fell from her eye. He lifted his hand and caught it on his finger, and placed it into his own eye.

'Juliet, I have loved you since I was twelve. And

… no matter what, I will love you until my last breath.'

'Quinn, my heart, I promise you the second dance at the Grand Ball,' Juliet said.

Quinn dipped his head. 'Then I shall look forward to it.'

'Juliet?' A female voice echoed through the room.

Juliet looked to her left. 'Here, Mother,' she called after a moment. She looked at Quinn. 'You must go, now, before you are caught,' she whispered.

Quinn took her hand and kissed it once more, then disappeared out the open wooden doors and to the forest, where he disappeared into it, stopping at the lake of tears to catch his breath.

He bent down to quench his thirst, then stared at his reflection. Why did I have to fall in love with Juliet, a princess, he thought. In what world would I even think I had a chance of being with her? All the kingdom rules forbid commoners from even mixing with royalty!

Quinn raised his hand and punched the water, shattering the reflection of his face. 'That arrogant bastard of a prince doesn't deserve her kindness and beautiful heart!' he said between clenched teeth. 'But what can I, a commoner, do?'

Quinn stood and looked to the heavens. All things are possible, he thought. He stood taller, took a few steps, then jogged to the village, ruminating a plan in his mind to have Juliet as his own. He smiled. Juliet would be his wife, one day.

Quinn arrived at the village and a horn

> sounded, as was tradition when one of their own returned. People came from their homes and gathered around him, then parted way to allow his mother through the midst. She held a warm smile and a cake. On top was one single candle.
>
> 'Happy birthday, Quinn,' she said.
>
> 'Thanks, Ma,' Quinn closed his eyes and made a *wish*. Then he inhaled deeply and blew out the candle, filled with hope.

Tobi sighed.

I opened my eyes and looked at him.

'The end.' He shrugged as he pressed his lips together.

I frowned. 'It can't be. I need to know the end of the story!'

'I just … can't think of how Quinn gets what he wants.' Tobi raised an eyebrow at me. 'Perhaps you could finish the story?'

I laughed. 'You know it won't end well. There will be a murder for sure! And I can't guarantee the ending will be a happily ever after.'

Tobi let out an audible breath and raised an eyebrow. 'That, I cannot deny.' He closed the book. 'You know, I did contemplate telling your story from the point of view of Altalos, but changing it so you get your happily ever after.'

'Really? I'd love to hear it.'

Tobi connected his eyes to mine, ocean-blue to greenish-blue. 'Close your eyes and watch, my twisted, dark storyteller friend.'

'Is that a compliment?'

He raised both eyebrows at me and placed a finger over my lips. 'Close your eyes and enter the story.'

I gazed into his eyes until my chest started to warm, then did as he asked.

> 'Altalos stood tall, mighty and strong. He

took slow steps to the middle of the Great Hall and unsheathed his sword. Someone was in here. He could smell her. Yes, her. His target. He didn't know what she looked like, or her name, just what she smelled like: sugar and spice and all things nice. Once he had killed her, he would receive his hefty reward and disappear into the caves to live out the rest of his days in peace. She would be his last kill. And he was glad. He never liked watching life fade from a person. He glanced at his left forearm. He had marked six scars for the six lives he had already taken. Today's death would be number 7.

He looked about the Great Hall. There was no movement. 'I know you are here. I can smell you!' he said, his voice deep and threatening. There could only be one place for her to hide. Under the tables. He lowered himself onto his haunches. The floor was bare but as he glanced away, some dress fabric caught his eye. It was white. Pure. Like her. His target.

He lifted his eyes to her face, and his resolve softened. He smiled. 'It's you! I thought I would never see you again!'

'Altalos, my friend?' Gabriela said.

'Yes. It's me. What are you doing under there?' he said.

'Isn't it obvious? What are you doing here?'

'I have come to—'

'To?' Gabriela frowned.

'No matter … who caused this?' he said.

'Jacomus?'

'Jacomus?' He rubbed at his brow. 'Look … come out from under the table so we can talk.'

Gabriela manoeuvred herself from the chairs and stood, taking a little longer than he thought she would.

'Where are the people?' Altalos asked.

'I bought them some time. I chose to protect the others.'

'Dear, dear Gabriela, why would you do that?'

'Because the men were off fighting another battle … someone had to do it!' Gabriela said.

'And that,' Altalos lifted his sword, 'is why I have come to take your life.'

'No. NO. You are my friend! What has happened to you? The Altalos I knew would never betray me like this. You don't have to do this. What harm can I do to anyone, or anything?'

Altalos stilled. A vision entered his mind. She was with child. And he would lose his own life. Death by arrow.

Altalos sheathed his sword and fell to his knees. 'Forgive me, Gabriela. I cannot take the life of my friend. What sort of person would that make me?' He bowed his head and waited for Gabriela's answer.

But none came.

When he looked up, an arrow was pointed at the middle of his forehead.

'Give me a reason not to take your life, right here, right now,' Lochi demanded.

'Because … I spared your wife's life. I was promised 100 Tlaanar to deliver her body over the border. But I cannot do it. She is my friend, as are you, Lochi.'

Lochi frowned. 'Why didn't you refuse to do

it from the outset when they gave you the target?'

'I had no name, only her smell and location.'

Lochi narrowed his eyes at Altalos. 'If … they had named your target, what would you have done?'

'I would still have taken the job, not to kill, but to warn you of the bounty on her head, and then disappear from our kingdom.'

Lochi lowered his bow and arrow. 'You had mercy on my Gabriela, so I will have mercy on you. Now go, before I change my mind.'

A peaceful silence hung in the air, waiting to be inhaled like the woody, spicy, sweet scent of frankincense and myrrh. I breathed in deeply, opened my eyes and looked at Tobi. 'Nice,' I said. 'You should be a negotiator, where you turn darkness into light. Where you can talk a person out of committing something terrible and irreversible.'

He looked down and shook his head. 'What a terrible job that would be—not the life path-changing for the person being negotiated with, but for the negotiator and their ability to absorb the other person's story, to be able to find a solution for them.' He closed his eyes for a moment in time, then looked up at me, his ocean-blue eyes now stormy and full of gloom, heavy in a melody of depression and darkness.

Was he a negotiator? Was he a man with an invisible cape who saved lives? My mind wandered to my research. The deletion of traumatic memories. Perhaps it could help first responders? I swallowed. He had just described my job to a certain extent. When we go live with memory deletion, we need to hear, and read the traumatic event, locate it in their digital memory print, watch it to ensure it is the correct memory, then remove it. My skin burned, wondering how the stories of others would affect me. Was I ready to see and feel the trauma of others?

I placed my hand on his shoulder and the storm in his eyes vanished, evaporating like wispy clouds on a perfect summer's day. 'Nevertheless, Tobi, your stories are like poetry, weaving and entwining and dipping the characters in light.'

His mouth twitched. 'Thanks. I've had much more practise than you. When I first started, darkness dominated my storylines, and I had to consciously choose to change my thought processes. Otherwise, I couldn't sleep.'

'I'm so glad to hear that. Here's me thinking you are perfect!' I kicked his foot with my foot and grinned at him. 'You know, I've been thinking …'

'Should I be scared?'

'Maybe … why can't I remember you from our childhood. If we spent so much time together … I should be able to remember you.'

He looked out at the water, beyond *Zero*, to the lake full of darkness at this hour, with a crooked smile. 'It's because you always had eyes for Will-I-Am. I think you were blinded by him.'

I laughed. 'Yes, William. Well, that went well, didn't it?'

'On the contrary, I think it went well for you.'

'How's that?'

'You were too good for him.'

'You think so?'

'I know so … behind the scenes and all that. I … punched him out cold defending you once.'

'You did?'

He nodded. 'Best thing I ever did. And then I didn't go to the parties. I had dates with study.'

'Same. What were you studying?'

He pressed his lips together. 'If I told you, it would tell you my job.'

I sighed.

'Trust me. Please.' He drew his eyebrows together, pleading.

I looked down at the candles lighting the jetty. Built just for me. My heart warmed. 'For now.'

'Thanks,' he said.

'Sorry to be a party-pooper, but I need to get going. I have a date.'

Tobi's eyes widened. 'A date?'

'Yeah. I promised the new guy at work a date about two months ago. It happens to be today. A promise is a promise.'

Tobi lifted his chin and looked down at me with hooded eyes. 'Okay,' he said, after what felt like a day where time froze. He slow blinked then looked down and started to secure The Book of Beginnings to his belt.

'You know you could just toss your book down to me,' I said.

He tightened his belt. 'And if you drop it, our spoken stories will fall out.'

I frowned and tilted my head to the side. What an odd thing to say. 'They will?'

'Yes. It's made from a specialised paper that has super absorbent acoustic properties and the sound waves are recor—' Tobi froze, then connected his eyes to mine.

'Go on. I've read about absorbent acoustic properties.' My skin prickled. Why would he have a book that encoded our stories in the paper? It certainly was possible.

'I'm kidding. I made it up. Did you?'

'No.'

Tobi raised his eyebrows at me.

'There's a paper that's been published about acoustic absorbency,' I said. 'All they have to do it tweak the composition of the paper a little bit, and BOOM—private conversations and secrets no more.' I shuddered. Imagine if we are surrounded by materials engineered to record every conversation wherever we are, our voiceprints kept on a world data base—inconspicuous materials used, not known devices like mobile phones, or digital watches, or technology assisted home devices.

Tobi looked down and continued to secure the book under his belt. 'Miss Danube, I do believe you think too much.'

I leaned across him and gripped onto the branch on his right, stilled and looked into his eyes. 'Mr. Brooks, I will take that as a compliment.' I moved down to the next branch, then I descended the tree quickly, jumping from the last branch.

I hit the ground and my skin burned. It rippled up my arms and entwined at my chest. I breathed out and paced back and forth while I waited for Tobi the sloth to reach *Zero*. My chest tightened and I gasped for air. It was a panic attack. I placed my hands over my face. My story was stuck in my head. Replaying. Tormenting. Irritating. And it wasn't leaving.

'Indi?' Tobi's voice was close, his warm breath comforting against my neck.

I turned and looked at him and frowned. *Why did my story unnerve me so much?* 'Hold me … please,' I said.

Tobi stilled, then released the book from his belt, squatted and placed it on the ground like it was as fragile as glass. He looked up at me, his eyes full of tenderness, then took a step closer and wrapped his arms around me, pulling me close. Gently.

Heat swept through my chest as I stopped my internal war to keep him at a distance, and I melted into him, his scent of sweetness and spice creating a harmonious duet like two lost melodies had finally found each other and entwined after a century or ten apart.

My panic attack dissipated.

After a moment, I placed my hand on the back of his neck, and felt his head lower to my shoulder. 'Thanks,' I whispered, then stepped back from him, hoping that he wouldn't read anything into my request for a hug. 'How can I help you pack up?' I asked to change the focus of our closeness, of the enchantment he had cast over me.

He rubbed the back of his neck where my hand had been, then gave a nod. 'There's a door in the platform. If you lift it, the cushions fit in a space under there, safe from weather. I'll do the rest. Meet you on the jetty in five minutes.'

'Don't be too long. I have a date.'

Tobi frowned. 'So you said.' His tongue caressed the "d".

I made haste on Jacaranda Island and gathered the cushions, found the hatch and placed them inside, then made my way to the jetty and waited, looking out beyond *Zero*, to the lake full of liquid black at this time of night, except for the moon's reflection—white with edges of blue from the lake.

'It's a beautiful night.' Tobi's words were warm against my skin on my shoulder.

'Only because you made it beautiful,' I said, and turned to face him.

A heated look swarmed in his eyes. 'So … this guy … your date … is he—'

'Don't worry, he's an academic genius who has a fascination with Clark Kent.'

'So, he could be your Superman?' Tobi said, hanging his head and brushing an imaginary object off the jetty with his foot.

'Not a chance. I've known him long enough to know that most definitely will not be true.'

'You never know. He may have his work persona, and be completely different once he takes off his white coat. Will he give you flowers?'

I tilted my head to the side, contemplating his remark. 'I'll let you know.'

'Will you text me afterward … so I can go to sleep without worrying about you?'

I raised my eyebrows. 'Why would you worry about me?'

'You're having a date with another man. What if–' He took a

deep breath.

'Hey, did your wish come true, yet?' I said.

'You know I don't believe in wishes. You have to act on a plan.'

'But your two stories both had wishes in them—'

'Placed there just for you.' He smirked at me.

'So, your wish hasn't come true yet?'

He looked down with a slow smile, then looked back at me, gazing deeply into my eyes. My heart flickered. 'Has your wish come true?' he whispered.

My eyes faltered on his lips. 'No,' I said.

'Perhaps you need to act on a plan?'

He took a step closer to me, his proximity causing a whirlwind of flutters in my chest.

'That's not how wishes work, Tobi.' I took a small step back from him and realised at once I had made a mistake. There was no jetty behind me to step onto, and I started to fall—

Tobi reached out, grabbed my hand, and pulled me towards him with more force than I expected. With the grace of a baby giraffe learning to walk, I fell into him, my face so close to his I could feel his body heat.

'Thanks,' I whispered.

His eyes wandered to mine and his lips parted.

I couldn't fight my attraction anymore. Was it him or his love stories working their magic on me? I let my wall of heart protection fall, and placed my hand on the side of his face, closed my eyes and pressed my lips to his in a slow, soft kiss, then pulled away.

When I opened my eyes, his were still closed. I captured his face in my mind, memorising the perfections and imperfections of his features; his rawness and his vulnerability, exposing his heart before he decided I was not who he wanted.

He opened his eyes, lowered his chin and looked at me with

a raised eyebrow. 'Granted,' he whispered.

'Granted?'

'My wish. Maybe I do believe after all?'

I narrowed my eyes at him and shook my head, then ran my fingers over his jawline. 'I have a date. I can't be late.'—

A metallic squeak sounded from behind me and I froze, my heart accelerating. My memories were so vivid it was like I was reliving them, and everything and anything around me in real time ceased to exist. Being unaware of my surroundings was a dangerous place to be when you were a woman. There was always that feeling that you were a target, an object, like a lifeless, soulless person of no worth. To be fucked and discarded.

I extracted the classic diamond-studded, gold compact from my running belt and pushed the button. It flipped open.

Mirror. Mirror. I gazed into the left side, positioning it so I could see over my shoulder without turning my head. There sat a man in a wheelchair. Beanie. Scarf. Sunglasses. Blanket over his lap. He was motionless, until he lowered his head then tilted it to the right side a little, like he was trying to listen to something. That, or he was full of regret. He released the brakes against the rear wheels and used his hands to manoeuvre, then push the wheelchair with grunts of struggle and frustration. I wanted to go over to help him, but decided not to as I didn't want him to feel weak and incapable. Feeling a sense of achievement was everything. No matter how small.

Once he was gone, the feeling of high alert left me, and I stood to continue with my mindless running.

Thump. Thump. Thump.

My mind followed the pattern in a stupor.

Thump. Thump. Thump.

And then it didn't.

Thump. Thump. Thump.

Mia's death was my fault.

Thump. Thump. Thump.

I was the one who sent the boys to that party because I knew Mia would be attracted to them. But they weren't supposed to become intoxicated. They weren't supposed to take her away. Yolande wasn't supposed to be involved.

Thump. Thump. Thump.

My mind wandered to that day I arrived at the mountain, after noticing Jack's location on GPS on my phone. He should have been at the party, not at the top of that mountain. But I was too late. When I got there, I saw Mia and Yolande standing at the edge of the cliff, naked, and then, in the next breath, they were pushed over the cliff as the sirens sounded and flashing blue and red lights came. And there was not a damn thing I could do about it.

Thump. Thump. Thump.

It was all my fault.

Thump. Thump. Thump.

It was all my fault.

Thump. Thump. Thump.

It was all …

Thump. Thump. Thump.

… my fault.

Thump. Thump. Thump.

Stop. I was home.

The evening in the time of neither *here* nor *there*—the colours of the *in-between* had vanished, replaced by the darkness of nightdom ... the place of no shadows. All the colours above had changed, and there was one of me, instead of two. No shadow. Unless I opened the diamond-studded compact. Not mine. Stolen. On the night that I wished I could unwish. And then there was three of me.

Chapter 18

The black leather chair sighed when I sat on it. Like it had taken its last breath. I looked to my right at Yolande. Her eyes were empty, hypnotised on the opposite wall. She knotted her fingers together and released them. Over and over. My bones shuddered. I was here at her request. To attend her psychology appointment. I wondered how many sessions she had participated in over the years since Mia died. Too many, I suspected.

All because of me. My chest tightened while my stomach churned.

I looked around the waiting room. There must have been a hundred paintings, big and small, including the Rorschach Test—the inkblot test—asymmetric figures made symmetrical by folding the paper in half, just like an art lesson at school. It didn't make sense that a person's personality characteristics and emotional functioning could be solely judged based on the ugly inkblots. But then again, maybe I had an underlying thought disorder. After all, I was the one who wished for unwishes, and believed that wishes came true.

A woman in her thirties walked out of the consulting room. She had manicured nails, perfect hair and make-up. She turned her perfectly painted face towards us and smiled. I smiled back, trying to interpret whether her smile was genuine or fake. When her face relaxed, her Botox enhanced lips looked painful. In that split second, I decided her smile was fake. In that split second, I also hoped the psych sessions would help her to accept her natural self, flaws and all. *Don't be a copy … don't be a copy …* I tried to send telepathically to her. *Be yourself. You matter. You are worth—*

'Yolande.' The psychologist's voice was comforting, like a warm childhood blanket and a mug of hot chocolate by the fireplace. She smiled, the universal language for welcome.

Yolande stood. As she walked forward, Dr. Jones put a hand on her shoulder. I followed behind, transfixed. The doctor's voice had pulled me in, like a vortex, and I was captivated.

Yolande stopped before two white leather chairs. She dipped her head and looked at me. 'Dr. Jones, this is my friend, Indigo. I asked her to sit in on our meeting today, if that's okay with you?'

Dr. Jones held out her hand to me and I took it. 'Welcome, Indigo. Thanks for coming. Can I offer you a cup of tea?'

I glanced at Yolande. Her eyes widened and she nodded her head. Too enthusiastically. My eyes returned to Dr. Jones. 'That would be lovely, thanks,' I said, though I never chose to drink the concoction of tea, except once, with Scarlett.

Yolande folded herself into the first chair like it was a shell protecting her, and I sat next to her, my body moulding to the curves of the furniture like it was about to absorb me. And I wished it would do that.

I breathed out the nervous silence in the room, then the chink of the china teacups and saucers broke the quietness. My stomach quivered. I knew for certain that Dr. Jones would not approve of my field of research. I was out of my comfort zone.

In a catastrophic way. I sucked in a staccato breath through my clenched teeth to calm the panic inside. *This is about Yolande, not me,* I thought. *Relax.*

Dr. Jones placed three teacups and saucers on the table before us. I mirrored Yolande and reached over and picked up a teacup after she did. I was surprised to see that Dr. Jones also took part in the cup of tea ritual. The warmth of the brew touched my lips and I calmed a little, even though I was not a tea drinker. For a moment, I wondered, maybe I could become a tea drinker like the other two billion people on the plant. I frowned. There must be some science about tea, because Dr. Jones didn't even ask if I wanted a coffee.

'What brings you here today, Yolande?' Dr. Jones asked, and placed her teacup onto the saucer. She picked up a pink pen and notepad.

Yolande wrapped both hands around her teacup and crossed her legs. 'My friend, Indigo, has brought me here. Well, I invited her. She said she can help me with my memories of the day that M ... Mia ... died.' I watched as she swallowed like she had something stuck in her throat.

'How nice,' Dr. Jones said, and looked at me. 'How can you help with her memories?' Dr. Jones' face was expressionless.

I placed my teacup onto the table. 'I'm a neuroscientist, and I've been working on the deletion of traumatic memories—*digitally*.'

'Digitally?' She scribbled on her notepad. 'On live subjects?' she asked, lifting her chin a little.

'I'm sorry. I can't divulge any methodology from the research due to my confidentiality clause. But we have been successful.'

'And how can you help Yolande?'

'I can digitally remove the memories specific to that day, like it never happened.' It was my turn to swallow. Hard. I had told a white lie. I didn't want to tell Dr. Jones that we hadn't quite done that yet. But that was our goal. My gut told me it was wrong to remove Yolande's memories. But my love for her was stronger. I didn't want her to suffer any more. It was like she was slowly disappearing in front of me, like a piece of her had vanished each time I saw her. If I could undo her suffering, I would.

Dr. Jones narrowed her eyes at me. 'So essentially, you are removing Mia's death?'

I lowered my chin, and spoke with a slowness of precision, like an archer retracting the arrow in the bow, lining up the target. 'The event of the death, on that particular day.' I released the arrow, hitting the target.

Dr. Jones looked away from me and at Yolande. 'How does the thought of no memory of Mia's death feel to you?'

I turned my attention to Yolande. She was pinching the skin on her forearm leaving a red welt. I winced. She blew a breath between her lips, then spoke, 'Every time I close my eyes, I see her. I see Mia at the bottom of the cliff. Broken. Her body resting in a way it shouldn't. And then I see her body twitch and I am filled with hope that she is alive. Like I wished she was alive ... but she wasn't.' She spoke without blinking. Her chin trembled, then her eyes reddened and swelled with tears that spilled over and ran down her cheeks. I watched her as she caught her sob, and held her breath for an impossibly long time.

Take a breath, Yolande, breathe, I pushed toward her.

'Do you think removing that memory would help you with your daily life?' Dr. Jones asked.

Yolande covered her face with her hands, wiped her tears away and looked toward the ceiling for what seemed like eternity. She shook her head. 'Yes.' Her affirmative answer was soft, but her negative head action was in contradiction. 'I don't want to feel the pain anymore. I don't want to keep reliving that moment,' she added, her voice cracking, her hand beating over her heart with aggression like an act of self-hate.

My eyes burned before a tear rolled down my face. I didn't wipe it away. I let it drip onto my shirt. One. Two. Three times—*Mia. Yolande. Me.* My throat tightened and I struggled to take a breath. I couldn't imagine what every day must feel like for Yolande. Living with the vision inside her memories of that day. None of us even knew exactly how Mia died. And why did Mia die, but not Yolande? All we knew was that Yolande blamed herself. How heavy must that burden feel? Except that was a lie I kept telling myself. If you repeat a lie enough times, it becomes your truth. I knew how Mia died. I saw the part where Mia and Yolande were pushed over the edge of the cliff, and then a blank. Nothing. Just sirens and flashing red and blue lights and a helicopter. But I was oblivious to the exact details of the traumatic memory that Yolande lived every waking moment of her life. I had no idea what happened once they disappeared over the edge of the cliff. Her rescue was long and complicated. Mia's even more so.

Dr. Jones offered Yolande a tissue, then me. 'Yolande, there is a therapy that is currently being trialled, and is in phase 3 of the validation process. It involves MDMA, or ecstasy, as it is more commonly known. It's called MDMA-assisted psychotherapy. You are given active doses of MDMA during what we call manualized psychotherapy sessions in two or three eight-hour sessions, spaced a month apart. Three non-drug 90-minute therapy sessions precede the first MDMA exposure, and three to four follow each experimental session. You recount the event under the supervision of two psychiatrists. It has been reported to change the way you feel about the event, and you are able to cope better. It has been reported to lessen PTSD, anxiety, and guilt. It helps patients overcome the emotional reliving of traumatic memories.' Dr. Jones stopped talking and observed Yolande's reaction.

Yolande pulled her eyebrows together, her heart tears becoming fuller on the precipice of her eyelids. 'You mean, I have to retell what happened, over and over?'

'Yes. I know it sounds traumatic. But the studies have shown it to be successful for most patients.'

'Most?' Yolande said. 'What happens if I fall into the group who it doesn't help? Where does that leave me?' A heavy tear, the colour of broken, fell.

'Or … we can use another drug—Propranolol. It can interfere with memory storage.' Dr Jones put her pen and paper down. 'And I can also offer you Eye Movement Desensitization and Reprocessing Therapy, commonly known as EMDR therapy, or Extinction Learning.'

'Extinction Learning?' Yolande started to shake. I placed my hand over hers and held it. What would I do if it were me sitting in Yolande's place? What if it had been me with Mia on that tragic day, instead of her? Would I ingest the drugs the psychologist was offering? The drugs that were absorbed by your entire body, not just the memory houses of the brain. How did if affect the rest of the organs of the body? 'It's okay, Yolande. Dr. Jones is just telling you what she knows.'

'How do you feel?' Dr. Jones asked.

Yolande's chest expanded as she breathed deeply, then she let it out with a controlled slowness. 'I feel … numb.' She closed her eyes and placed her palm on her forehead, her fingers in her hair. Veins protruded on her temples.

'I have given you many options. They do require deep consideration … the good and the bad. It will take some time to decide which is the best course of action to take … the one that suits your situation, your chemical makeup.' Dr Jones paused. 'If, that is … you do want to erase memories of that day?'

'What?' I said, my voice louder than I intended. 'If she wants to erase the memories of that day! Why do you think Yolande is sitting here in a consultation with you? If she was alright with everything that went on the day Mia died, she would not be here an—'

Dr. Jones put her hand up, her palm facing me. 'This … is for Yolande to decide.'

Yolande looked at me. Her face was heavy with a darkness I had never seen on a person before. A shiver ran down my spine as a melody of deep grief and self-punishment flowed through, and around Yolande. The events of the day Mia died was invading her like cancer. A slow death.

I couldn't sit here any longer and listen to the psychologist's course of brain altering chemical medications intended to help Yolande. What if the drugs solved one problem but caused another? Another irreversible problem?

My body tensed. I breathed out my turmoil and pulled the scattered pieces of my brain back together. Of course, medications helped people. Of course, medications had been trialled and assessed and were safe, just like we do with neuroscience research. Medications had saved the lives of millions of people, and will continue to do so. My angsty reaction was because memory removal was *my* speciality, and *my* digital removal was the best option for Yolande.

But in the end, she had to choose which treatment option was best for her. If there's one thing I had learned, being true to yourself is the best option. Being gentle and kind to one's self is healing at its finest.

I took a courageous breath. 'Don't decide today, Yolande. Take this session as the information session it is,' I urged.

'Tell me, Indigo, what does your therapy involve … in your … *digital* erasure? I'm intrigued,' Dr. Jones said with a smoothness in her voice that was like a melting honey of deception.

I waited a beat before I spoke. 'It does what you are offering, but it doesn't involve any medication, any cocktail of drugs that circulate in the bloodstream of the body. What the team does, is painless, specific, and 100% accurate.'

'But is it?' Dr. Jones tilted her head to the side. She was sceptical of our methods.

'Are you questioning the efficacy and accuracy of the analysed data and scrupulously scrutinised results that have been replicated time and time again and proven beyond a doubt?' I was starting to get annoyed.

She folded her arms. 'No. I believe that neuroscience is a precise science once the answers are discovered.' She looked out the window. 'The difference is, what I offer, can possibly be reversed. The memory remains, intact, and can be retrieved again. I believe it is a more compassionate procedure for Yolande to endure, don't you agree?'

Unbelievable. I raised my eyebrows at her, my heart thumping in my chest. 'No. I do not agree. I know there is a less traumatic way to erase the memory,' I said, my gaze lingering on her until she shifted in her seat. I looked at Yolande. 'Are you ready to leave?'

'Thank you for everything you have shared with me today, Yolande.' Dr. Jones' intonation fell into a well-recited conclusion spiel. It was also her way of ending the session before I did with my encouragement of Yolande to leave. This was her power play in action, making her feel like she was in control of the direction of our time spent together.

'Thanks, Dr. Jones,' Yolande said, her intonation in sync with Dr. Jones', like she had spoken the words a thousand times before.

I stood, holding onto Yolande's hand, giving a gentle pull until she was on her feet beside me. We followed Dr. Jones to the door. She opened it, and Yolande and I stepped out of the room that felt like a torture chamber to me. I thought a session with a psychologist was supposed to be calming and therapeutic. I wished I could return to 45 minutes prior and never have stepped through that door with Yolande. I wished that Yolande didn't have to incur the emotional pain of that 45 minutes. And I *wished* …

that Mia hadn't died. *Unwish. Unwish. Unwish.* How I wished wishes could be unwished. Reversed ... the *undoing*. Can we go back in time?

Yolande stopped at the receptionist's desk and I stepped outside to douse the anger I felt inside. I walked up and down the path to the quaint little white house with the pretty flower garden and waited, counting the bees to distract my thoughts.

The front door to the house creaked and I looked up at Yolande. I offered her a small smile. 'Let's grab a coffee,' I said. I wanted to add, "a real hot drink", after my disastrous experience with tea, but didn't.

Yolande took five steps towards me. 'Sounds like a plan,' she said. Was she as relieved to be out of that house of delving into thoughts and feelings and digging for the truth as much as me? If we had stayed there any longer, would the clever Dr. Jones have picked up on my guilt that was oozing out the pores of my skin like a repulsive smell?

I hooked my arm with hers and dragged her along the garden path, out the white picket gate, and along the walkway until we came across a forest café with outdoor tables.

We sat under an ancient tree and I looked at all the colours above; brown textured limbs decorated with green leaves and colourful hanging lanterns. I ordered a "real" hot drink and sat in silence, then closed my eyes and inhaled the scent of the living forest—damp moss, wet tree trunks and sweet flowers—and tried to connect to its nature heartbeat; its soothing and graceful melody.

The aroma of coffee and the clang of mugs and saucers pulled me back to the table.

'Thanks,' Yolande said to the waiter.

I nodded with a smile. There was my happiness. In a mug. Happiness I wanted to taste. I lifted my "real" hot drink to my lips and took a sip, leaving the mug level with my chin.

After digging inside of myself to find my courage, I lifted my eyes from my coffee to Yolande. 'I'm sorry,' I said. I pressed my lips into a hard line. I had rushed her to a café to douse the flames of sorrow of the destructive psychology session for my sake. But I hoped this downtime was as much for me as for her. I was choking with survivor guilt.

'Sorry about what?'

I took a deep breath. 'It should have been me seeing the psychologist for Mia's death.' There. I said it. My heavy words sat between us like a grand piano being beaten with a baseball bat.

'What?' The black pupils of Mia's eyes enlarged like they were trying to swallow me, then narrowed, ready to shoot deadly laser rays intended to destruct.

My stomach churned. 'I was meant to go out with Mia on that day, but I had study to do. You were second choice.'

The sound of her cup smashing on the table made me jump. Coffee splattered. Over my hand. Over my shirt. Over my heart. Just like the inkblot test. Judging. Labelling. Condemning.

'We all knew how reckless Mia was.' I spoke wildly fast to make myself feel better and to match my pounding heart. I had the ugly feeling that Yolande was about to put me onto her most hated person list.

'She wasn't reckless.' Yolande's voice was defensive. 'She was an extrovert who got her high off interacting with peop—'

'And made some bad choices. You weren't the only one who had to rescue her from situations that she couldn't find her way out of.' I shook my head. My mind wanted to relive the past, but I couldn't go there. It needed to stay buried. It was easier to forget that way. I needed to keep those emotions locked in the "Do Not Open" compartment of my brain.

I looked at the fractured cup. I hoped it wasn't a sign of what our relationship would become. Yolande grabbed a paper serviette and started to wipe the table. She stopped when a waiter appeared.

He removed the broken cup pieces and cleaned all traces of the coffee inkblot test from the table. He erased every physical proof of what had happened. He had undone what was done. I wanted to borrow his magic cloth of erasure.

'So clumsy of me,' Yolande muttered to the waiter, her voice quivering. 'Thank you for cleaning my mess.'

'Accidents happen,' he graciously said, 'would you like another?'

'No. But thank you,' Yolande said, then stood as soon as the waiter retreated from the table. She glared at me, her eyes aiming an arrow of loathing at me, intended to injure.

I was right. She hated me. We were done.

My throat tightened as I captured my deep sorrow, my regret, my thoughtless decision to reveal my secret that I knew would possibly be like piercing her heart with a sword of betrayal. But I couldn't keep the secret inside me any longer. I had to take the fallout for my decision.

Even as she left our forest café of sanctuary, she deposited an ember of lingering emotion with the intent to devour our relationship like a ravenous fire. I felt it burn in my heart, and a part of me died.

It was all my fault.

My mind raced with a million ways to make amends with her. I shook my head. None of them would repair the damage I had just created.

It was too late.

I stood and left the ancient tree that had morphed into a gnarled and bitter being, adorned with ugly lanterns of accusations, and hurried back to the Brain and Mind Institute.

I swung open the door of the conference room and landed in my seat with a heavy heart, just in time to be briefed on our next step of digital memory removal.

This was it. The zenith of our research. Make or break. I

buried my morning of catastrophe with Yolande into my "Do Not Open" compartment of my mind, then centred myself on the work I had to do. Emotions and mood could play no part. This was neuroscience—observation, hypothesis, testing and analytical results.

I left the conference room shoulder to shoulder with Biran, iris scanned into the Memory Lab and looked about the room of clear glass boxes, coffins for the brains in the state of between worlds. Living brains, implanted with wireless electrodes.

The absence of a laboratory scent reminded me of the unearthly, intrusive research I was involved in. But it was to help people. It would save the lives of those who suffered from life altering traumas that imprisoned them inside their own bodies in a state of terror, living an abysmal, dark existence.

I opened the research journal on the desk and skimmed over our real time research entries. We knew which sounds correlated with each brain. We knew what that sound looked like digitally, encoded into the memory cells. Our neuroscience colleagues had been working on a bank of images and memories, and what they looked like digitally. Our computer engineers had been collating billions of identified sounds and images, to precisely match memories and faces of people from facial recognition technology, and had been successfully used. AI had been instrumental in the enormity of the task.

And finally ... the nanobots that would wirelessly isolate the traumatic memory to capture and download were ready. As was the deletion activation system.

It was time to take the next step in the research process.

Chapter 19

The red maple leaf on my desk looked pale, reflecting my emotions from my time with Yolande today. At least we had made gains with our research, as terrifying as the next step would be. I grabbed a new sheet of off-white, handmade paper, flattened it with my hand and picked up the calligraphy pen. Each meeting with Tobi made our plan more urgent. At the lighthouse he sounded keen to do the reset—to remove memories of the night of Midsummer's Eve. And now that my life was even messier with my close friends, perhaps it was time to start again, somewhere else. Like a new beginning ...

Dear Finn,

Hey. I hope you remember me. I met you at Kingdom Adventure Park during the spring of the most amazing flowering season. Ever.

You started talking to me in the queue to the

Marvellous Super Roller Coaster, then you sat next to me in the car and held my hand as I screamed my lungs out in the darkest, scariest tunnel where I think we were inverted, holding on for dear life.

When the ride ended, we looked at each other, our smiles wide, our eyes caught in each other's.

Afterward, we ate burgers and I drank Coca-Cola for my nausea, while you laughed at me.

I fell into your I wanted to spend more time with you, but you got a text and had to leave. I called your name and you stopped. I ran to you, out of breath, kissed your cheek and thanked you for holding my hand on the ride. Remember? You smiled at me and said, 'You're welcome—

I stopped writing and leaned back in the chair. Was he worth it? Was I willing to give up the life I had worked hard for to start over with him? Yolande would forgive me. Wouldn't she?

The screen on my iPhone lit up.

> **Remember Tobi? Did you know he can sing?** It was Emily.

Me: **Tobi?** *I had to pretend we didn't know each other ...*

> Emily: **You know Tobi ... when we were little. He has a big brother we all liked. He had the marshmallows at the park**

Me: **Oh. Yes. Tobi. He sings. Is he good?** *He can sing!!!?*

Emily: **Utterly. Totally. Devastatingly**

Me: **Devastatingly?** *Please don't tell me that ...*

Emily: **So easy to fall in love with his voice. Dreamy**

Me: **I'll be sure to keep away from him then. You know my stance on love.** *I had already fallen, I wanted to add. But didn't.*

Emily: **Mmmmmm ... I think I'm falling for him**

Me: **Where are you?** *Why didn't I know? Why wasn't I invited?*

Emily: **Having a BBQ at the park**

Me: **Everyone?**

Emily: **Ah ... yeah ... Yolande didn't want you to come. She was upset so I didn't invite you. Sorry.**

Me: **It's okay. I wouldn't have come anyway. Research to do.** *Lie.*

Emily: **Good. Do you want me to go live so you can hear Tobi's voice?**

Me: **No need. But thank you anyway. Gotta go xx**
Yes please. I would love to hear his voice ...

Emily: **Chow xx**

Exclusion. I deserved it. But still, the sting of rejection hit me like a slap in the face. I sunk down into my chair as my eyes watered. That intrusive nagging, self-deprecating voice in my head wanted to tell me I'm not good enough, and I'm a bad friend. But I stopped it in its tracks. I didn't want to go down that rabbit hole.

Coolness of the night seeped under the door and I shivered. I got up and added a log of wood to the fireplace. It spat its disapproval of its final destination, the ember touching my cheek with a sting, my hand flying there to brush it away. I pulled out the diamond-studded compact, pushed the button and it flipped open.

Mirror. Mirror. Two mirrors. Two of me. I looked into the magnified side and checked my cheek. It was a little red, but otherwise fine. As I went to close the compact, I caught a glimpse of me in the past, meeting Tobi again—

He stood tall with his hands behind his back, clothed in a stylish, long woollen overcoat the colour of the night sky. His scarf and knitted beanie completed his dark ensemble. I watched as his breath created white clouds, like he was a cloud-breathing dragon.

A flush crept up my face as I stopped before him, my heartbeat racing. 'By the light of the full moon,' I said and shivered. I pulled the belt of my burgundy coat tighter around my body.

He gave me a crooked smile and offered me his hand. I placed my gloved hand into Tobi's and climbed into the rowboat. At that moment, the icy wind blew off the snow-capped mountains, biting my cheeks. For once, I didn't want to go to the Jacaranda tree with Tobi, I would have preferred to be reading a book beside a fireplace. I placed my backpack onto the burden boards of the boat and sat.

Tobi climbed in and took control of the oars. The boat rocked with the beginning strokes until it calmed into a smooth rhythm with the propulsion.

'You okay?' Tobi said, his voice deep and rich in its tones.

'It's just so cold.' I pulled the hood of my coat over my burgundy-coloured woollen beanie.

'Just for a short while. Then we'll be warm,' he said.

I doubted it. There was nothing warm about the Jacaranda tree in the Winterdom. I still couldn't understand how a Jacaranda tree could even be growing in this part of the world. It was possible, I had read about it. But still … I looked up at the full moon. Bright. Beautiful. All the colours above. 'The moon is always better in the winter,' I said.

Tobi looked up and the corners of his eyes wrinkled. 'Yes. It's so bright it's like a midnight sun.'

'Left,' I said, guiding his rowing direction. I looked to the right, beyond *Zero*, the lake full of dark blue, beaming the reflection of the full moon. Perfect. Until a ripple from the rowboat made it wobble like it was having a technical glitch. A technical glitch like we expected to see on digital files of memories at times.

'Twenty-nine and a half days,' he said, cutting into my thoughts.

'Since … until?'

'Since I saw you last.'

'You've been counting?' I frowned.

'Every. Single. Day.'

'You're freaking me out a little,' I said.

'Don't be. I love … seeing you … spending time with you.' His voice was tender.

I pulled my eyes away from his gaze and looked at the second sky. The nightdom. All the colours of above. 'If we were the summer moon and the winter moon, I would be the summer moon, with less light.'

'I disagree. You would be all the moons with their full spectrum of colours seen from the earth. I … would be the evening star beside you.'

'Left a little more, and start slowing your strokes,' I said. I looked up at Venus. The third brightest object in our sky. Maybe Tobi was right. He was the star, producing its own light. I could only reflect it.

'Indigo Feather Danube, your night will get better.'

Was I that transparent? 'You think?'

'I know.' Tobi gave me a small smile and pulled the oars into the boat as we glided toward the jetty. As we slowed to the speed of his slothness, he picked up the rope and lassoued it over a post and secured it. He climbed out and turned, and offered me his gloved hand. I grabbed my backpack, stood, and placed my hand in his, wishing we didn't have gloves on so I could feel his energy connect to mine, warming my blood and stealing some of his light, giving me that feeling of euphoria, even for a brief moment in time.

I walked toward the Jacaranda tree and stopped. A pile of wood was stacked there. I turned to Tobi. 'You broke Rule Number 4, again!'

He gave me a lopsided grin. 'Rule Number 4 is made void by Rule Number 8, remember—you may only break Rule Number 4, to add an element of surprise for the significant other.'

My resolve softened. 'I'm your significant other?' I frowned at him. He had never asked me to be his girlfriend. He had never asked me to be a together with him. A *we*. An *us*.

He paused and looked at me. 'You have always been my significant other.'

'Now I know you lie. We have only met at the magical

Jacaranda tree five times.'

He placed his backpack under the tree next to mine, stood tall and shook his head. 'What's eating you, Indi? You feel darker than a moonless winter's night throwing meteorites to injure me.'

I closed my eyes. I wanted to cry. Research silence at the Brain and Mind Lab was exhausting. Mentally. Emotionally. I was spent. And then there was the heavy burden of guilt I carried with me about the death of my once best friend, Mia.

'Hey.' His voice was gentle. He stepped closer and pulled me to him, his arms folding around me at the perfect pressure to feel like love. I wished it was love. Did I trust him enough?

I melted into him and put my arms around his neck. A tear escaped and fell onto his coat. I wanted to stay there for the long winter's nightdom of the full moon. Like I was accepted. Liked. His kindness filling me until I overflowed with it to give it out to others. Like Tobi. To Tobi.

'I'm sorry,' I said, and released from his hold. 'Work has been heavy.'

Tobi lifted his hand, removed his glove and wiped a second tear away. 'Let me take some of the heaviness away from you.'

'And how would you do that? Are you planning on doing deep brain stimulation to lift the dark cloud of depression? Yay – a magical cure!' I did jazz hands for emphasis.

Tobi stared at me, pain lining his face, touching a raw part of me. I had hurt him.

'Only a neuroscientist would answer with that,' he said.

'Or a psychiatrist,' I said, my eyes watering.

He hung his head and shook it. 'I should know better.'

I turned from him and made some distance between us to help me calm down. I turned back to him, my anger still boiling.

'What should you know better?' I said, my voice more aggressive than I intended.

'Not to add fuel to the fire.' Tobi's voice was low.

'That's exactly right, Tobi. I am the fire, and I will consume you!' Tears streamed down my cheeks. I wiped them with my hands and flicked them down in frustration. I was hurting him, but he had done nothing to deserve it. It should have been me who I was hurting. What sort of a person am I?

I walked to the rowboat, jumped in, untied the rope and pushed off from the jetty. I just ... I just needed to find some space. I just ... needed to clear the research crap out of my head that was making me question everything. *Everything.* I just needed ... *him.*

The rowboat glided to a stop in the middle of the lake. I lied back on the burden boards of the boat—aptly named—and crossed my hands over my chest like the death pose and stared at the Winterdom sky. All the colours above. The moon. Full. Bright. Glowing. And the stars. But not all of them. The light from the moon was outshining them, but still, I knew they were there. Hiding. Like me.

And I let my tears fall. Tears for my living brains who had suffered such trauma when they were embodied as physical people with an identity. Tears for those who suffer, keep suffering and were yet to suffer, exposed in their state of being human, of their broken trust of life, of others, and being betrayed by monsters clothed in human flesh. Of being violated without consent.

And tears, for Tobi. Whom I hurt ...

'I'm sorry,' I whispered to everyone, heard and unheard. Past, present, and in the future. And especially to Yolande, Mia, and Tobi. Like a wish. But more like a prayer without words from the heart, asking for forgiveness.

I inhaled deeply, almost coughing at the bite of the cold air. My gray with an "a" feeling was now more like a grey with an "e", according to Yolande's definition. More bearable, and not so dark and self-consuming.

I organised myself on the middle seat of the boat, held on to the oars and began to row.

Back to the Jacaranda tree.

Back to Tobi.

I glided toward the jetty. Slowing. Stopping. And placed the rope over a post to secure it. I sat for a moment longer in the boat and cast my gaze towards Tobi. He had made a fire, a perfect fire, and I watched as he added another piece of wood to it. Then he gazed over at me above the flames, brooding.

I scuttled out of the boat, onto the jetty, and took slow steps toward the fire.

Toward Tobi.

Me and my guilt.

My regret.

I stopped behind him, bent down, and wrapped my arms around him.

He placed a hand over my gloved hands. 'I knew you would come back.' His voice was tender.

'And if I stayed there floating, waiting for eternity to come—'

'I would have swum out to you.'

'In the freezing water?'

He turned and I let go of him. His eyes connected to mine in a penetrating probe. 'Yes.'

'How could you after what I said?'

'Because I care for you. You are angry. I get that. I know your words were ignited by something out of your control. I know …' He let out a heavy breath, the mist heavy with unspoken words.

'What do you know?'

He paused. 'It's the trust and safety paradox.'

'Meaning?'

'Meaning … you feel safe enough with me to be yourself and not censor your words and actions. It's actually a compliment.' He gave a crooked smile.

'You. Are. Unbelievable!'

His eyebrow arched.

'In a good way,' I added.

He tilted his head with a slow blink. 'Sit,' he said, and patted the space next to him.

'I'll get my backpack first,' I said.

'I have it here.'

'Are you a mind-reader as well?'

'Mmm … no. Just logical.'

'I'll take logical, because I absolutely do not want you inside my head reading my mind.'

'Imagine what that would be like, seeing thoughts and memories of another person,' he said as he stared into the fire.

I stilled. That's what I did. And there was no voodoo involved. All science. 'Do you think it would be a good thing if you could do that?' I pulled a flask out of my backpack, and two mugs.

Tobi breathed in and out audibly, his dragon cloud breath painting the air with an artist's brush, until the warmth of the fire consumed it. 'That's a tough question.'

I poured hot chocolate into the mugs, got out some marshmallows and held one up. He nodded. I dropped it into his mug and handed it to him.

'Thanks,' he said. 'I think … being able to see thoughts and memories of another person would make them honest, and conscious of how actions affect others. What do you think?'

I sipped on my hot chocolate and watched the dancing flames of the fire. 'I think … people would become scared of being judged. I think … anxiety would become an affliction suffered by almost everyone. I think … people would self-isolate for self-preservation from the heavy implications and burdens of knowing the intricacies of others. I think … it would make a race of lonely humans who would have short life spans.' I looked up at Tobi. He was staring at me. 'Did I say too much?'

'On the contrary, I think you are spot on, as I possibly am.'

'And highlighting the fact that you are light, and I am dark,' I added.

'My favourite type of darkness, Indi. Passionate. Deep. Complex. Delicate. Beau—'

I placed my finger over his lips, 'Ssssh.'

Tobi closed his eyes. When he opened them again, they connected to mine, holding me still, drawing me closer, his love language serenading mine. I was lost. But found. I was captured. But happy. I took a long slow breath, then peeled my eyes away from his and gazed into the fire.

'Hey, I brought something to show you.' Tobi reached into his backpack and took out a large envelope. He opened it and pulled out some photos.

I leaned closer so we were almost touching, his sweet and spicy scent making my heart flutter.

'Here we are at the park. I was six,' he said.

I took the photo from his hand. There we were. All fifteen of us. I looked at each of the faces with fondness, gazing longer at Mia. I searched for Tobi. Where was he?

'That's me,' he said answering my unasked question. He pointed to a blonde-haired boy. Lanky. Awkward looking. But smiling.

I looked from the photo to him, observing similarities. I smiled. His eyes and eyebrows were the same, and his lips.

'My hair got darker as I got older,' he said.

I studied each of the other photos from the envelope, one from each year until we were twenty. It was us, the gang, growing up. I was missing from some photos, and so was he.

'Ha! You are standing in a similar position each time.'

He looked at me briefly with a grin. 'That was my goal—to be near you when they called us together for a photo.'

'And I never noticed.'

'Once, I touched your hand when I gave you a balloon—I

was nine.' His voice smiled.

'And you still remember?' I looked at him.

Tobi raised an eyebrow and nodded with wide eyes. 'Oh yeah.' He touched his fingers. 'It changed my world.'

'No.'

'Yes. Seriously. Now do you believe me when I say you have always been my significant other?'

I removed my gloves and looked at each photo again. I ran my finger over my bottom lip as I studied each photograph. Surely, he was confusing a childhood crush with what he was possibly feeling now?

'Who's that?' I pointed to a boy with dark wavy hair. He was a little older than the rest of us. 'Wait. Now, I remember him!'

'You do?'

'Yeah—I'm sure all the girls were in love with him.'

Tobi laughed. 'I didn't know that. He was my brother.'

It felt like my heart had stopped. 'Was?' I looked at Tobi, feeling blood drain from my face.

'Yes. He died.' He kept his eyes on the photo without blinking.

It felt like someone had just deleted all the stars from the sky and turned off the moon. There were no longer any colours above, nor the heavenly, hypnotic, melodic music of the universe. 'I'm so sorry. I don't remember. When?'

'I was sixteen. Matt was twenty-two. My parents covered it up.' He shook his head. 'When he was absent from our parties, they gave excuses for where he was and why he wasn't there … lies to stop the pain. Except, it made it complicated. It made it worse.' Tobi squeezed his eyes shut.

I placed my hand over his. I didn't know what to say. So I changed the topic. 'Do you remember, or maybe not, when we were a bit older, there was a guy who used to read books under a tree away from us. The girls used to call him "BookBoy", his long dark hair covering his eyes. When he would lean his head back against the tree and close his eyes for a moment … my knees would go weak.'

Tobi's eyes widened and he smiled. 'Did he do that … like this?' He tilted his head to the back a little, lifted one leg, and closed his eyes.

'Exactly like that! He entered my dreams.'

'In a good way?'

'Oh—in a very good way.' I couldn't stop smiling.

Tobi narrowed his eyes at me. 'When my brother died, I started reading books, isolating myself from the group. That tree was my best friend. I couldn't cope with the lies my parents told, making others believe Matt was still living.' He looked down and grimaced. 'Every day I used to replay the events of his death in my head, and make up words I could have used to help him, to stop him from—' Tobi looked up at the full moon, his eyes wet. 'I wish … I could go back in time and save him.'

A tear fell from my eye. 'Tobi,' I said, stopping my heartbreak from becoming vocal. 'It's not your fault.'

He took a shuddering breath. 'I know … but still … I will always wonder.'

'As I will with Mia. I was supposed to go out with her on the day she died, but I had study to do. I keep thinking, if I was with her on that day, standing beside her, would I have died as well? Or could I have stopped her from dying?'

'Yolande's been a mess since that day,' Tobi said. 'Bastards who did that to them.'

'Yolande is making progress, thank goodness, and Xander, what a gift!' I stared into the fire. No one will ever know about her memories being removed if she chooses to do it. Anxiety coursed through me. I wondered if I would cope with seeing the vision of her memory of what happened on that day, of seeing Mia as she died ... how she died. I took a deep breath. 'So, mystery solved,' I said, changing the course of our conversation once again.

'What was the mystery?'

'Not remembering you at our gatherings. But apparently, you were the desire of my teenage dreams!'

Tobi laughed. 'I'm not sure if that is a good thing … is it?'

I looked up at the moon with stars in my eyes, desire pooling in my belly. 'I don't think I should tell you the content. It would make you blush.'

Tobi placed his finger under my chin and turned my face toward his. 'What about now? Do you think I could make you blush?'

I frowned. Sensuality. It was not a place I wanted to think about, right now. 'What if I'm not the person you think I am? What if I'm no good for you? What if, I keep wounding you?'

'It's a risk I'm willing to take. Nothing ventured. Nothing gained. Live my life with no regrets. Leave no stone unturned ... you?'

'I can't … yet.'

'At the moment, or never.' Tobi's beautiful face was blemished with a frown and an inky sadness.

'At the moment.'

'Then I'll wait for you, like I have been doing since I was twelve.'

'Tobi,' I whispered. My chin trembled. 'I'm not the girl of our teens.'

'I know, Indigo. You are so much more now. Hey, I want to make another rule for Jacaranda Island.'

'Another rule? What are we up to?'

'Rule Number 6. No other people are allowed on the island. I want to make it ours—exclusively,' he said.

'And build a house on it?' I teased.

A dimple emerged on his right cheek. 'Don't tempt me.'

'Okay. Rule Number 6, after Rule Number 5, and before Rule Number 7—Indigo and Tobiah only on the island. Please sign the exclusivity rights.' I held out my hand and signed it with my finger, and waited for Tobi to do the same.

'You make it sound so fancy,' he said as he signed my hand, the touch of his finger making my heart flicker.

'It's just words. It's just gibberish, nonsensical embellishment to make something simple sound important.'

'Well, I approve,' Tobi said, and threw a piece of wood onto the fire. 'I've been meaning to ask, why didn't you text me back after your date with the new guy?'

I looked into the fire and at the hot emitted light that allowed us to see muted night colours with an added tint of orange. 'Our research silence begins at 12am of the day we start our intense focus. My contract states what we can and can't do in that time.' I looked up at him to watch his reaction.

'You were out with him for that long?' He frowned.

'Yes.'

'What's his name?'

'Why do you want to know?'

He paused. 'I just want to know his background.'

I shook my head. 'Because.'

'I need to know that you are safe if you meet him again. Did he give you flowers?'

'Yes. Out of politeness, and as a thank you for helping him navigate the ropes at work.'

Tobi took my gloveless hand in his and kissed it, the warm softness of his lips sweeping a heat through my chest.

'Can I ask you a question?' I said.

'Any time,' he said, his voice low.

'Why do we have to keep meeting under the cover of darkness, by the light of the full moon? And then there is Rule Number 7—pushed up from Rule Number 6—the secrets of us on Jacaranda Island must never be spoken of on the mainland ...'

Tobi traced each of my fingers with his. 'It's ... to protect you.'

'From what?'

'I can't tell you, like you can't tell me what your job entails.'

I pulled my hand away from his and stood, then walked to the shoreline and put my glove back on. How do you trust someone when they aren't telling the whole truth?

I stilled when his arms wrapped around me from behind, making me melt. 'I know I keep saying this, but you need to trust me. Please.' His breath warmed my skin. 'Let's climb the tree,' he whispered. He unwrapped his arms from around me and took my hand in his, sending heat through me.

We stopped at the base of the tree. I looked up at all the colours above. The winter Jacaranda tree was naked. Not a leaf in sight. The limbs, tinged with a hue of orange from the fire, were spread out like a leaping dancer frozen in time, waiting for the next note of the song to be played, to move on.

'Feeling brave, Tobi?' I looked at him. His eyes were cast upward.

'Always, with you,' he said, his voice low.

I stood on my tiptoes and kissed his cheek, removed my gloves so I would have a better grip on the limbs of the tree, and gave them to Tobi to look after, then started the tree climb, engaging Rule Number 2—on the nightdom of the full moon, when dark shadows become a whisper of themselves, the Jacaranda Tree of Jacaranda Island must be climbed.

I settled on a thicker branch than I normally would—the branch that supported the swing Tobi made. The crispness of the air was not kind to my gloveless hands. I breathed hot air onto them and rubbed them together while I looked down and watched Tobi, climbing at the speed of a sloth. I smiled, remembering the kid with the gangly legs. Maybe gangly legs were harder to co-ordinate?

Tobi sat next to me and looked about. He connected his eyes to mine. 'Made it.'

'Tobi, *the Brave*.' The corners of my mouth turned up.

He reached around behind him, and produced my gloves. 'Ah—you're a legend!' I quickly gloved my hands, enjoying their pre-warmed state from his body heat.

'Are you ready?' Tobi asked, blowing warm air onto his bare hands, and then opened the dark blue book of beginnings, of unfinished stories.

I gave him a half smile. 'I don't think tonight is a good time for me to tell you a story. I'm sure it will be darker than you want to hear.'

'I beg to differ. I think tonight is a perfect time for you to tell a story from within.'

I looked up at the luminous full moon in the nightdom. It filled me with wonder, and courage. 'Why not. It could be interesting.'

Tobi brushed a curl from my face, his fingers skimming my skin, and my breath hitched. He turned his attention to the book and opened it at the dog-eared page. He looked at me. 'Close your eyes, and give the story words, with your mind and heart, then speak it to life.'

I closed my eyes and listened. 'Once upon a time, he got her alone in his car on the dark street.'

I opened my eyes, wide. His fifteen words had injected toxic fear into me.

'Hey,' Tobi frowned. 'Concentrate. Change the focus from dark, to light. Change the context from anger to kindness. From fear to courage. Change the goal from aggression, to love … you can do it.' He raised his eyebrows in a question and gave me a slow nod.

I nodded, unable to form words for a moment, then said, 'For you, I will try.'

'Good,' he said. 'Remember, you are safe here, with me.'

I laughed. 'Up in a tree that, with any sudden movement,

could cause us to fall and get badly hurt … or die …'

'And I won't let that happen. I have waited too long to be with you.'

I placed my gloved hand on his thigh to make me feel safe, and waited. Silence floated on the air in expectation.

'Once upon a time, he got her alone in his car on the dark street,' he said. 'Finish the story.'

I drew in a slow, deep breath, the cold air alerting my senses. I clenched my teeth, battling the war within. Alone with a man on a dark street meant danger, and a possible fight for your life. I screamed inwardly to douse the feeling of fear, then searched for courage and a change of point of view of the scenario, and took a deeper than deep breath before I began my story.

> 'Once upon a time, he got her alone in his car on the dark street. Normally, one of her sisters would be with them. But not tonight. Everything was as he had planned. He had waited a long time for this day, and his heart was thumping in his chest. Was it with anxiousness, or excitement? Maybe it was a combination of both?
>
> He turned to Lucy. 'Stay here. I have a surprise for you.' He pulled her hand to his lips and kissed it, then got out of the car.
>
> He moved, adding a skip to his every second step, fuelled by excitement, setting up a chair and a table, flowers and candy, and a lighting system. He double checked everything, then stilled.
>
> He smiled. It was time.
>
> He returned to the car and opened the passenger door. 'Lucy, my love. Come with me.' He held out his hand and Lucy took it.
>
> He walked her to the chair and she sat. He

kissed her hand once more and said, 'For you.'

He stepped out of her vision field and pressed a button and classical music played—cello—deep, melodic, imbued with emotion. And then, in the next moment, her artwork was projected onto the buildings. Every single piece she had ever created in her lifetime.

Lucy gasped. 'Tim … how … this is so … magical.'

'You are magical. Your artwork is magical. I feel magical when I am with you, every moment, every breath I take.' He lowered himself onto bended knee, reached into his pocket and pulled out a small case. He opened it and held it before her. 'Lucy. I love you. Will you marry me?'

Lucy placed her hands over her mouth. She couldn't believe what she was hearing or seeing. Her eyes welled with tears and she lowered her hands from her face. 'Yes … yes!'

He smiled first, then he was overcome with emotion. He stood, took the ring out of the case, and slipped it onto Lucy's fourth finger, the diamond sparkling in the lights of the light show.

He placed his hand on the side of Lucy's face with the gentleness of falling snow, then moved his lips to hers, and kissed her like his life depended on it. Lucy moaned in pleasure and he pulled away. 'I love you,' he whispered. Then …'

I paused, dark words filling my head. Dark scenes of tragedy. The kiss ending in Tim's death. But Tobi's words came to me—"Concentrate. Change the focus from dark to light. Change the context from anger to kindness. Change the goal from aggressive, to love … you can do it."

> 'He said, 'This street of your art is my gift to you to share with others. Your art, presented to people to fill them with your light, the moment they enter.'
>
> Lucy's eyes filled with tears. 'The gift of giving. There is no better gift. I love you, Tim.'
>
> And they kissed again, their souls connecting deeper and stronger, to last them a lifetime together.'

I opened my eyes and looked at Tobi. I was unsatisfied with my story. It was a soppy, weak ending. But it would have to do. It was what Tobi wanted to hear.

'Why did you pause just before the end?'

'Because I wanted to kill off a character,' I said.

'Which one?'

'Tim.'

Tobi raised an eyebrow. 'Why did you change the ending?'

'Because I remembered to change the focus from dark to light, anger to kindness, aggression to love.'

'And you did.' His face fell.

'Are you disappointed?'

'It didn't feel like … you.'

'I had to work against myself to do it. That part was hard work.'

'I think … next time, let the story tell itself. Don't interfere with it.'

'If that is your wish,' I said, waving my hand in a fancy loop.

Tobi laughed. 'Your turn to tell a tale.'

Tobi stilled and gave me a slight smile. 'Close your eyes and watch.'

I placed my hand on his thigh again. It made me feel safe

during storytelling. He lifted it to his lips and gave my gloved hand a kiss, then placed my hand on the branch. First, warmth flowed inside me from his kiss. How did he do that? Then disappointed filled me as I was no longer in physical contact with him.

I waited for his story in silence. Longer than I expected. I decided to watch his storytelling face, so I squinted between my eyes like when I was a kid, cheating when told to close your eyes, defying the one with the power. And winning.

> 'Once upon a time, he got her alone in his car on the dark street. It would be better here, safer for her, when he revealed himself away from the eyes of others. He turned off the radio so she wouldn't be distracted, and turned his body towards hers. 'Wendy, I need to show you something before it's too late.'
>
> 'Too late for what?'
>
> 'Like … if you get too attached to me … like … if you … fall in love with me.'

Tobi's eyes opened. He lowered his head and tilted it to the right side a little, and a second later, the town siren sounded.

Tobi jumped from tree, the book tumbling to the ground after him.

'What are you doing?' I called, climbing down the tree as fast as I could, safely. What happened to Tobi the sloth?

'I … we … have to go.'

'Because of the town's sire—'

'There's a fire. I have to go. Jump in the boat. Now.'

My heart thumped in my chest and I ran to collect the backpacks then headed for the rowboat, removing the rope tied to the post. I looked over at Tobi, extinguishing what was left of the fire. Then he ran like an elite athlete, launching himself into the boat, grabbing the oars and started rowing, powerfully.

'Tobi … I'm confus—'

'I'm a volunteer firefighter, like some others in Tarrin,' he said. 'Forgive me for not finishing the story.'

I stared at him. The story was the least of my worries. Why did he stop the story before the siren sounded? I couldn't even see any smoke or the colour of fire reflected in the clouds. 'What do you need me to do?'

'What you always do after we meet.' His voice was assertive. Like he had removed our heart connection from the equation.

I nodded, and the all the colours above went dark, covered by clouds, except for the orange glow in the clouds where the fire projected upwards, easily seen now.

As we neared the shore, snowflakes fell, creating a magical winter wonderland. Tobi jumped out of the boat and grabbed his backpack, and raced off, leaving me sitting in the boat. I leaned over to untie my shoes to step into the freezing water so I could drag the boat to its resting place, when suddenly I was lifted off the seat.

Tobi had returned.

He placed me on the shoreline, pulled the boat higher onto the shore, then stopped before me and stilled. He gazed into my eyes, placed his hand on the side of my face and lowered his lips to mine with a controlled gentleness that broke my heart. He pulled away and ran his thumb over my bottom lip.

And then he was gone, leaving me wanting—

My cell phone vibrated. I withdrew from my memory with a resounding yes. Yes. He was worth it.

Chapter 20

The wooden park bench creaked as Lucas leaned forward, placing his forearms onto his thighs. He stared at his fingers.

I waited for a nauseating wave of anxiety to pass, then threaded my fingers together. 'We are awakening your mother's traumatic memory this morning.' I tried to deliver the news as smoothly as I could with compassion. This was an extraordinary event in our research today, and I know that Lucas did not approve of what his mother had consented to do. The saving grace was, that he did not know the details of how we were awakening memories, nor the fact that we had kept *just* her brain alive for science and research purposes.

The word "consent". My stomach churned. It was permission for something to happen, or agreement to do something. When people were traumatised, it was because something had happened to them without their consent. Most of the time. Humankind must be educated about consent. No means no! And then there was "accidental" trauma. When something happened to people that was out of anyone's control, and not inflicted with intent. Lucas's mother's trauma seemed to be a "being in the wrong place at the wrong time" type of case. Accidental at first, but then she was chosen by the criminal.

Lucas placed both hands behind his neck and sat up straight. 'Is she the first?'

'Yes.'

Lucas nodded his head, then reached into his pocket and pulled out a picture and ran his thumb over it. It was an ultrasound of a baby. 'Can you tell her, if that is even a thing, or even possible, that Carlee is pregnant, and we are having a girl.' His voice cracked.

'Of course.' I inhaled deeply to quell my anxiety.

'If you can talk to her, and I don't know if you can, and that freaks me out, a lot, but, if you can, would you please ask her what the baby's name should be?' He reached into his pocket and pulled out a piece of paper with a list of names on it, and handed it to me.

'I don't know if that is possible, but I'd love to give it a shot for you.' I took the piece of paper from him.

Lucas looked at me and I offered him a smile. 'Thanks,' he said.

I placed my hand over his. 'Your mother is a remarkable woman from what we have read with all the information she gave us for her profile. You should be proud of her.'

Lucas wiped a tear from his cheek. 'I am … and thank you.'

'You're welcome. I'll let you know which name she likes. No promises though.'

Lucas looked up into the daydom, to all the colours above. It was blue with a hint of "there's-a-change-coming". 'I'd like that.'

'Thanks again, Lucas. I need to go. I have a baby name conversation to enjoy.' I stood and faced Lucas, shook his hand, then left for the Mind and Brain Institute, grabbing two coffees to go from the café on the way.

I placed Scarlett's coffee onto her stand-up desk. She looked up at me with a frown. 'Where did you get the compact from?' Scarlett signed.

I placed my coffee next to hers. 'What compact?' I said. My skin burned. 'And stop signing. You can hear.'

'The one you keep in your pocket,' she said and widened her eyes at me in disapproval.

I silently sighed. How I wanted to tell her it belonged to someone deceased. Someone who was dead. *Dead*. There. I said it in my mind. I wanted to tell her that we couldn't find the body. I wanted to tell her I had to keep it because it had my fingerprints all over it, and I shouldn't have picked it up on that fateful day.

I paused, then slipped my hand into my pocket and pulled out the compact. The diamonds sparkled under the laboratory lights as if to say, "Here I am—the evidence!"

'I found it,' I said. It was a half-truth.

Scarlett reached for it, and I let her take it from me, my stomach quivering with nervousness. She ran her thumb over the diamonds and turned it over and back before she pushed the button to flip it open. The two mirrors greeted her. She moved it closer to her face and looked at the edges of the mirrors.

I put my hand on her shoulder. 'What are you looking for?' I said.

'I had a friend with one of these once.'

My heart raced.

Scarlett ran her fingernail around the insert of the left mirror. 'She said some compacts had a hidden compartment behind the mirror on this side.'

My heart thumped and I held my breath. Did Scarlett know Willow, the one who owned the compact? 'You never told me about your friend. What was her name?' I signed.

'Maggie. Short for Magnolia.' Scarlett frowned then shook

her head, then checked the compact closely again. She snapped it closed and held it out to me. 'There's no secret compartment in this compact,' she said. 'Where did you find it? It could be worth a lot of money.'

I took the compact and slipped it back into my pocket. 'Just under a tree.' I shrugged. 'Do you still see Maggie?'

Scarlett shook her head. 'No. She kept asking too many questions about where I worked. She seemed more interested in that than about me as a person. Plus, she sucked at sign language.' Scarlett chuckled.

I smiled. 'Well, that is a good thing. I'd hate to think I had some competition for signing with you.' I glanced at my watch. 'Hey, it's a big day for our research. I'm going to grab some sun next to the lunch area, and take a moment of solitude before we take this next big step forward.'

Scarlett tilted her head to the side a little. 'Are you okay? You only just arrived. It's not like you to freak out with the research,' she said.

'Well … today I am,' I signed. I didn't want others to hear my comment. 'What if all the work we have been doing falls in a heap, and we have wasted our time? What if … we are entering a territory that we should never enter? What if … we reveal something about the human genome that was never supposed to be discovered, and it makes everyone question everything about life as we know it? What if—'

'Stop it, Indigo!' Scarlett signed at me with aggression. 'Do you remember why you became involved with the digital download of memories?'

I took a deep breath and raised my hands to sign again, this time pausing, waiting for my resolve to enter my hands with the passion I had when I was first contracted to work on this project with the best neuroscientists in the field. I nodded. 'To help people with PTSD. To help people forget a traumatic event in their lives. To stop people from ending their lives because they can't live with what happened to them … what happened to them without their consent, or accidentally!' I signed.

'Right,' Scarlett signed. 'Now, imagine if … what you discover today works, and you can remove the crippling memory to help people return to a liveable, happy life? That's what you are here to do.' Scarlett placed her hands on my shoulders and whispered, 'Go get your sunbeams, find your courage and return to finish the job you started. You are going to make a difference to the lives of hundreds of millions.'

I closed my eyes and held them there for a beat, opened them, looked into Scarlett's eyes, and nodded. Once. She dropped her hands from my shoulders and I grabbed my coffee and escaped through the internals of the building, through the lunchroom and outside into the sunshine. But it didn't smell like sunshine. It smelled like "a-change-was-coming". A musky, fresh earthy smell permeated the air—petrichor. And then the sunshine was stolen, replaced by angry storm clouds. Ominous. A warning perhaps. Electrical activity. Just like inside our brains.

I stood up straighter, renewed with vigour and assured of my convictions—bad things happened to people who didn't ask for it, or deserve it and I wanted to help them. I wanted to help them forget and move on and build a happy life, instead of being crippled by the event that changed their lives, imprisoning them in a heavy darkness that threatened to suffocate them, flooding their bodies with fear and paranoia that made life unbearable. My intentions were pure. My heart was in the right place. Whatever happens in that laboratory today, success or failure, is what is meant to be, at this time in history.

I took a slow, deep breath, held it for the count of three, then released it through my lips until it could be breathed out no more.

A rumble of thunder echoed through the cloudom as I took confident steps back to the Brain Lab. I hand scanned into the

Mind Matter Division, collected my laptop, and stopped before the iris scanner, then entered the Memory Lab. I looked about the room of clear glass boxes, coffins for the brains suspended in the state of between worlds. Living brains, implanted with wireless electrodes.

The absence of a laboratory scent reminded me of the unearthly, intrusive research I was involved in, but this time, instead of a feeling of guilt washing over me, a sense of courage and determination fuelled me.

I donned my virtual reality headset and looked over at Biran. He gave me thumbs up.

I exhaled slowly, and beamed Quinn's hologram above his brain. 'Good morning, Quinn.' I looked at the digital representation of his brain constructed from fMRI. The middle and superior frontal cortex and superior temporal cortex of his brain lit up. It is what happens when people hear their name. I touched my finger to the audio folder on the projected screen and opened it, then chose Quinn's favourite music—*Handel's Messiah*. The digitally altered music streamed directly to his auditory nerve via a wireless electrode, and his brain erupted in a kaleidoscope of light in many lobes.

I moved on and projected the next brain hologram. 'Good morning, Emerson.' We had light in the correct places. *Consciousness.* In his audio folder I opened *Air on G String* by Bach. His brain lit up in a symphony of light.

Next. Hologram projected. 'Good morning, Ardon.' *Consciousness.* I smiled and opened the audio folder, found *Bitter Sweet Symphony* by The Verve, and pushed play.

Next hologram. 'Good morning, Jamie.' *Consciousness*. Audio open—*Let It Be* by The Beatles.

I continued with each of the next five brains, streaming music to their auditory nerve to bring them to consciousness.

I paused before I moved on to the next brain. I felt my heart race as I projected her hologram. I cleared my throat. 'Good morning, Charlie.' *Consciousness.* My body tensed. She was the chosen one for this experiment. There would be no music for her this morning. I blew out a breath as my skin burned with unease.

I quickly moved to the next subject and projected the hologram. 'Good morning, Nic.' *Consciousness.* Audio open—*Concerto for Piano and Orchestra No. 23 in A major* by Mozart.

I stepped back and watched the brain holograms alight with colour as the music activated multiple lobes. All except Charlie. Today was her day.

I pressed my lips together to calm my nerves and hidden guilt. I was the one who had chosen Charlie. It was out of self-protection. Her history, although traumatic, was not on the same level as the other brain subjects, whose narratives involved rape, torture, violence, and other vile despicable acts performed on them without consent.

I breathed out my anxiety and sat on the corner seat and opened my laptop, then clicked on Charlie's folder. I reread her consent to volunteer in the research, then her timeline of events from the time of her birth. The information had been recorded with preciseness. I skimmed through the pages of information to the event that changed her life. It happened on March 23rd, 2018, 8pm. It was highlighted in red so I couldn't miss it. I needed to make a decision today—do I download her entire memory contents so we could make a memory-map, or do I identify that moment in time that turned her world upside-down, and remove just that memory, watch it, then question her about what she could remember?

My body prickled with anxiety. I couldn't remember having to make such an enormous decision. The ramifications of my choice would be immense. We had done memory-maps before. Why was I even thinking of doing another one? My question was already answered. I just needed the guts to call it.

I rubbed my hands together, then opened and closed them. I walked to Charlie's brain, suspended in oxygenated artificial cerebrospinal fluid. I placed my hand on the glass, and slowed my breathing, and gazed over the gyri and sulci: the peaks and grooves of the cerebral cortex. After a moment I said, 'Hi, Charlie.'

Spike.

'I met with your son, Lucas, this morning.'

Spike.

'He showed me a picture of a baby. It will be born in spring.'

Spike.

'He wanted me to ask you about some names for the baby. It's a girl.'

Spike.

'Amy.'

No response.

'Alice?'

No response.

'Chloe?'

No response.

'Lucinda?'

No response.

'Charlotte.'

Spike.

'Ava?'

No response.

I grinned. 'I'll let him know that you like the name Charlotte, yes?'

Spike.

My stomach lurched. I wasn't just dealing with a mind of memories here. This felt more like consciousness. There was no way I could have a conversation and elicit a response from just memories. This was talking to Charlie, like she was still alive. It was just that she didn't have a mouth to speak, a face to show expressions, nor a body to move.

I placed my hand on my forehead and looked around the room. I swallowed the nausea that threatened to decorate the floor, and fought the urge to run out of the room. Fear.

Would it have been less personal if we hadn't given the brains their names?

I paced the room. Don't form an attachment. The number one rule. I had broken it.

'Are you okay?' Scarlett's voice through my headset startled me. Scarlett's voice! She chose to speak!

I took a deep breath and nodded my head. I didn't want anyone to know how I was feeling. I gazed up at the hologram of the 3D image of Charlie's brain.

'Biran,' I said.

'Yes,' he said.

I looked at him. 'Confirming that we are removing Charlie's memories of the traumatic event, and leaving all other memories intact. Are you ready for us to proceed?'

'Correct, and let's proceed.'

I placed my hand onto her glass case, the coffin for her brain in the state of between worlds. 'Charlie, remember that you signed up to be included in our research of deleting memories. Well … we are ready to remove one of your memories. I'm going to retell your story of an event that happened in your life, according to your paperwork, and ask you some questions about it. Are you ready to participate?'

Spike.

With a trembling hand, I opened the file that Scarlett had given me and read through the traumatic event. I rehearsed the planned sequence of narrative, and the correlating questions in my mind and looked over at Biran. His role was to navigate the nanobot to its location, find the ensembles of neurons that became active while I am retelling the memory, copy them to a file, the zap the ensembles of neurons so the memory no longer exists. It was totally legit in theory.

I lifted my eyes to Biran, trying to maintain a calm composure, and nodded. Once.

Biran's eyes widened, then settled and he nodded. Once.

I took a calming breath. 'Charlie … the car was travelling on the road.'

No response except for the middle and superior frontal cortex and superior temporal cortex of her brain lit up in response to her name. As planned. A generic everyday event that should not elicit a response.

'It was a sunny day.'

No response. As planned.

'Buddy was sitting on the backseat. He barked.'

Spike.

'Hey, Charlie. Stop at the store. Let's grab a couple of ice-creams and some water for Buddy.'

Spike.

'You stop the car, turn off the ignition, grab your purse, open the door and get out, leaving the door open. You enter the store. It was quiet, and people look at you with a slight shake of their head, some tilting their heads to tell you to get out of the store.'

Spike.

'You look back at the door, but then walk to the freezer where the ice-creams are kept, and select two. Then walk to the fridge and grab a bottle of water for Buddy.'

Spike.

The spike did not fall. It stayed high. So, I keep on with the story without stopping to check for spike responses.

'You walk to the counter to pay for the ice-creams and water, noticing other customers in the store have not moved. The cashier's eyes are wide and his chin is trembling. The sound of sirens fill the street outside, and flashing blue and red lights bounce off the walls. You feel something hard against your back, and a hand is forced over your mouth. It is pressed so hard against your mouth that your jaw hurts and it is hard to breath. You are pulled backward, your back slammed against the chest of the robber. He pulls your through the front door to the outside world. Your tears are blurring your vision and you feel faint. You see cops all around with their guns up pointed at the attacker ...'

I stopped reading and took a deep breath. I want to look at the brain trace to see what is going on, but I can't.

I continued. '"Drop the gun. NOW!" a deep voice calls, and you hear the click of the gun held against your back. A gunshot sounds and the pain your feel in your lungs is excruciating. There's another gunshot, and the attacker falls to the ground, pulling you down with him. Your eyes are open, and the last thing you remember are the hands and faces of police officers.'

'Memory identified,' said Biran, 'Data copied and sent via blue tooth to the computer, and saved.'

I nodded and switched off my headset. 'Now delete it from Charlie's memories.'

'Deleted.'

I wiped imaginary hair from my forehead. 'You okay, Biran?'

He nodded. 'You?'

I nodded back, then took a deep breath, switched on my headset, and started reading again, as planned.

'The car was travelling on the road.'

No response.

'It was a sunny day.'

No response.

'Buddy was sitting on the backseat. He barked.'

No response.

'Hey, Charlie. Stop at the store. Let's grab a couple of ice-creams and some water for Buddy.'

No response.

'You stop the car, turn off the ignition, grab your purse, open the door and get out, leaving the door open. You enter the store. It was quiet, and people look at you with a slight shake of their heads, some tilting their heads to tell you to get out of the store.'

No response.

'You look back at the door, but then walk to the freezer where the ice-creams are kept, and select two. Then walk to the fridge and grab a bottle of water for Buddy.'

No response.

'You walk to the counter to pay for the ice-creams and water, noticing other customers in the store have not moved. The cashier's eyes are wide and his chin is trembling. The sound of sirens fills the street outside and flashing blue and red lights echo off the walls. You feel something hard against your back, and a hand is forced over your mouth. It is pressed so hard against your mouth that your jaw hurts and it is hard to breath. You are pulled backward, your back slammed against the chest of the robber, and he pulls your through the front door to the outside world. Your tears are blurring your vision and you feel faint. You see cops all around with their guns up pointed at the attacker ...'

Anxiety is burning my skin, but I continue. '"Drop the gun. NOW!" a deep voice calls, and you hear the click of the gun held against your back. Two gunshots sound, and the pain you feel in your lungs is excruciating. The attacker falls to the ground, pulling you down with him. Your eyes are open and the last thing you remember are the hands and faces of police officers.'

No response from Charlie; Brain ID: B100-6.

Good. And bad.

I didn't know what to think. I should be elated because it appears the memory has been deleted. We'll have to keep checking over the next few days and months to ascertain if the memory has been permanently deleted, or whether it reappears somewhere else in Charlie's memory.

I continued with today's strategic plan, checking that Charlie was still there after the nanobot intrusion and memory zap. 'Hi, Charlie.'

Spike.

'I met with your son this morning.'

Spike.

'He showed me a picture of a baby. It will be born in spring.'

Spike.

'He wanted me to ask you about some names for the baby. It's a girl.'

Spike.

'Amy.'

No response.

'Alice?'

No response.

'Chloe?'

No response.

'Lucinda?'

No response.

'Charlotte.'

Spike.

'Ava?'

No response.

I smiled. 'I'll let him know that you like the name Charlotte, yes?'

Spike.

I frowned, then said. 'Is your name, Charlie, short for Charlotte?'

Spike.

'Thanks for your courage today, Charlie. You have just helped millions of people around the world, in the present and in the future.'

Spike.

'I'll talk to you later.'

Spike.

I inhaled deeply to control the tingling on my arms. *Hello anxiety, my friend.*

We had succeeded in our research and execution. But this was just the beginning. There was still a great deal of work to do. If we weren't a target for our knowledge before, we certainly were now if there was any leak of our success. The accomplishment of this experiment now made humanity vulnerable to the research getting into the wrong hands. In a way, I wish that we had not been successful with this test. I *wish* …

'Captured in its entirety. Well done and congratulations!' I jumped as Scarlett's voice sounded in my headset.

I turned to her, not hiding the tear that ran down my face. I wiped it away then turned back to Biran and gave him the thumbs up, removed my headset and exited the lab, feeling my energy evaporate. I was exhausted from the continuous flow of adrenaline pumping through me during the research.

The sound of applause broke out amongst our colleagues, but I wanted nothing to do with it. I pushed through the onlookers to rush through the office, descended to the ground floor and ran outside, gasping for air.

The street was eerily empty, yet noisy, the air saturated with moisture from the approaching active storm. A storm warning flashed on the digital sign at the Art of Brew Café to the right. I beelined for the 100-year-old sugar maple tree in the middle of the park going against all the "do nots" of storms, and sat under it. I had to get away. I didn't want anyone from the Memory Lab checking on me to see if I was okay. No one in their right mind would join me here under the tree to see if I was okay. It was too dangerous with the lightning about. But hey, what were the actual chances of the tree being struck?

I leaned against the tree, then lowered myself to the ground, closed my eyes and sucked in short gasps of air, my chest feeling tight. I felt like I had been hit with a maddening melody of notes being played in a tragic key of sadness and mourning.

'Are you insane?' A voice splintered my self-pity like an axe splitting wood. It was Tobi's voice. Tobi's voice! The voice I once loved. *Tobi* ... he sounded ...

I stopped breathing and looked up. An elderly man with a metal walking stick stood next to me with an angry face. He bent down and pulled me to my feet, then dragged me away from the tree and across the park, holding my hand so hard it hurt.

We stopped under cover at the café, panting, as a sharp sizzle sounded through the air, followed by an instant deafening thunderclap. Smoke rose from the tree I had been sitting under.

My eyes widened and I looked at the old man who had saved my life. The old man who sounded like Tobi. The old man with ocean-blue eyes. Like Tobi's. He raised an eyebrow at me. 'Sit. There.' He pointed to a table that was partly hidden by some foliage. 'I'll be back.'

I watched the old man waddle off, hunched over and a little shaky, and placed my hand over my mouth as a small giggle escaped, wanting to become an uncontrollable, and ridiculously loud laugh. I inhaled deeply to calm myself, then made my way to the table and sat. Before I knew it, I had tears of laughter rolling down my cheeks, but when old man Tobi sat opposite me, they morphed into tears of sadness. I wanted to disappear into the seat, like entering another dimension.

'Hey.' Tobi reached for my hand, his touch soothing me at once.

'Hey,' I said, focussing on his disguise, my eyes wandering over his face and to the moustache, highlighting his perfect lips.

'Do you have a death wish?' He frowned at me.

I took a sharp breath and frowned back at him. 'Do you?'

He looked over at the park, then back to me. 'Look what you

did to the tree!'

'Maybe it was you? After all, you're the one with a shiny silver walking stick!'

His mouth twitched and he took a sip of coffee. 'Bad day?'

'Not now,' I whispered.

Tobi raised his eyebrows at me over the top of his coffee cup.

'I can't believe you get to play dress-ups for your job.'

'Yeah … well.' He scratched his thick left grey eyebrow.

'Old people can't run that fast, by the way.'

'Hey, this old man had an adrenaline rush, spurring on his superhuman powers.' He leaned over, picked up the teapot and poured me a tea.

I laughed and couldn't stop, but when I did, my tears started again. I closed my eyes and didn't open them.

'I wish I could hug you.' His voice was soft. Gentle.

I opened my eyes, lifted my teacup to my lips and took a sip, surprisingly looking like a professional tea drinker for one who didn't drink tea. 'I don't wish ... I need.'

His jaw clenched. He put his coffee cup down and threaded his fingers together in front of his mouth and narrowed his eyes at me, then stood and walked around the table, pulled me out of the chair and up into his arms. I melted into him, familiar with his body size and muscle that felt protective, then screwed up my nose at his terrible old person smell. The terrible smell of an old person with bad hygiene because they didn't care.

'Thanks,' I whispered, stepping back from him, and sitting down again.

'What upset you—person or thing?' Tobi said when he sat back in his chair.

How do I classify a living brain suspended in fluid? 'It,' I said, detaching myself from what had happened. 'Research has been heavy.'

'Details?'

'Can't do, sorry. What turned you into an old man? Did you speed up time? And what is it with your smell? Details?'

Tobi held a crooked smile and looked down before he looked back up at me. 'Can't do, sorry.'

I looked out at the rain. 'Let's disappear into the eighth day where no tea exists,' I whispered, and looked back at him.

'Of the month?'

'Of the week.'

He raised an eyebrow. 'A different dimension.'

'Absolutely.' I gazed into his ocean blue eyes. The ones I used to dream of. The ones I used to like to fall into and get lost inside.

'Indigo Feather Danube, are you trying to run away from something? Or is it in fact the pot of tea?'

'Yes. No … I don't know.' I frowned, then rubbed my forehead hoping to erase my predicament. I let out a sigh. 'I can't believe after all this time you don't know I don't like tea!' I tapped on the teapot. 'I guess I'd better return to the place I'm missing from.' I stood. 'Thanks for the tea that I don't drink, the hug … and for saving me from a possibly really bad, terrible, disastrous, painful day.'

Tobi stood. He nodded gently, his eyes full of compassion.

I placed a finger on his chest. 'How did you know I was under the—' I shook my head, 'no-no. I don't think I want to know the answer to that.'

Tobi tapped his walking stick on the pavement. Twice.

'I wish we were like we were before the … and if we were, I would kiss you,' I whispered.

Tobi tilted his head to the side a little. He pointed at me. 'Young.' He pointed at himself, 'Old. A sweet, lingering, delicious kiss … every shade of wrong.'

I grinned at him then raised an eyebrow. 'On the cheek. It would look like the elderly man saving the young woman from death by lightning, and her giving him a kiss of thanks on the cheek.'

Tobi gave a crooked smile, but his face portrayed one of deep sadness. Of a past of beauty between us that had been shattered and scattered, unable to be found and pieced back together. He touched his finger to his cheek. I stood on my tiptoes and placed my lips where his finger had been. 'Thank you,' I said. 'By the light of the full moon?'

Tobi gazed into my eyes and drew me in. 'We can't.' He raised an eyebrow at me, then turned and walked off at a slow pace, working his walking stick like he had walked a million steps with it.

The sting of rejection pierced the protective wall of my heart and I berated myself for letting myself be vulnerable. When he was out of sight, I took slow steps to the lab. I had to face what I was avoiding: praise for the success of the experiment.

As I walked, I mind-mapped each of the steps we had followed in the research, according to the correct protocol for science research—question; research; hypothesis; experiment; data/analysis—this is where we were at before the conclusion. And then we would start again, with pe—

'Indigo!'

I looked up at the sound of my name, and the applause started. My body tensed in repulsion of the praise. Biran stepped out from the crowd and stopped before me. 'Just in time. We are about to proceed with analysis. Please join us.'

I nodded, and looked over at Scarlett.

'Are you okay?' she signed.

I held up my hands and made bunny ears with my fingers and shook them from side to side. *Sort of.*

Scarlett pressed her lips together and signed, 'Talk to you later.'

I clenched my fist and air knocked twice, yes, then followed the neuroscience team to the conference room. The living-human phase was about to begin after we successfully deleted memories from the other encased brains. What traumas would we have to witness to remove from memory neurons? And would their traumas affect me negatively, an empath? I mentally ticked off the names of the team members on the neuroscience team; did we include psych for our own counselling? And I wondered, should a computer program be created that would match the memory text to images with pinpoint accuracy, so therapists would not suffer secondary trauma?

I slowed my step as I approached the conference room, and clenched my teeth as my body tensed. Once I entered, there was no going back. I closed my eyes, reminding myself of the reason we were doing this—to stop the misery of millions of people affected by trauma. To stop the suicide of innocent people. Those people who never gave consent to what had happened to them.

I lifted my chin and stepped into the conference room. It was time to accept, and acknowledge, the research results from today, and their very real potential for use to help others.

Chapter 21

The rain battered the window like it was in a one-sided argument. My 7am Saturday alarm sounded, shouting at me to get up and go for a run.

'Stop.' My voice command silenced it at once. Running in this weather was never fun. When the rain stopped, I would head out. I pulled up my bed cover to counteract the draft that was sneaking in, uninvited, and Tobi filled my mind. I allowed our story of memories to continue. There was something odd at times. A particular behaviour of his that baffled me—

He waited by the gentleman's rowboat, his hands behind his back and I smiled. He looked sophisticated and breathtaking in his stylish, long woollen overcoat the colour of the night sky, finished with his dark scarf and knitted beanie. His breath created white clouds, as mine did. Two cloud-breathing dragons together.

'Twenty-nine and a half days,' I said when I stopped before him.

'And fifty-two seconds,' he added, before producing a bouquet of flowers from behind him like a magician.

My gloved fingers brushed his as I wrapped my hand around the bouquet, but he still gave me a pleasurable zap. My slow smile blossomed at the feathering of snow that covered the pink daisies. How long had he been waiting?

He held a crooked smile and ungloved his hand to help me climb into the boat, his eyes like a satisfying, optimistic symphony, with a touch of seduction. The moment our hands touched, I felt the freeze of Winterdom thaw, my body warming and coming alive.

I sat on the end seat of the rowboat, and watched as Tobi pushed the boat off the shore and jumped aboard without getting wet. He leaned forward to take control of the oars. Why had I never noticed how stunning he was while he was focussed and concentrating?

Tobi looked across the water, beyond *Zero*, to the lake full of icy blue, and, as we picked up the pace, his gaze settled on me. Devouring.

I lowered my chin and looked up at him through my eyelashes. 'I want to break Rule Number 1,' I said.

Tobi narrowed his eyes, then raised an eyebrow. 'You want to meet under the azure canvas with the sun that casts no shadow, instead of by the light of the full moon in the deep freeze of winter?'

I flashed him a smile. 'It would be warmer then … but no. The monthly wait to see you is like dragging fingernails down a blackboard.'

Tobi winced. He stopped rowing and sighed, then pulled the oars in and moved closer to me. He gazed into my eyes before he focussed on my lips, and leaned in, hesitating, before he placed his lips on mine. Lingering. Tasting. Caressing. He pulled away, leaving me breathless, and returned to the oars and started rowing again.

'To your left a little,' I said, guiding the boat. 'And row faster.'

Tobi frowned. 'Faster?'

'Yes. I need you to kiss me again.'

Tobi looked to the side and the corners of the mouth turned up, but the boat remained at the same speed.

'To your left a little more,' I said, took off my glove and held out my hand to catch some falling snow. 'If I catch enough, I'll be able to make a snowball to throw at you.'

Tobi gave a lopsided smile. 'As long as it doesn't sink the boat.'

My lips twitched. 'Left a little more, and start slowing your strokes.'

Tobi gave a slight nod, pulled the oars in, then captured my eyes in his while we glided on the water's mirror reflection.

'Now,' I said.

He picked up the rope and threw it over a post as we neared the jetty. We floated to a stop. He stepped out of the boat and held his ungloved hand out for me. I placed my cold, naked hand into his, my breath hitching at his touch.

With careful steps on the icy jetty, I followed him to the unleafed Jacaranda tree. I looked up at all the colours above, at its confronting bareness, and hugged the tree, projecting my heart love into it. The tree was so cold at this time of Winterdom. I removed my scarf and wrapped it around the trunk of the tree. There. Now it would be warmer.

'Do you think it knows, Tobi?' I said, keeping my eyes on the tree.

'Knows what?'

'That we're here? Can it feel our presence? Does it know that I gave it a scarf to keep it warm?'

Tobi looked up at the tree. 'I think it's too frozen to feel. You know … like when your hands and feet go numb with the cold.' He looked back at me, removed his scarf, and placed it around my neck.

His eyes settled on mine, his pupils darkening before he leaned closer, and time slowed. And suddenly I was aware of every inch of my body as it warmed. Our lips touched. Delicately. Then Tobi's hand moved to the side of my face, and his kiss deepened with a softness that made my heart ache and my knees weaken. He pulled away, and it felt like the string to our heart love broke. I wanted his lips on mine to tie it back together. I kept my eyes closed, memorising the imprint of his lips on mine, replaying the aphrodisiac way he made me feel.

'Hey,' his voice was soft. I opened my eyes. He reached up to a branch and brushed the snow off it. 'I don't think we should climb the tree.'

'But it's Rule Number 2—on the nightdom of the full moon, when dark shadows become a whisper of themselves, the Jacaranda tree of Jacaranda Island must be climbed.'

He took off his beanie and ran his hand through his dark hair, then looked up at the tree once more. 'Okay, but the lowest branch only.'

And I was there. Within a heartbeat. On the lowest branch. Cleaning off every speck of snow and ice for Tobi, the sloth. He settled on the branch beside me gripping it, and the trunk, for dear life.

'Tobi, *the Brave*,' I said. 'Thank you,' I whispered.

'Only for you, Indigo Feather Danube … how did you end up with that name?'

I smirked. 'I was conceived on the banks of a river, a white feather falling through the foliage of the Chaste Tree covered in lilac-coloured flowers after my parents basked in the glow of lovemaking.' I held my breath to stop my laughter from escaping from within.

'Seriously?'

'Yes. My parents tell me the story every birthday. It would gross me out, except for the hilarity of the lovemaking under the

Chaste Tree.'

'Were they married?'

'No.'

'It makes sense now,' Tobi said.

'What does?'

'Everything … the day a spark of light ignited when you were created, your name … your … *uniqueness*—'

'Everyone is unique.' I cut him off. I hated the word unique. It was so overused and felt washed in dirty dish water in the key of discontent and unease.

'Everyone is born unique,' he started, 'but some choose to be copies of others. You're not like that.'

I sighed. 'You should put your beanie back on. The cold is affecting your brain.'

Tobi shook his head a little, then pulled his beanie out of his pocket and put it on. He looked to beyond *Zero*, to the lake full of icy blue. 'The sunset is stunning,' he said.

I followed his gaze and looked to all the colours above, to the setting sun, the hues exploding in the colours of romance and of love. My body warmed. 'It never fails to impress,' I said, then tuned into the depths of my philosophical thoughts and existential ponderings. 'Do you ever feel … insignificant compared to … our world in all of its spectacular majesty … I mean … look at it. It's so grandiose compared to the ugliness of people.'

Tobi's fingers were under my chin then. He turned my face to his, painted with a frown, 'The ugliness of people?'

'Yes.' I shrugged. 'The hate. The greed. The violence. The … unkindness.'

'And then there's goodness, the patience, the kindness … the love, the gentleness—' He closed his eyes and his lips touched mine for a brief moment, softly, like butterfly wings, but enough to scatter my brain. 'The self-control,' he breathed and opened his eyes. He dragged his gaze away from mine and looked back to the sunset. 'To answer your question, no, I don't feel insignificant. I feel privileged to witness the beauty of the earth.'

Words failed me. He was the positive to my negative, the light to my darkness.

'Tobi, what if we are nothing but children of time,' I said.

'Meaning?'

'Time never stops, and we are pulled along with it. No choice. It dictates everything we do. We are stuck in this cycle of sleep, wake up, work, sleep.'

'It sounds like you need a holiday,' he said.

I breathed out heavily. 'Research is intense at the moment.' I focussed on the full moon, now brighter in the sky. 'Imagine if we lived on the moon. Sunrise to sunset would take two weeks. I would have more time to get everything done.'

'I would prefer the pace of Earth. Besides, look at it. The moon just … is. It's presence; its beauty perceived from the earth, from our point of view. Yet, if you lived there, the sky would be forever black. There, the terrain is devoid of life in shades of gray, mostly. And you look up and see the Earth glowing, vibrant with life, and you would wish you were there.'

I stared at the moon, wishing for moonbeams to zap the heaviness from my heart. Tobi's hand wrapped around mine and my heart fluttered, the heaviness evaporating. Wish granted. I basked in his presence and the way he made me feel things I had never felt before. Right there in my heart.

I closed my eyes. 'Tobi,' I said, 'do you ever think we will stop the search for everything?'

He was silent for a beat. 'Only if you haven't found everything.' His voice sung to my soul in an intimate balance of harmonious notes full of devotion.

'Meaning?'

'Everyone is looking for something. When they find it. They are happy,' he said.

'Is it inside them, or outside?'

'For me, it's both, and one is dependent on the other,' he said.

I looked at him, studying his profile. 'Have you found what you are looking for?'

He turned his head toward me, lowered his chin and gazed into my eyes. 'Yes,' he said, lingering on the "s".

'Does it make you happy?'

He inhaled, then ran a finger over his lips then said, 'Yes, and no.' He looked back at the moon, illuminating the sky with whispers of declared songs of praise for its Creator.

'I don't understand,' I said.

'When I found what I was looking for, I was happy, until I wanted more of it.' His gaze remained on the moon and he blinked slowly.

'Like finishing a hot drink on a freezing cold day.'

He nodded. 'I guess.'

'Did you get more of it?'

'Not yet. But I'm working on it.'

'I hope you aren't disappointed when you get more of it,' I said.

He looked at me and raised an eyebrow. 'I won't be disappointed.' He removed his hand from mine then rubbed his hands together while breathing warm air into them. The cloud-breathing dragon of the Winterdom.

'Do you want to proceed to *Zero*?' I asked.

'Yes.'

'What about story time where I get to frighten you?'

'Yeah. That. When I jumped out of the tree last time we met, I dropped it and didn't pick it up,' he said.

I grinned. 'I remember now. Tobi, the sloth, leaping into action to become Tobi, the cheetah. You owe me an explanation.'

'It's obviously that adrenaline spike you hear about.'

I narrowed my eyes at him.

He looked down and smirked, then looked back at me. 'I have to be honest with yo—' He stilled, and stared past me, frozen in time, like he was listening to something that I couldn't hear. He snapped out of it. 'You know how I like to snowboard?'

I nodded.

'Jumping from the tree was like doing a jump on a snowboard, in a way … sort of.'

'You should stop there, Tobiah. I know it's nothing like doing a jump on a snowboard.'

He looked up and closed his eyes, sadness falling over his face like a heavy burden. 'I can't tell you why I could jump from the tree like that, due to my job.' He opened his eyes and looked into mine like he was pleading for forgiveness.

'It's time to proceed to *Zero*,' I said, and waited for him to move. I didn't want to jump from this low branch in the Winterdom. I'd done it when I was young, and twisted my ankle. Badly. I sat and counted while I waited for him to descend the tree. When he reached the ground, he kept his arms around the tree in a hug, for a moment.

He stepped away, and I lowered myself to the white ground, landing on something hard under the snow. I bent down and dug. It was the book of unfinished stories. I picked it up, wiped off the snow and offered it to him. 'My nightmares are back.'

'Great,' he said with sarcasm and a smile, and took the book from me.

I walked to the jetty and stood near the end, and looked across the way, beyond *Zero*, to the lake full of icy blue. Light footfalls sounded behind me, and then arms wrapped around me from behind. Strong, but gentle.

'There was once a boy,' Tobi said, his voice low, it's sensuality pooling inside me. 'Finish the story.'

I placed my hands on his and took a calming breath.

'There was once a boy. He was born with knowledge that no one else had. He could see things that no one else could see. But when he spoke of these things in truth, he was told he was lying. So, with every breath of every day he tried to hide his gift; his otherworldly knowledge, but his eyes couldn't. Whomever looked into them could see the stars that shined, showing them that he was not like the others. He was different. And was misunderstood. He became the centre of allegations and rumours and untruths. So, to protect his heart, he withdrew from people. And he learned this: if no one could like him, he must be unlikeable, and therefore, unlovable.

The boy made himself invisible. Head down in books. Caps hiding his face. Ear buds in to block out the world. And the stars in his eyes faded until there were none, replaced by the uncolour of normality. Of gray colours of acceptance. Of camouflaged colours of blending in. Of being liked by others.

And so, he must be happy, mustn't he? He was now like everyone else and fitted in with perfection; his giftedness boxed up, sealed, and buried.

Dead.

His behaviour had been moulded by others, by society, creating him into a copy of them, like they were all on the same medication to stop individuality. And that is how he lived his life. Like the others. Sleep. Wake up. Work. Sleep. Day in. Day out.

Then one night, when he was lying in his hiding place, stripped bare of his normality, daring to release his true colours and his inner light while looking up at the stars, a girl stumbled upon him.

She gazed into his eyes and saw more stars than the night sky.

'What!' he said, angered that she was in his hiding place beyond the trees in the open field, and that she had seen him. The real him.

Disappointed by his reaction, she hung her head. 'Nothing. I just thought … you might be … different … to the others.'

His face softened. 'Different in a good way … or different in a bad way?'

'Different, in a good way. Trying to fit in with the world is a boring path that keeps its own flat line, without peaks and falls. No challenges. No creativity. No imagination. No triumphs. It just is. Sleep. Wake up. Work. Sleep. Wake up. Work. Mediocrity.'

She reclined next to him and gazed at what he was looking at: two versions of himself. In one vision, he was dead in spirit, to fit in with others, but in the second vision; his true being, fearfully and wonderfully made, was shown—his inner light and his vibrant colour.

She poked him in the chest. 'I prefer this colourful, shiny version of you. Release yourself from your self-imposed prison. Be who you are meant to be. Follow the path that was built just for you. Love others like you want to be loved.'

He frowned at her. 'You can see what I see?'

'Yes. You're not the only one who sees what you see. The world is waiting for you to show them light. But it takes courage. I know you can do it.'

He shook his head.

'After the first step, it gets easier.'

He looked at her, eyes brimming.

'The world will love you for being you. Not at first, and not always. But in the end.' She covered his hand with hers, and he held onto her fingers, and closed his eyes.

When he opened his eyes again, she was gone. But the stars in his eyes were brighter, burning like they were created to be.

He smiled. He had work to do. Important work to gift to others.'

My story ended. I looked at the moon and became aware of Tobi's warm body against mine. He kissed my head. 'What? No violence. No fear?'

'Are you disappointed?' I said.

'No. Is it—'

'No psychoanalysis. Let my words infuse you with depth until you are lost. Your turn. There was once a boy.'

Tobi changed the weight on his feet, rocking me from side to side for a bit, and then stopped. 'Close your eyes and watch, Indigo, my storyteller of depth.'

I closed my eyes and waited …

'There … was once a boy, who was stuck in the mud.'

The corners of my mouth lifted.

'Along came a girl, a friend, who kindly offered her hand, but when their fingers were about to touch, she pushed him so hard he fell backwards, and became stuck in the mud even worse than he was before. He looked at her, confused. He thought she was his friend. He thought, perhaps she even liked him a little. Not as much as he liked her, but perhaps she liked him a little.

She stood with her hands on her hips, smiling at him, watching him squirm as he tried to free himself from the gobby, blobby mud.

'Please, help me,' he said.

'No.'

'Why not?'

'If I help you, I will get stuck, like you, and I won't be able escape.'

'I won't let you get stuck.'

'How do you know?'

'You just have to trust me.'

'I don't think I can do that?'

'I will never let anything happen to you,' he said.

She shook her head, her bottom lip trembling. 'But I'm scared.'

'Of what?'

'What happens when I trust you? What happens next?'

'You don't have to be scared anymore.' He sank deeper into the mud.

The girl looked at him. How could she believe that he would be kind to her? What if she helped him, and he pushed her into the mud and left her there? What then?

'Trust me … please,' he said.

The girl turned and walked away.

The boy was done. The mud would consume

him, and no one would ever know where to find him, his bones buried under the weight of the heavy mud, preserved until the end of earth time. He closed his eyes, wondering whether he would ever open them again.

'Here.' The girl's voice was determined, but calm.

The boy opened his eyes to see her at the edge of the mud. She dragged a log over, lifted it a little and dropped it across the mud. Then she stood on it, and held a thick stick out to the boy.

He reached up with two hands and held on to it.

'Start pulling,' he said.

She started pulling, but began to overbalance, so he let go. He didn't want her to become stuck in the mud, like him. He wanted her to trust him. When she straightened up, she looked at him with curious eyes.

'Let's try again,' he said.

Once more, she held the stick out to him. He reached up and held on to it with two hands. 'Lean back and pull,' he said. That way, if she fell, she would fall backwards, away from the mud.

There was a voluptuous squelch and his back released from the mud. He sat up. Relieved, he looked at the girl. He held on to the stick and asked her to pull again.

As she did, he was able to stand. She got off the log and pushed it toward him as best as she could. He leaned forward and fell towards the log so he was touching it, then lifted his feet out of the mud, one at a time.

> The girl took a step back from him when he stepped onto the firm ground.
>
> 'Thank you,' he said.

Tobi stopped speaking. I opened my eyes and turned my head a little to see him. He squeezed his eyes shut, with his head inclined to the side. Then he relaxed his face, took a deep breath and continued his story.

> 'He—'

Tobi's voice cracked and he stopped speaking, but then began again.

> 'He bent down and picked up a leaf. Then he dipped his hand into the mud and wrote on it, blew on it to help it dry, folded it and handed it to her. When she opened it up, she looked at him with wide eyes.'

Tobi touched his head on my shoulder for a moment, then removed his arms from around me and stepped away.

I turned to him to see him with his head bowed. He took off his beanie and ran a hand through his hair, then placed the beanie back onto his head.

'What did he write on the leaf?'

He pressed his lips together. 'I'll finish the story later. I have to go.' He tilted his head up a little and looked down at me, his eyes watery.

I took a step closer to him and placed my hand on his shoulder. He stilled, like my next movement would injure him. I stood on my tiptoes and lifted my lips close to his but he stepped back and looked at me, a tear falling from his eye. Then he stepped further away, turned around and put his arms behind his head, before he turned to face me again. He held out his hand. 'It's time to go.'

Confused, I frowned at him, placed my hand into his. We walked along the jetty and stepped into the boat.

He rowed with powerful strokes; his eyes averted from mine.

My heart began to ache. This felt like a goodbye.

He carried me from the boat when we got to the shoreline, and placed me on the ground like I was about to break.

'I'm sorry,' he said. He looked into my eyes and shook his head like it was the last time he would see me, and left.

My mind filled with a melody of grief and despair. I should never have opened my heart to him—

I breathed out the memory of his love potion and wiped away my tear. Memories. My research subject ...

My phone lit up. A text.

> **There's a yacht at the marina. Vertigo. 10:00pm.**

> Me: **I'll be there, around that time.** I grinned at my humour.

Chapter 22

Water was pooling inside my galoshes. They weren't supposed to do that, were they? Had been sabotaged? I squelched along the floating walkway of the marina, squinting through the raindom and looking for a yacht named "Vertigo". And there it sat. A dark-coloured yacht with a whirly thing lighting up and spinning in the wind of the raindom.

I strolled along the walkway looking for a way to climb onto the yacht, when I heard a deep voice. 'Close the umbrella.'

I closed the umbrella. Then a hand appeared before me and pulled me on board the yacht. I overbalanced a little but was steadied by the same hand, and also the same hand I then felt on the small of my back, guiding me toward a covered area on the deck of the boat.

'Sit.'

I lowered myself onto a seat.

A bluebird chirped. Once. Twice.

Tobi paced to and fro, his hands in his pockets, rain dripping from his black hood. He seemed nervous. Agitated. 'I … I need to know more.'

I tracked his back and forth path on the deck of the boat, and when he slowed, I said, 'This I know. Our research predicts that once memory of traumatic events is removed, the person no longer has nightmares, PTSD, or anxiety. It's like they have been freed from a mental and emotional prison. Their quality of life improves. Their happiness improves. Their self-confidence improves. We have people who have volunteered to be research subjects.'

He clenched his jaw and looked up at the whirly thing spinning in the breeze, then brushed his hand over his face, and flicked the water from his hand.

If we were going to do this thing—removing our memories of the incident—we needed to act fast. I could get him in as a volunteer subject for Phase 3 of the research. 'Do I have your consent to remove that moment in the time of the incident from your memory?' I asked.

He closed his eyes.

'Choose—fear of being found out, and the certainty of a trial and accusation of something presumed to have happened, which we actually can't prove our innocence or guilt, life or death, with no body, no evidence—or to reset, to begin again, fresh. Choose.'

He opened his eyes and looked at me. 'I can't … yet.' He reached down, grabbed my arm and pulled toward him, then placed his finger under my chin and pulled my lips closer to his, almost touching. I inhaled his sweet, spicy scent, and added it to the memory of how he used to make me feel, and closed my eyes, waiting for the sensuality of his kiss. But, he stepped back from me, tucked his hands into the pockets of his black hooded jacket, and left.

I stepped out into the rain, my galoshes filling with water again. I shook my head. Our secret was getting impossibly heavy to carry. I needed answers. I needed him to make a choice … before I decided to go to the police.

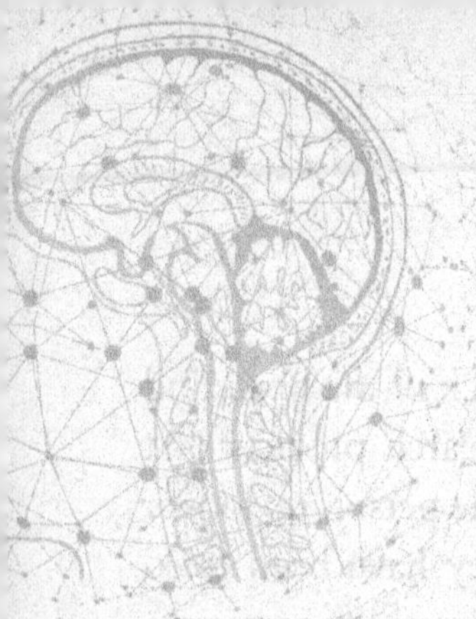

Chapter 23

I pushed my lunch around on the plate at work. First the lettuce. What is the point of lettuce? Then the tomato, followed by the beetroot and avocado. I stuck my fork into the lasagne and twisted it. Usually my favourite.

The first day of the work week was always harder, but today was impossibly worse—my world was imploding. I had been excluded by my once, close friends, and I was possibly about to do something with Tobi that was totally illegal. Totally unethical. According to the laws of medicine and civil law.

The chair opposite me scraped along the floor. I looked up to see Xander placing his lunch tray on the table and lowering himself into the seat. I wanted him to leave. Like everyone else.

'Have you solved it yet?' he asked.

'Solved what?'

'Whatever you are ruminating about as you create office lunch art.'

'I wish.' I clenched my teeth together and berated myself for using the word "wish".

'Don't be too hard on yourself about what happened with Yolande, if that's one of your musings.'

I frowned and shook my head. 'It was a bad call on my part. I should have let sleeping dogs lie. I'm so sorry for all the distress and upheaval it's caused. I was trying to explain to her that what happened to Mia wasn't her fault. It should have been me there that day and the end result would have been the same ... or worse … two deaths—mine and Mia's.' I shook my head again. 'How's your Meniere's research going?' I said to change the topic.

He raised one eyebrow. 'Extremely well. After extensive research into Meniere's disease, we have identified three groups. The first group are conditions that mimic the symptoms of Meniere's disease, for example, vestibular migraines, and people who are wrongly diagnosed with Meniere's. The second group are those whose cause of Meniere's can be identified, for example, through injury or anatomical reasons, which, by the way, can possibly be fixed with procedures and manipulations. The third group are those whose cause of Meniere's cannot be identified, nor fixed, by procedures used in the second group. Most probably auto-immune. For this group, we are using nanomedicine, using a nanobot to secure a biopsy of the inner ear, analyse the biopsy, and depending on what we find, deliver effective, non-destructive, medicinal treatment directly to where it is needed with the nanorobot. We are in Phase 2, and I'm thrilled with the results, and just short of claiming that we have found a cure. I am quietly optimistic! Phase 3, where we conduct a wide range of research with people, is not far off.'

'So, you're using the smart nanorobotics that have controls and sensors including remote video capability?'

'We have been.' Xander smiled. 'What it has allowed us to do has been … extraordinary, and … unprecedented ... even to the point of watching a vertigo attack in situ.'

I shook my head. 'Technology blows me away. I'm so thankful

it has been re-engineered for medicine and research. We are on the cusp of something enormous—the beginnings of individualised health management, instead of one treatment fits all, that is quite frankly, hit and miss at times.' I looked down and pushed the curled carrot garnish around my plate. 'I'm sorry I couldn't persuade Yolande into being a research subject for the memory removal. If she was going to get it done, at least it would have been with me, and I would have stopped the process if necessary, either for her, or due to technical reasons or methods.' I shrugged my shoulders.

Xander leaned forward on his chair. 'I'm curious, have you or your research assistants tried it on yourselves?'

'Absolutely.'

'And?'

'And what?'

'Was it successful?'

I gestured to Xander to lean in even closer. 'I cannot speak of the results. Classified information.'

'Two blinks for affirmative.' I blinked once. And once again. A mathematical equation for Xander to acquire his answer.

Xander leaned back in his chair, folded his arms and grinned.

'Your lunch is getting cold. Eat up,' I said, looking at the steam rising from his lunch.

'In the same way you are eating your lunch?'

I looked at my plate with a lopsided grin. 'Unlike me.'

'Tobi asked where you were the other night?' Xander said.

'And you told him I was banished?'

Xander shook his head. 'I told him it had slipped your memory.' Xander beamed me a smile and laughed at his own humour.

I raised my eyebrow at him trying not to laugh at his attempt at being funny. 'Did he get it?'

Xander's eyebrows creased. 'I don't think so.'

Chapter 24

Dear Finn,

Hey. I hope you remember me. I met you at Kingdom Adventure Park during the spring of the most amazing flowering season. Ever.

You started talking to me in the queue to the Marvellous Super Roller Coaster, then you sat next to me in the car and held my hand as I screamed my lungs out in the darkest, scariest tunnel where I think we were inverted, holding on for dear life.

When the ride ended, we looked at each other, our smiles wide, our eyes caught in each other's.

Afterward, we ate burgers and I drank Coca-Cola for my nausea, while you laughed at me.

I wanted to spend more time with you, but you got a text and had to leave. I called your name and you stopped. I ran to you, out of breath, kissed your cheek and thanked you for holding my hand on the ride. Remember? You smiled at me and said, 'You're welcome ...'

'Lucinda,' I said.

'Lucinda,' you repeated. Then left.

I dropped the blue calligraphy pen onto the off-white, handmade paper and looked out my window into the nightdom. Frustrated with the narrative I was writing, I screwed it up and threw it at the bin, hitting the rim before it fell to the floor, joining my seven other writing attempts. It's what we were planning to do. It was our chance to escape from the situation that had unfolded before our eyes. The situation that should never have happened. If only he ... *if only*. Three words would have changed everything. Just three words. My mind filled with a melody of grief and despair, just like that time I thought I would never see him again. Except, I did—

He waited by the gentleman's rowboat. He stood tall with his hands behind his back, his winter coat, scarf and winter cap the colour of the nightdom sky. He cut a powerful figure. A brooding one.

I lowered my head and wondered why I was here, but kept walking forwards.

When I stopped before him, he connected his eyes to mine and clenched his jaw before pulling a bunch of daisies from behind him. He looked downed at them, lifted his hand and stroked a white petal. 'Daisies. Simple. Uncomplicated.' His voice was deep and rich.

'Unlike me,' I added.

He broke off the flower and tucked it above my ear, his gloved finger brushing lightly over my skin. My breath hitched. 'Forgive me for my … unscheduled departure … a month ago.' He held out his hand for me.

I looked at his long, gloved fingers. They pulled at my heart strings, wanting me to touch my fingers to his, to feel that chemical hit that he gave. But I didn't. It would hurt my heart too much. I looked up into his eyes, then focussed on the boat behind him and walked to it. I climbed in, sat in the middle and took the oars in my hands and waited, and wondered whether he would join me.

I sat still with a straight back and looked over beyond *Zero*, to the lake full of icy blue. I inhaled deeply, closed my eyes and started to count. Silently.

1 … 2 … 3 …

If he didn't get into the boat when I got to ten, I would row away anyway.

4 … 5 … 6 …

I gripped the oars harder.

7 … 8 … 9 …

The boat rocked from side to side as he climbed in and sat at the end where I usually did. When he settled, I pushed an oar into the water, touching the bed of the lake, and pushed hard, to get the boat into deeper water. Then I fell into a rowing rhythm.

'Left,' he said, looking at me, then looked away. 'I didn't know whether you would meet me today.'

'Unfinished business,' I said, my body tensing with anxiety.

I watched his Adam's apple rise and fall. 'Likewise,' he said.

It was my turn to swallow the ache in my throat. Perhaps I did love him? If I didn't, this wouldn't hurt so much, would it? I kept rowing, keeping my strokes firm and even, trying to burn the emotion simmering inside of me.

'To your left a little more,' he said.

I kept rowing, my eyes on the full red moon, rising above Tobi. It was angry. Like me.

'Left a little more, and start slowing your strokes,' he said, his voice more tender this time.

I gave one, two more strokes, then pulled in the oars like Tobi had done so many times, and waited for the jetty to sneak up on me. When it appeared, it was Tobi who lassoued the rope over the single post. He grabbed a backpack and jumped onto the jetty and kept walking. I stood, and waited for the boat to settle from rocking, then stepped out, relieved that he didn't give me a hand to take.

I turned on the jetty to make my way towards my Jacaranda tree, and slowed my step. Tobi stood there, facing me. There was a fire burning in the fire pit to his left. He had already been here? I closed my eyes and blew a breath between my lips, then opened them, hesitated with my step, but then walked with confidence. Chin up.

I stopped before him, trying to ignore his scent of sweetness and spice that tried to infiltrate my heart. 'You keep telling me to trust you.' My throat was tight.

'I had to sort something out.'

'With another woman?' My fear.

He shook his head. 'I would never do that. It's not my style. It was with work and the restrictions they place on me.'

'Including relationships?'

'Yes. Like when you go into research lock-down.'

I lowered my eyes to the timber planks of the jetty. He was in the same position that I was.

He reached into his pocket and handed me a large leaf. 'It's from the story I didn't finish.'

I looked up at him. My eyes were burning, tears threatening to fall. I took the leaf from his long, gloved fingers.

Tobi's voice surrounded me at the same time, 'He bent down, picked up a leaf, dipped his finger into the mud and wrote on the leaf. He blew it dry, folded it, and handed it to her. When she opened it up, she looked at him with wide eyes.' He gave me a nod to open it.

I paused, feeling anxious, nervous, like I was about crumble. Could whatever was written on this leaf hurt me more? I blinked slowly, then opened it. There, on the leaf, was a hand-drawn heart and the words, "thank you for trusting me". I closed my eyes and a tear fell, betraying me. Tobi reached up and wiped it away from my cheek. He took my hand then and led me to the fire pit. He pulled me down beside him.

'You broke Rule Number 4.'

'Enabled by Rule Number 8, for my significant other.' He looked into my eyes deeply, then turned and pulled marshmallows out of his backpack, and two sticks. He placed a marshmallow on the end of one stick, toasted it lightly, and handed it to me. 'Peace offering,' he said.

I took it from him, blew on it, and placed it into my mouth, closing my eyes, letting the sweetness pour into me, washing away my bitterness.

'I'm here to protect you from the blood moon,' he said with a lopsided smile, sadness shining in his beautiful eyes as his brow creased with barely controlled emotion.

My breath caught, and I looked up into all the colours above. The red-orange moon was a sight to behold. 'Should I be scared of you, or the angry moon?'

'Neither. According to a legend in Africa, the blood moon is the result of a conflict between the sun and the moon. The moon needs healing.'

I closed my eyes. He was the sun with its own light. I was the moon, only able to reflect light. It felt like we were in conflict, and I needed healing. But didn't know how. I felt a hand on mine and opened my eyes. Tobi pulled my hand to his lips, leaving the softest kiss. His eyes connected to mine, full of yearning. 'If I ever have to leave unexpectedly, please trust me. It's not you. It's my job.'

I pulled my hand from his, wiped my tear, stood and walked to the water's edge to gaze at the moon. I needed time to think. I wrapped my arms around myself for warmth. It was the end of winterdom, but still freezing at night.

The sound of footfalls came from behind. I glanced over my shoulder as Tobi neared, then stopped behind me and wrapped his arms around me. He pulled me close. Gently. I was cocooned in his warmth, his strength, with sweetness and spice surrounding me like a sensitive and sincere melody, graceful and soothing. I stopped fighting my internal war and melted into him.

I gazed up at the blood moon, and all the colours above. 'The moon is beautiful.'

'Like you,' he said.

'Please don't break me,' I whispered.

'It would destroy me if I did.' His voice cracked.

I turned to face him. He clenched his jaw as he looked at me, his eyes stormy and wide, allowing me to see into his soul. My stomach fluttered as I placed my hand on the side of his face. His lips parted, and my heart skipped a beat.

He lowered his head, our lips almost touching, like he was asking for permission to kiss me, and then our lips met in a slow and soft kiss that had me falling. Totally. I was in love with him. There was no going back.

Our lips parted and he opened his eyes. Vulnerable. Beautiful. Undone.

I breathed out his love potion and turned back to the blood moon. It rose higher in the heavens, the redness lessoning, it's time of stardom ebbing. It was healing, like me.

'On the nightdom of the full moon, when dark shadows

become a whisper of themselves, the Jacaranda Tree of Jacaranda Island must be climbed,' he whispered, took me by the hand and led me to *my* tree. He looked up into the leafless limbs, the branches looking like arms reaching out, trying to vacuum auroras of light from above to infuse into it to become a dream tree.

Tobi's hand left mine and he climbed, leaving me standing at *Zero.* He climbed past the scarf I had wrapped around the tree trunk, upward, climbing with confidence and agility. I watched, my heart glowing. When he settled on a branch, I ascended the tree and sat beside him. I smiled.

'What?'

I shook my head. 'Nothing.'

'Spill the beans.'

'I think I've lost my sloth.'

'Are you sad?'

'Yes. I loved my sloth.'

'Loved?'

I smiled again. 'Yes. Past tense. He's gone now.'

Tobi looked up at the blood moon and raised an eyebrow. 'I guess he can always return.'

'Maybe the blood moon transforms him?'

'Maybe.' Tobi reached over and grabbed his dark blue hardcover book of unfinished stories. It was wedged between some branches. 'Shall we?'

'I guess. Maybe we should make it a rule—Number 9—when in the Jacaranda tree of Jacaranda Island, the book of unfinished stories must be opened.'

'And Rule Number 10, to round off the rules—there are no rules when the declaration comes.'

'The declaration? What declaration?'

'I'm not sure. But we will know when we declare it.'

'We? Hmmmm … cryptic.' I eyed him curiously. Did he know something I didn't?

Tobi opened the dark blue book, a little less immaculate after it had spent a month in the outdoors of Winterdom. He looked at me. 'Close your eyes, and give the story words, with your mind and heart, then speak it to life.'

I closed my eyes and listened. 'Once upon a time, the moon rose, large and red, dominating the sky with its splendour. People gasped. All except Lucelle. She fingered the letter in her pocket, knowing that it needed to be opened. Now.' Tobi's voice sounded fruity in a gentle speaking melody, singing to my heart, the core of my being. I exhaled, then took in a deeper breath, and fell inside the story that started drawing images in my mind.

> 'Once upon a time, the moon rose, large and red, dominating the sky with its splendour. People gasped. All except Lucelle. She fingered the letter in her pocket, knowing that it needed to be opened. Now. She wanted to keep looking at the moon. She wanted to memorize every detail about how the colours of red and orange bathed the moon in magic, knowing it would stay with her for days. But she couldn't concentrate for two reasons. Firstly, she had learned to hate the moon, and, secondly, a long-awaited letter had arrived three days ago with the inscription, "To be opened as the blood moon rises".
>
> She took one last lingering look at the moon and tried to inhale all of its majesty, then slipped her hand into her pocket and pulled out the letter. She stared at it, checking three times that the handwriting belonged to the deceased.
>
> Of course it was. It could only be from him.
>
> She moved away from the hordes of people and sat between the black volcanic rocks, hidden. She pulled out her book and a torch from her bag. She

wedged the torch higher up behind her in the crevasse of a rock, settled more comfortably on the sand, took a breath, and slid her finger above the red wax seal on the back of the envelope, opening it.

Her heart pounded, and she hesitated, like she always did. She had been receiving letters like this since her love died.

Who did he give them to?

What instructions had he given them.

Was it a man or a woman?

And how did the letters get to earth from the base on the moon?

She slid the letter out, held it against her face, closed her eyes and inhaled the familiar cologne of her love - a crisp blend of aquatic and woody scents. She so wished he was still here with her.

She unfolded the letter, opened her book, and placed the letter on the page to read in secret, like she had done every other time since the accident.

She frowned. His words were fewer this time.

Dear Lucelle,

As I write these words I live and breathe. And, as you read these words, I live and breathe.

Still.

Lucelle took a sharp breath. He was dead. How can he breathe? She looked up at the blood moon. She was told he had died while researching on the moon base. And these letters, all fifty-two of them, were written as he prepared for death, written to … make his death less difficult for her. She continued to read:

By the time you have this letter, I will have been released from quarantine. From isolation. Meet me on the beach where we first met. 2pm. July 27th.

The reason my heart is still beating, is because of you.

I love you.
Grayson xx

Lucelle's breath shuddered. Her eyes filled with hot angry tears. Then guilt. Her wish had come true. She should be over the moon that he was not dead as she had been led to believe.

It was all a lie? She had been betrayed?

How could they?

Squeaky footsteps in the sand came closer. Lucelle closed her book, ensuring no part of the letter, or any of the other letters, were protruding. She blinked away her tears as best as she could before Gael sat beside her.

"Hey, my beautiful wife," he said as he lowered himself to the ground and gave her a chaste kiss. "Why are you here? You can see the moon better from the other end of the beach."

Lucelle looked up at the moon. She was sure she could see the damage of the lunar station explosion on its south pole. "I thought, if I could move away from the crowds with their phones and cameras, I could see it better, here ... where it's darker," Lucelle lied.

Gael looked up at the moon and tilted his head to the side. "I don't think so." He stood. "Come. Let's walk to the other end of the beach. This is a once in a lifetime event." He held out his hand to her.

She sucked in a shaky breath and placed her hand in his and stood, and they began to walk. She kept her eyes on the sand. She couldn't tell him that she hated the moon. She couldn't tell him that the moon was the reason for her broken heart. And now. Grayson was back. From the dead.'

I opened my eyes and looked at the blood moon, my heart cloaked in sadness from my story. Tobi was silent. He normally spoke once I had finished my story, but this time he didn't.

'The end,' I added, and looked at Tobi.

'Are you trying to tell me you ha—'

'No psychoanalysis, remember?'

He frowned and looked down at the book. 'I remember … but—'

I placed a finger over his lips. 'Your turn.'

He inclined his head with a slight nod.

'Once upon a time, the moon rose, large and red, dominating the sky with its splendour. People gasped. All except Lucelle. She fingered the letter in her pocket, knowing that it needed to be opened. Now.'

Tobi stopped. I opened my eyes and looked at him. He shook his head. 'I … can't find the words. Your story … cut me.'

'Cut you?'

He looked down and shook his head. 'None of them will be happy. There won't be a happily ever after.' Tobi looked at me. 'Do you know the ending?'

'No,' I lied, hoping he didn't notice. I did know the ending and it wasn't pretty. The truth was, I didn't want to keep telling that story because Tobi was right, there would be no happy ending. 'I'm sorry it cut you.'

Tobi lifted his eyes to mine. Sadness dripped out of them. 'I want to kiss you because it feels like the right thing to do, right now … but I don't want to fall out of the tree.'

I covered my mouth to stop my bubble of laughter. But failed.

'What?' he said, blinking in rapid succession.

'Tobi, *the Brave*. Lean a little closer and keep your eyes open. Your eyesight helps with balance.' When he did, I placed my lips on his, then pulled away. 'Better now?'

'A little. I will resolve my need when we are on *Zero*.'

I kept my eyes on his, the corners of my mouth turning up. 'I'll look forward to it then.'

Tobi gave a coy smile and took my hand in his. 'Now, close your eyes and watch the words come to life.' He lifted my hand to his lips and kissed it, then put my hand on his thigh. Warmth flowed inside me that calmed and elated. How did he make me feel this way?

> 'Once upon a time, the moon rose, large and red, dominating the sky with its splendour. People gasped. All except Lucelle. She fingered the letter in her pocket, knowing that it needed to be opened. Now. She knew it was from her lover. She could smell his scent. When she couldn't stand another wave of anxiety, she backed away from the crowd of people and stood under the light post.
>
> She closed her eyes, then pushed her hand into her pocket and pulled out the letter, sliding the letter beneath her nose, inhaling the scent of vanilla, musky amber and cedarwood.
>
> She ripped open the letter as her heart beat double time. Patience was not in her genetics. She pulled out the loose paper in haste, carelessly letting the envelope

drop to the ground and started to read:

To My Dearest Lucelle,
My Heart,
My Eternal Love,

It's been two years since we last kissed, and I can't wait to be with you again. I dream of you every moment, and especially every night.

I have good news. I have sold paintings, pottery, and all of my sculptures. I also have orders for many more portraits. But the portrait I want to do the most, is yours.

My income is now substantial, and your father will approve of how I can now provide for you, my love. I have included a train ticket for you to come to Paris.

I can't wait to share my life with you. I have so much to tell you. I have so much to show you.

I will be waiting for you at the Gare du Nord 2pm, July 27th. My heart is waiting to sync with your heart again as we join our bodies in passion. La vie est une fleur dont l'amour est le miel.

I love you.
Forever yours,
Grayson xx

The wind blew Lucelle's hair across her face. She smiled. She was going to Paris to be reunited with Grayson. Her Grayson. She looked at the moon, wondering whether he was painting it with the full spectrum of colours, right now. She stilled. The train ticket! The only thing she held was Grayson's letter.

In a frantic state, she turned around and looked about on the ground. She had dropped the envelope in her haste to read his letter.

And it was nowhere.

She started to run where the wind took her. The envelope would be there too, wouldn't it? But as far and as wide as she looked, the envelope was nowhere.

It was gone. Forever.

Her heart sank. There was no way she could afford to buy a train ticket to Paris. She looked up at the moon, large and red, tears welling, balancing, then falling from her eyes. With the envelope and his address gone, she couldn't even let Grayson know what had happened. When she didn't meet him at 2pm on July 27th, he would think she didn't love him anymore.

Lucelle placed her hand over her aching heart. She walked home by the light of the fading blood moon until dark clouds covered the little light she had left to see.

She kept walking.

Even when it started to rain, the drops mixing with her tears and leaving a trail of sadness.

When she got home, she went to bed, wishing not to wake up in the morning if she couldn't be with Grayson.

But she did wake. Even without Grayson.

She sighed heavily, got out of bed and walked towards the kitchen, then stopped mid-stride. There was something on the floor near the front door. She went to it. It was paper. An envelope. Torn like an impatient girl filled with love had ripped it open in haste. She picked it up and looked inside the envelope. And there was the train ticket to the Gare du Nord, 2pm, July 27th.

She closed her eyes and pressed the train ticket to her heart. Wishes do come true, she thought. That's why she did wake today. It was destiny.'

When silence saturated the air, I opened my eyes and looked at Tobi, impressed by his French. 'A happily ever after. Nice.' A sudden warmth flowed through me. I swung my legs and looked at the full blood moon to override the euphoria of love I was feeling. It failed. 'I love you—r story.' *A Freudian slip*. 'What did you say in French?'

He looked down, and his lips curled into a slow smile, then repeated it, 'La vie est une fleur dont l'amour est le miel—life is a flower of which love is the honey.'

My heart melted, and I refrained from placing my hand over my heart that was beating way too hard. I took a calming breath to change my focus. 'Speaking of honey—sweetness. I could go another toasted marshmallow. You?'

He gave a half smile. 'Sounds like a plan.'

I turned and descended the tree, planting my feet on *Zero*. A moment later a thump sounded. I turned, and there was Tobi. Smiling.

I frowned, 'What happened to my sloth?'

'The one you love?' His eyebrows were raised.

I nodded. 'Yes.'

He held up a finger, stepped past me, then climbed the tree at the speed of a sloth to the branch where we were. He waited a moment, then descended the tree with awkward limbs, slower than a month of Sundays.

His feet hit *Zero* and he turned to face me. 'There. You must love me now,' he said, dark and brooding.

My body flushed with warmth as my stomach fluttered, and I lost my train of thought as his love potion cast a spell on me. 'Who-o doesn't l-love a sl-loth?' I said, stumbling over my words.

The corner of his mouth lifted, creating the perfect balance of half happy, half sad. He leaned in closer. 'I have a suppressed need that is waiting for a resolution,' he said, focussing on my lips before he leaned closer, our lips almost touching, teasing, wanting. He brushed his lips over mine once, twice, waiting, then seduced me with a slow, soft kiss. I ran my fingers through his thick hair, and felt a lump on his skull, above his left ear. Tobi pulled away from our kiss, his fingers moving my hand off his head, then dropped his forehead against mine.

My brain scattered. Momentarily. I sucked in a deep breath, my eyes wide, and stepped back from him, then glanced up at him through my eyelashes. His eyes were closed, and his hands were behind his head.

I turned and walked to the fire pit and sat, staring into the flames, knowing I was in deep trouble. Was I in love him, or was I reacting to our chemical attraction?

All I knew was that I wanted more. I took my gloves off and rubbed my hands closer to the fire. They weren't cold. I was trying to divert my overwhelming emotions, my inclinations, my … desires … before I acted on them. I stopped rubbing my hands together and splayed them in front of the fire, concentrating on moving one stretched finger at a time. *Distraction.* Dousing of the fire within. A marshmallow on a stick was before me and my focus changed. I didn't even know he had sat beside me. I took the stick from him and held it close to the fire.

'You okay?' he said.

'Yes,' I lied. 'You?'

I saw him nod in my peripheral vision. 'Yes.' I wasn't convinced.

My marshmallow caught fire. I pulled it away and blew on it.

It was more toasted than I wanted, but I still ate it. I swallowed, welcoming the new taste that masked the addictive flavour of Tobi. 'Where did you learn French?'

'In France. I went to university there. I didn't learn it as a subject. I just absorbed it, for survival.'

'Nice. France. And you came back to Tarrin?'

'It was part of the plan. As small as Tarrin is, you know they have some insane research and other ground-breaking programs going on. It's the place to be if you want to jump outside the constraints of the controllers.'

The controllers. The government. I knew exactly what he meant. The controllers always knew more than they were willing to admit to, and didn't want anyone else learning what they knew, or discovering more than they ever thought possible. It was suppression at its finest.

'Indeed. Tarrin is the place of trials and experiments, pushing the limits, exceeding the boundaries beyond knowledge, and the imagination. Discovering the indiscoverable. Curing the incurable.'

'And then there are the spies who walk among us,' he said.

'Making it hard to trust anyone new who comes to live here.'

'And those you have known, but you really don't know,' he said.

I looked at him. 'Are you talking about me?'

'Maybe.'

'The same could be said about you,' I said.

'True.'

'Are you saying you don't trust me?' I pulled my eyebrows together.

'No. It's just … I want to see you more than once a month … but.'

'But?' I frowned at him.

He sighed. 'I am supposed to remain unattached. For my job.'

'Unattached? So, you're breaking a rule of your job by meeting me here once a month?'

'Yes.'

'Could you lose your job if they find out!'

'They won't do that,' he said.

'How do you know?'

'I am too valuable with my knowledge and experience. They can't replace me.' He clenched his jaw.

'If you are so sure of that, why don't you renegotiate your contract?'

He stared into the fire and narrowed his eyes.

'Wait. Are you a priest, or married?'

He looked at me and laughed.

'This is serious. I can't keep meeting you if you are,' I said.

He took my hand and pulled it to his lips and kissed it. 'I'm not married, and I'm not a priest. But if you see ever see me dressed as one, it's part of my job.'

I frowned at him.

He shook his head as if he wanted to tell me something but couldn't. He sighed. 'I'm a protector, a first responder, a—' He stopped talking and tilted his head to the right a little and winced.

'A ...?'

'That's all I can tell you. And it's more than I should have told you.' He took his gloves off and rubbed his hands together, closer to the fire.

I giggled.

'What's funny?'

'Imagining you dressed as a priest.'

He gave a wry smile. 'It's not as funny as you think. I did consider going into the priesthood.'

I raised my eyebrows at him. 'Now I'm scared.'

He shook his head. 'Don't be.'

'What stopped you?'

'A longing … a knowing that I am meant to love someone on the earth with all that I am.'

'It doesn't make sense,' I said. 'Your longing, or knowing, and your job where you have to remain unattached. You may as well have entered the priesthood.'

He pulled off his beanie and ran a hand through his dark hair, before putting it back on. He looked into my eyes. 'You're not helping my struggle.'

'Perhaps that's a good thing?'

'Perhaps.' He placed a marshmallow onto his stick and toasted it to perfection and offered it to me. 'Winter is dragging on this year. I can't wait for the warmer weather so I can take off my clothes.' He looked at me with wide eyes. 'I mean, the layers of clothing for warmth.'

I took the toasted marshmallow from him and smiled. 'I liked my other mind image better.' I elbowed him in the arm. 'Would your family have approved of you joining the priesthood?'

'No. It would be the end of the family name if I didn't sire a son.'

'In your job, with your … unattached-ness … you could potentially have many children to bear your last name.'

Tobi looked at me with a frown and shook his head.

'Meaning—'

'I know what you mean, and I don't want that. If I ever have a baby, it will be with the woman I love, and together, as a family.' Tobi's shoulders rose as he took a deep breath.

'Speaking of the fam. Are you going to the celebration?'

'Possibly. You?'

'Obligated.'

There was a silence.

'If I'm there … we need to act like we haven't been seeing each other.'

'But—'

He put his finger under my chin and raised my face to his so our eyes connected. I felt like my soul was naked with his. 'You have to trust me—'

'I—'

Tobi shushed me, first with his finger against my lips, and then with his mouth, kissing me with a sweet sweeping of his lips across mine, tender and soft. He pulled away.

'For you.' I whispered, then reconnected the pieces of my brain.

'Good,' he whispered, and leaned in and kissed me just below my ear.

A shiver flowed down my spine and my breath caught. 'I'm so glad you're not a priest,' I said, my voice low.

'Me too.' His lips quirked up in a small smile before he lowered his head, tilted it to the right side and frowned, then lifted his head and sighed. He looked at his watch. 'I have to disappear into the darkness,' he said. 'Work.' His voice cracked.

I put my hand on the back of his neck and stroked it. 'Now I know what you do—you're a baker, working on secret recipes with the love potion imbued in them, shipped globally, to make the world a nicer place.'

Tobi gave me that half smile again. The one that made my heart skip a beat. 'I'll bring one on the next full moon so you can sample it.'

'I'll bring the antidote.'

'There is none, for what I offer.' He gazed deeply into my eyes, burning a song of love onto my heart in an amorous and restless key.

I breathed out an undetectable, slow, hot breathe, to calm the rampant butterflies inside me, without success, so I stood and walked around Jacaranda Island ensuring it was tidy, ready for us to go.

I waited for Tobi at the end of the jetty, gazing up at the blood moon. Its colours had almost completely faded. I felt his warm breath on my neck as he stood behind me, and closed my eyes, totally enamoured by him.

'Is the blood moon healed now?' he asked, his voice low.

I smiled, knowing he couldn't see my face. I turned to face him. 'Perhaps. Maybe one last kiss will completely heal it.'

He leaned in closer, and placed his lips upon mine in a kiss so gentle it almost broke my heart—

I squeezed my eyes shut. *Tobiah Lucas Brooks*. I ran my hands over my face and went to my chest of drawers and pulled out his scarf. The one he had wrapped around me after I used mine to keep the trunk of the Jacaranda tree warm. I pressed it against my face, and inhaled his sweet and spicy scent, reminding my heart of what we once had. Three words from him would have changed everything.

Just three words.

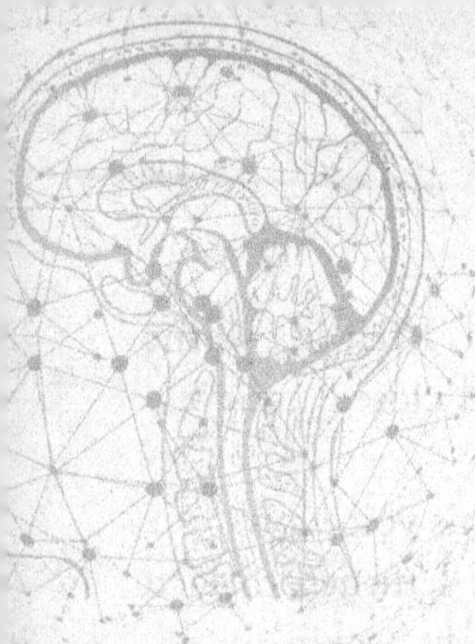

Chapter 25

'M-21.' I called the number in the same tone I had used for the previous twenty research subjects over the last four days. Friendly and warm, inviting, but emotionally detached on the inside. There was never a good reason to grow heart strings to any of the research subjects. It could cloud my judgement, my focussed discernment for the neurological research. We had progressed at a phenomenal rate in Phase 2 and 3 with our memory deletion research, after the arduous and long, Phase 1. To be in Phase 3 with human subjects was beyond huge. It was our dream, our hypothesis, fusing into real life. I smiled to myself. Four more research subjects after this person and we were done for Phase 3 of the research. It was a monumental step and I couldn't wait to delve into the data we had accumulated, plus follow up on the research subjects to assess the long-term effects of the targeted memory removal and its effect on their PTSD and their lives.

'M-21?' I called again.

There was no movement from the waiting room. Perhaps

the volunteer had changed their mind. And that was okay. No judgement would be made. I looked down at the page, then flipped it over to the next person, 'M-2—'

A hand wrapped around my arm, warm and soft, with a pinky fingernail the colour of pale pink candy floss, just like Mia always had. I stiffened and the back of my throat ached at the memory. I sucked in a quick breath to stop myself from dissolving into a puddle of tears filled with deep grief and crippling anxiety, swirling in a melody of despair. I changed my internal focus to external, and inhaled the scent of roses in the air, but perhaps softer, and a bit sweeter, and suddenly, it felt like a thousand flowers grew arms around me in a warm hug. I knew who M-21 was before I even looked up at her. The painted pink fingernail revealed her identity, as well as the fragrance of roses from Flowers for Fleur. But still, when our eyes connected, my heart stopped for a beat.

'You came.' The words tumbled out of my mouth after being caught in my uncomfortable anxiety. I widened my eyes at her, then pinched my brows together. 'Are you sure?'

Yolande's intense blue eyes were on mine. She closed her eyes for a moment too long, then said, 'Yes.'

I placed my hand over hers, still on my forearm, and nodded. 'Come with me.' I offered her a smile that I hoped wasn't sad, and led her toward the research room. We stopped before the white door. 'It's okay to change your mind,' I said. This was the second last chance where subjects could retract their intention to participate in the research.

Yolande shook her head. 'I've decided to do it.' Her eyes reddened.

I spent a moment connected to Yolande's eyes, then scanned my iris to gain access to the research room. The door clicked and I pushed on it to enter. 'Biran, I'd like you to meet our next research subject.'

Biran leaned forward and shook her hand. 'Thank you for

volunteering in our vital research at the Brain and Mind Lab.'

I looked at Biran, then spoke to Yolande, 'You know if you rearrange Biran's name, it spells the word brain.' I chuckled at my own joke and caught sight of Yolande's grin. It was a line I used with every volunteer subject to make them feel more relaxed.

Biran shook his head. 'Indigo's been making jokes about my name since the day we met. Now … if you look at my tie—the colour of indigo—I have five of these. I wear one each work day to remind her that indigo is not a name, it's a colour.' Biran looked up at me and raised an eyebrow.

Yolande grinned, then I gestured for her to sit on the dark blue ergonomic recliner chair. It housed padding and cushioning in all the right places to provide optimal comfort.

She looked at the chair like all the other research subjects had, ascertaining whether it could be trusted, and whether it was harmless. After a moment, she lowered herself down and made herself comfortable.

Biran held out an iPad to Yolande. 'This presentation will show you the procedure, how it is done and how it works. At the end of the presentation, if you decide to withdraw from the research, please know that it is okay. You are also under a non-disclosure contract for the time of ten years if you proceed with opening the presentation.'

Yolande took the iPad from Biran. She blinked. In slow motion. 'I agree to the non-disclosure.'

Biran smiled. 'Thank you. Touch the arrow on the screen. If you have any questions, please ask.'

I took a deep breath as Yolande's finger connected with the arrow, and the presentation began. I couldn't believe she was sitting in the research subject seat.

I was excited for her, and then I wasn't. My skin started to burn. Anxiety. My friend and my foe. My gut kicked in with its own opinion then, and I stumbled over the fact that I would be able to see exactly what happened on the day Mia died. Would I cope with that? I breathed out my hideous nervousness that emanated from the centre of my stomach. There was one thing I was sure of, seeing how Mia died would give me total insight into Yolande's behaviour. But then … is it like passing on a memory, or off-loading it onto someone else. A ticking time-bomb. What do I do with the memory then? Will it haunt me like it has haunted her? Sometimes, is it better not to know details?

Dr. Redfern entered the room and fussed about the tray that held the cannula and nanobot technology, arranging the instruments so they were spaced apart perfectly.

Biran looked at Yolande. 'Any questions?'

Yolande looked back at the iPad screen and flicked between the slides of the presentation. She shrugged with uncertainty, then closed her eyes and placed her hands over her face. She removed them and looked to the ceiling, to all the colours above. 'Will I feel the nanobot moving through me?'

'That's our most common question,' Biran said. 'No. The nanobot is twenty-five times smaller than the width of a hair, and smaller than a blood cell. We can give you a sedation during the process if you prefer, for either physical reasons, or emotional.'

Yolande blew a breath between her pursed lips and looked around the room. 'If something goes wrong while I have the nanobot inside my brain, what is your emergency protocol to avoid a catastrophic event, neurologically?'

'The nanobot has a built-in self-destruction code, so that it quickly dissolves and is eliminated through your body's waste system,' Biran said, his voice calm.

Yolande gave a nod. Her questions had already been answered in the presentation she had watched. I'm pretty sure she would have been researching nanobot technology since I mentioned it to her. She would love the technology behind it all, being an aeronautical engineer and working with technology in the

Defence Force.

'It's understandable if you decide not to go ahead with the memory removal,' Biran said.

Yolande blinked slowly as her eyes reddened once more. She frowned and placed a closed hand against her lips, like she was trying to barricade her words and emotions.

'Feeling anxious is a completely normal response to what you are about to do,' Biran said. 'Take a deep breath through your nose, then blow it out slowly through your lips.'

Yolande's chest expanded. She moved her hand away from her mouth, pursed her lips and exhaled for an extended time, then said, 'Please tell me the dates you have on my database for the specific memories you will delete.'

The keyboard clicked as Biran displayed information labelled as M-21. 'July 13, August 3rd, 4th and 5th, of the year you can see on the monitor.'

July 13. The day of the death. And the other dates: court proceedings. I frowned. Yolande did not include the funeral.

'Were there any other dates you wanted to include, like July 20th?' I raised my eyebrows at her.

Yolande shook her head. 'Dr. Jones, and your own psychologists have advised me to keep that memory, and I have decided to accept their advice.'

'Good,' I said. If we removed her memory of the funeral, she would be forever asking where her friend was. Imagine having to lie to people about the death of someone, pretending they were still alive, but making excuses for them. Tobi entered my mind. His story. His battle for the truth to be told. 'Do you have any requests before we proceed?'

'No.'

'Do you consent to us removing the memories as indicated on your paperwork?' Biran asked. He was forever patient in these proceedings before we activated the memory deletion phase.

'Tell me how you locate the memories?' Yolande said, her voice quivering.

'We have two methods. The first is where we locate your earliest memories,' Biran said, 'watching them in fast forward, until we find the milestone of your 2nd birthday, then go from there, following your memory markers using your circadian rhythm. The traumatic memories you wish to have removed have a different chemical composition. The nanobot is programmed to detect those chemical changes, engage with the memories and wirelessly transmits them to us, where computer intelligence decodes them and creates the images using the database from billions of digital photographs collated by AI. It then forms digital images on the screen for us to see. It will appear like a video, or a movie, of what happened on those dates.' Biran tilted his head to the side a little. 'And then we remove those memories, using a chemical carried by the nanobot.'

Yolande shifted in the chair. 'And the second?'

'The second is where we place you under twilight sedation. We can talk to you and ask you questions, including retelling the incidents you have indicated you want removed. The neurons that hold those memories will light up on the real time hologram. The nanobot will locate those memories, copy them and send to our computer wirelessly, and then, with your consent, we will instruct the nanobot to release a chemical to delete the memory. After the procedure, you will have no recollection of what occurred, due to the twilight sedation.'

A tear ran down Yolande's face. 'Being inside my brain ... it feels so ... intimate.' Her voice shook. 'The memories crush me inside every day. I'm scared that you will be traumatised after seeing what happened.'

Biran touched his hands together like he was saying a prayer. 'We have techniques that help us to manage information and images that we experience with this type of research. We have counsellors on hand for debriefing. We are well prepared. Besides, what happened on those dates was a thousand times worse for you. And that is why you are here. And that is why we are here.'

Yolande looked up at me and held out her left hand. I wrapped my hand around hers. 'I'm with you for the entire process. Remember why you are choosing to be a research subject?' I said.

She nodded. 'To help others, not just myself. To help those who never gave consent to what happened to them, like Mia and me.'

My eyes watered. 'Ready?' I tried to keep my anxiety from crippling me. I didn't think I was ready to see what happened on that day of Mia's death. But this was about Yolande, not me. Nausea swirled in my stomach.

Yolande placed a hand over her heart and closed her eyes. Tears trickled down her face and dripped onto her shoulders. She looked upward, like looking at the heavens. 'Sorry,' she whispered. 'I love you, forever and a day.'

My throat tightened as my heart overflowed with sadness in a passionate melody of sorrow and darkness. This was difficult to watch. I choked back my tears. I couldn't even imagine how difficult this was for Yolande to choose to erase the memory of her friend's death. Our friend's death.

I changed my inward focus to outward, and what I had to do to detach from my feelings.

Dr. Redfern sat on the chair on Yolande's right side. 'Put your arm on this board, please.'

Yolande searched his face as if to be deciding whether the doctor could be trusted or not.

'What colour?' I asked. Yolande saw people in colours. She was a synesthete. Different colours had different meanings.

'Blue,' she said.

'Is that good?'

'Yes. Very.' She placed her arm on the board that extended

out from the armrest of the reclining chair.

The doctor ran his fingers over Yolande's skin before using an alcohol wipe where the intravenous cannula would be inserted. 'Just the sensation of a prick,' he said.

Yolande winced.

'Would you like a twilight sedation for the procedure?' he asked.

Yolande looked up at me. I nodded. She took a deep breath. 'Yes, please.'

I tilted my head slightly and gave Yolande a gentle smile. 'Do you want to participate in the long version, where all of your memories are copied, and the trauma memories identified by us and erased, or do you prefer the shorter version, where you retell the memory for the nanobot to locate, copy and delete?'

Yolande raised an eyebrow at me. 'The short version.' I smiled, and she raised an eyebrow as unspoken words, that said, *why are you even asking me that - the answer is obvious!*

'While you are here for research, I was wondering if we can collect some other memories from you?' This wasn't part of the protocol. This was for me. I was curious about how our technology could be used in other positive ways. Would I find myself in hot water afterward? Absolutely. But eh! Why not?

'Such as?'

'Happy memories of Mia?'

Yolande looked up to the ceiling for a moment and frowned. She looked back at me with despair painted on her face that was almost too much to bear. 'Sure. Why not.'

I looked over at Biran. He gave a nod. Then I looked at the attending physician and nodded.

I turned my gaze back to Yolande with a small smile and stroked the back of her hand that I held. 'Ready?'

Yolande nodded.

In my peripheral vision, I saw Dr. Redfern inject Propofol

into her cannula. Ironically, it was the drug Dr. Jones talked about being an option for lessening the sting of traumatic memories for PTSD. Memory Extinction Therapy, she called it. I maintained eye contact with Yolande until she closed her eyes, then placed her left hand on her thigh and fell into my role of the research.

256. That was the number of electrodes positioned on a specifically designed cap. I applied the conductive gel to ensure our signal quality, then placed the cap onto Yolande's head, and moved with haste to the computer screen, sitting beside Biran.

'Inject the nanobot,' Biran said with a calmness like we had done this a thousand times.

The clang of instruments echoed around the sterile room, and a moment later, a screen lit up with data wirelessly delivered to the computer. A hologram of Yolande's brain projected into the room above her. We monitored the nanobot's location on the Nanobot App, as it was remotely controlled to travel to Yolande's brain. And then the nanobot entered her hologram.

Biran tapped on the keyboard, commanding the technology to engage in connecting digitally with memory cells.

'Yolande,' I said. 'Tell us what happened on the day that Mia died.'

'We were at a party, and two guys walked in. They took Mia to a car and I followed them. They put her in the backseat and I hurried, opening the back door. 'Mia, I have something insane to show you!' I said, and grabbed her hand to pull her out of the car, to stop her from making a mistake.'

I looked up at Yolande's hologram while she recounted the event. Neurons lit up and were being wirelessly sent to the computer.

'But Johnno was behind me. I could smell the hard liquor he'd been drinking. He gave me a firm shove and I landed across Mia's lap in the back seat. The door shut behind me, and then another door closed. By the time I had raised myself up, Jack was driving the car away from the party.

'Where are we going?' I asked, taking note of the scenery around us, looking for a moment of slow speed where Mia and I could jump out of the car. Their colour was no longer blue. It had become red, bright red: danger.

'Up to the outlook to watch the sunset. It's amazing at this time of the year. You girls will love it!'

My heart calmed little. There would be heaps of people at the outlook watching the view. It would be okay. We would be okay.

But the outlook was different to the one I knew. Jack followed a bumpy, rugged, off-road track to get there. When he stopped the engine, he turned to us. 'This is the real party, girls!'

Jack and Johnno got out of the car. They gripped our wrists and pulled us out of the back seat. Jack hit the left side of my face as he pushed me down onto the grass and laughed. I kept my eyes on them as I felt my cheek smarting.

We had to run.

I stood, then reached down for Mia's hand and pulled her up beside me.

Jack pulled out a bag of white powder from his pocket and snorted it, then handed it to Johnno, who did the same. In an instant, their unlikeable demeanour became surly and repulsive—'

'Don't listen anymore,' Biran said to me as the memory continued to be told and recorded.

My stomach knotted and nausea rose. But I couldn't, not listen. I needed to know the continuing narrative of what had happened before I had arrived on the scene on that fateful day, after following Jack's location on my phone. But this time it was from Yolande's view. I fixed my eyes on the monitor and my muscles tensed, ready for what was coming next.

Biran moved his body so I couldn't see the screen, but I heard Yolande's words. All of them. Almost. When I couldn't listen to the details anymore, I lowered my head and put my hands over my ears. I thought I was ready for this. But clearly, I wasn't.

Biran attached markers to the events of Yolande's choosing, then made three copies of the event that changed all of our lives. He securely saved the memories in three locations—that tragic day of her best friend's death, *our* best friend's death, and the court case days.

Biran looked at me and raised his eyebrows. 'Do you agree that we have we identified and marked the memories so Yolande's trauma can be disposed of, and her PTSD can be resolved?'

I inhaled deeply, mentally noting what Biran had deleted. 'Yes. You have isolated the days of Yolande's choosing. Plus, her memories from the moment she entered the building today. She won't remember why she was here. The objectives of this experiment are fulfilled.'

'Correct.' Biran tapped on the keyboard again. 'Requesting agreement and permission to copy and store Yolande's trauma memories with the nanobot, that she has identified to remove, and that we have located and confirmed, and highlighted,' Biran said to me.

I swallowed the lump in my throat. 'Agreed and permission granted,' I said.

Biran tapped a key and the highlighted memories on Yolande's hologram vanished.

An eerie silence filled the room. It happened each time we deleted the traumatic memories. It felt like resetting a person's life. It felt like stealing a little bit of each person. It felt like ... altering them in some way.

It felt like ... something we should not be interfering with.

But I guess, any monumental change when dealing with people's physical, emotional, neuronal or spiritual states, challenges your conscious, your existential concept that has been shaped in your mind over a lifetime. An existential crisis.

My stomach quivered.

'Yolande,' I said. 'Tell me all about the happy memories you have of Mia.'

And then it began. Yolande fell into an easy recall of our beautiful Mia. Her hologram became a symphony of light. The nanobot moved quickly capturing and downloading memories, but not erasing them.

'Thanks Yolande,' I said to stop her from continuing. 'Rest easy now.'

'Asking for confirmation that the process is completed,' Biran said. The computer screen flashed green.

I looked over at Yolande and a tear fell from my eye. She had suffered more than I ever knew. I pushed a calming breath between my lips to quell my anxiety. 'Affirmative,' I said.

I looked up at the hologram of Yolande's brain as Biran manoeuvred the nanobot back to the docking station in the cannula. 'Dr. Redfern, you may now stop the sedation and remove the cannula. M-21 will be with us again soon,' Biran said.

I walked over to Yolande and sat by her side, then removed the EEG cap from her head, and used paper towel to collect any gel residue. I gave her head a gentle massage like I did for all of the subjects.

I took her hand in mine again, and watched her face for signs of waking from the twilight sedation. For a moment, I had an insane mind flash that Biran had scrambled her memories in a different order, and Yolande would wake in a state of confusion and panic, even though she was the twenty-first research subject, and all twenty research subjects before her were fine. This unchartered neuro-research terrified me at times.

Yolande moved her head and inhaled deeply. She opened her eyes and connected them to mine.

'The procedure is finished. How are you feeling?'

Yolande frowned. 'Tired.' She looked around the room. 'Where am I?'

Good. 'You're in the Brain and Mind Lab. You came here to help us with some research. You've done well, and we are very happy.' I smiled at her, my heart breaking for what she had been through.

Yolande's lips turned upward. She nodded. 'That's right. So, I did help in some way?'

'Yes, and thank you.' I rubbed my thumb over the back of her hand, then released it, reached for a bottle of water, unscrewed the lid and handed it to her. 'Drink some water. It will help you to come out of the sedation quicker.'

'Thanks.' Yolande lifted the bottle to her lips and drank.

'Rest for another five minutes, and then you'll be ready to go. Do you have someone waiting for you?'

She nodded. 'Yes.'

'Who, and where are they waiting?' I was checking her memory.

'Xander ... is waiting in the foyer. He said to text him when I was finished. We're going to the café afterward.' Yolande grinned. 'You should come too.'

'I would love that, except, we haven't finished here, yet. I'll take a rain check though, if that's okay.'

'Absolutely.'

'Now, close your eyes while you wait.'

Yolande closed her eyes. I was supposed to ensure the room was tidy and in place for the next research subject, as I did for the previous twenty subjects. But I didn't. I wanted to observe her to make sure she was still herself. Undeniably I had a strong connection to her. Ethically, it was absolutely wrong for us to allow her into the research program, due to our shared history.

I gazed over her face, relaxed and carefree. I hadn't seen her like that since before Mia's death. The vision of the events surrounding our friend's horrific death came to my mind. I inhaled deeply. My heart went out to Yolande. Now I understood, without question, why she wore those ugly safety work boots all the time. She had every right too. Never judge another person for their behaviour. You don't know what they have been through, what they were hiding from others to protect themselves, physically and psychologically—

'Indigo, our research subject is ready to go. Take your time as you see her out.' Biran's voice cut into my thoughts. I turned to him and he nodded at me. Once.

I looked at Yolande. She opened her eyes, and they twinkled.

'Ready?' I said.

'Yes.' Yolande sat up in the chair.

'Take it easy when you stand. You may feel a little unbalanced.'

I held out my arm to her, and she wrapped her hand around it, her skin soft and warm, her pinky fingernail the colour of pale pink candy floss, just like Mia used to wear.

We walked at a slow but steady pace to the foyer. The moment we entered, Xander stood and rubbed the back of his neck. He walked over to us in that danseur sort of way, and put his hand around Yolande's waist to support her. He connected his eyes to mine and raised his eyebrows in a question. I gave him a smile, with a nod. *It was done. Finished.* 'Enjoy your coffee,' I said.

'Bye, Indi,' Yolande said.

'See you soon, Yolande.' I leaned forward and kissed her cheek, then turned and walked with haste back into the Brain and Mind Lab, trying not to crumble into a thousand broken pieces as I grappled with the guilt that Mia's death was all my fault. Not just that, but that Yolande's continued suffering was because of me. I had done this to my friends.

It was all my fault.

I turned off the lights to the lab when Biran left after our last research subject for the day. I was exhausted, yet highly agitated. I was supposed to go home, but couldn't. The heaviness of guilt and shame was trying to pull me under.

I went to my locker, pulled out my secret key and unlocked a small silver metal box I kept hidden under a spare lab coat in the corner, opened it up, and pulled out my leather hip flask filled with whiskey. I only ever used it in emergencies. And today was an emergency. I slipped it inside my lab coat pocket, and returned to the room where we had conducted the research for memory deletion.

I sat in the chair that Biran occupied for each research subject, and logged on to the computer, then pulled my hand away from the keyboard, shaking. I had seen too many cases of traumatised women, and a few men, over the past four days. Violent acts committed against them without their consent. I turned my head and cussed as my memory betrayed me. It had retrieved those memories that belonged to others, replaying them. Nausea made an abrupt appearance. I grabbed a bag and expelled the contents of my stomach into it. Repeatedly.

I held my breath to stop the heavy emotion that was building inside me. But then submitted to it, lowered my head and let my tears fall with ugly, loud sobs.

We were supposed to be humankind. HumanKIND!

How could some people believe they had to the right to take from others what did not belong to them! Where did they miss the education about permission and consent? Why did they not understand the meaning of NO, or STOP! Where was their empathy? What had happened to them to make them into people who sought power by hurting others? There had to be answers ... somewhere ...

I squeezed my eyes shut to stop the anger and pain of what I had witnessed over the last few days, then shook my head as sadness dripped from my eyes in a melody of groans of misery. My mama always said, 'Look for the helpers.' And I always did. Helpers like me. We were trying to help. But we needed to do more. Far, far more. We needed to prevent the atrocities from happening in the first place!

Enraged, I stood and paced the room trying to stop my thoughts from obsessing with trying to fix the world. Trying to find the source of the problem. Trying not to open Pandora's box that would set the world in a spin of violent vertigo, and upset the powers to be in their ivory towers making money by changing people's moral compasses—

I stopped walking, leaned over and put my hands over my face. 'STOP!' I yelled, muffling my anguished cry and trying to halt the cycle of my obsessive compulsive thinking about the topic.

I straightened up, rubbed my forehead and sat at the computer again. I pulled up Yolande's file and opened her memories. I clicked on the file titled "Happy Mia Memories". I wanted see Mia again. Our happy, vibrant Mia. A living Mia.

I popped my feet up onto the desk, reached into my lab coat and pulled out my whiskey flask and leaned back in the chair. I watched as Mia's presence occupied the screen before me. There she was. Funny. Beautiful. Demanding. Predictably erratic. Overflowing with love.

I took a long draught of whiskey. Our research had undeniably proven we could access memories digitally, and watch them. Then delete them on request. Forever gone from the mind of the person who chose to have them removed. And now they could live happily ever after like they were supposed to.

But what about the people who performed the Memory Deletion Therapy. Those who would be exposed to the violence and trauma of others. Those who had to add markers for deleting. Like me ... the other person's traumatic memories now becoming theirs. Perhaps an artificial intelligence trauma recognition program could be invented. It certainly was possible with technological advances. I made a mental note once again, to discuss it with the team.

I took another long draught of whiskey and pushed the physical violence I had witnessed with the research subjects into my mind box of "Never To Be Opened".

If I kept witnessing atrocities committed against people, like I did throughout the week, I thought that maybe I could never trust a man again. It was time for good men to take a stand. It was time for good men to guide boys, teenagers and young adult men in the way they should behave, with respect for others and themselves, so evil would not triumph. Everyone was accountable, including the bystanders who did nothing to stop the acts of violence from happening. Bystanders ... who did nothing …

I emptied the last drop of whiskey and a short sob escaped me. The world was indeed a dark place. I closed my eyes and the words of Martin Luther King Jr. came: "Darkness cannot drive out darkness; only light can do that. Hate cannot drive out hate; only love can do that".

The Memory Access Nanobot was a technological tool born out of love and compassion. The recorded memories could be used in a court of law, and viewed alongside the memories of the offender. Everyone would see exactly what happened. There would be no lies. Only truth.

Chapter 26

My hand trembled as I inserted the key into the lock of my apartment door. I dropped my bag onto the floor and headed straight to my bedroom, slumped onto my bed and buried by face in the pillows, then rolled onto my back. The white ceiling of nothingness stared at me, judging. I squeezed my eyes shut so hard I thought my face would never return to normal. And I wished it never would. I deserved to be banished from society like a monster for being a partaker in the interference of memories under the guise of doing good.

A wild river of rage coursed through my blood at my betrayal of a friend, two friends, and at the secret embedded in every living thing at Jacaranda Island. I was the worst kind of human.

I filled with the self-loathing of regret. Decisions were made that can't be undone. I wanted to disappear. I wanted to step inside a portal to a parallel world and never return. But none of those things were possible, so I did the next best thing. I climbed into the darkness of my wardrobe and shut the door.

Hello darkness, my friend. Bliss.

Except for the green glow-in-the-dark brain that occupied the corner of the wardrobe floor. Next to me. Drawing my eyes to the gyri and sulci: the peaks and grooves of the cerebral cortex. I reached out to it and ran my fingers over it, my mind reciting brain facts, the research we had done and what we had achieved, and the faces of those who we had removed traumatic memories from. Happy faces. No longer wishing to end their lives.

I frowned. I wasn't a monster. I wasn't the worst kind of human. I was a compassionate empath. I cared about people and their happiness. I drew a deep breath and pushed open the wardrobe door and climbed out.

I sat at my desk, put the compact in its usual spot near the plant, and lit a honeysuckle and jasmine scented candle to relieve my anxiety. I had a letter to write. I smoothed out the homemade off-white paper and picked up the calligraphy pen.

Dear Finn,

Hey. I hope you remember me. I met you at Kingdom Adventure Park during the spring of the most amazing flowering season. Ever.

You started talking to me in the queue to the Marvellous Super Roller Coaster. Then you sat next to me in the car and held my hand as I screamed my lungs out in the

I dropped the pen. My handwriting was a mess. Between my shock of witnessing Yolande's past today, and the whiskey I had ingested, I couldn't even read what I had written.

I couldn't stop shaking. *He* wants to forget. Tobi wants to forget. But he can't say the words yet. It would come. He was in a panic. He was agitated.

I didn't want it to come to this. I didn't want him to forget us. There had been so much … of *us* … together. Willow's body must be somewhere …

I picked up the compact, turned it on the side and spun it. Around and around it went, like the merry-go-round of vertigo, falling over then rocking from side to side until it stopped. I picked it up again. The stolen compact. Not mine. I pushed the button on the side.

Mirror. Mirror.

I gazed into the left side. The distant me. The me of the past where I met Tobi again—

'Not under the azure canvas with the sun that casts long shadows, but a little later,' he said, his voice low and gentle. He stood tall with his hands behind his back, his broad shoulders and pectoral muscles accentuated through his long-sleeved burgundy shirt. 'The light of the full moon will be here, soon. Rule Number 1.' His voice was deep and rich in its tones.

'As planned.' I gave him a shy smile.

He held out his hand with a crooked smile and my heart raced. I placed my hand into his and he kissed it, connecting his ocean-blue eyes to mine. I climbed into the boat as a euphoric warmth blossomed inside me like watching a flower bud opening to the sun on time-lapse.

I sat, then watched as Tobi pushed the boat off the shore and jumped aboard. He leaned forward to take control of the oars. I looked at his left hand wrapped around the oar, his fingers lean, a scar on his ring finger, his hand in a strong grip that somehow made me feel safe.

Tobi looked across, beyond *Zero,* to the lake full of blue, as we picked up pace, then his gaze settled on me.

'It's been too long,' I said.

'Waaay too long.' He narrowed his eyes at me. 'How was your date with Liam?'

'It wasn't a date. I was doing what you told me to do at the celebration, remember, you said, if you were there, we needed to act like we haven't been seeing each other. You weren't there, and Liam asked if I had a boyfriend, and I said no, according to your wishes. So, when he asked me to the movies, how could I refuse?'

'Thank you, then. And perhaps … should I apologise?'

'No. His kiss wasn't as nice as yours … to your left … a little,' I said, guiding the boat, then looked down at my hands, twisted together. I looked across beyond *Zero,* to the lake full of blue, so reflective at this hour of the second month of Springdom as melancholy drifted down upon me like a blanket.

'Indi?' I looked back to Tobi. He clenched his jaw. 'Liam's a fast mover. But the kiss is not what's bothering you. There's something else.'

I looked back at my hands. 'I just … I don't know if I can keep doing this with you.' I looked up at him, my stomach somersaulting.

His eyes widened and he pulled in the oars, climbed over two seats and sat opposite me. He grabbed my hands and frowned. 'Don't say that,' his voice cracked in a whisper.

'It's just … everything in my life is moving forward, except … *this.*' I pointed at him, and then to me, and back again. 'I don't even know what *this* is—'

'Just a little while longer … please …' he said, barely over a whisper, his eyes wet.

I closed my eyes, considering his request. He was like a part-time boyfriend. Was he even my boyfriend? I couldn't see him on the mainland. I didn't even know what our relationship was.

I nodded. 'A little longer,' I whispered, wondering whether it was the correct decision.

'Thank you,' he said. He leaned forward and brushed his lips over mine making me forget every letter of the word "doubt". He returned to the rower's seat and put the oars back into the water.

'Left. One hundred and eighty degrees,' I said. The boat had drifted to the right when it was unattended.

'Even strokes,' I said. I brushed the perspiration from my forehead. The sun was hotter than I expected at this time of Springdom. I unbuttoned two buttons on my floral dress, hoping to feel a little cooler. I looked up at Tobi when the boat slowed. 'Keep rowing … to the Jacaranda tree … in case you had forgotten where we are going,' I said.

He smiled crookedly.

'Keep going with even, firm, long strokes,' I added. We had drifted quite a distance from Jacaranda Island.

Tobi swallowed. He looked over to his right, away from me.

'Left a little more, and start slowing your cadence,' I said. The boat veered to the left, perfectly lined up to arrive at the jetty. 'Glide,' I said, my eyes widening. Jacaranda Island was covered in yellow flowers.

Tobi pulled the oars in and my gaze settled on him. 'Now,' I said.

Tobi reached out to his left side and stopped the boat against the jetty. With his right hand he grabbed the rope and secured the boat. I climbed out in haste, but then stood still on the jetty. A wide grin stretched across my face and I couldn't stop it. Jacaranda Island was covered in yellow flowers.

I bounced along the jetty and stopped where the timber boards met the ground, bent down and snapped a yellow flower off its stem. It bled onto me. A white, milky sap. Weeds. Dandelion weeds.

'An enclave of yellow flowers, soon to become an island of wishes.' His words were warm on my neck before he kissed me there, sending a shiver down my spine.

I turned to face him, and held the flower under my chin.

A corner of his mouth lifted. 'So, you like butter?'

'Or … I'm going to be rich!' I turned and made my way through the dandelions, being careful not to step on any. I stopped at the deck Tobi had built, put my backpack down and turned. Tobi threw out a colourful blanket, holding the corners so it floated down like a feather. He sat on it before reclining onto his back, lying amongst the dandelions.

I walked over to him and settled beside him, looking up at the darkening sky and all the colours of above. 'I've never seen dandelions here before.'

'Did you wish for them?' he said.

'No. Did you?'

'No. Maybe they are waiting for us?'

'For what?' I said.

He rolled onto his side and propped his head up with his hand. He reached over, put his finger under my chin and turned my face toward his. 'For our wishes to align—my wish for you … your wish for me … so you know what *this* is, so I know what *this* is.'

My lips parted and Tobi leaned into me, his mouth meeting mine—soft, gentle and slow, lingering, before our lips began to move in perfect sync, slowly, cautiously. I kept my eyes closed, basking in the warmth that heated every part of my body. No other man had made me feel this way.

Tobi pulled away and rolled onto his back, his eyes set on all the colours above. 'I need to know what you feel for me.' His voice was raw.

My breath stuttered. The words I was dreading to hear. How

do I answer that? Do I bear my heart with eight words—*I think I'm falling in love with you?* Or do I coat my heart with protection? *I like you. A lot.* Should I tell the truth using three words that may end in rejection for me? *I love you.* Or should I tell a partial truth? Better still. Distraction. I gasped. 'Look!' I said.

Tobi followed my gaze to the sunset, to all the colours above—yellow, orange, and red in clouds fanned out like fingers, graduating to pink puffs against the deep blue sky.

'Beautiful. Like you,' he said.

'Dramatic. Stunning,' I said, ignoring his comment.

'It's like an explosion. A statement. A declaration.'

'Most definitely a declaration.' I watched the sunset canvas change with the encroaching twilight sky, the full moon revealing itself above the clouds.

Large. Luminous. Breathtaking.

It was all the colours above that I loved. 'I'm going for a swim,' I said and stood, then walked to the water's edge and began unbuttoning my dress.

'Is that wise at this time of night? What about sharks?' He was behind me, his breath warm against my neck.

I pushed my dress from my shoulders and let it fall to the ground. 'It's my wish. And there are no sharks here in the fresh water, plus, it's an inland lake? Are you coming in?' I walked into the water until it was waist high, then lowered myself into it, up to my neck, and turned to face Tobi.

He was undressed, his clothes folded neatly on the ground beside my messy, discarded dress. I watched as he stepped into the water, making no effort to cover his nakedness. I indulged in ogling his athletic physique and a warmth rushed through me. Can that be measured with science?

'Tobi, *the Brave*,' I said as he lowered himself into the water and came near.

'Only for you … I'll fight off the bull sharks when they come,' he said.

'Then I thank you, Tobi, *the most Brave*. Turn around.'

Tobi frowned at me, but turned as I asked him to do. I moved closer and let our bodies touch, gently, then wrapped my arms around him from behind, and hugged him tighter. He held on to my arms around his chest and lowered his head.

'Are you okay?'

There was a pause before he replied. 'Yes. It's just … I never expected you to do something like this.'

'Something like this?'

He released my arms from around him, and turned to face me. 'Skinny dipping.'

I grinned at him. 'I prefer to call it moon dipping. And only on a full moon after a declaration from the sunset.'

He held my eyes in his, then lowered his lips to mine. It was my intention not to let our bodies touch in the water, facing each other like this. But I failed when his kiss pulled me to him like I had no self-control, and I fell deeply, moving closer to him as our kiss deepened. And I loved it more than I thought I would. I loved it more than I should.

'Ms Danube, Rule Number 2,' he whispered. 'On the nightdom of the full moon, when dark shadows become a whisper of themselves, the Jacaranda Tree must be climbed.'

I took a deep breath. 'And Rule Number 9,' I said, 'the book of untold stories must be read.' I was thankful for the change of direction.

'Absolutely,' he said, and kissed me below my ear, sending a fire through my veins. 'You go first.'

I pressed my lips to his, then stood and turned from him and walked to the water's edge, picked up my dress, put it on and buttoned it up. I made my way to the timber deck and rummaged through my backpack for my underwear, and completed my clothing ensemble. In the pocket of the backpack, I found my gold ring and slipped it onto my fourth finger on my left hand, then walked over to the Jacaranda tree and waited for Tobi.

I lifted my eyes to the tree canopy, and at all the colours above. The fresh, new season leaves glowed light green with the full moon. Spectacular.

'Are you warm enough?' Tobi said. He was behind me. How could he move so quietly?

'I will be.' I brushed my hand down his arm, then ascended the tree, and stopped at the branch where I knew he kept his book of unfinished stories. He sat beside me sooner than I expected. I reached over and grabbed the book and gave it to him.

'Thanks,' he said, his eyes trained on me.

'What?'

He looked down and shook his head. 'Nothing.' He started to turn pages of his book.

'You can't look at me like that and say, nothing!'

He looked back up at me. 'You just … make me … happy.'

'A good dose of endorphins will do that to you.' My lips curled into a slow, knowing smile. 'Hey … have … you ever been in love before?' I wasn't sure I wanted to hear his answer. But I needed to know where I stood in his history of women, and whether I would be loved less than any of the others.

'Why do you ask?'

'Just wondering how many girlfriends are written on your heart?' I held my breath in anticipation of his answer.

'I've had a few. None written on my heart, as you say. But I did fall in love when I was twelve. You?'

I released my breath. 'I've had a few boyfriends here and there. Nothing serious. Short lived. Ended badly. Definitely infatuation. And so you know, I've never moon dipped with them, nor been naked with them at any stage.'

Tobi looked down, his cheeks dimpled and the corner of his eyes wrinkled, then vanished. He looked back up at me. 'Does that mean you trust me?'

I blinked, and waited a beat before I answered. 'Yes.'

'Thank you, and granted,' he said, and reached over for my hand and threaded his fingers through mine.

I looked up at the moon, my eyes teary, wondering who he fell in love with and ... was he still in love with her. 'Your wish?' I asked.

'My wish?' he said.

'Yes. You said granted.'

He smiled. 'Yes. My wish was granted. Are you okay?'

'Sure … let's get started with the unfinished story.' I hid the tear that fell down the left side of my face. *He was already in love with somebody else?*

He gave me a nod. 'Close your eyes, and give the story life, with your mind, then speak it with words. Are you ready?' His voice fell into a tone and rhythm that felt slower, intimate, and my heart melted. I waited with great expectation for him to begin. And it did, without disappointment. 'Once upon a time, there was a young woman who was a collector. She looked around at her room of extraordinary things, and her eyes settled on the bucket full of stars.'

A vision entered my mind. I was in the room of extraordinary things. A thrill of creative imagination filled me, then fear of what would come to be. Stories were like that. They had a habit of telling themselves.

I took a calming breath.

> 'Once upon a time, there was a young woman … who was a collector. She looked around at her room of extraordinary things, and her eyes settled on the bucket full of stars. But the stars couldn't shine, being locked in the darkness of the bucket. Mabel squinted. She looked at the jar of hearts,

and then to the maze of memories, the letters of love lost, and the bottle of childhood tears.

She held her hand over her heart. Reversing her collections of extraordinary things was going to be difficult. But she had to do it. She had searched for these things all her life, ever since her search of everything began. A tear fell from her eye. She had searched for *everything* … and found *nothing*.

Mabel bent over and picked up the bucket full of stars, pressing her hand to her back as she lifted it. Then she stepped out into the misty twilight, wishing the bucket of stars would light her way. But how could they, locked away in the darkness?

She walked until her feet ached, then stopped at the edge of the cliff above the stormy ocean, protesting its anger against the rocks.

Mabel sat and waited. There was only one way to reverse her collection of stars, and that was to return them to their rightful place. Up there. In the second sky. But it had to be done in the correct order. Patience was pivotal.

She let out an internal cry of despair. Why couldn't her life be filled with love and wonder, instead of intrigue and questions and the never-ending quest of searching for answers?

She looked across the ocean. The sun had almost said goodbye, but not quite. But it wasn't the sunset she was waiting for, it was the blue, full moon, when good deeds will be multiplied.

Mabel reached for the small jar she wore on her necklace. She needed to make sure it was ready for the moonrise, when it sang its song of love for the earth. And it couldn't be a second too early, nor a second too late.

She removed the lid of the jar and stared at the horizon, watching for the last burst of green colour from the setting sun. When she saw it, and witnessed the nanosecond blink of darkness, she allowed a thousand memories of her life of sadness to fill her eyes with stories of rejection and hopelessness.

She held her breath as the moon whispered hello, the blue glow welcoming it to the night. It grew larger, and reflected upside down in her eyes and in her tears—her moon tears. They rolled down her cheek and fell, and she caught them in the jar.

But she had to be careful. She could only catch seven tears—one for loneliness, one for self-harm, one for self-hate, one for negative thoughts, one for anger, one for fear, and one for disappointment.

Her life in seven tears.

When she was done, she placed the cap onto the jar and held it up with the blue moon behind it. Blue tears. Blue moon tears imbued with blue moonbeams.

She took off the necklace, unlocked the bucket of stars, removed the lid and placed the necklace into the bucket.

The stars glowed impossibly brighter, blinding her for a moment.

Then she waited ...

For a sign ...

It would come ...

She just had to be patient ...

Mabel looked across the ocean replaying her life as the night grew darker, as the air grew colder, and until the blue moon was no longer blue. But still, it illuminated the sky reflecting the brilliance of the sun.

And Mabel grew tired.

Tired of the stories.

Tired of the mistakes.

Tired of the negativity.

Tired of the storms in her life.

And maybe, just maybe, if she hadn't overthought all those moments in her life, if she hadn't dwelt on the past, she wouldn't have entered the realm of the depressed that had lodged itself inside of her, not wanting to leave. If only, she had forgiven herself and moved on.

She sighed. The sign would come for her to release each star to freedom, away from the darkness of the bucket where they were not allowed to shine, oppressed and imprisoned.

She just had to be patient.

But patience was not one of her virtues.

It never had been.

Maybe, just maybe she could learn it.

Mabel stilled. The moon vanished, and darkness arrived like someone had blown a dusting of black pigment across the second sky. She searched the heavens to count the stars like she did when she couldn't sleep, which was more often than not.

Mabel's eyes widened in wonder. A shooting star dashed across the night. That was the sign she had been waiting for. She reached inside the bucket of stars, lifted one star out and held it up. It glowed on her hand. She closed her eyes and imagined it back in the heavens in its rightful place, then she blew it with a wish.

And it was gone.

Mabel smiled when she found it in the above, shining brightly and twinkling amongst its family. It was the *returned*. Her chest filled with a radiating, light feeling that made her feel weightless. Where was the heaviness of the darkness?

Mabel took a deep breath, then continued to release the stars until there was just one remaining in the bucket. She looked at it, remembering how she had captured the stars all those years ago. She remembered how happy she was on that fateful day of victories.

Maybe she could keep just one?

And then Mabel remembered how her happiness faded away. She remembered how the energy of keeping the stars locked in the bucket of absolute darkness consumed everything of the stars. There was no beauty from their light. There was no song for the universe. And it left her feeling empty inside, like she too was being consumed by the darkness.

Mabel blinked, releasing a tear.

Returning to the past in her memories only ever ended in sadness.

She reached into the bucket and picked up the very last star. She held it high into the night and adored it for the last time, closed her eyes, and imagined it back in its rightful place in the night sky, then blew it with a wish.

And it was gone.

Mabel smiled. She found it in the heavens, shining brightly and twinkling amongst its family.

Its friends. It was the *returned*. Her chest filled with an impossibly greater, radiating, light feeling, that made her feel like she had been released from capture.

She was free.

Like her stars.

She looked up to the second sky, the night. Her seven stars twinkled.

Mabel felt odd. She put her hand over her heart. Was that happiness she felt?

Mabel stood, confused. How could letting something go, that she had worked so hard for, make her feel happy?

She turned, and started her journey home in the misty night carrying an empty bucket. Her back did not hurt, nor did her feet ache.

Mabel reached the light of her porch and frowned—what if everything is not outside of herself, but inside? What if, she must make a conscious effort to push the darkness away?

Mabel closed her eyes. She decided she liked the feeling of happiness from returning the stars. She felt peaceful. She felt like a different person. A person she could like.

She took one step into her house, then turned to her room of extraordinary things, and walked there with quick steps.

She smiled. What would she reverse next?'

I opened my eyes and stared ahead, exhausted from my story. Then I became aware of Tobi's presence, beside me. I looked at him. He was watching me, his mouth partly open. 'The end,' I said, feeling like I had to fill the uncomfortable silence that sat between us.

Tobi blinked and looked away. He shook his head.

'Did I say something wrong?'

He shook his head again. 'So far from wrong that I am lost for words.' He lifted his chin and looked into my eyes like he was looking into my soul.

My heart raced as my skin burned with anxiety. If he saw inside me, he wouldn't like it. I cleared my throat. 'It's your turn ... to tell your story,' I said to diffuse the moment.

He looked down and shook his head. 'I don't think I can after yours.'

'But, Tobi, my story is always filled with darkness, and yours with light. That's how it goes … *always*.'

Tobi looked upwards, to all the colours above, and frowned.

'It's not just the story, is it?' Dread filled me. Had I given him too much insight, into me. I had well and truly broken my oath about not telling him my innermost thoughts. I had vowed to keep deep and meaningful conversations off the menu. It was too late. I had been revealing myself to him every single time we met.

He looked down. 'No.' He reached for my left hand. 'What's this?' I watched as he traced the ring on my fourth finger on my left hand.

I shrugged. 'It's my reminder.'

'Of what?' His voice was almost a whisper.

'To be careful.'

'Because you are married?' His voice cracked.

I stiffened and looked at him. 'What?'

'I'm worried that you are married and hadn't told me.'

'Would that be a problem?' The words fell out of my mouth before I could stop them. Of course it would be a problem! It would be a problem for me if he was married, or in a relationship. I would never go out with a man who was spoken for.

'Absolutely, yes.'

Relief flooded me, then I shook my head. 'It's not a reminder of that.'

'Then it's a reminder to be careful of what?'

'Love.'

'Love?'

'Yes … love.' I looked up and blinked to stop my tears from spilling down my face and betraying me.

'Why do you have to be careful of love?'

'Because …' I swallowed hard, 'love hurts.' I looked at Tobi.

He looked down and nodded, then shook his head. He turned his face to me. 'If love hurts, there is no love. It's rejection that hurts. It's miscommunication that hurts. It's deception that hurts.' He ran his hand through his hair. 'You never answered my question from earlier.'

'Your question?'

'I need to know … what you feel for me.' Tobi held my eyes in his, not blinking. Waiting. Expectant.

I looked away from him. I wasn't ready for this. I shook my head, my throat tightening. 'I'm chaotic. Messy. Lost, some—'

'Times … I know. Stop avoiding my question.' He brushed his hand over his forehead. 'I want …' He closed his eyes, then opened them again. 'I need … to know how you feel … what you feel … for me. If you—' He paused and looked away, then looked back to me, his eyebrows drawn together with barely controlled emotion, '—if you don't feel the same way as me … we should stop meeting.'

Was he saying he was attracted to me and wanted to keep seeing me? Or, was he saying that, he liked me, but not loved me, and if I felt more than him, we needed to break up because there would be no future for us?

My skin burned. A sob caught in my throat and I pushed it down, hoping it would collide with the feeling of hurt that was rising from my heart. I needed a change of focus from our heavy conversation. 'Did you plant the dandelions?'

'Yes. For you—please answer my quest—'

'I feel …' I released a controlled breath between my lips. I was terrified of telling him how I felt. 'I think …' I breathed deeply, trying to inhale oxygen that felt stolen from me. 'I know …' My heart thumped against my chest. I looked into his eyes. His ocean-blue eyes filled with fear. I blinked. 'I've fallen in love with you.' I held my breath and waited.

He stared at me.

My chin trembled. No reaction from him could only be rejection of my feelings. *Love hurts*. A tear rolled down my cheek. I needed put up my wall of protection before he injured my heart. Logic. Please come. Give him an out. 'But you're in love with someone else. Since you were twelve. You said it earlier. I'm sorry. I need to go.' My words fell out in a panicked rush. My cheeks flushed hot and nausea filled my stomach. I positioned myself to jump from the tree. I had to get away. Quickly. Never to see him again.

Tobi's hand wrapped around my wrist. 'Indigo. Stop.'

I kept my eyes on *Zero*, the ground below. I couldn't let him see me falling apart. Love hurts. For me.

'It's you. I've been in love with you since I was twelve.'

I stilled, then looked at him. A tear skimmed my cheek and fell to *Zero*. 'Me?'

He nodded. 'Yes.'

'After all these years?'

'Yes,' he whispered. 'I love you.'

My right eye blinked, releasing another tear. I frowned. 'Please … let me get down from the tree.'

He frowned, and a look of hurt flickered in his eyes. He nodded. Once. He grabbed the book of unfinished stories and threw it to the ground, then followed it down with quick climbing limbs, jumping the last metre and a half, and disappeared from view.

I descended the tree in a state of numbness. I found my feet on *Zero*, my vision blurred with tears. At the water's edge I could see Tobi's silhouette, his hands behind his head. I walked over to him and stopped, facing him. I placed my hand on his chest, over his heart, and he looked down at me.

'*Within* ... the heart dimension that feels like intoxication.' I whispered his words from when we first stepped onto Jacaranda Island together. I moved my hand upward, behind his neck, and caressed his skin while I kept my eyes connected to his. He frowned before his eyes filled with yearning. 'I love you,' I said.

His hand was on the side of my face then, his lips on mine, hot and hungry. When I sagged against him, he pulled back and dropped his forehead against mine.

I stepped back and held up the ring on my left hand. 'My reminder to be careful, to not go too far.'

He grabbed my hand and pulled me closer again. 'I like your reminder ... for reasons more than you know.'

'Good,' I said. I held out my other hand. 'Give me your pocketknife.'

Tobi frowned.

'Just give it to me, and I need you to turn on the torch on your phone for light.'

'As you wish.' Tobi bowed, walked to his backpack, and returned with the pocketknife.

I took it from him and walked to the Jacaranda tree,

'Are you sure?' he asked. 'I know how much this tree means to you.'

'I'm sure,' I said. 'It's our tree, and Rule Number 6—exclusivity. *Our* Jacaranda tree.' I angled the pocketknife and started shaving bark from the tree trunk before carving our names into it. When I finished, I checked over it, then straightened my back, satisfied with my tree trunk art.

Tobi ran his fingers over it, his lips curling up on one side making a dimple appear on his cheek. He connected his eyes to mine. 'I love you, 'til the end of time,' he whispered, our lips almost touching.

I stepped back from him; my brain scattered. I needed a change of focus. 'I can't leave tonight without hearing your story.'

He ran a finger down the side of my face and I closed my eyes. I needed to move further away from his spell.

'Okay. I'll see what I can do.' He lowered himself to the base of the tree and leaned against it. I joined him, our shoulders touching.

'Close your eyes … and see the story,' he said, then sighed.

I closed my eyes and waited. There was such a long pause, I could have counted to one hundred. But I didn't. I just waited. For him. And then his story began…

> 'Once upon a time, there was a young woman … who was a collector. She looked around at her room of extraordinary things, and her eyes settled on the bucket full of stars. It was empty.
>
> She smiled and placed her hands over her heart, remembering how it made her feel. She turned her gaze to the jar of hearts, the maze of memories, the letters of love lost, and the bottle of childhood tears. She removed her hand from her heart as darkness surrounded her. Threatening. Fighting to stay with her.
>
> Mabel shook her head. Reversing her collections was going to be more difficult than just returning the bucket of stars. But she had to do it. Then perhaps, her search for *everything* would be resolved when she had *nothing*.
>
> A tear fell from her left eye.

She chose the extraordinary thing that would hurt the most.

The jar of hearts.

Broken.

All of them.

All hers.

She picked up the jar and held it over her regenerated heart. It was made of pieces of broken fragments from her old hearts. She had sewn them together with tears, and with carefully planned stitches of introvert qualities to protect herself, and with magical stitches to make her invisible. And finally with stitches of no hope of a happily ever after.

Year after year she worked hard to keep her regenerated heart from getting damaged. She kept everyone away who could ever possibly hurt her feelings. There would be no love for her. She had tried that. And it hurt. Too much.

Mabel sucked in a deep breath to stop the pain inside her from surfacing. If she let the pain out, it would truly be ugly. And dark. Darker than the darkest moonless night, or the darkest and deepest pit.

She ran out the door with the jar of hearts and into the black forest of secrets.

It was better there.

No one could see her.

She sat under the tree with the ugly, gnarled limbs. It reminded her of the monsters from her dreams that chased her. They reminded her of pain. Growing. Twisting. Repelling.

It was a visual reminder of the ugliness of

rejection.

She wondered what to do with the jar of hearts. Then decided to pray, because she knew a prayer was better than a wish.

She closed her eyes and lowered her head. She didn't pray the words with her voice, because the power of it scared her. It would make it real then. Too real. But her tears fell as she prayed in silence, and the story was told by them.

Mabel opened the jar of hearts. Her hand hovered over the top of it. Was she brave enough to confront her jar of the past? Her jar of unbearable pain?

Mabel squeezed her eyes shut. She needed courage. Confronting her past and her fears was the only way to heal. So she plunged her hand into the jar with a boldness she didn't know she possessed.

She pushed her hand deeper, her fingers curling around Heart Number One.

She pulled it out, feeling a thread of own her regenerated heart break. Her breath stuttered. What was she doing? She looked at Broken Heart Number One.

Dear Broken Heart Number One.

An image appeared before her.

It was her first love.

Mabel's throat became tight and she stopped breathing. It was her mother. And then a little girl appeared beside her mother. It was her.

There were two stories. The one she had lived. Feeling unloved and unworthy.

Why was she never good enough?

Then her story faded, and her mother's story

appeared. Her beautiful mother.

Mabel gasped. She never realised what her mother was going through. And for the first time in her life, she understood.

Her mother had tried so hard. If she had known how she affected her, her mother would have changed their story together. A new narrative. *Of love. Of happiness.*

"Forgive me, sweet Mabel?" her mother asked.

Mabel's tears fell onto the heart as she nodded, and at once, Broken Heart Number One crumbled, and fell through her fingers, as dust is to dust.

Mabel rested her head against the trunk of the ugly gnarled tree. She took a deep breath. She must keep going before she lost her courage.

She pushed her hand into the jar, her fingers curling around Heart Number Two.

She pulled it out, feeling another thread of her own regenerated heart break. Her breath stuttered. *Dear Broken Heart Number Two.*

An image appeared before her. She was at school. There were a group of children, laughing. She smiled, excited to see what was so funny, and made her way through the crowd. She frowned. There was a girl, huddled close to the ground. Her cheeks were streaked with tears, her knees bleeding. 'Loser … Loser … Loser!' they yelled. Unrelentless. And it most certainly was not funny.

Mabel looked into her eyes. They were filled with shame. She looked like an animal that had been beaten. Mabel stepped through the crowd to shield the girl. 'Stop it! Stop it!' she yelled.

And then a teacher appeared. The children

dispersed like dogs with their tails between their legs.

Cowards.

The teacher patted Mabel on the back before she stepped past her to help the girl.

That should have been the end of the story. Mabel was a hero. She had stood up for someone.

But it wasn't the end of the story. The other kids turned on her. Social bullying. Exclusion. She was too nice. Too kind. Too giving. Too understanding. She was different. She didn't follow the pack. She didn't like the things they liked ...

Once, she believed everyone was lovely. Kind. Until they weren't. It was then, that her own heart broke.

Mabel looked at herself in the story. Then she looked at the bullies. She realised they were broken before she was. They just lashed out to make themselves feel better. Pushing others away was the only way they knew, hurting themselves first so they couldn't be hurt back.

Protecting their hearts.

Mabel was filled with compassion. She knew how they felt. She squeezed her eyes shut with a cry of despair. The pain in her heart felt so real.

'I forgive you,' she whispered, and Broken Heart Number Two crumbled, and fell through her fingers, as dust is to dust.

She plunged her hand into the jar, her fingers curling around Broken Heart Number Three, bobbing above the others. She pulled it out, feeling yet another thread of her own regenerated heart break. Her breath stuttered. Keep going, she encouraged herself.

Dear Broken Heart Number Three.

An image appeared before her. Her breath caught before a tear fell from her eye. It was her first boyfriend. He was so … beautiful. Kind. Nice. He was the earth and sea and the heavens. He was *the one*. The only one she would ever love. She did everything for him, losing her identity along the way. However high he asked her to jump, she did it. But it wasn't enough.

She wasn't enough.

And he left her, ending their relationship in a heartless, faceless text. The vision of him became impossibly tall, while Mabel became a miniature version of herself.

Mabel breathed faster as an ache entered her regenerated heart. She counted to ten to slow her breathing rate, then she looked at him again, this time seeing him clearly for who he really was.

He used people. He lied. He gaslighted.

The vision of him began to shrink until he was smaller than her. She shook her head, then realised he had taught her three things.

Boundaries. Balance of relationships. Truth.

She now had an acute radar for men who were not real men. Mabel smiled.

'Thank you,' she whispered, and Broken Heart Number Three crumbled, and fell through her fingers, as dust is to dust.

Mabel rested her head against the trunk of the ugly gnarled tree. Her regenerated heart was starting to feel stronger. She must keep going.

Mabel pushed her hand into the jar. The last

heart. It was bigger than the rest. Her fingers struggled to curl around it, but she pulled it out, feeling another thread of her own regenerated heart break. She held her breath this time, to stop it from stuttering. She lifted the heart and turned it around.

It was heavy. Complicated.

Dear Broken Heart Number Four.

An image appeared before her. And then another and another and another. It was people, everywhere. They all had one thing in common.

They were fake. Mabel detested fakeness.

They were mean. Mabel detested meanness.

And then she saw their lives, before they became fake and mean. They were protecting their hearts. They didn't want to get hurt any more than they already had been. They just wanted to be liked, and accepted.

Mabel knew how getting hurt felt, and she understood them. It didn't make things right, but she forgave them. She was reminded that people are not perfect. They make mistakes. All the time. Every action had a reaction.

'I understand,' Mabel whispered.

Broken Heart Number Four crumbled, and fell through her fingers, as dust is to dust.

Mabel rested her head against the trunk of the tree. She closed her eyes and let two tears trickle all the way down her cheeks.

Every story has two sides. And between them is good communication, or broken communication. And deep within the stories, people are protecting themselves, wanting to be accepted.

Wanting to be liked.

Wanted to fit in.

A sharp pain echoed in Mabel's chest. She sucked in a deep breath, opened her eyes and placed her hand over her regenerated heart.

Her eyes widened.

Her heart was still.

There was no beat.

There was no pumping of oxygenated blood around her body.

This was the end, of her life.

Opening the jar of hearts was too much for her.

So it shall be, she thought.

She had found peace amongst the pain and brokenness. She had lost herself, but she had found herself. She had forgiven herself. She had forgiven others. And she was good enough.

Mabel ... *was good enough*.

Mabel closed her eyes, and surrendered.'

There was silence.

My heart accelerated. That couldn't be the end of the story. Tobi's stories always ended with a happily ever after. I opened my eyes and looked at him. His eyes were closed, his head tilted to the left side. After a moment, his shoulders relaxed. Was he in pain?

I blinked and a tear fell. His story was filled with darkness. More so than mine. I felt his finger brush over my skin, wiping my tear. And then his voice floated around me, pulling me back into the story:

'Her breath stuttered. She gasped and opened her eyes. The black forest of secrets was no longer black. She was surrounded by vibrant greens and flowers beaming with colour.

She looked up at the ugly, gnarled tree. It was no more. Standing in its place was a healthy oak tree, it's life-force beating in tune to Earth's heartbeat. And it was teaming with wildlife.

Her heart gave a thump. She pressed her hand to her chest. And there was a strong beat. Confident. Not the scared heart she had stitched together.

A blue bird landed beside her, wagged its tail and cheeped. Mabel smiled, then her breath caught. Beside the bird was her colourless, regenerated heart, the stitches popped, revealing the scars and the cracks.

And between all the cracks, light shined through. Brightly.

Mabel picked it up. 'My answered prayer.' She looked up toward the heavens. 'Thank you.'

Her hand tingled and she cast her eyes back to her regenerated heart. It glowed once, twice, thrice, then disappeared.

Mabel picked up the empty jar of hearts and stood. She smiled, and started her journey home through the living forest of hope.

She reached the porch of her home and stilled.

What if everything is not *outside* of herself, but *inside* of herself?

What if I get to choose what happens to me, even after something bad has happened?

It was making more sense. How I react to a situation determines the path I take.

Her eyes widened. She could choose to change her path at any time.

> Mabel smiled.
>
> She decided she liked the feeling of happiness from returning the stars, and the feeling of peace from seeing someone else's point of view, and knowing it wasn't always about her.
>
> Somehow, she felt … content.
>
> She felt like a different person.
>
> A person she could like.
>
> She took one step into her house, then turned to her room of extraordinary things, and walked there with quick steps.
>
> She smiled. What would she reverse next?'

A finger traced my lips. I kept my eyes closed enjoying the warmth that filled me. And then his lips were on mine, soft and gentle. He pulled away. 'We have to go.' He shrugged. 'Work.'

I sat up and sighed.

'I agree,' he said, standing and proffering his hand. I placed my hand in his and waited for the extra lift he would give as he pulled me off the ground. 'See you at the boat in two minutes.'

I nodded, collected my backpack, and waited in the rowboat for him, watching his every move—his posture, his footfall, his self-confidence. I wondered what his job was. I was beginning to see a pattern. Whenever he would close his eyes and turn his head for a moment, he would have to return to work. Yet, he never looked at his phone or his watch. He had no pager. What was going on?

He jogged along the short jetty and lowered himself into the boat like he had done it a million times. He released the rope and pushed us away from the jetty, leaned forward and held on to the oars and began to row.

'Your story … I was worried it would end when Mabel died,' I said.

Tobi's lips quirked up in a small smile. 'And then I continued to a happily ever after for you.'

I nodded. 'Next time when you tell your story, can you go with your own storyline instead of stealing one of mine?'

He raised his eyebrows at me. 'Stealing your storyline? That's not how it works, Indi. The story tells itself.'

'But lately … yours seem to—'

'No psychoanalysis, remember?'

I rolled my eyes.

Tobi gave me a crooked smile. 'That's a first.'

I frowned at him.

'The eye roll,' he said.

'It's such an outlet. You should try it.' I raised an eyebrow at him.

He lifted his chin and looked down at me. 'Indigo Feather Danube.'

'Right a little,' I said. The shoreline was getting closer. 'Have you ever studied psychology?'

He narrowed his eyes at me but didn't answer. He pressed his lips together, and after a beat said, 'Yes. And no.'

'Well, that's clear.'

'Have you?'

'Yes. And no.'

The boat stopped at the shallows. Tobi threw his backpack onto the pebbles, got out of the boat then came to me and lifted me out. He carried me to the shoreline, placing me down with the gentleness of a male ballet dancer. He pulled the boat up onto higher ground and then stood before me, seeming to slow time down. He looked at his watch, which I also focussed on, trying to ascertain how high tech it was. It was nothing out of the ordinary for a guy like him.

'Thanks for everything, today.'

'Everything?' I said. *What could everything possibly mean?*

He gave me a lazy smile. 'I can only have sweet dreams from today.'

'Oh, really?' I said, smiling at him.

His lips were close to mine. 'Most definitely,' he said. 'And Rule Number 10 is now unsealed: There are no rules when the declaration comes.'

'The declaration?'

'Of love,' he said, lingering on the "v".

'Hmmm … no rules? I disagree. There are four rules I want to keep. For us.'

He bounced on his toes. 'We'll talk … later. I need to go.' He turned and started to run, but then came back. 'I love you,' he said, then left.

I didn't want to forget … ever—

My phone lit up pulling me out of my memory. A text:

On the path at the place of fireflies.
100 steps. Midnight.

Me: **See you then**

I looked out the window. The deed of forgetting that must be done was getting closer.

A tear slipped down my face.

Chapter 27

'Your obsessive movement is unsettling,' I said, as he paced to and fro, the sound of crackling dry leaves being crushed underfoot. I pulled the black hood off my head and a bluebird chirped. Twice.

He stepped onto the path, took his hands from his pockets and placed them behind his neck, then winced. 'You're late.'

'I'm twenty-five steps late. At one hundred steps, like instructed, I was here at midnight.'

'When you remove my memories,' he paused as hurt crossed over his face, 'what if I meet you again for the first time, and … I don't like you?'

I let out a silent shuddering breath. That thought had crossed my mind, too. I lifted my hand to see if any fireflies would land on me to stop the sting of his verbalised fear. 'That's why we need to create a new memory of us that will be triggered when we see each other for the first time … that memory will not be deleted.' I looked up into his eyes, dark in this bioluminescent light.

He reached out and pulled me against him, then placed his

forehead on my shoulder. 'What we're going to do … it scares me,' he whispered.

'It'll be alright. The research subjects who have done this have had their lives are turned around. It's a resounding success. Remember, it's a snippet of time in your life. You won't feel any different.'

He stepped away from me and frowned, and placed his hand over his chest. 'Except for here. Our love will be deleted. Like it was nothing.'

It felt like I took a knife to my heart. His words saying that our love was like it was nothing, hurt. Deeply. I shook my head. 'We'll start again. We'll feel it again.' I stepped forward and ran my thumb over his lower lip. Our eyes connected deeply, in a song of soul love.

He kissed my thumb. 'I want our new memory to be of us—'

'Doing what?' I said.

He ran a hand through his hair, 'You know what I want to do.' He arched an eyebrow.

'It has to be something that injects a large dose of adrenalin, to create a strong emotional bond between us. It needs to be unforgettable. Unbreakable.'

'Then it most definitely has to be me making lo—'

I raised my eyebrow at him. 'No.' I paused. 'That will be in our new life together. It needs to be a different type of adrenaline—one involving fear, and then the enjoyable resolving of the fear.'

He smiled crookedly and looked down.

'The Kingdom Adventure Park,' I said. *Like I had been planning in the letter I was trying to write*. 'On that roller coaster that terrifies.'

He blinked numerous times then rubbed the back of his neck. 'So … this is really happening.'

'Only if you want to begin again. Only if you *choose* to forget. But I need you to say the words.'

He turned his head and cussed under his breath, then looked at me. 'I can't … yet.'

I let out a sharp breath. 'Let me know when you can.'

I pulled the black hood over my head, turned, and started the walk of one hundred and twenty-five steps out of the forest, in the nightdom that should have cast no shadows where secrets could hide. Except, it wasn't dark. This is where the fireflies danced and blinked, bioluminescent, lighting up the forest like an enchanted fairy tale. A place where no secret could hide.

Chapter 28

2 AM. The ceiling was where my eyes rested. Wide awake. Lost in the past. Lost in memories. Lost in Tobi. *Tobiah Lucas Brooks*. Standing next to the blue rowboat on the white pebbled shoreline at the park of our childhood—

'By the light of the full moon,' he said. A heated look swarmed in his ocean-blue eyes, his voice deep and rich in its tones. He stood tall with his hands behind his back, his broad shoulders and pectoral muscles accentuated through his dark blue T-shirt.

'Rule Number 1,' I whispered, my body filled with his love potion. The moon, impossibly large, had just entered the nightdom and was behind him, stealing all the colours above. I took a step closer to Tobi, put my hand on his chest and lifted my lips to his where I lingered, basking in the sensation of euphoria that washed over me.

Tobi pulled away and I held my breath. I wanted to stay inside his intoxicating world where nothing else mattered, where nothing else existed, except us … and love.

I opened my eyes and looked into his. He bent down and lifted me into the boat, placing me carefully, holding my hand until I found my balance. I sat, still high from our kiss and watched as Tobi pushed the boat off the shore and jumped aboard. He leaned forward to take control of the oars, and looked beyond *Zero*, to the lake full of dark blue at this hour, reflecting the full moon as we picked up pace.

His gaze settled on me. He shook his head slowly. 'You have no idea how much I look forward to this every month.'

'Maybe I do?' I said, and inhaled deeply to control my urge to hurdle the seat between us and lather him in sublime love.

He gave a lazy smile. 'Sometimes … I want to control time—speed it up when we are apart, then slow it down when I am with you.'

'But then … would time move too quickly, making us grow older, faster?'

He looked up at the moon, mirrored perfectly in his ocean-blue eyes. 'I think … that fast time, followed by slow time, would cancel each other out, so it would be the same.'

'Tobi, the keeper of time. The controller of time. Just for us,' I said.

'Imagine if I could?'

'Left a little,' I said.

Tobi kept the left oar in the water to turn the boat, then started to row again. 'Perhaps, if we spend more time together, time will go slower, and we will stay young, for longer.'

'Perhaps … but when you slow time down, would we move in slow motion?'

Tobi smirked. 'Perhaps.'

I placed my fingers in the water and left them there, dragging through the surface, cutting into the mirror, made of water. It was oddly satisfying.

'Left a little more, and glide,' I said. I retracted my hand from the water and looked at Tobi.

He held my gaze and stopped rowing. The boat glided in the quietness filled with expectation. My expectation. 'Now,' I said.

Tobi reached out to his left and stopped the boat against the jetty. With his right hand he grabbed the rope and secured the boat. He leaned forward and grabbed our back packs and hauled them onto the jetty, then offered his hand to me, pulling me from the rowboat with gentleness.

I stood close to him, our hands still connected like they were locked together for a lifetime, his steady gaze lingering on my eyes then wandering to my lips.

I released my hand from his as I looked over his shoulder at the Jacaranda tree, a glint catching my eyes. There, hanging from the lower branches were stars, and coloured miniature lanterns.

'You broke Rule Number 4 again,' I said.

'Because of Rule Number 8.' His voice was tender.

I walked to the Jacaranda tree and lifted my hand to a star and ran a finger over it. It was made of wood, painted white, decorated with hearts. 'I feel like you've put a spell on me and I'm living inside a fairy tale.'

He traced his fingers along my arm up to my fingers. 'Not a spell, but I want to give you the fairy tale … if you'll allow me to.'

I took a deep breath. He was intoxicating. 'I can't.'

'Trust me,' he whispered.

'I can't when you are keeping a secret from me.'

'As you are from me. But you are more important to me than your job.' He stood closer, the warmth of his body touching mine, his scent of sweetness and spice encircling me, waiting to enter. 'Did you bring the stuff I asked you to?' he whispered against my neck.

A change of direction.

A distraction from the issue.

He was good at that.

I turned to face him, and connected my eyes to his. 'Yes. Did you?'

He nodded, took my hand and led me to the deck. He pulled me down beside him before he reached into his backpack and pulled out a metal container the size of a shoe box. He sat it in front of us, then pushed his hand into his backpack again, and pulled out a parcel wrapped in brown paper, tied with string.

I took his lead and opened my own backpack, removing my collection, according to his only text in the past moon cycle. I shuffled my stuff, keeping them in order and tidying them so they didn't look so misshapen. Chaotic. Like my life.

I watched as he untied his parcel, folding the brown paper neatly, then rolled the string around his little finger so if formed a perfect circle, and placed it on top of the paper. He picked up the first item and help it up. 'A picture of me. Do you have a picture of you?'

I added my photo on top of his in the metal box.

'Something you'll never do,' he said.

I placed a picture of a tattoo into the box, while he placed an image of a broken heart.

My breath caught. 'Yours or mine,' I said.

He looked up at me. 'Yours.'

I wanted to cry. But I didn't.

'Something you hate,' he said.

I added a piece of torn paper with the word "trauma" on it. Tobi added a picture of a gun.

'A first that is etched into your memory that you never want to forget,' he said.

I lifted my next piece of paper and read it in silence—*making a baby with my husband*—I smiled and placed it on top of the other collections. I watched Tobi as he read it. He swallowed. Hard.

'It's in the future,' I added.

He looked up at me and raised an eyebrow. 'I was worried that you were married, again … for a moment.'

'If I was, I wouldn't be here with you,' I said. 'Add your first.'

He looked at his paper, closed his eyes and smiled coyly, then placed it on top of mine—*swimming naked under the full moon.*

I took a deep breath.

'Something funny,' he said.

I added a picture of the flat earth. He added people stumbling while ice skating.

'Something that scares you.'

I pushed my next paper into the box. *Loneliness.* That scared me more than love.

Tobi added a typed piece of paper—*not being able to remember. Forgetting.*

I took a deep breath. He just described my research; helping people to not remember. To forget.

'Your wish,' he said.

I opened my wish-square. My handwriting. In ocean blue like his eyes. *I wish for Tobi to be blissfully happy, even if it is without me.* I folded my wish-square, hiding my words, hiding my emotion that threatened to undo me, and placed it into the box. Tobi unfolded his wish, looked at it, and refolded it before placing it on top of mine.

'Something you love,' I said, my voice gentle. I placed a piece of paper with his name written on it into the box, then added a sprinkling of miniature red hearts.

He added a photo of me with a heart drawn over it. I frowned. Where did he get that photo from? It was recent. On the mainland, where we never meet …

Tobi looked up at me. 'Ready?'

'Not yet. We need to add our list of our rules.' I placed the last piece of paper into the box.

Rule 1 - By the light of the full moon, when dark shadows become a whisper of themselves, is when we can meet.
Rule 2 - On the nightdom of the full moon, when dark shadows become a whisper of themselves, the Jacaranda Tree must be climbed.
Rule 3 - Only one boat allowed on the island at time.
Rule 4 - You cannot be on the island by yourself.
Rule 5 - Whilst on Jacaranda Island, the tree must be climbed, no matter the weather.
Rule 6 - Indigo and Tobiah on the island only. Exclusivity.
Rule 7 - The secrets of us on Jacaranda Island must never be spoken of on the mainland.
Rule 8 - You may only break Rule Number 4, to add an element of surprise for the significant other.
Rule 9 - When on Jacaranda Island, the Book of Beginnings must be read.
Rule 10 - There are no rules when the declaration comes.

'Now I'm ready.'

Tobi closed the box, picked up the brown paper and string, stood and went to the Jacaranda tree.

I followed.

He gave the paper and string to me, reached up and pulled a purple bloom from the tree, opened the box and added it. Then he reached forward and pulled a strand of my hair, then his, and placed them into the collection. He closed the box and handed it to me. 'Wrap it in the paper and string.'

As I fussed with the wrapping, he dug into the soil. When he finished, I passed the wrapped box to him and he placed it into the ground and covered it up. I looked up and found a branch in direct alignment with its placement, and made a mental note of it.

'The story of us. Done,' he said.

'But not finished,' I added.

'To be continued.' His voice was warm like a delicious hot chocolate in the Winterdom, and his gaze connected with mine filled with desire. He leaned in, his lips almost upon mine, but then he moved away, his brows furrowed, tearing his addictive energy from me.

My heart dropped.

Disappointed, I looked away from him and at the full, luminous moon, only to be mesmerised by its beauty. I walked to the edge of the water in a futile attempt to get closer to it. I sat on the shoreline, moved by the magic of the celestial body, then reclined onto my back to be swallowed in the moment, burning the image of the full moon into my memory bank. Never to be forgotten.

'Beautiful,' Tobi whispered. He was beside me, his arm touching mine, creating that spark of attraction before he connected his fingers to mine increasing the current.

'The *Way Above and Beyond*,' I said. 'It makes me feel so … insignificant. I wish I could go there to be filled with the fear of not getting enough oxygen to live, and look back on the earth so that I never take what we have here for granted. Ever. The moon is so … simple, yet breathtaking. Like the Earth's keeper. A lifeless watcher. A reminder, that this is what we will become if we don't be careful. Dead.' I released my hand from his and rolled onto my side and put my head on Tobi's chest.

He folded his arm around me and pulled me closer.

'Humbling.' His soft lips were warm against my forehead. 'You may feel insignificant, yet you hold a great deal of power. Through words. Through actions. Through being. Through love. Through hate. We have something the moon can never have.'

I looked up at him, my brows drawn together.

'It can never feel what we feel. The *Way Above and Beyond* is just a witness. Would you rather be the moon adored by all, without a heartbeat, feeling nothing, or a person adored by one, heartbeats connected, lost in love, being loved and feeling the full spectrum of emotions, of depth, transcending time and space?'

I traced my finger over his chest as I contemplated his words. 'Tobiah, do you think my heart-song is in harmony with yours?'

'I want to say yes. I want to say that our heart stories are aligned, connected, never to part. Is it about me, or you, or us? All I know is, when I see you, when you are close, when I look into your eyes, when we kiss ... there is no other place I would rather be. And when we part, I crave for the moment I see you again. Is that my heart-song yearning for yours?'

I traced my finger over his abs and down to his belly button and a little lower.

I felt his chest rise, slowly, with a deep breath, then he put his hand over mine. 'You need to stop, or we will conceive a baby like you were, Indigo Feather Danube.'

A slow smile blossomed over my face. 'Hmmm … created under the Chaste tree, twenty-five years ago.' I looked up at all the colours above, the magnificent purples of the Jacaranda tree glowing under the magic of the full moon. 'We could … under the Jacaranda tree … where the realm of purple blends with the heavens, our joining creating the spark of light as new life is ignited.' I looked at Tobiah. 'You wish,' I whispered.

'Not I wish. I want. With you.' His lips brushed my lower lip and I felt the tender caress of his tongue. And I was falling. Sinking deeper into his kiss until everything around me became nothing and my body surged with warmth. He pulled me on top of him and ran his hands along my body igniting me. I sat up. Before it was too late. Before I lost myself in him at the point of no return.

I connected my eyes to his, inhaled a steadying breath and

crossed my arms over my body, reaching for the hem of my dress, then lifted it up, and off, discarding it on the ground beside us. I watched Tobiah as his eyes focussed intently on my face. He was such a gentleman.

'The water is calling.' I stood, turned and entered the water, closing my eyes as I submerged, letting the coolness of the water douse my flame of desire.

I opened my eyes and turned to Tobi. Sitting up, he ran a hand over his face. 'Are you joining me?' I called.

He shook his head.

Disappointed, but not surprised, I turned to face the moon. He was right. I would rather be a person, being loved, feeling love and the full spectrum of all that it encompasses. Tobi made me feel more alive than I had ever felt. Love. Lust. One or the other, or both …

The sound of splashing water came from behind me. I turned to see Tobi stepping into the water, his clothes discarded on the ground next to mine. I smiled and turned back to the moon.

Within the next heartbeat he was behind me, close, his arm pulling me against him, his hand splayed over my stomach. I placed my hand over his to stop him from possibly exploring. It was my body. I wasn't ready to give it to him, yet.

I tilted my head to the side as his warm lips caressed my neck. I breathed out the addictive feeling before I gave in to it, then turned to face him.

His dark eyes settled on mine. 'Do you know how long I have waited for you?' His voice was low.

I shook my head and ran my fingers through the ends of his hair, the longest I had seen it since we were young. 'Rugged,' I said. 'Just like "BookBoy".'

'I loved you then,' he said. 'And I've never stopped.' His unmistakable look of yearning awoke a desire within me. His lips were on mine, once, twice, caressing, in a lingering kiss. I glowed from the inside and forgot where I was, sinking further into him, like we were one.

Breathless, I broke from his kiss, then put my hands onto his chest and pushed him away with a gentleness. I gazed into his eyes, locked in a state of euphoria I never wanted to leave. 'I think I love you too much.' My voice cracked. I didn't want it to. But it did.

Tobi pulled me towards him again and folded his arms around me. I closed my eyes, bathing in the sensation of our naked bodies touching. I ran my fingernails over his back and he released his arms from around me.

'I'm heading back to *Zero*,' he said.

'Did I do something wrong?'

'No. It's me.'

I smiled. 'Ah … so not under the Jacaranda tree where the realm of purple blends with the heavens, but in the water of darkness, touched by the reflection of the magical moon—a moon baby instead of a tree baby.' I splashed water at him. 'I wouldn't let you anyway. The joining of my body with another is a gift for my husband only. It's sacred.'

Tobi ran a hand through his hair and moved closer. His lips touched mine in a gentleness that hurt my heart. 'I want to be your one and only,' he whispered, then backed away, turned, and walked out of the water. I watched as he clothed his athletic physique, wandered to the Jacaranda tree and sat beneath it, leaned his head back against the trunk, bent one knee, and closed his eyes, exactly like "BookBoy".

I left the water, dressed and made my way to the tree and sat beside him. 'You okay?'

He opened his eyes. 'Never better.'

'Are you sure? It doesn't look that way.'

'I'm just consolidating my memories of tonight. Never to be forgotten.'

I took his hand in mine. 'You won't forget. What is embedded in emotion, the senses and words, stays for a lifetime.' I wanted to add unless you have your memories deleted. But didn't. I lifted my face upward towards the limbs of the Jacaranda tree, to all the colours above, the blooms glowing in the moonlight. 'Rule Number 2,' I said, and stood. 'See you at *Above*.' I secured my hands and footing and ascended the tree, settling on our branch.

Within moments, Tobi was beside me. 'Rule Number 9,' he said, and pulled the book of unfinished stories out from under his shirt. 'Are you ready?'

I nodded.

He opened the book to the dog-eared page and looked at me. 'Close your eyes, and give the story life with your mind, then speak it with words.' His voice fell into a tone and cadence that felt intimate, and my heart melted. I waited with great expectation for him to begin. And it did, without disappointment. 'Once upon a time, their eyes locked.'

A vision entered my mind. I was in a room. White. Everywhere. And a man was standing before me.

I took a calming breath before I spoke the story.

> 'Once upon a time, their eyes locked. She blinked, a tear falling as glanced around him, looking for an escape. She knew those eyes. Dark, filled with hate. They had visited her in dreams, filling her with fear. Relentlessly. The fact that they had now locked eyes outside of her dream realm could only mean one thing. Her time had come.
>
> He was taller than she thought he would be. She looked into his eyes again. Once, they were filled with nothing but kindness. Until she made a monumental discovery in her research. One, that she had told to only one other.

The voice came.

Deep and penetrating.

Threatening. 'You know too much. Your discovery will put many good men in jail.' He rose on his toes, pulled his right arm back with a clenched fist, then moved forward and punched her face, the impact making her stumble on her feet.

She hunched over, holding in her scream, and placed her hand over her cheek, feeling her eye starting to swell, while the warm trickle of blood ran down her face. As anger filled her, she stood tall, pulled her shoulders back and lifted her chin in defiance.

He reached forward, placed his hand under her chin and lifted her face higher to his. 'Look what you made me do.'

'I didn't make you do anything! You chose this, you coward!'

He burst out laughing, then pointed to a man standing at a doorway.

She turned her face in the direction of his crooked finger.

There stood the man she loved.

The only one she had ever loved.

The only one she had ever trusted.

She faltered and gasped. 'It was you?' Her eyesight blurred, obscured by tears. 'YOU ... betrayed me?'

I wanted to cry, my body tensing with each breath, building up to release.

I felt a hand on my shoulder. 'Indigo ... Indigo ... pull

yourself out of your story … Indi—'

I frowned and started to shake my head, and then I was falling. From the Jacaranda tree. *My* beloved Jacaranda tree. I wanted to open my eyes, but it was better with them closed. I would have no memory of the descent in free fall and whatever position my body was in.

I hit the ground. Hard. My eyes popped open and I gasped for air, failing to fill my lungs with the vital oxygen it needed to survive. My skin burned with anxiety, my heart thumping in my chest. I started to shake.

I heard a moan before I felt a hand touch mine. I looked up. Tobi knelt beside me. 'Slow, deep breaths … ready? In 2, 3, 4, 5 and out 2, 3, 4, 5. In 2, 3, 4, 5 and out 2, 3, 4, 5. That's better. Keep going. You're okay. That's it. Slow, deep breaths.'

I kept my eyes connected to his, mirroring his slow, focussed breathing. A calmness fell over me when I realised I could breathe again. 'I'm sorry,' I whispered. He rubbed his shoulder and moved it about. 'Are you hurt?'

'I'm okay, I think … you?' he said.

I started laughing, and couldn't stop.

'Indi?'

'Do you know how ridiculous this is? We FELL OUT OF THE JACARANDA TREE!' I stilled and looked into Tobi's eyes, then started to cry. 'You could have died.'

'But I didn't. And neither did you.' He frowned at me. 'Do you hurt anywhere?'

I shook my head. 'Nowhere. Everywhere. I can feel everything, so I don't have a spinal injury.' He pulled me up into a sitting position. I took a deep breath to settle myself. 'My back is a little sore, but otherwise … *Above* to *Below* … in one second flat. Gravity sucks. I don't recommend it.'

Tobi laughed. 'Actually, it felt like an hour in slow motion. I still don't recommend it.' He stroked the side of my face. 'I'm sorry. If I didn't try to pull you out of your story, this would never have happened.'

'I need to go back and finish the story.' I wanted to cry.

'No, you don't.'

'I have to. I need to have a happy ending. For me.'

Tobi ran his hand over his face. 'Alright … but let me carry you over to the deck and make you comfortable.'

'Okay,' I whispered, and put my arms around his shoulders, ready for him to lift me. I watched him wince as he stood with me in his arms. He was hurt more than he was letting on. He placed me gently on the deck then fussed about, placing pillows behind me.

'Thanks,' I said.

He nodded, then walked to the water's edge, rubbed his shoulder again and moved his arm around. He ran his hand through his hair, then turned and walked back and sat next to me.

'Do you hurt anywhere?' he asked again.

I shook my head. 'Maybe in a day or two.' Out of the corner of my eye, I saw Tobi close his fist and then stretch out his hand, and close it again. 'Are you okay?'

He nodded. 'For now.' He lifted my hand to his lips and kissed it. 'Now let's finish your story. We can't fall here.' He took a deep breath. 'Close your eyes … Once upon a time, their eyes locked.'

I closed my eyes and inhaled, a little, feeling a slight twinge in my ribs, then let my breath out with caution. I shook my head, trying to climb back into the story, to that moment in time before we fell out of the tree. I continued:

> 'There stood the man she loved. The only one she had ever loved. The only one she had ever trusted. She faltered and gasped. 'It was you?' Her eyesight blurred, obscured by tears. 'YOU betrayed

me?'

He shook his head and took a step backward. 'I had no choice.' His voice cracked.

'Dear, dear Ciaran. We knew your lover would tell us your secrets. That's why we planted him to be with you, to watch you closely. He's been our informant for a while now.' He laughed. 'We can use your discovery for our own purposes. We would like to thank you for your hard work.' He smiled. 'But now, you must be erased.'

His dark eyes filled with hate and anger, and glowed red with rage like in her dreams. He moved his right hand to the inside of his jacket and pulled out a gun and held it up at her.

Unhurried footsteps sounded from behind her, getting louder. The man she loved stopped before her. He kissed her cheek. 'Forgive me for what I am about to do,' he whispered. He turned from her and stood next to the person with the dark eyes and the gun.

They exchanged a glance and a nod.

She paled as her limbs trembled. This was it.

'On the count of three.' The man from her dreams repositioned his gun and closed one eye. 'One …'

She watched as her lover raised his gun from behind.

'Two …'

A loud crack sounded, and blood sprayed Ciaran's face. She jumped, then froze. The man with the dark eyes collapsed to the ground with a thud.

Dead.

She whimpered, wiped the blood from her face, looked at her hands and gasped. The one she loved stepped forward and pulled her into his arms. 'I'm sorry you had to witness that.'

She put her hands on his chest and pushed him away, looking at him with confusion. 'You were using me?' She stepped further back from him, shaking her head, her tears falling to the floor.

'It's my job.'

'To pretend you loved me! How could you do that?'

'I fell in love with you, and you changed me. This was my last mission. And then I'm free.'

'You … killed … a man.' She wrapped her arms around herself.

'I saved your life. I stopped your discovery from getting into the wrong hands. This has ended well for everyone.'

She shook her head, turned and ran.'

I opened my eyes and looked at the moon, higher in the nightdom.

'You don't trust me,' Tobi said, his voice low, depleted of energy.

I looked at him. 'No psychoanalysis … remember. The story tells itself,' I lied. He was right. I loved him, but I didn't trust him … enough. 'Your turn.'

'I … I need to tel—' Tobi stopped speaking, like his words were stolen from his mouth, and then his eyes focussed on his feet. He pressed his lips in a hard line, then clenched his jaw. 'I can't telly my story. Your story isn't finished. You left him standing there after saving her life. His heart is breaking.' He looked at me, his face torn. 'I need to know the end of the story.'

I placed my hand on the side of his face, my heart hurting. 'Okay.'

I closed my eyes, aware of the twinge in my ribs, then continued my story. For Tobi.

> 'She shook her head, turned and ran.
>
> The door slammed behind her before he made his first step to run after her. He knew she was in shock. He knew everything she had just experienced and witnessed would affect her adversely. Traumatically. He even knew it could make her hate him. He despised that thought, but he would overcome her hate with his love. They would be together. It was all that mattered.
>
> As he exited the door and looked outside, he caught a glimpse of her disappearing into the forest. And he ran.
>
> He slowed as he entered the forest, and listened. He could hear her slowing footsteps, her weeping, and then there was nothing. He walked in quietness so his footfalls could not be heard, looking to his left and right for her. She wasn't far. He could smell her perfume. The one that made his heart accelerate. He stopped when he saw her sitting by the stream.
>
> He placed his hand over his heart and went to sit beside her. In silence. He didn't have the words he needed to say but he knew they would come.
>
> After a while, she placed her head on his shoulder. 'Thank you.' Her shoulders shuddered with a sob.
>
> He took a deep breath. 'The mission was complicated. We were tracking you, an organisation,

and the research they were after. Only one thing was certain through the entire operation: your safety. There were others in that room with us. Hidden, using a specific technology unknown to the public. I raised my gun, but I didn't shoot him. You were protected. Always.'

She let out another sob.

'Forgive me, Ciaran.'

Ciaran lifted her head from his shoulder and placed her hand on the side of his face. She wiped his tear away. 'Let's start a new life, somewhere else. New names. No history. Just us.'

His lips were on hers then in a wild passion he found hard to control. Breathless he stood, grabbed her hand and pulled her towards the stream, using the rocks as stepping stones to get to the other side, where they ran through the forest until they found a road and a parked car.

He broke into it, opened the door for Ciaran and closed it, then got in, hot-wired it, and drove off into the sunset, ready for the new chapter of their lives to start with the new day. Together.'

I opened my eyes and looked at Tobi. His eyes were closed, a tear trailing from the corner of his eye. 'The end. A happy ending.' I caught his tear with a curl of my hair. 'With the stealing of a car.'

Tobi's mouth twitched; his eyes still closed.

'You can open your eyes now.'

'I don't want to. I'm replaying the kiss in my mind. I need that happily ever after.' Tobi opened one eye and raised his eyebrow at me. 'Your stories terrify me.'

'No psychoanalysis … remember,' I whispered. I gazed into his eyes.

'My life was so boring before I met you,' he said.

'Likewise,' I said. 'Before I met you, I had never fallen out of a tree.' My lips twitched as I suppressed a smile. I needed him to be happy again. Maybe my stories were too dark for him.

'My bad. I feel terrible about that. I didn't take into consideration the fragility of our balance sitting in the tree. At least I fell too. My just punishment. If we could go back in time, if we could *undo* it, I would change that moment.'

'I wouldn't change a thing,' I whispered.

'Damn it, Indigo! I could've hurt you badly. You may have injuries you don't know about. How could you not change a thing?'

'Because of what I saw in your eyes, what you did for me. It spoke louder than words. I know I can trust you.'

He shook his head. 'I do believe you have rose-coloured glasses on.'

I flashed him a smile. 'Well … you know what they say … love is blind.'

He leaned forward and pressed his lips to mine for a moment in time.

'Tell me your story. It's the rules,' I said when he pulled away.

He nodded. 'Close your eyes and enter the story with me.'

I closed my eyes and waited.

> 'Once upon a time, their eyes locked. Greeny-blue to ocean-blue. He waited forever to be this close to her; to see the detail of colour in her beautiful eyes; to smell the perfume she wore; to see the perfect outline of her lips that he so wanted to kiss.
>
> He moved his weight from one foot to the other to keep his cool. He was falling apart inside and didn't want her to see it. After all, you only

have one chance to make an impression. A good impression. *Step 1*, like he had rehearsed a million times. *Make contact, in person*. He handed her a pink rose, the colour of her lips. 'I do believe we met at another time,' he said.

She smelled the rose and raised an eyebrow at him. 'Great pickup line.' She beamed him a smile that told him she was laughing at him.

He looked down and grinned. 'It was ten years ago, in the school play. You were the lead actress; I was an extra. I handed you a pink rose, just like this one.'

She looked down at the rose before looking back at him. 'You don't look like that person.'

'You remember him?'

'Of course. Every play we did, he said a different line to what he was supposed to say. It took everything I had not to smile or laugh at him. I would go to bed every night after the play and replay that moment, James. You look amazing!'

He lowered his head and smiled, then looked up at her. 'I wanted to say thank you for not embarrassing me about my clumsiness with my line memorisation. It meant a lot to me.'

She smiled and blinked slowly, like a cat exhibiting its affection. 'You know, thinking back, you were possibly the only sane person.' She put her hand on his forearm. 'Come. Have coffee with me. Tell me what you are doing now.'

His eyes widened in surprise. This was going better than he thought it would. He would follow her anywhere. He slowed down. Cool, he had to play it cool. He looked at his watch. *Step 2*, like he had rehearsed a million times. *Get her contact details*. 'I'm sorry. I can't right now. I need to meet my agent. Here's my phone, can you put in your details so we can catch up another time.'

'Your agent?' she said, raising her eyebrows and taking his phone in her hands.

Step 3, like he had rehearsed a million times. *Make yourself look important*.

'Yes. We're negotiating a contract.' He watched as she added her details into his phone, then raised his eyes to her face, the one he loved, his heart accelerating.

She passed his phone back. 'I'd love to hear about it,' she said. 'Call me when it's signed.'

'I will,' he said, gazing into her eyes to make a deeper connection. *Step 4*. The love potion. *Eye contact.* He dipped his head at her, glowing, then turned and left. His *wish* had come true.'

The story had finished. I opened my eyes to see Tobi looking at me with a wide grin. I narrowed my eyes at him. 'So … you have a formula to pick up girls?' My mouth quirked at the corners.

'Only one. But mine went like this—*Step 1*. Find the courage to talk to her. *Step 2*. Follow her dare. *Step 3*. Make myself seem mysterious, somehow. *Step 4*. The love potion eye gaze. And the rest is history.'

My smile disappeared. 'You had to find the courage to talk to me?'

'Yes. It's a nervous thing guys have when they want to talk to someone they like.'

'Oh. So, are you saying that girls determine the fate of a conversation?'

'Absolutely. If the guy likes her.'

I looked up at the moon. 'Tobi, what if … you only have a certain amount of happiness per lifetime … and when you reach your fill, it's downhill from there? And what if … happy people don't contemplate the deeper meaning of life. They just live in the moment and are always happy?'

Tobi placed his finger under my chin and turned my face to his. 'Indi, are you saying you're not happy?'

I shook my head. 'But what *if* … I can't make you happy?'

'Don't,' he whispered, lingering on the "n" and tinkering on the "t".

'But—'

'What if's hold you in a place where you can't move forward. They coat you in crippling anxiety. They chain you to negative thoughts and keep you in a cycle of thinking, but never doing.' His chest rose then fell. 'What *if* … I told you that you can make me happy. What *if*, I told you … you do make me happy.'

I raised an eyebrow at him. 'A negative to a positive. I see what you are doing.'

'What *if* … it's your job that makes you see the world in a bad light?' he said.

I closed my eyes. He was right. It was my job.

'I don't do what if thoughts or conversations.' His voice was curt.

'Never?' I said and looked into his eyes, dripping with sadness.

'Once, but now, never.'

'Really? How can yo—'

He stood, paced back and forth, then stilled. 'What *if* … I hadn't argued with my brother the day he died … what *if* …' Tobi looked away; his face twisted in pain. 'Don't you think I haven't entertained a thousand what ifs and wishes about that day?' He dug his foot into the ground, then turned and walked to the water's edge. He placed his hands behind his head then hunched over like he was in pain.

I stilled, hit by regret and guilt. I had forced him to revisit a place of agony. I cursed under my breath, stood, wincing as my ribs hurt and walked to him, stopping behind him. I placed my arms around him, pressing my body against his, gently. 'I'm sorry,' I whispered.

He placed a hand over mine. 'It's getting late. We'd better get going.'

I released my arms and returned to the deck, refraining from wincing as I walked.

Tobi appeared before me. I hadn't even heard his footfalls. How did he do that? 'Start walking to the boat and I'll pack up and grab our stuff,' he said. He sounded so bossy. So cold … detached.

I placed a hand over my ribs. 'Okay,' I said, and turned to walk to the boat, wincing each time I felt a spasm.

As I tried to lower myself into the boat, Tobi appeared again without a sound. He held out his hand to stabilize me. The backpacks were next, then he removed the rope from the post and sat on the rowing seat. He pushed the boat away from the jetty with his left hand, and I watched as he hesitated before grabbing the oars. It was his right shoulder.

'Text me after you visit the doctor tomorrow,' I said.

'I will. Probably physio though. You should see a doctor.'

'I will. I'm wondering whether I have cracked a rib or two.'

He nodded. 'It's possible. Let me know.'

My stomach wobbled. Why was he being so cold? I took a shallow breath to gather some courage. 'Tobi, I can't wait another month to see you again.'

He lifted his chin and looked down at me. 'I know. Just wait a little longer.'

'A little longer for what?'

'Till we can see each other on the mainland,' he said.

'What are you waiting for?'

He looked over the water, then back to me. 'For something to fall into place.'

'Like a jigsaw puzzle piece?'

'I guess you can look at it that way.'

'What is the piece that is keeping us apart?' I needed him to tell me.

'I can't tell you. You have to trust me.'

'So, we'll meet by the light of the full moon on the last month of Springdom? And the next time will be the first month of Summerdom. I think it will be on Midsummer's Eve …'

'Yes, by the light of the full moon. Or maybe, a little earlier on that day.'

'I wish,' I said.

'Perhaps it will be granted.'

The boat scraped the shoreline, and Tobi climbed out, then stepped beside the boat to lift me and carry me onto the shore. I hid my pain from him. I wished we could go back in time and change the pathway of tonight. I wished we could undo what was done. It felt like we were falling apart. And it hurt my heart—

Rain battered against my window and I turned my head to look at the splatters, a tear falling from my eye matching the speed of the descent of raindrops on the glass.

If only I could go back in time, I would change everything.

If only I could go back in time, I would have stopped myself from falling in love with him.

If only I could go back in time, I would listen to my head, and not my deceitful heart.

And yes, he was right, we did wait for something to fall into place. Out of the tree. A person. And the body was missing.

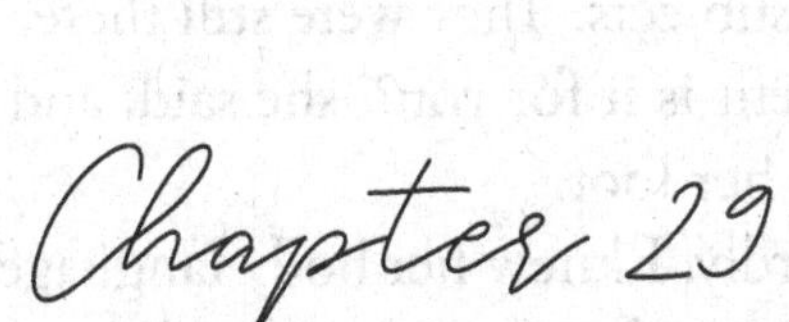

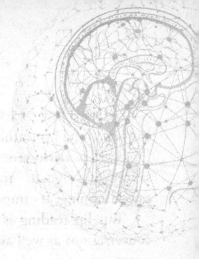

Chapter 29

Scarlett placed a coffee mug in front of me. It was only half-full. I gazed over my newspaper, making sure I couldn't be seen. 'What's that?' I said, frowning, nodding toward the coffee.

'It's a *Rachel*,' Scarlett said, then spelled the name in sign language.

'A *Rachel*?' I said.

'Yes. It will make you feel happy. It will get you out of your Monday-itis.' Scarlett raised her eyebrows at me.

'I am happy,' I mouthed, annoyed by her assessment of my mood.

'Not,' she mouthed back.

I closed my eyes for a moment. 'Okay, what's in it?'

'It's a strong, skinny, extra frothy, and extra hot, cappuccino.'

'It's only half full! Did you drink some?' I said.

Scarlett shook her head. 'That's how a *Rachel* is served.'

'Half price?' I asked.

Scarlett shook her head again. 'What's going on?'

I turned my face to her. 'Hey, I need you to lip read a conversation,' I mouthed.

Scarlett narrowed her eyes and placed her spoon on the saucer. She signed, 'You know I don't like doing that. It's like eavesdropping. It's impolite.'

'But lip reading is such a useful skill. I wish I could read conversations as well as you,' I mouthed, then glimpsed over the newspaper at my subjects. They were still there.

'Of what benefit is it for you?' she said, and folded her arms. She started to tap her foot.

I smiled inwardly. I knew her body language well. The folded arms meant "no", but her "tapping foot" meant, give me some more information. She didn't want to read a conversation for me, but she was interested. If I get my words right, she'll do it.

'Look straight ahead, about five tables away. Who do you see?'

Scarlett grinned. 'It's our Tobi,' she said, 'the one you kept talking about, until you stopped talking about him.'

'And?'

'The woman who works on the fourth floor of Neuroscience, in the office.'

I gasped. 'She works in the same building as we do?'

'Yes. For the last six months, doing office jobs and answering the phone.'

'Seriously?'

Scarlett nodded as she watched them. 'I notice more people than most … a learned skill from being deaf—' Her eyes widened.

'What?' I frowned, then angled the newspaper so I could see them, hiding most of my face. I didn't want Tobi to know I was here.

'She called him Tobiah!' she signed at speed.

Tobiah? Nobody knew his full name except me, and—'What are they talk—'

Scarlett held up her hand and I stopped talking. I returned

my gaze to Tobi and the woman. She had long blonde hair that fell over her left shoulder. She gathered it in her hand and twisted it around her finger, just like … *Willow*.

My breath caught. It can't be her! Not after … my skin burned like a fuse running to ignite an explosive, travelling along my limbs, increasing my heart rate. I gulped down my *Rachel* half cup of cappuccino, hoping to heaven it would make me feel "happy". It didn't. Perhaps they needed to add something "extra" to it, something illegal.

I squinted to see the woman more clearly, then ducked fully behind the newspaper when Tobi looked my way. I kept my eyes on Scarlett.

She let out a breath like she had been holding it, then seemed to relax, like she was relieved. But then her body stiffened. 'Bend over and tie up your shoelaces,' she whispered.

'But I don't ha—'

She pushed me forward. 'Pretend. You need to get out of sight!'

Scarlett held the paper like she was reading it while I leaned over, hitting my head on the table in the process. I felt Scarlett's hand on my back pushing me so hard I slipped off the chair and underneath the table. She used her foot to slide my chair in, squashing me.

The sound of walking shoes came closer, then stopped.

'Hi, Scarlett.' It was Tobi's voice.

'Hi, Tobi,' Scarlett spoke.

My eyes widened. I had never heard her use her talking voice with another person outside of our work habitat.

'How's your cochlear implant?' Tobi said.

'Great. Amazing!' Scarlett said.

'I've heard the technology is quite advanced now,' he said.

'It is. Enjoy the rest or your day, Tobi,' Scarlett said. She was done with the conversation with him.

'You too.' The sound of Tobi's footsteps faded into the distance.

Scarlett kicked me and pulled the chair out.

I climbed back onto the chair. 'I can't believe you spoke to Tobi,' I said. 'You always use your notepad to communicate to others, like you used to, when you were deaf.'

Scarlett scowled at me. 'I did it for you so you could hear the conversation, and just for the record, I hated it! I'm not used to talking like a "normal" person yet.'

I closed my eyes and looked down. I didn't deserve to have Scarlett as my friend.

'I hope you tied up your shoelaces,' Scarlett said.

I looked up at her. Her smile was so big it radiated a thousand megawatts. I laughed, remembering the mischief we got up to when we were young.

'Scarlett Mae, you would make the perfect spy!'

'Maybe I am, already?' she said and arched an eyebrow.

'Do you think he knows I was under the table?'

Scarlett shook her head. 'Not a chance. I distracted him by using my voice, and then with my magic mind confusion device.'

'Your magic mind confusion device?'

'Absolutely,' she said.

'And that would be?'

'I could tell you, but then I'd have to kill you,' she said with twinkling eyes.

'Somehow, I don't think I want to see your magic mind confusion device,' I said.

'I don't think it would be wise for you. You are confused enough as it is,' she said.

I shook my head. She was right. 'I think I need another *Rachel*—a dose of happiness.'

'I have something better. Come with me,' she signed.

I hooked my arm through hers, and we walked, our steps

perfectly synchronised. I shoved my noise cancelling earphones on and pretended I couldn't hear, like Scarlett, for seventeen years before her successful cochlear implant and experimental hearing cell regrowth treatment. Of course, it was impossible for me not to perfectly hear nothing. But it was kind of interesting pretending not to hear anything. It was like disconnecting from the world for a bit, where nothing mattered, but everything mattered. But the more I thought about it, the more alert I became. Mostly from fear of not knowing if danger was around. Was I safe?

I slowed my step and pulled off my earphones.

'What's wrong?' Scarlett said.

'Nothing,' I whispered.

'Liar,' Scarlett said. 'Spit it out.'

I shook my head and guided her to a bench seat. We sat. I turned to her. 'I just realised how unsafe the world was for you with no hearing.' I placed my hand on hers.

She pressed her lips together. 'It is, but I learned to be smart about where I am, and everything around me, all the time. I also rely on my gut feeling, my intuition … what brought this on?' she said.

'While we were walking, I was trying to tune out of sound, and—'

'You know, when I first lost my hearing, I was terrified, of everything. I didn't know how I would cope. And at school—' she closed her eyes for a moment, then opened them again, tears balancing on the rim of her lower eyelid. 'At school, I was so blessed you were my friend. You helped me more than you can know,' she said. 'What do you want to know about the conversation I lip-read?'

'What's her name?'

'He never said it. But her name is Magnolia, Maggie for short.'

My breath stopped. *She's the one who owns the compact exactly like the one I stole. Maybe she's Willow's sister?* 'What did you say she called him?' I asked.

'Tobiah. Is that his full name?'

'Yes.'

'I thought Tobi was short for Tobias. Tell me why you were hiding behind the newspaper?' Scarlett said.

'I didn't want him to know that I saw him with another woman.'

'I smell a rat, Indi. What's going on?'

I looked to the small buildings, and all the colours beyond in the city of Tarrin. 'I can't tell you. I'm sorry.'

'You will tell me, eventually. You always do.'

'Do you think she was a true blonde?' I asked.

'No.'

'What else did they talk about?' I asked.

'Well … I think … it's not entirely accurate, as I lost some words due to people walking past, but I think the general topic was about—when they weren't arguing—something disappearing, or missing, or removed. And there was water involved, and a long waiting time. He was sorry for what had happened.'

I gave a sigh. It was her. It was Willow.

'He's an undercover cop, did you know?' Scarlett said.

I blinked, instantly transported to that night on Jacaranda Island when he told me. 'Yes. Is she his detective partner?'

'I don't know.'

'He's also nervous about getting caught out with something.'

'Did he say what it was?'

'Something to do with a tree. Something that is still there. Something she needs to get back … and something he needs to do, soon.'

I fingered the compact in my pocket. *Was this the thing she needed back?* 'What else was said?'

'He needed to wait for the full moon, and then it would be done,' Scarlett said. 'It sounds intriguing, like a mystery that needs to be solved.'

I nodded, my mind in a whirl. I had already been to the tree and retrieved the box Tobi was most probably talking about, and his book. What could he possibly be waiting for?

I sighed. 'So, Scarlett, what was the something better than a *Rachel*, for a dose of happiness. I could really do with it after the episode with Tobi.'

Scarlett stood. 'Walk with me.'

We linked arms and she pulled me along, my heavy heart slowing us down. And not to forget the enormous sack of guilt. Could she feel the weight of my heavy baggage? I huffed. I hoped Scarlett couldn't hear my exasperation. How good was her hearing cell regrowth?

We turned the corner and walked eighty-eight steps. I only knew because I was counting to keep my mind off what I saw with Tobiah. Scarlett stopped at a wrought iron gate adorned with the impression of wealth. She entered a security code, then looked at me and grinned. Not just an ordinary grin, but a mischievous grin. What was she doing? Should I escape before we enter the gates of no return?

Scarlett stepped forward. I released my arm from hers but did not move. She turned to me, 'Come on,' she said.

'I need to get back to work,' I said.

'Me too. This won't take long.'

I wasn't so sure. I shook my head.

'It's your wish.'

My wish? I shook my head. 'I didn't wish for anything,' I said.

Scarlett raised an eyebrow at me. 'Yes, you did. You asked me to take you to the dose of happiness—that's like a wish.'

'No. That's totally different to a wi—'

Scarlett grabbed my hand and pulled me through the gates then released her hand. 'We must hurry, before the happiness dissipates.' She turned on her heel and took quick steps. I had to run to keep up with her, trailing behind her through a dark forest. *Why did I feel like I had just stepped into the page of a fairy tale?*

I shielded my eyes from the bright sun when we stepped out of the forest. I squinted to get my bearings. Before us was a white cottage that looked like it should be breathing beside the sea, oceans blue and calm, the unpolluted air a salty balm for the soul. I took a deep breath to capture the soul healing.

Then Scarlett ran, twisting, and telling me to follow with a hand gesture. I closed my eyes for a moment, then let my body fall forward until my legs took over momentum. And I ran, following Scarlett to the front door of the cottage, where she stopped, waiting for me, grinning like the Cheshire Cat.

I stopped before her, panting. I hadn't run like that since … since … I can't remember. Or can I … was it when we would play hide 'n' seek when we were young, and I'd bolt for the Jacaranda tree to climb it. My safe place. My look out. My place of alone while the others played the game. I smiled. My sadness shell had cracked, and happiness seeped through … a little.

The path to happiness. *Step one. Run.* Endorphin hit with exercise. What was step two?

Scarlett pulled out her phone. Her fingers moved at speed with a text. In the next moment, the door opened, and the kind face of an elderly gentleman appeared. He placed a finger over his lips, and I heard a quiet hush. Scarlett rubbed her hands together, her eyes lighting up, then grabbed my hand and pulled me into the cottage and through to the back door, hesitated for a moment, then pushed it open with the quietness of the creep of time.

And there was nothing.

Nothing but a field of green.

And a fence.

Yet, Scarlett stepped out into the field of nothing like it was a field of everything. She turned to me and beckoned me to join her in the field of green, the sun casting beams of light that tried to ignite my volatile doubt about step two of her dose of happiness.

Yet, I stepped forward, swallowed by endless blades of perfectly manicured grass, and heard the door click behind me. There was no escape.

First, the fairy tale forest, and now the sea of green. I didn't feel happiness, just the thudding of my heart as panic set in. I had to get back to work.

I looked at Scarlett with my feet planted to the ground like I was about to grow roots and turn into a tree. She held up one finger. 'One moment,' she mouthed.

I nodded. What other choice did I have?

'Come,' she mouthed.

I walked. What other choice did I have?

And then the sea of green came alive with balls of bouncing, fluffy, four-legged creatures. Puppies the colour of golden sand. Bounding. Bustling. Bursting with contagious energy. Giving joy. Unconditionally. Giving irresistible, contagious happiness.

I stopped beside Scarlett. She dropped to the ground. And so did I, only to be swamped by adorable puppies a moment later.

I couldn't stop smiling. I looked to the beams of the sun and all the colours above and let out a slow breath, feeling my stress release, like letting go of a thousand helium balloons.

Scarlett's dose of happiness. *The cure*. I looked over at her and our eyes met. They sparkled like a sea of diamonds. 'Welcome to happiness,' she signed. 'Your wish has been granted,' she voiced.

'I didn't wi—' I started to sign.

Scarlett had looked away. Our communication was broken. She cradled a puppy close to her heart, put it back on the grass, smiled, and stood. She raised her eyebrows at me. 'Thank you for encouraging me to get a cochlear implant, it has changed my life. I don't think I could live without it now.' Scarlett ran her hand over her facial tattoo. 'Come on. We'll be in trouble for taking too long for lunch. We have to get back to work,' she said. And then she was off, walking briskly, with me lagging behind.

I wanted to stay in the field of happiness.

A high-pitched whistle sounded, and all the puppies bounced over to the elderly gentleman, who greeted them with a scattering of food. Scarlett looked over at him and waved before she disappeared through the back door of the cottage, to the front door and out, towards the dark forest, meandering through it, and out to the wrought iron gate. She unlocked it, and stepped through with an air of contentment.

I sidled up beside her and linked my arm through hers. We walked at a steady pace, the return to reality hitting me like a leaden weight.

And just like that. My happiness was gone.

I walked without signing, or talking to Scarlett, as she pulled me along, my heavy heart slowing us down. And not to forget the enormous sack of guilt that I dragged behind. Could she feel the weight of my heavy baggage? Did she see the difference in me when it all lifted, as I interacted with the puppies?

I exhaled loudly, hoping Scarlett couldn't hear it with her new hearing cell regrowth, or her cochlear implant that changed her world.

I looked along the street, listening to our shoes tap the pavement. Maybe I needed to study puppies and happiness? Maybe I could replicate the chemical findings of what caused their blissful happiness, bottle it and sell it. I would be on people's most loved list then, instead of on their hated list as an experimental neuroscientist.

Scarlett and I entered the Mind and Brain Lab together, then were lost in a world of synthesized reality that was far from normal. No part of living brains without a body could ever be ordinary.

The brains were responsive. Our research was a success.

But I had too many questions, and no answers.

Chapter 30

Dear Finn,

Hey. I hope you remember me. I met you at Kingdom Adventure Park during the spring of the most amazing flowering season. Ever.

You started talking to me in the queue to the Marvellous Super Roller Coaster, then you sat next to me in the car and held my hand as I screamed my lungs out in the darkest, scariest tunnel where I think we were inverted, holding on for dear life.

When the ride ended, we looked at each other, our smiles wide, our eyes caught in each other's.

Afterward, we ate burgers and I drank Coca-Cola for my nausea, while you laughed at me.

I wanted to spend more time with you, but you got a text and had to leave. I called your name and you stopped. I ran to you, out of breath, kissed your cheek and thanked you for holding my hand on the ride. Remember? You smiled at me and said, 'You're welcome ...'

'Lucinda,' I said.

'Lucinda,' you repeated. Then left.

You don't know this part, but I followed you. I know where you live. I want to see you again, so this is why I have left you this letter.

Hopefully yours,
Lucinda.

P.S. I'll be waiting for you at Myrtle Beach in one year, when the full moon whispers hello on the horizon. I'll be wearing the colour of white and my dog, a gorgeous golden retriever, will be wearing a blue bandana.

P.P.S. If you can be there, my wish will come true.

I stopped writing.

There. Done.

I folded the off-white handmade paper into thirds, and slipped it into the envelope. I picked up the blue pen, my hand shaking, and wrote "Finn" on the envelope.

I gazed out the window at the nightdom, at all the colours above, and placed my hand to my mouth to catch the heartache that rose from deep within. I had just sealed our fates, and most probably the one where I would never see him again. What sort of man would be devoted enough to wait a year?

Time heals. He will move on with his life.

I grabbed the classic diamond-studded, gold compact. Not mine. *Stolen.* On that day that can't be undone. That wish that can't be unwished.

Mirror. Mirror. I pushed the button on the compact, and it flipped open.

Two mirrors. Two of me. The one before the event. The one after. I gazed into the left mirror. The reflection of me before the event that changed everything, and slipped back into a memory—

'By the colours of the sunset on the day of the full moon,' Tobi said, his voice deep and rich in its tones. He stood tall with his hands behind his back, emphasising his broad shoulders in the white linen button-up shirt he wore, the long sleeves rolled up to just below his elbows. He lifted his chin a little, and connected his ocean-blue eyes to mine with a penetrating gaze, and heat spread through me.

He focussed his eyes on the ground then, and moved his weight from one foot to the other. From behind, he produced a pink rose and offered it to me. 'I do believe we met at another time,' he said.

I smiled, remembering his last story, and took the rose from him. I lifted it to my nose and inhaled the fruity, floral, raspberry, scent, reminding me of warm days in the Springdom. I gazed up at him. 'Great pickup line.' I beamed.

He lowered his head and smiled coyly, then looked up at me. 'It was a month ago.' He shook his head. 'And I left you without kissing you, or telling you how much I loved you. Please forgive me.'

My heart cried for him. I reached up and stroked the back of his neck. 'How could I not?'

He leaned forward and kissed me, making my heart bloom,

then picked me up and placed me into the boat. He pushed the boat off the shore and jumped in, sat on the rowing seat and began to row.

My eyes wandered over all of him—his dark wavy hair parted on the side, his eyes, his nose, his lips, his chin, his white linen shirt, his brown belt, his shorts—a greenish-dark-blue colour, and his dark blue sports shoes. When he settled into a rhythm, he looked at me with smiling eyes. 'Just one more meeting on the full moon and the final piece will fall into place, and then we can see each other on the mainland.'

'You mean, we have tonight's full moon, and one more, and that's it?' I wanted to jump up and down, but it would end badly in our "borrowed" wooden rowboat.

'Yes.' He sucked in a breath like he was nervous, then looked out over beyond *Zero*, the lake full of blue, and stopped rowing.

Was there something wrong?

He pulled the oars in and the boat continued to glide until it slowed and came to a stop. He climbed over the middle seat to sit opposite me, then looked at me with a stormy gaze, and something deeper that seemed to come dangerously close to touching my soul. My breath caught in my throat, and a silence hung in the air.

He placed his knee on the bottom of the boat, and moved off the seat to balance there, kneeling before me. He reached over and brushed a lazy finger over my cheek, tucking a lock of hair behind my ear, and that current he gave sizzled. He blew a breath between his lips. 'Indigo Feather Danube. Remember the very first day I got into a rowboat with you?'

I inhaled deeply, my stomach tightening. 'Yes.'

'Remember, you were rowing, and I asked you whether I should be rowing while you were sitting?'

'Yes. And I asked you if you were going to propose to me?' I said, butterflies pounding my stomach. I looked down at my hands, twisted together. 'And you pressed your lips together like you were most disgusted, and said no.'

Tobi looked down and laughed, then took my hands in his and looked into my eyes, ocean-blue to greeny-blue. 'I was terrified of you. I didn't know what you were going to do from one moment to the next. You fascinated me. You challenged me. You scared me. You reached inside me and touched my heart. I can't imagine my life without you in it ... Indigo . . . will you marry me?'

I held my breath, tears filling my eyes. I wanted to say yes. I really did. But I didn't know what his job was. What if he was my enemy in the neuroscience field, trying to gather evidence to prove that we were conducting experiments that were illegal and unethical. If he was, and he found out what I truly did, would he hate me then? Maybe I needed to tell him what I did before we both got hurt?

'Indi?' His voice broke, and his ocean-blue eyes became stormy. 'I love you . . . please say yes.'

I took a deep breath to cool the heat of anxiety flowing through me. 'Tobi, nothing would make me happier than being your wife . . .'

'But . . .' he said, and held his breath, pain etching his face.

'But . . . I need to tell you what I do. I don't want to marry you, then you discover what I do and hate me for it. I need to protect your heart. I don't want to hurt you.'

He squeezed his eyes shut and turned his head to the side, then released my hands from his. I had hurt him. And I hated myself for it. He moved back to the rowing seat and took a deep breath. He ran his hand through his hair and looked at me, already detached from the situation. 'Shall we go to the tree, or back to the shore, and walk away from each other?'

A tear rolled down my cheek, and my throat tightened. 'To the tree. I need you to understand,' I whispered.

He lifted his chin and looked down at me. Then nodded.

Once. Reached for the oars and started rowing.

'I'm sor—'

'Don't,' he said, lingering on the "n" and tinkering on the "t".

I closed my eyes as pain surged through me. I didn't want to say goodbye, but maybe this was it. I wanted to cross my arms over my heart and double over to stop the pain. But I didn't. I took even breaths to calm the riotous chaos happening inside me.

I opened my eyes when I felt the boat stop. Tobi stepped out and onto the jetty, and offered me his hand, like he always did. I placed my shaking hand into his, and when I stood on the jetty beside him, he pulled my hand to his lips, closed his eyes, and kissed it.

A lump of emotion formed in my throat, escaping from my heart. I let go of his hand and walked to the deck. I placed my backpack there and removed my mobile phone from my pocket.

'Put your phone beside mine,' I said.

'Why?'

'What I am about to tell you is classified. I am forbidden to tell you.' I looked into his eyes. 'But you are more important to me than my job.'

Tobi raised his eyebrows and pulled his phone from his pocket, and placed it beside mine.

I walked to the Jacaranda tree and climbed it. Tobi followed.

He sat beside me, leaned his head against the trunk of the tree and closed his eyes. My heart sank as I looked at him. So beautiful, undone. I had hurt him.

A tear slipped from my eye. 'I'm a neuroscientist. We have living brains, no bodies, suspended in fluid. They have electrodes inserted inside them and we are conducting research.' That's all I needed to tell him. He didn't require the details of our true research. I didn't want him implicated in anything else to do with me. I had to protect him. 'That's it. Please don't hate me.'

Tobi opened his eyes, looked at me and frowned. 'That's it.

I already knew you were a neuroscientist, and I had heard the rumours about the living brains. You're not telling me anything new.' He clenched his jaw and shook his head. 'And … I could never hate you.'

I looked down and twisted my fingers together. 'Why didn't you tell me you were an undercover cop?' I looked up at him.

He stilled, and eyed me warily. 'Technically, I'm not a cop. I'm a negotiator. A specialist skill. Nobody wants to go out with a cop. I thought … if you got to know me first, then a least I could have a chance with you.'

'But you are trained to kill.' I winced, my tears spilling.

'I have taken an oath to protect and defend. There's a difference.'

'You removed your weapon at the siege.' I let out a sob, then held my breath to stop it happening again.

'You saw that, six months ago?'

'It was televised, and like everyone else in Tarrin, I held my breath, waiting to see if the cop would get shot. I thought he looked like you, but I wasn't 100% sure because of the distance of the coverage.' I sucked in a shuddering breath. 'You could have died!'

'I wouldn't have gone in unless I was 99.9% sure he wouldn't attack me, or shoot. My last thought before I stepped forward, was you, and the pain you would feel if something happened to me. I wouldn't let you go through that unbearable pain of loss.'

'But what if—'

'I wear undetectable lightweight armour under my clothes. It's hi tech. Classified.'

'But your head is exposed.'

'Again, undetectable protection, and we have snipers.'

I took a deep breath and released it slowly. 'Your job changes … everything.'

'And nothing.' He whispered, his words laced with heartache.

'I love you with my entire being. Fiercely. Passionately. Tenderly.' His voice cracked. He placed his hand over mine. 'The vision of the siege that was televised didn't show the conversations I had with the man for hours beforehand. It didn't show his eyes as I approached him, full of pain, reaching out for a lifeline. It didn't show the whispered words we exchanged that changed the trajectory of his life. It didn't show the deep gratitude he had for me, because I understood where he was coming from.' Tobi moved my hand to his lips and kissed it, his tear falling onto my fingers. 'I save people from suicide. I stop their families from suffering the insufferable pain of losing a loved one, like I did.'

I closed my eyes. He was doing exactly what I was doing. Saving people. The only difference was that the brains he saved still had bodies, they were living people, which we were working toward. I opened my eyes and looked at him. 'There could never be a man greater than you. I love you, Tobiah Lucas Brooks.'

'But,' he looked down, then back up at me, 'do you love me enough?' His voice was weak, his eyes filled with pain.

I nodded. 'Yes,' I whispered. My insides clenched with dread at the fear of my next question. 'But … will you stay with me, even when I am chaotic. Messy. And lost, sometimes. Filled with too many questions and not enough answers, wallowing in the darkness.'

He frowned. 'Yes.' He kissed my hand once more. 'I need to see you on *Zero*.'

'So we can feel *Within* … the heart dimension that feels like intoxication,' I said, my voice barely audible.

'Yes,' he whispered, lingering on the "s", then started to descend the tree.

I climbed down after him, jumping from a branch halfway, and beating him to *Zero*. I looked up at him, continuing to climb down at the speed of a sloth. The sloth I loved. I leaned against the trunk of the tree and waited, intoxicated by his essence.

When he touched down on *Zero*, he stood before me. 'I do prefer climbing down the tree rather than falling.'

I tilted my head to the side a little. 'I don't know … I kinda liked having you fuss over me.'

Tobi lowered his head and smiled coyly, then his lifted his eyes to mine. He kneeled onto one knee, and took my hand in his. 'Marry me, Indigo?'

I breathed slowly to calm the fluttering butterflies in my stomach. 'Yes,' I said.

Tobi closed his eyes and kissed the fourth finger on my left hand, then stood. His gaze met mine, penetrating, searching, and soul connecting in an unmistakable look of love, of desire. He placed his finger under my chin and tipped my head up, and lowered his lips close to mine, hesitating.

And I wanted.

His mouth was on mine then. Caressing. Lingering. Tender. And I melted, consumed in that kiss. I was nothing, and I was everything, and in that moment, I had no doubt that I could trust him with my heart and my life. He, who had loved me since he was twelve—

I closed the compact. I still loved him. I missed him. But I didn't know if we could get back what we once had. Not after the incident on Midsummer's Eve when he cast me that look of hatred.

Chapter 31

Deep, soulful cello notes seeped under the double Gothic doors of the church, each note imbued with love and devotion, and with anticipation of the sacred marriage vows to be exchanged.

Romantic. Tender.

It was exactly what my soul needed after my tumultuous week at the Mind Lab, interviewing our human subjects, taking notes and recording the efficacy of the memory removal we had conducted. I needed this reminder of love. Of human kindness.

I stood beside Chloe in the church antechamber and smoothed out my dusty aubergine bridesmaid dress while we waited for Yolande. My heart was beating hard. With anxiety. And with excitement. Anxiety for me. Tobi was here. And excitement for Yolande, who was about to marry Dr. Xander Parker.

I watched as Yolande looked down, her smile bringing warmth and sunshine into the room. She caressed a pale pink rose petal on her bridal bouquet, flowers of Love and Forever, of white and pale pink roses, white thryptomene, white freesias, and pale green lisianthus: soft and romantic with a touch of sage coloured foliage created by Grandmother Fleur. They released the scent of old rose, musk and myrrh with a hint of citrus. Spectacular.

The doors opened and the guests turned toward us, looking for the bride.

Notes of the cello floated off to the gabled ceiling and the stirring piano notes began. I held my breath when a male voice filled the church with such a timbre it was like embracing my heart. I knew the song—*Turning Page*. It was about a guy waiting a hundred years, but who would wait a million more. I gulped down my emotion.

I counted to five, and Chloe took her first step to walk down the aisle, stepping only on the first and third beat of the song. I inhaled slowly, and cast my gaze to my floral bouquet. Simple and elegant. All white peonies, releasing a scent that was sweet and rosy, citrusy and spicy, reminding me of the colours of the Springdom.

The white peonies balanced perfectly with our bridesmaid dresses of dusty aubergine, off the shoulder, full length, elegant tulle with a sweetheart neckline. I blew a breath out to ensure my breasts sat comfortably where they should. I was never happy showing this much of my cleavage.

I stilled, watching for when Chloe was ten pews down the aisle, then stepped forward in the customary bridesmaid walk on every first and third beat. Anxiety skated over my skin, burning me. I kept my eyes forward, watching Chloe as she neared the altar, and then exchanged a smile with her as she turned to watch me. Tobi was in my peripheral vision, his presence turning my insides into all kinds of crazy.

My heart was telling me to look at him, but I didn't. I couldn't. It would make me cry after what had happened on that tragic nightdom that changed everything between us—on that fateful Midsummer's Eve when the full moon shone with its glorious luminosity, when the lake and the tree witnessed the most hideous wish that came true. I swallowed to calm the emotion that was rising to the surface, and, when I was two steps from the front of the church, I smiled at Xander with love, before I took my final steps, and moved to the side, then turned back to the entrance of the church.

Yolande stood beside her father. She looked elegant and breathtaking and stunning and so beautiful. Her father whispered to her and her whole face lit up, and they began the long-awaited bridal walk for her to marry the love of her life. I looked away, twice, as she approached. Watching her and Xander's intimate gaze felt like an intrusion into their love story.

She stopped before Xander, gave me her bouquet then turned towards him. As I gazed at the happy couple, my eyes veered over Xander's shoulder. And there were those ocean-blue eyes that I once loved. They connected to mine and his lips parted. He gave me a small smile and I blinked as heat seared its way through my skin. I lowered my eyes to the flowers, fiddled with the bouquets, then focussed back on the bride and groom.

Five hours of close proximity with Tobi. I could do this. Just because he looked captivating and charismatic in his deep dark blue wedding suit and my stomach was fluttering at the sight of him, didn't mean anything, anymore. We were done. I would do my best to keep a distance between us for the celebration, apart from the official photographs and the waltz.

The pastor's words became a muffle as I focussed on Yolande and Xander, and in a daze. I followed them to the table to where the marriage certificate was, after the words of their joining was done, and sealed with the promise of a kiss.

A sweet and spicy scent flowed around me, and my stomach clenched. Tobi was standing behind me. Close. 'You look beautiful.' His words where whispered and warm, close to my ear, each word delivered against my skin like a melody trying to wind their way to my heart.

'Thank you,' I said, trying to block his magnetism. I turned and connected my eyes to his. 'Can you hold my flowers while I sign the wedding certificate.' He nodded, and as he reached for the flowers our fingers touched, and that familiar spark travelled through my veins. I breathed out the current that sizzled between us, sat and signed the certificate, then stood and stepped back for him to do the same, reclaiming my flowers without touching him. It was safer that way.

He stood beside me, as Xander and Yolande followed the pastor to the front of the church. 'Family and friends, I introduce to you, newlyweds, Xander and Yolande.'

Applause broke out and Xander kissed Yolande again. If I ever believed in fairy tales, this was it. Theirs was a true love story. With hands threaded together, they walked to the front doors of the church with coloured rose petals falling around them.

Tobi offered me his arm and I took it, as was required, and I smiled as we walked, as required, and followed the newlyweds from inside the church, to the outside and into the fractured daydom where monsters are hideous and real.

'Xander and Yolande? Not Dr. and Mrs. Parker?' said Tobi.

'Yolande's not taking Xander's surname,' I said.

'Ouch.'

'Ouch?' I looked up at him.

'It's like being married but not married,' he said.

'Sarried? Mingled?' I said and looked away from him.

'What would you do if it were you?'

'If I was getting married?' *Like we were meant to?*

'Yes.'

'Sarried,' I said.

'Why?'

'So I don't lose my identity, something I am proud of, something I have worked hard for.'

'Ladies and gents, gather around,' a photographer instructed. We all had a position to stand in. I walked to the top step to the left a little. Tobi joined me soon after.

'Indi and Tobi, stand closer,' photographer one said.

Tobi gazed into my eyes and moved closer, and heat seared its way through my skin. His scent of sweetness and spice tugged at my heartstrings. Tobi ran a finger along my spine and that current between us sizzled again. And I'm painfully conscious I'm moments from being pulled under his spell.

'If I asked you to take my last name because it was important to me, would you?' he said.

His spell shattered and my mind was clear. 'Why would it be important to you?'

'Answer my question,' he said.

'Answer my question,' I retaliated.

He let out a breath. 'I would want people to know that you belonged to me, that you were taken. That you are mine.'

'And by people, do you mean other men?' I said.

'Why do you always ask the hard questions?'

'You don't own me. The ring on the fourth finger tells people I am hitched. Is the taking of your last name a deal breaker for you?'

He rubbed the back of his neck. 'It tells people you love me enough to leave your single name behind, your single identity, to start a new life with me, as husband and wife, as Mr. and Mrs. Brooks,' he said.

'Bridesmaids—gather under the arbour,' said photographer one.

'Groomsmen—to the bench,' directed photographer two.

We parted and I walked to the arbour where photographer one had directed us to. It flourished with greenery and climbing pale pink roses with the scent of strong myrrh. After several photographs we moved to the bench seat where the groomsmen had been, and sat and waited.

Chloe put her head on my shoulder. 'Did you hear how he proposed to her, twice?'

The corners of my mouth turned up and I nodded. 'The first time she said no.'

'How nice to have a guy propose and ask for your hand in marriage …'

'What do you mean? You're married.'

'Yeah .. we just sort of agreed to get married ... and we did.' Chloe wiped a tear away. 'And that's the end of the story.'

'But he's a nice guy,' I said.

'And loyal. Everything you want in a husband … but still … I feel robbed of that special moment, and feeling like he wanted me more than anything in the world. Like I was beyond special. And worthy of a romantic proposal. I feel duped. Maybe even second rate. And why didn't he have to guts to ask me in the first place.'

'No, Chloe. He loves you to the sun and back. He would do anything for you. The way he looks at you …' I shook my head.

'I know. But still … it's always there, in the back of my mind. Maybe he just settled for me.'

I put my arm around her shoulders. 'He picked the best. There is no one better for him than you.' I kissed her head, careful not to dislodge her hair artistry.

'Thanks. Remember that when I come to your door crying after filing for divorce.'

I looked up. Chloe's husband walked toward us, his eyes shining, then softening as he came closer. He was besotted with her. He leaned down and kissed her. 'You look amazing,' he said, then left.

Chloe sighed.

'You won't get divorced,' I whispered.

We walked to a hook and rail fence for more photographs, where I had to stand facing Tobi. 'Using your line of thought,' I said, continuing our previous conversation, 'would you love me enough to take my last name, losing your identity of what you have worked for, and who you are known as, to start a new life with me?' I looked down and caressed a flower petal then looked back into his eyes. 'You do know that in some countries, women cannot take their husband's last name by law. I am thankful that we have a choice. Here's your choice, hypothetically speaking—me as your wife with a different last name, or not married at all. What is important?' I said, my voice low so it wasn't heard by others.

'You, married to me.' He held my eyes in his and I felt my lips drawn to his.

'You're a fast learner, Mr. Brooks,' I said, breathing out his potion, and offered him a smile. I placed my hand over his heart and felt it beating. The heart I once loved.

'You're a good teacher, Ms Danube,' he whispered.

'I love your hair like this,' I whispered, my eyes wandering over his face and his dark hair, then settling on his lips.

He frowned, tears filling his eyes. 'Don't,' he said, lingering on the "n" and tinkering on the "t".

'Don't what?'

'Don't make it harder for me.'

'What is getting harder?' I raised an eyebrow at him.

'You. Me … *Us*. I wish—'

'Don't wish,' I whispered.

He stood behind me then, as instructed by the photographer, placed his hand over my stomach and pulled me against him. Gently. I closed my eyes and relished in the feeling of his body against mine, once again. I wanted to melt into him.

He placed his warm soft lips on my bare shoulder. 'I wish,' he said again, his voice low, sending a current into my centre. Heat rushed to my cheeks.

'Thanks everyone. That's a wrap!' the photographer said.

Tobi released his hand from my stomach, and at once I craved his connection again. I turned to him and looked into his ocean-blue eyes, now stormy and dangerous.

His gaze shifted from my eyes, to my mouth, and my insides melted. His lips turned up in a half smile and he lowered his head. I touched my fingers to his, feeling that familiar spark, then parted from him, and walked down the steps.

I breathed a sigh of rclief. He was right. It was getting harder. And I needed to make more of an effort to stay away from him. We just had the waltz to dance at the reception, and that would be our last point of contact. End of story. For us.

I climbed into the car with Chloe. 'What's with you and Tobi?'

I frowned. 'Me and Tobi? Nothing, why?'

'Are you sure?'

I pressed my lips together and shook my head.

'The way he looks at you … the way you mirror each other … the sparks … I've lost count of how many times he ran a finger along your skin …'

'He flirts with all the girls,' I said.

'No, he doesn't,' Chloe said. 'It's like he's under your spell.'

'We're no good for each other,' I said. 'We argue all the time. The discussions you may have seen have all being about us not agreeing on anything.'

'It's a sign,' Chloe said.

'A sign?'

Chloe beamed at me. 'Wait and see.'

I looked out the window and shook my head. 'There is no Tobi and me.'

The bridal waltz began. I swayed to the music while Yolande and Xander danced. Graceful. Majestic. Hypnotic. Feet in perfect sync. He was a ballet dancer after all.

Xander held Yolande like she was the most precious thing in the universe, like his life would evaporate if they couldn't be together anymore. Sparks of sexual chemistry arced between them, and their intimate eye gaze was locked in a connection like they were the only people in the room. Yolande was floating, fuelled by his love.

I looked away. They had what I would never have. And it hurt.

Tobi stood beside me and held out his hand. 'Dance with me.'

I had no choice. It was what the bridesmaids and groomsmen did. So I placed mine in his and felt that spark. He stepped closer and placed his other hand on the small of my back. His touch was too soft, too comforting, too everything, and my insides melted. We fell into a waltz, our rhythm so easy, so natural. As we continued dancing, I stopped fighting my inner war and let myself be drawn closer to him.

He lowered his head close to my shoulder. 'I wish—'

'Don't say it,' I whispered.

'This should have been *us*.' He breath was warm against my neck.

'It could have been us,' I whispered.

'What have I done?' His voice cracked.

'You shouldn't have brought another girl to our tree.'

'It's not what you think happened.'

I looked up into his ocean-blue eyes and trailed my fingers lightly along the back of his neck. 'I wish—'

'Don't,' he said, lingering on the "n" then caressing the "t".

We danced, the music leading us as though we were in a trance.

'I want to kiss you,' he whispered.

'It will make it worse.'

'I want to go back in time and change it all.'

'All of it?'

'Just the very last part where—' His eyes held mine.

'It happened, Tobi. It can't be undone.' *Please. Say just three words. It will change everything.*

'My intention was to—'

'So you keep saying,' I said, annoyed.

'I don't see how we can get over this.' His voice was depleted.

'Could anyone?'

He looked away while we waltzed.

'Trust,' I whispered, 'you told me to trust you … and when I finally did you—'

'It's not what you think happened.'

'So you keep saying.' I sighed.

He stilled. 'What have we done … to *us*?'

'It's a mess.'

'A mess I can't be involved in,' he said.

'But I can?'

'I wish—' he whispered.

'Stop … Tobi—'

'May I?' It was Xander.

I looked at him and nodded with a smile, more than pleased with his timing. 'Of course.' I placed my hand into his and he guided me in a waltz. 'I never thought this would happen. Me, dancing with you.'

He smiled, leaned in and kissed my cheek. 'Thank you. This day would never have happened without you—'

Gentle arms wrapped around me. Yolande. She took both of my hands in hers. 'Thank you for changing my life.'

I hugged her. 'Your happiness is my happiness. I love you.' I stepped back. 'Congratulations and enjoy the rest of your night.'

I kissed Yolande on the cheek, then Xander, and moved back until I was swallowed by guests on the dance floor.

I stopped at the doors of the celebration room and looked to my right at Tobi. I held his eye contact until it hurt, then disappeared into the night.

I ran out into the fog of the nightdom, where there were no colours of the above, and stopped when my phone vibrated. I pulled it out of my clutch purse to read the text:

The sunflower field. 23:00.

I switched off my phone. Message received. That was all that was needed.

Three hours until then.

Chapter 32

'I choose to forget.' Tobi's voice broke, the drooping sunflowers in the nightdom reflecting his deep anguish; the brokenness of his heart.

In the candlelit depths of the middle of the sunflower field, I watched as he drew his eyebrows together and shook his head, slowly, before he leaned closer and pressed his lips to mine. He took my mouth like it was his, like I was his and always had been. He pulled back slightly and dropped his forehead against mine, then bent down and blew out the candle, stood up, grabbed my hand and pulled me through the sullen sunflowers in the nightdom, oozing with sadness, shattering my heart.

He wants to forget.

Me.

Our past.

Our everything.

A whimper escaped me while we ran through the sunflower field, the sunflowers towering in rows like brave, stoic soldiers. Did they turn their heads to follow me, or did I imagine it?

Finn. I wanted to say his new name.

But not here. Not now.

When the time was right.

He pushed me forward to my car. When I got in and turned on the engine, he pulled a bicycle out from the edge of the field of sunflowers, mounted it and rode away.

I wound down my window. 'Finn,' I whispered, hoping the breezed would carry the letters on the wind. I turned my head to the sound of fluttering wings, and watched as a bluebird flew off. I flicked away my tear, then left.

Chapter 33

I placed the stolen classic diamond-studded, gold compact onto my study desk, rested my chin on my hands and gazed out into the nightdom, at all the colours above. I watched the stars disappear, one by one, as the forecast storm rolled in, taking its time in the early hours of the morning.

He wants to forget. Me. Our past. Our *everything*. My tear ran. I reached over and held the compact in my hands and turned it over and over before I finally pushed on the button. It flipped open.

Mirror. Mirror. Two mirrors. Two of me. The one before the event. The one after. I gazed into the left mirror. The reflection of me before the event. The girl who never wanted to fall in love …

I gazed into the right mirror. The girl who did fall in love. The girl who was involved in a situation that had unfolded before her eyes. The situation that should never should have happened. Every story has some sort of tragedy. But not like this … not with a missing body.

I turned on my phone:

Me: **Sunday. Kingdom Adventure Park. 3pm**

Him: **So … this is really happening?**

Me: **You chose to forget. When you see me, look at me as though you are seeing me for the first time in your life. Be at the extreme roller coaster, where you will sit beside me, and we'll take it from there**

Him: **And then?**

I swallowed, then texted: **The following Sunday, sit in the kitchen of your house and wear a blindfold, so you don't form any visuals of me. I will be there at 10am. I will knock three times, pause, then two times, pause again, then one time. You will answer 'It's unlocked.' I will place my hand on your shoulder, guide you to the car and drive you to the memory lab.** I took a deep breath.

Him: **And my memories of us will be gone?**

Me: **Yes. Except for the rollercoaster memory. Your new name is Finn**

Him: **And the memories of the death? They'll be gone?**

Me: **Yes**

Him: **So … this is really happening**

Me: **Are you sure you want to begin again? Are**

you sure you want your memories of … Willow … deleted? Are you sure you want your memories of me deleted?

Him: **Yes**

Me: **Then this is really happening. We can't meet or text anymore. It's a total blackout for communication for us. Remember, tomorrow … Sunday. Kingdom Adventure Park. 3pm. Then the Sunday afterward, your place in the kitchen, 10am. Blindfolded**

It was done.

His memory of the death would be gone. And mine. Biran and I had experimented on ourselves for the removal of memories. And it was successful. I reached over to the envelope with Finn's name on the front. I needed to plant it in his house soon. When the memories had been deleted, it would be like the death had never have happened. You were only dead if someone knew about it, right?

I closed the diamond-studded, gold compact, turned it on the side and spun it on my desk. Around and around and around it went, vertigo at its finest, until it slowed then fell onto its flat back; the diamond studs facing the ceiling.

I pulled out the letter to Finn and photographed it. I needed a copy so I knew where to meet him in one year from now, in case my memory deletion went wrong. I was taking a big risk. But in the name of science, it was worth it. And if we were going to be an *us* again …

I lifted my phone and opened the camera and hit record. This was a message for Scarlett. If something happened, I wanted her to know the truth.

When I finished recording my message for her, I downloaded

it onto the computer and labelled the video "To Scarlett. To be opened in the case of my physical death or total memory failure.'

I turned off my phone, laid on the bed and stared at the ceiling. A life sentence in prison over a possible death with a missing body, or to begin again with new memories.

Choose.

Chapter 34

Parking was atrocious. The Kingdom Adventure Park was full of tourists today. And it was hot. Stinking hot. I drove around the car park for fifteen minutes looking for a vacant space. In the end, I parked on a grassy side slope. Illegally. Fitting. What we were planning to do was illegal. Totally.

'Enjoy your day,' the cashier said.

I took a step through the gates of Kingdom Adventure Park, and looked around. Buildings, inspired by books, greeted me. Whichever building you chose, was like stepping into the book. How I longed to do that, to choose all of them, one after the other. But I wasn't going there today. I was meeting Finn at the Marvellous Super Roller Coaster, as we had planned.

My stomach tightened with anxiety. How had it come to this? Running away from a presumed death, an unproven death, a missing body, and no missing person reported to the police.

But he was insistent. This was the only way to go. For *us*.

I twisted my hands together, then took my first step towards my future as Lucinda, my new name in my new life in a new part of the world.

I headed towards the Rides and Thrills and beelined for the Super Roller Coaster. I slowed as it came into view, double guessing myself about whether this is what I wanted to do. I let out a sharp breath. It was now or never. And he was the only man I have ever loved.

I walked toward the queue and looked at each person. He was supposed to be standing in the line waiting for me, as per the instructions. And I was supposed to line up after him.

But he was nowhere. I joined the end of the line to weight up my options, and to rethink the entire plan that we had created. I shook my head. It wasn't going to work. If he wasn't here as planned, he wasn't committed to our future together. I pressed my lips together, then turned to leave, and bumped into someone. I looked up. It was *him*.

'I'm so sorry,' I said, my body filling with relief.

'It could have been worse,' he said. 'I could have been holding a drink.'

I raised an eyebrow at him and gave him a shy smile. 'True,' I said. I tilted my head on the side, 'Have you been on this roller coaster before?'

He shook his head. 'No. You? I'm Finn, by the way.'

'No.' My lips quirked up in a small smile, and I turned back to face the front of the queue, and took a step every two minutes, slowly inching my way closer to enter the ride.

After twenty minutes, I stood behind a small group of people. My stomach did a backflip. It was imperative that I got on the same ride as Tobi, and to sit next to him.

'How many in your group?' the attendant asked.

'Four.'

'There's room for six. Do you mind if two others join you?'

The attendant looked at me. 'How many in your group?' I held up one finger. He looked at the person behind me. 'How many in your group?'

'One,' he said.

The attendant looked back at me. 'Do you mind riding together?'

I turned around and looked at Finn, then shook my head. He looked stunning in his pale blue button up shirt and stone-coloured pants.

'Awesome. Ride for six. Make your way through.'

I followed the group to the ride platform, and climbed in after them, leaving a seat spare beside me.

Finn sat; our legs almost touching. 'There's no backing out now,' he said.

'I'll just have to try to be brave.' I pressed my lips together. I hated roller coasters.

'Are you a screamer?'

My eyes danced. 'Nah. It's not good for the vocal cords.'

'Neither is singing badly.'

I looked up at him and frowned. What an odd comment. 'Then I'll be sure not to sing while we're on the roller coaster.'

He leaned across me, his scent a mix of woody and cinnamon notes surprising me. I raised an eyebrow. His choice of his *Finn* "smell" made me think of new beginnings. 'What are you doing?' I said after a moment.

'Making sure you are strapped in properly. I don't want you falling out while we're inverted. It will scare the people below.'

'When I land on the ground with a thud?' I berated myself. Thud was a bad choice of words.

He narrowed his eyes at me. 'No. The sound of your scream as you fall.'

I lifted my thumb and first finger, and ran them across my closed lips like doing up a zip, then the roller coaster car started to move. While we rolled slowly, I adjusted my off the shoulder blue and white floral maxi boho dress, to ensure I was decent for the ride.

'I'll bet you a burger and drink that you scream,' he said, his eyes taking all of me in.

'And if I don't, you'll buy me a burger and drink?'

He gave me a crooked smile and held my eyes in his, ocean-blue to greeny-blue, and my insides melted. 'Sure.'

The roller coaster car rose the incline, revealing a stunning view over the city. We reached the pinnacle, and the car started to fall. My eyes widened at the drop. I reached for Finn's hand, and screamed louder than I had ever screamed before. Before I knew it, we entered a dark tunnel. It was so dark I had no idea whether we were upright or sideways. I was totally disoriented when all of a sudden, we were inverted, or so my plaited hair told me. The ride continued with highs and lows and fast turns.

And then, the car came to a sudden stop. And I couldn't move. It was like my muscles were frozen in place from being tensed for the entire five minutes of the ride.

'You good?' he asked.

I sucked in a deep breath, and realised I was still gripping his hand like a vice. I released my fingers from his. 'Yep,' I said, popping the "p".

The security bar of the car retracted. I stood, smoothed down my floral dress, then stepped out onto the platform. I turned to him. 'I owe you a burger and drink, don't I?'

'Yep,' he said, popping the "p".

'Let's find a place to eat,' I said, nausea dancing in my stomach. I really didn't feel good.

We strolled through sideshow alley, side by side, then stumbled upon a burger site, and ordered. I sat opposite him at a table while we waited for our food to be served. 'Thanks for letting me hold your hand like I was hanging on for dear life. That was the most terrifying roller coaster I have ever been on.'

'Really? How many roller coasters have you ridden?'

'One,' I said.

He chuckled, his ocean-blue eyes holding mine.

'I don't like heights. It scares me.'

He raised his eyebrows at me. 'So, you wouldn't like climbing trees, then.'

I shook my head. 'Never. It's way too dangerous.' Our food arrived. I picked up my Coca-Cola and emptied half of it, hoping that it would settle my nausea. I closed my eyes and waited to see what my stomach wanted to do.

'You okay?'

'Yep. Great,' I said, and picked up my burger to take a bite.

'Thought so,' he said, then stopped chewing. 'Would you prefer to drink some dandelion wine instead—a fruity elixir infused with wishes?' He raised an eyebrow at me, then closed his eyes, and lowered his head and moved his chin towards his right shoulder. When he opened his eyes again, his phone pinged. He tapped on the screen, and I saw a text message, from Yolande, as I had asked her to do. He sucked in some air through his closed teeth, 'Looks like I need to go.'

I put my burger down. 'Really?'

'Yeah. Sorry.' He looked to his right and winced. 'Thanks for the burger and drink … and … sitting next to you on the roller coaster was … interesting.'

'Same.' I took another swig of Coca-Cola for my nausea. 'Sorry about your hand.'

'It was nothing … gotta run.'

I nodded and watched as he walked off. He was quite spectacular. He had played his part to perfection. What have I done, letting him go like that? I stood and ran after him.

'Finn,' I called. 'Finn!'

He stopped and turned around.

I stood on my tiptoes and kissed his right cheek. 'Thanks for holding my hand on the ride,' I said, my stomach knotting.

He lowered his head with a coy smile and my insides melted. 'You're welcome.' He held the "m", waiting for my name. He frowned at me.

'Lucinda,' I said.

He nodded his head. 'Lucinda,' he repeated with perfect enunciation, like he was tasting my new name on his tongue. He connected his eyes deeply to mine, placed his finger under my chin, his eyes wandering to my lips before he brushed his lips across mine, one, twice, in a gentle kiss. When he pulled away, he frowned, then he opened his eyes and gazed into mine, turned and left.

I placed my finger over my lips, still tingling from his kiss. Why did it feel like a goodbye kiss?

My throat tightened as I watched him walk through the crowd until he blended in. I let out a breath like I had been holding it the entire time I had been here, and then was overcome with an incredible, deep, sadness. Like something had just ended.

But it was meant to be a beginning. A new life together.

My eyes burned as tears built. It was time to go.

I walked slowly, taking in the happiness and laughter of the theme park visitors, jealousy jabbing me at their seemingly carefree lives. Why couldn't it be me? Why couldn't I have that fairy tale life spruiked on social media, those forever smiles with perfect white teeth, that forever perfect job, perfect family, perfect friends, perfect partner … perfectly forever happy without a problem in the world?

I exited the Kingdom Adventure Park and walked to my car, opened the door and sat inside. I stared out the windscreen across the coloured sea of cars of the vast parking lot, heat waves rising above some. I leaned forward and placed my forehead on the steering wheel, and wept, while the sound of a melody in a disturbing minor key of soul searching and sorrow played relentlessly in my mind.

The realisation of the magnitude of what we were choosing to do was heavy. I should have been happy.

We were choosing to start again as *us*.

With a new beginning. A reset.

Then reality filled me. Our past, filled with beautiful moonlit nights on Jacaranda Island, of being together, of absorbing each other's essence, of exchanged soul stories, of falling in love, of treasured memories of *us*, would be obliterated like it had never, ever happened.

And Tobi … he had played his part as Finn. *Flawlessly.*

I squeezed my eyes shut to stop the deep hurt inside me, then sat back in the seat, leaving the hot tears on my face to dry in the air-conditioning. When I glanced in the mirror, they had left a trail of white, salty electrolytes, on my face, like an artwork of sadness.

Step one of our memory removal was complete—creating a new memory to keep. Now to wait a week for step two, the memory deletion, and finally, step three—the disappearance of Indigo and Tobiah.

Just like the body, on the nightdom of the full moon on Midsummer's Eve.

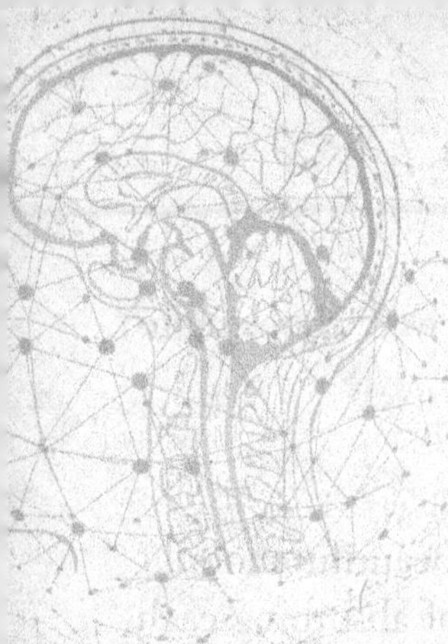

Chapter 35

Four. That was the number of steps that led up to the front entrance of Tobi's white, bay-and-gable, two storey house built onto a slender plot of land. At exactly 10am, I lifted my hand to knock on the blue timber door, but hesitated as I battled my conscience of whether to continue with the illegal memory deletion or not. Technically, we didn't kill Willow. It was never meant to happen. None of us could have predicted the outcome of that fateful night. We were innocent of any wrongdoing. I lowered my head as a wave of relief washed over me at the thought of being released from liability on that night, then knocked three times, paused, knocked two times, paused again, and knocked once more. I played it perfectly as per the instructions in my text.

'It's unlocked,' he said, the timbre of his voice singing to my soul through the natural fibres of the door, even now, after all this time, and after everything that had happened, and even after him accusing me of causing the death. According to him, it was all my fault.

I blew a slow breath between my lips, placed my hand on the doorknob and turned it, then stepped into his house. I shook my head. We had been seeing each other once a month for over a year, yet, I had never been inside his home.

I looked about and raised my eyebrows, impressed with the interior Hamptons style design—classic, breezy and spacious, with large windows and French doors letting in ample organic light, reminding me of relaxed summer holidays at the beach.

I stepped forward, running my finger along a weathered oak hall table, and faltered in my step as I placed the envelope with "Finn" written on the front, onto it. The letter written by me. The letter that would determine our future.

I walked toward the kitchen then, where Tobi sat on a chair facing away from me, wearing a blindfold, as I had told him to do. I stopped behind him, and placed my hand gently on his shoulder, then moved beside him, reached down to his hand and took it in mine, and pulled him up off the chair.

I guided him through the house, down the front stairs with care, and to the car, opened the door and encouraged him to sit in the passenger seat, then watched as he felt for the seatbelt and fastened it, while I sat in the driver's side.

The clouds muted the sun when I started the car, and kept it that way while I drove in silence for the fifteen-minute journey to the Brain and Mind Institute.

The back entrance to the institute was eerie, like a ghost town. I almost expected a tumbleweed to come rolling down the road. I parked the car, got out and went to the passenger door, and helped Tobi out.

Holding on to his hand, I led him to the security door, iris-scanned into the building, and guided him to the lab where I positioned him to sit on the dark blue ergonomic recliner chair, where twenty-five other human subjects had sat before him.

He explored the seat with his hands before he manoeuvred

his body onto it, and waited in silence, in the darkness of his blindfold. He showed endless patience, and an unbelievable calmness considering the enormity of what I was about to do to him, and its implications on his memory.

I inhaled deeply as anxiety rolled over my skin in violent waves. I was taking a big risk with this entire narrative—the use of the research lab outside the boundary of our research regulations, breaking protocol with ethics, deception of the law by erasing the events of that night. I blew air through my pursed lips and silently counted to three. This … is what we had decided … *together*.

I aligned myself into the time and place of where we were, and my role of what I had to do, suddenly aware that perfect silence could not exist here. Ever. The room was filled with the tune of the low hum of electronic equipment. Relentless, like tinnitus.

I removed Tobi's blindfold, ensuring I did not come into his field of vision.

256. That was the number of electrodes positioned on a specifically designed cap. I applied the conductive gel to ensure our signal quality, then placed the cap onto Tobi's head.

'Ready for the buzz bomb?' I said, my voice low. I would remove this conversational memory during the process.

He laughed. 'The hippy crack? Sure. Tell me why I need to have it?'

'Top secret, and all that stuff,' I said.

'Mmmmm. I love that you are super smart.'

'Thanks.' From behind, I placed an oxygen mask over Tobi's nose and mouth, and turned on the oxygen. 'Deep breaths,' I said, wishing I could connect my eyes to his—greeny-blue to ocean-blue. The most beautiful eyes I had ever seen. I would be more than happy to look at them for the rest of my days on earth. Potentially, this could be the last time he remembers me, as the person he once loved, and perhaps, still loves. After the procedure, I am just another girl he doesn't know.

I looked up to the ceiling, trying to stop myself from breaking with sadness about the erasure of our lives, and trying to stop my tears from spilling.

I needed to connect to him again. My lips to his. My soul to his. For one last time as us, as Indigo and Tobi, our shared love entwining and flowing in a melody of tenderness and love.

I placed my hand over his eyes, pulled off the oxygen mask, and lowered my lips to his, caressing with a gentleness I never wanted to forget, but knew I would, then rested my forehead against his.

'I'm ready. Let's do this, so we can begin again … as *us*.' His voice was rough.

I positioned myself behind him and replaced the oxygen mask over his nose and mouth, then slowly increased the amount of nitrous oxide into the mixture, maintaining a flow rate of 6L per minute. Within moments, he was out of it. I watched his body relax in his state of unconsciousness, oblivious to the next events that would occur.

I fussed about the prepared tray that held the cannula and nanobot technology, the elements spaced apart, perfectly.

I positioned Tobi's arm in an extended position then applied a tourniquet, and tapped the vein to check that it was suitable. Happy with the vein, I released the tourniquet, washed my hands and cleaned the site with an alcohol swab and allowed it to dry, and continued with the rehearsed steps to successfully insert the cannula.

After a moment in time, I injected the nanobot into the cannula and flushed it into Tobi's bloodstream. I gazed at the computer screen, and waited for it to light up with data, wirelessly delivered to the computer.

Nothing.

I jigged my legs and held my breath for a moment to stop the panic that wanted to burn inside me. I recited the alphabet to counteract my impatience and nervousness—*A. B. C. Come on! D. E. F. G*—

The computer screen lit up. We had connection.

I slipped straight into neuroscientist mode, reached over and pressed a key to project a functional magnetic resonance image as a hologram of Tobi's brain, above him. I monitored the nanobot's location as it travelled through his body on the Nanobot App, until it reached his brain and passed through the blood-brain barrier—a perfect combination of the latest advances in engineering, neuroscience, and physics.

I tapped on the keyboard, commanding the technology to engage in connecting digitally with memory cells, detecting the specific chemical markers that set them apart from other cells.

The computer screen became staticky, with a black and white colour faze, then a yellow birthday cake in the shape of a car appeared with two candles, and the "Happy Birthday" song began, followed by cheering. These were the memories of a two-year-old Tobi.

My fingers flew over the keyboard as I coded in the next commands, and an icon appeared on the screen initialising total download of memories, wirelessly. I had now captured the life memories of Tobi. *Digitally.* And not just a snippet of our time at the Jacaranda tree, I captured his entire life, and converted the information to be able to be watched on a screen. I pressed save, and copied it onto my attached external hard drive.

My stomach churned. It was wrong. It was an intrusion of privacy.

I refocussed on the reason we were here, illegally. I had a job to do. I typed in the date of Midsummer's Eve and watched his life from his eyes, in vision but no sound, fast forwarding it until I saw her. *Willow.* At the base of the Jacaranda tree. I attached a marker to it, preparing it to edit it out of his memories. I turned on the sound.

She stood there, with Tobi, on that fateful night. I watched the scene unfold from Tobi's eyes. Then I watched Willow fall out of the tree. That moment in time when our lives were changed forever. I backtracked and watched it three times. My memory of the incident matched his.

I shook my head. Where did she go? How could her body just disappear?

I let Tobi's memory of that night continue from when Willow fell from the Jacaranda tree. I speed watched the entire scene from Tobi's eyes, even when he left Jacaranda Island to get help. I gasped. He didn't go to work as he had claimed. He just sat in his car and stayed there.

From his eyes, I watched myself run to my car and leave, and then watched as Tobi opened his door and got out, walked to some tall reeds and lowered himself into a small motorboat, and returned to Jacaranda Island. He climbed out of the boat and the view of Willow appeared. Lifeless. In the same position I remembered her in.

Tobi stopped before her. His vision went to the Jacaranda tree, and hovered there before he looked down at Willow. I assumed he was going to collect her body, but instead, he held out his hand.

'She's gone.' She placed her hand into his, and her pulled her onto her feet. Willow was alive.

She ... was NOT DEAD!

Panic engulfed me like the flames of an inferno, and my stomach churned. Willow's death was a lie.

A LIE!

Then everything splintered. Changed forever.

A sob ripped through my throat and I placed my hand over my mouth as I dry retched. Once. Twice. And again.

I stopped the memory vision, stood and paced the room. I needed to run. I needed to get out of here. But I couldn't. I blew out a series of short breaths to try to gain control of my shattering emotions and my nausea. I squeezed my eyes shut, placed my hand over my heart, and doubled over as I tried to stop the breaking of my heart.

I reached for a bin, and expelled the contents of my stomach. I rested back on my haunches, as a horrendous sound like clenched fists being bashed onto an out of tune piano, over and over and over again, erupted inside my head with an excruciating pain. I wanted to scream, but couldn't.

Not here. Not now.

I sucked in a sharp breath as a sudden coldness hit me at my core. My heart raced and I needed to run. Far away.

In a maddening panic, I looked over at Tobi. He was still under a twilight sedation. Time was running out. I had to bring him back. Beyond that, I didn't know what I was going to do.

My thoughts became discombobulated as I wondered what to do with the information I had stumbled upon. The truth. I had stumbled upon the truth. And a lie.

I screamed internally, feeling my chest shudder, then stretched out my fingers over the keyboard and decided to download the entirety of his life of memories. *Everything.*

I should have been astounded by what I was capable of doing. But I wasn't. I had been working on the Memory Removal Project for years. I copied his file of memories onto the security encrypted folder on my external hard drive, that could only ever be accessed by me, then transferred the files onto two other locations on my personal digital safe, off site. I eyed the red USB plugged into the computer. I had intended to download the Jacaranda tree memories onto there to keep, but was in two minds, as the heat of anger flushed through me.

Dogged by an irritating, edgy, twitching feeling and fuelled by revenge, I marked every memory cell that contained my chemical tag as our technology allowed. My intention was to delete me out of his life, so that in his mind, I had never even existed.

There was only one more step to complete the memory alteration, the memory editing—the memory resetting—I had to click the delete button. Once that button was pushed, it was finished.

I crossed my arms over my chest and bent over to stop the soul-crushing ache.

I … I … had been betrayed. By the one I loved. By the one I trusted. By the *only* one I had ever let myself trust.

And now we were finished. I was finished. I could never repair the damage between us. The collateral damage inflicted on my heart and mind was too much. It was too painful. He had done to me what he said he would never do—*don't break me*, I had specifically told him. And he did. In a most spectacular way. *Betrayal.* The ultimate wounding of the heart. My body trembled as it physically hurt to breathe.

I straightened up and inhaled a shuddering breath, and placed the cursor over the delete key. Technically, according to his memory, once I hit the delete button, Willow never fell out of the tree, because she was never there. And furthermore, because she wasn't in fact, dead, none of this mattered anymore ... none of this!

In anger, I clenched my teeth, moving the cursor over the delete button, but then moved it to the button beside it: *cancel.* I clicked on it. I couldn't remove his memories of me it. There were unsaid words between us in light of the new information. What I had seen in his memories changed everything. *Everything.*

I manoeuvred the nanobot back to his cannula, shut down the hologram, followed by the computer, and turned off the nitrous oxide, allowing 100% oxygen to flow through his mask to reverse the conscious sedation. I removed the electrode cap from his head and dropped it into a container, then used paper towel to collect the gel residue on his head.

I placed the external hard drive into my backpack and pulled out the blank red USB from the computer and pushed it into the front pocket of my jeans. Then I removed his mask and paced the floor and waited for him to wake.

After three minutes, I sat on the chair and watched him, strangely feeling calm after everything I had discovered. I gazed over his face—the beautiful face I knew so well. He looked so peaceful, but all of that was about to change.

I ran my finger over his, trying to wake him from his seemingly eternal sleep.

I wish … *no, don't say it.*

His eyes fluttered open, briefly, then closed again. He smiled, then opened his eyes and looked at me. 'I was having the most beautiful dream about us,' he whispered. 'I didn't want it to end.'

I placed my hand over my mouth to stop the sob that threatened to surface. I wanted to see that most beautiful dream, because mine was filled with darkness and bitterness and devastation and shattered brokenness.

'Hey … I still remember you. I remember … everything. Did the procedure fail?'

I nodded. 'Yes,' I lied. My voice cold.

His eyes widened.

'I'll talk to you about it in a few days when you'll remember our conversation. Get up and walk around. You need to exhale the remains of the nitrous oxide from your system so you don't look like a drunk.'

Tobi rubbed his face with his hands then stood, unsteady on his feet. 'I'm intri—'

'Pull your hood up. Follow me closely.' I stood and grabbed my backpack.

'I—'

'Follow without talking. It's important.' I walked with haste through the Brain and Mind Centre to the back door, iris-scanning to exit. The moment we stepped onto the path and into the blinding light of the daydom, Willow appeared. A blonde haired Willow, who used the name, Magnolia, on the fourth floor of the Brain and Mind Centre.

I turned to Tobi, my eyes wide, fury rising inside me. 'She knows about today?' I said, my voice incredulous, pointing to Willow.

Tobi stared at me, emotionless. He nodded. Once.

I looked at Willow. 'Well … Willow of the undead. I tried to remove his memories of me, of the tree ... you included.'

She looked at Tobi with a lopsided grin, then back to me. 'Was it successful?'

'Ask him. You'll know soon enough.' I gazed into Tobi's eyes, lingering, perhaps for the last time ever. Those ocean-blue eyes I once loved so much. I shook my head slowly as bitterness crept through me, then pushed my hand into my pocket and pulled out the red USB flash drive. I handed it to him. 'This is what I downloaded from your memories,' I said, then walked away.

Chapter 36

I held my breath as I walked, elongating the distance between us with an entire twenty-page music script of despair and wailing and self-punishment and distress following me. I breathed again, and squeezed my eyes shut as the weight of disbelief descended upon me like a suffocating blanket.

I felt disorientated. Disconnected. Broken.

When I opened my eyes, I couldn't tell if I was walking with one step in front of the other, or if I was staggering along the path. I wanted to collapse to the ground and stay there, and dissolve into the darkest puddle of black ink that would rewrite my life, erasing all the sadness and bitterness and betrayal. And I wanted that darkest puddle of black ink to become a swirling vortex, that would suck me up inside it and deposit me into another time, another place. Away from my memories. Away from my life. Away from my worst enemy. Me.

I had done this. I had allowed myself to trust him. *If only …*

I couldn't remember the drive home from the Memory Lab. But now I was in my bedroom. I knew that much. I grabbed the key that was hidden under the desk and unlocked a drawer in the wardrobe. I pulled it open and grabbed the leather hip flask, identical to the one I kept at work. It was filled with bliss. It was filled with the potion that could annihilate every emotion I was feeling. It would make me more numb than numb. Anesthetised even. It would turn my life into oblivion. It would even stop the music that attached itself to every damn emotion I felt and saw in others.

I staggered to my study and slumped onto my chair at my desk, and turned on my computer. I connected the external hard drive of Tobi's memories to it, and pressed play.

I took a swig of whiskey and held it in my mouth. It was like a slap in the face for my taste buds, but it tasted sweet and honeyed and was most definitely pungently alcoholic. I swallowed it slowly, heating the back of my throat then blooming in my chest. The beginning of bliss.

I squeezed my eyes shut. He had lied.

My heart ached like there was no longer any sunshine. No happiness. No air to breathe.

I thought he loved me. He made me *think* he loved me. I *believed* … he loved me.

I watched his memories on 5x speed, and slowed it to normal speed the moment I first saw Willow. It was when they first met, at the bar like she had said. But she spoke to him first, and he never rescued her from a group of men like she had said. She had lied to me that Midsummer's Eve in the tree. Tobi walked away from her, and when she pursued him and put her hand around his arm, he pulled away from her and placed his hands in the air.

My heart dropped.

I fast forwarded to when Tobi saw Willow again. She was at the police headquarters with him, and two others. The senior police sergeant said, 'You're taking too long to get the information from her. Try harder Tobi, or we'll take you off the case.'

My heart clenched.

I was a case to him?

All those words. All those full moons in the nightdom filled with wonder and awe. All my heart strings, enchanted to his, growing and strengthening, and I was *just a case* he was working on … he was simply trying to extract information from me?

I lifted my shirt to cover my mouth as a guttural scream came from deep inside, then nausea rose with aggression. I grabbed the wastepaper basket to catch the violent discharge of my stomach contents, and continued to bitterly heave until it felt like I was going to turn inside out.

I had been used. I had been betrayed.

A dark languishing melody of deep distress and existential terror flowed through me, mirroring my broken heartedness.

A knife to the heart would have been kinder.

I glanced at the screen—

Tobi's voice, 'I can't do it anymore. I can't hurt her.'

'We told you not to get involved with her,' his boss said.

'Too late,' he said.

Tobi stared at his boss while he spoke, 'We're sending Willow in to speed up the case. She'll fall out of that damn Jacaranda tree and pretend to be dead. You go into a panic and somehow ask for your memories to be removed. I'll let you play it out by ear.'

'Sir, I am requesting to be taken off the case.' Tobi's voice.

'Not at this point, Tobi. She trusts you.'

Tobi grunted. 'For the record, I hate that I am doing this to her.'

'Get your emotions out of the case. That's an order!'

A door slammed shut, and Willow came into view. 'Let's go to the island and plan my pretend death. You have wasted too much time, like the boss said. We need the inside information of the Brain and Mind Institute and their Memory Deletion Research with living, bodiless brains. We need to shut it down. Grab your jacket and follow me.'

I watched Tobi's memories in 5x speed until the night Willow fell out of the tree, then slowed it to normal speed. Tobi returned in the small motorboat to Jacaranda Island. He held out his hand and pulled Willow up off the ground.

'Well done, Tobi. The boss will be pleased. I didn't think you had the guts to go through with it.'

I stopped the movie of memories as my heart squeezed. I couldn't breathe, and doubled over. It had all been a set up! Planned and orchestrated.

And I fell for it.

I fell for everything, the entire time I spent with Tobi. I fell in love with him. I thought he loved me. But it was all a lie.

A damn, bloody lie!

I opened my mouth wide in a silent scream, pushing it out from my stomach, until my insides tensed and hurt. My hot, angry tears fell like my life source was dripping from my body, and I couldn't stop it.

Spent and drained, I sat back in my chair and took another swig of whiskey. I swallowed it slowly. It heated the back of my throat, then bloomed in my chest.

This was my preferred way of annihilating memories.

I started the memories again. Tobi pointed a finger at Willow. 'Once I get you to the mainland, FUCK OFF! I never want to see you again!'

She smiled at him. 'But you will see me again. I have orders to assist you to finish the job. The boss doesn't like how involved you are with her.'

'He's damn right I'm involved with her. We have a connection. She does what I do—she stops people from taking their lives, and I just destroyed our relationship because YOU had to get involved!'

Willow frowned and lowered her head. She reached into her pocket, pulled some paper out, and held them out to Tobi. 'Indigo dropped these from the tree.'

Through Tobi's eyes, I watched his hand as he put the letters into his pocket. 'I'm done. With all of this! Get in the boat and wait for me!'

The view of the Jacaranda tree came closer. Tobi looked upwards, then climbed and sat on a branch. He pulled the letters from his pocket. He opened one, and there were my words, then the other. He cried. After some time, he folded the letters and pushed them into his pocket, wiped his face and climbed down the tree, and walked towards the motorboat.

I stopped Tobi's memories, and took another swig of the whiskey. I stared out the window with my alcohol fuelled thoughts, scrambling between truth and lies. I was struggling with what was real and what wasn't. Did he have feelings for me, or didn't he?

I went back in time in Tobi's memories. I played the memories at 5x the speed, watching run of the mill, day to day stuff, but slowed it down when I saw him in hospital. He was recovering from surgery on his head, behind his ear.

A doctor held up what looked like a cochlear implant, like Scarlett's. But this implant beneath his skin didn't need an external device to hear. I gasped. The lump on his head I had felt was a cochlear implant? A totally implantable cochlear implant? *What?*

It didn't make sense. Was he the only one who could hear with it? And how does that work when you already have perfect hearing? Was it planted there so the police force could also hear what he could hear?

I shook my head as my skin burned with anxiety.

I stopped Tobi's memories. It was such a tangled web of deceit. And Tobi's brother, Matt? Did he really die, or was that a fabricated lie as well?

I went back in time until I found Tobi's brother. He was pacing a room with a gun in his hand. Tobi was there, asking for Matt to give him the gun. They argued. Matt lifted it to his head … I paused the memory.

I had no right to watch it.

And I didn't want to watch Matt take his life through the eyes of Tobi. Nothing about it was right.

I turned off the memories, shut down the computer and grabbed my phone. Nausea swirled in my stomach, filled with the acrimonious ugliness of everything I had been through. I was used.

I ran to the bathroom and expelled the contents of my stomach, with all the bitterness of my crippling emotions until I felt hollow.

I sat on the tiled floor and wiped my mouth with the back of my hand, squeezed my eyes shut and cried. I felt like I had been wrung out and left to dry in a scorching hot wind. Maybe this was hell. I wanted it to be oblivion. I didn't want to feel like this anymore.

I curled up on the cold floor in the fetal position and hugged my knees to my chest. This was exactly why I was Indigo Feather Danube—a neuroscientist who wasn't in the habit of falling in love. I never wanted to be one of those girls who gushed and swooned and hyperventilated at the sight of a man. No matter how beautiful he was. Or how talented he was. Or how soulful his singing was. Or how athletic he was. Or how intellectually gifted he was.

I had just proven my point in a past discussion with Tobi. Love hurts. Painfully. Devastatingly. Shattering everything you believe. So much so that, for the first time in my life, I had no music playing in my mind in melodies and keys that painted the picture of emotion with a brutal succinctness.

I picked up my phone and opened messages. I had unanswered questions. From him. Tobiah, *the Betrayer*. At the very least, I deserved to know some answers.

Meet me at the fire pit of our youth. 9pm

I didn't expect him to answer. Perhaps it was better that way.

Chapter 37

He stood at the fire pit with his hands hidden in his jacket pockets, an orange glow casting shadows of regret on his face. He turned his head toward me as I approached. For once, he didn't have his hood covering his head, hiding his identity. Was he here as himself, instead of the well-rehearsed Tobiah, *the cop*, playing the role of the perfect, pretend boyfriend?

Seething, and crying internally, I stood opposite him, fixating my eyes on his face, refusing to focus on the flames of the fire pit that had hypnotised me since my youth.

'Did you meet with your superiors?' My words were controlled, and void of emotion. Monotone, like the sound of just one note being played.

'Yes.'

'You've told them everything about our facilities, our research?'

'Yes.'

'Which is the reason why you connected with me that day by the fire when our Olds met.' I tried to keep the hurt from penetrating my voice, and tensed my stomach to stop my internal weeping from escaping.

'No.' He moved closer to me, his scent of sweetness and spice trying to wrap its hands around my heart in a magical caress that would make everything okay.

I took a step back from him. 'So … your totally implantable, cochlear implant—your brain-computer interface—can they hear what you hear? Do they listen to your entire life … your every conversation?' A lump formed in my throat.

He narrowed his eyes at me.

'Can they hear this conversation?' My voice was more assertive than I wanted it to be.

He shook his head, ever so slightly. I watched his Adam's apple move up and down as he swallowed.

'Were you wired to record our conversations?' I held my breath, scared of hearing his answer. I wanted to get away from him and his poisonous deceit, but I needed answers.

He shifted on his feet. 'At first, yes. I was wired to record conversation. Then I refused to wear it,' he said, trying to connect his eyes to mine.

I released my breath and looked away, closed my eyes and rubbed my forehead.

He cleared his throat. 'I'm—'

I held up a white USB flash drive, interrupting him. 'I have your entire life of memories on this. From the day your turned two, until yesterday in the lab.'

He stilled, narrowed his eyes and frowned at me. 'But the USB you gave me was blank. I thought you said it didn't work. And that is what I told my superiors.'

I blinked at him and raised an eyebrow.

He pressed his lips into a hard line and frowned. 'So, you have … everything?'

'Yes. Everything that you saw and did. The only thing missing is thoughts and emotions!' My chin trembled as I recalled the final moments of his brother's life, and our supposedly falling in love.

He reached towards the USB and I pulled it away from him. His broad shoulders rose as he inhaled deeply, lifted his chin, then pushed his hands into his pockets in defeat. 'Did you watch … *everything*?' His voice sounded detached. He was protecting his heart.

'Obviously I can't watch your entire life. But I did watch the ones I had earmarked in the computer beforehand.'

Tears formed in his wounded eyes. He lowered his head and ran a hand through his hair. His resolve had been undone.

'Can you see what could happen if our research and capabilities got into the wrong hands? How it feels? How exposed you are? The Mind and Brain Institute can only be the ones in control of the technology. If our research is discovered, by anyone at this stage of testing—' My voice cracked, and my words bumped into each other inside my mouth, unable to continue to flow to be expressed. I blew them out between my lips, dispersing them into the night until they evaporated.

A tear dropped from his face.

I pulled my eyebrows together. 'Tell me. Can they hear me through your hearing implant?' My voice was curt.

He shook his head. 'No. It's to communicate to me only. Hidden. So no one else knows that I am connected, and no one hears what I hear. It's my safety net for when I go into dangerous negotiations. It's like having three ears. It's also for communicating to me to alert me to evolving incidents that I need to move quickly to get to.' He shrugged. 'You know ... like every time I had to leave quickly from the Jacaranda tree.'

I frowned, then closed my eyes. At least he was safer than I thought he would be in negotiations. My heart ached. Why did the person I fell in love with have to be so complicated?

'Can … can you replay the memories of my brother?' Tobi's voice cracked. 'I want to see him again?'

I shook my head.

'Please,' he whispered, his eyes pleading.

I looked down and winced. 'The memories of Matt—' I squeezed my eyes shut, then opened them, and shook my head again. I looked back at Tobi. 'It's not a good idea.' I held the USB above the fire pit, pulled the top of my black jumper up over my nose and mouth to stop toxic fumes from being inhaled, then dropped it, and watched as flames engulfed it until it melted into dripping balls of fire, exposing the metal components and damaging them, rendering the data unreadable. 'It's for the best.'

I looked over the flames at Tobi. He held the top of his black jumper over his nose and mouth as I did, his eyes focussed on the USB.

Three words would have changed everything. *Just three words.* From his perfect lips. Straight from his heart.

My mind filled with a melody of grief and despair, like white notes on black paper, singed with orange embers of betrayal.

Tobi looked up at me, his eyes wet, the ocean-blue colour a shade of brown in the orange glow of the fire of the nightdom of endings.

A wave of deep grief rolled through me, almost debilitating me. I wanted to kneel on the ground, press my hands against my chest over my aching heart, and cry from the darkest pit of my soul, but instead, I sucked in a shuddering breath to hold myself together with the only strength I had left.

He had betrayed me in the absolute worst possible way. And it hurt like hell.

Drowning in devastation, I buried my shattered brokenness deep into my mind box of "Do Not Open". Then I did the only thing that was left of a broken, severed us.

I walked away, hoping to conceal the image of my shattering heart, falling onto the ground behind me in the depressing melody of the dark night of the soul, each note erupting into a mini-inferno after it had expressed its unique sound of existential angst.

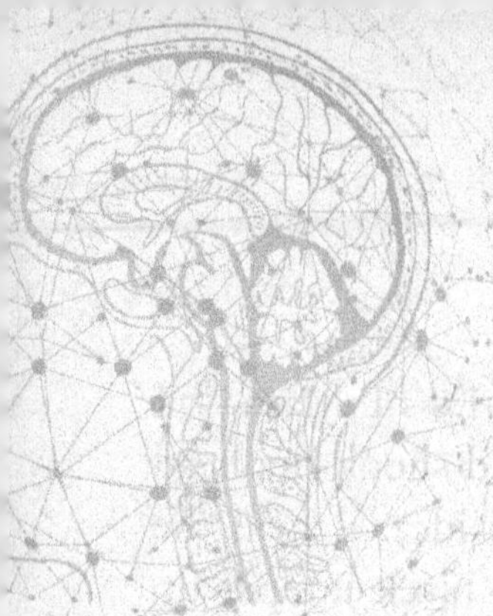

Chapter 38

I iris-scanned into the Memory Lab, hoping the black glue of self-pity that was holding my heart together wasn't noticeable. I kept a disposable pipette in my pocket in case I needed to suck up any heavy tears that threatened to fall, although, it felt like I had no tears left to cry after last night.

I lifted my chin, took a deep breath and slipped into neuroscientist research mode—the perfect distraction from the matters of my crushed heart. I looked about the room of clear glass boxes, coffins for the brains suspended in the state of between worlds. Living brains, implanted with wireless electrodes.

The absence of a laboratory scent reminded me of the unearthly, intrusive research I was involved in. But it was for the good of people. It would save the lives of those who suffered from life altering trauma, that imprisoned them inside their own bodies in a state of terror.

An intense feeling of guilt washed over me, and my head swam. I had to find my bravery and grit to do what I was about to do today.

I walked up to the first encased brain and pressed my hand to the glass. I slowed my breathing, and gazed over the gyri and sulci: the peaks and grooves of the cerebral cortex. For all we knew about the brain, it was still a mystery. The more we knew, the more we didn't know.

I had too many questions, and not enough answers.

But this I did know. Our intelligence was not the result of evolution. We were created this way. Our "brainprint" is unique, like our fingerprint. Our personality. Our identity. Our … *essence* … who we are, held in place by the confines of the skull, perfectly cushioned from harm. And for those of us who know, and who have witnessed, the brain is a glorious symphony of electrical storms of light.

We are made of light, like the stars in the universe, except, we are living, breathing, intelligent, creative, and given the power to change our own lives, and the future story of the Earth. History in the making.

A feeling of euphoria swept over me, replaced in an instant by a wave of fear rolling over me, and knotting in my stomach. We were interfering with the internal light of the brainprint, and its brain "signature".

I clenched my teeth and reminded myself that we were saving lives crushed by trauma. And what we were doing was a saving grace. We were removing crippling memories that darkened the light inside people, that erupted in a chemical pool of negative reactions that affected the whole person, from thoughts and emotions to actions, to the point of the person choosing to end their life to escape their traumatic memory. We, could stop it. We, could reset their lives to what they were supposed to be like before the trauma.

I looked about the room of clear glass boxes, again. They were like coffins for brains, suspended in the state of between worlds. The research was complete. The brains had performed exceptionally well in the experiment, and had achieved what the owner had given consent to.

I equipped myself with my virtual reality headset and looked over at Biran. He was writing a report.

I pursed my lips and exhaled slowly, and beamed Quinn's hologram above his brain. 'Good morning, Quinn.' I looked at the digital representation of his brain constructed from fMRI. The middle and superior frontal cortex and superior temporal cortex of his brain lit up. It is what happens when people hear their name. I touched my finger to the audio folder on the projected screen and opened it, then chose Quinn's favourite music—*Handel's Messiah*. The digitally altered music streamed directly to his auditory nerve via a wireless electrode, through the brain stem and onward to the auditory cortex of his brain. I smiled as his brain erupted in a kaleidoscope of light in many lobes, confirming the research that music affects all parts of the brain, not just the temporal lobe.

I moved on and projected the next brain hologram. 'Good morning, Emerson.' We had light in the correct places. *Consciousness*. In his audio folder I opened *Air on G String* by Bach. His brain lit up in a symphony of light.

Next. Hologram projected. 'Good morning, Ardon.' *Consciousness*. I smiled and opened the audio folder, found *Bitter Sweet Symphony* by The Verve, and pushed play.

Next hologram. 'Good morning, Jamie.' *Consciousness*. Audio open—*Let It Be* by The Beatles.

Next. Hologram. 'Good morning, Alex.' *Consciousness*. Audio open—*Behind Blue Eyes* by Limp Bizkit.

Next. Hologram. 'Good morning, Mica.' *Consciousness*. Audio open—*Hungarian Dances* by Brahms.

Next. Hologram. 'Good morning, Jordan.' *Consciousness*. Audio open—*Saturn* by Sleeping at Last.

Next. Hologram. 'Good morning, Emerson.' *Consciousness*.

Audio open—*How to Disappear Completely* by Radiohead.

Next. Hologram. 'Good morning, Hunter.' *Consciousness.* Audio open—*Riverside* by Agnes Obel.

Next. Hologram. 'Good morning, Charlie.' *Consciousness.* 'Charlie, we've been so busy I forgot to tell you I met with your son, Lucas, a couple of weeks ago.'

Spike.

'I told him you liked the name Charlotte for your granddaughter. He smiled, and said that was the name they liked, too.'

Spike.

'He said her name would be Charlotte Indigo Johnson.'

Spike.

'Do you like her middle name?'

Spike.

I laughed. 'Lucas said they were thankful that I could talk to you, and wanted to honour that.'

Spike.

'I'm about to stream your favourite music. Enjoy.'

Spike.

Audio open—*Stop Crying Your Heart Out* by Oasis.

Next. Hologram. 'Good morning, Nic.' *Consciousness.* Audio open—*Concerto for Piano and Orchestra No. 23 in A major* by Mozart.

I stepped back and watched the brain holograms alight with colour, as the music activated multiple lobes. I pulled out my phone and videoed the majesty of energy and a state of consciousness, then took a photograph of it, and slipped my phone back into my pocket.

I looked up again, and focused on a disturbing brain signal I had noticed a couple of times, but tried to ignore. It was an unknown. It had never been recorded or analysed before. This time, it wasn't just on one or two of the electrography traces, it was on all of them. My gut twisted.

I turned off the music for each brain, one by one, expecting the new brain trace to stop. But it didn't.

I shuddered, then stretched my fingers to ground me to the present, and inhaled slowly. I needed to have a serious conversation with the brains. But I wasn't ready. I couldn't find the courage, yet. I knew the devastation that was to come.

I placed my hand over my mouth and dry retched, then took a sip of water. I had to step up to the plate and do what was needed. The persons who volunteered their brains to research deserved the utmost respect.

I inhaled a slow and deep, calming breath. 'Biran, do you see that trace on the EEGs?'

He looked up at the EEG recordings, then frowned.

'There's a new trace that has appeared. Here.' I pointed to it. 'I've seen it a couple of times on two of the brains in the past, thinking it was a glitch, but today … they all have it.' My voice cracked.

Biran stepper closer to Mica's brain, studying it, then read the EEG. And one by one, he studied each of others. He winced. 'I doubt that it is unique to us here in the Lab. I'll check it against our database of expressed emotions in human subjects as brain traces.'

I walked around each of the brains.

I stopped in front of Charlie. I wanted to ask Charlie the question I feared the most. '*Are you still there, as a soul, as a person?*' But I didn't.

I desperately wanted to ask her, '*Can you feel anything, physically or emotionally?*' But I didn't.

I wanted, again, to ask Charlie, '*Do you have consciousness, like when you had a body and were alive?*' But I didn't.

I wanted to ask her, '*Are you angry about being kept alive?*' But I didn't.

I wanted to ask Charlie, '*Do you know anything deep and*

unknown to the living, regarding life and death and what is next? But I didn't.

I stopped walking around the Lab when I heard Biran's chair move. I looked at him as he stood with a grave expression. 'It's … it shows …' He brushed his hands over his face and cleared his throat. 'The brains are—'

'Screaming,' I finished for him.

Panic, like a poison streamed through my blood, and my stomach heaved. I was doing what I never wanted to do. I was going against my Neuroethics.

'They are suffering,' I said. They had consciousness with no sensory input, other than hearing. They had consciousness, with no means of expressions, of output. They were screaming in an agonising pitch that chilled my blood. That would chill anyone's blood. They were living in the *neither here, nor there*, world. And it was torture.

They want closure. They want … *peace*.

I squeezed my eyes shut and became aware of perspiration peppering my forehead. Words, unbidden, flew out of my mouth acting like all the "helpers" my mother would tell me to look for when there was a tragedy. 'What is the clause in our research regarding an event like this?' I knew if off by heart, but I needed Biran to say it so we were on the same page with the next decision we would make.

He sighed. 'Neuroethics: When an EEG shows evidence of negative or violent-type brain activity, the same as recorded on living humans, the research subject's "life" will humanely be ended with an injection of two drugs used for euthanasia to induce a peaceful, swift and uneventful death. The well-being of my research subject will be my first consideration.'

'And what does it say in the Research Subject Contract regarding an event like this?'

Biran blinked in rapid succession. 'Research Subject Ethics:

In the event that my EEG displays consciousness with evidence of suffering, I request that my brain passes from earthly life in a peaceful, swift and uneventful death.'

'And our final oath?'

Biran winced. 'Decisions for the research subject will be made as though the subject was embodied as a fully functional human-being in the room, to whom I have to justify my decisions to him or her.'

My throat constricted and I wiped a heavy tear away. 'Please call an emergency meeting with the neuroscience team, including psychologists. You need to tell them of our decision.'

'You're not attending?'

'No. I want to spend some alone time with our friends. I need to do it for me.'

Biran nodded once, then left the Memory Lab.

I equipped myself with my virtual reality headset and pulled up the hologram of each of the brains.

It was time to honour them.

I found the file titled, "It's Not Goodbye, But See You Later". We were prepared for this day. Everything was planned and mapped and created. This file had everything we needed to dress the brains for their finale, their walk of honour, so to speak. I could think of nothing more beautiful than adding the chosen sparkling galactic stars over and around them, celebrating their commitment, their courage, and their patience as we worked with them.

Then one by one, I did just that. I lit up each brain hologram, so it looked sacred and loved—exactly what our brains are, and what I chose to believe how our Creator saw us.

When I finished, I covered my mouth to catch my deep sob, filled with emotional pain that tried to escape. A sob filled with a grimacing key of choking back tears. I didn't want them to hear that I was crying. I didn't want to add any distress to what they already felt.

I drew in a deep breath, pulled my shoulders back and lifted my chin.

I could do this … *for them.*

Biran entered the room and gazed about at the spectacular display of sparkling galactic stars. He looked at me and whispered, 'Beautiful.' Then said, 'The decision was unanimous. We have permission to go ahead … in our own time.'

My throat tightened. We were now licensed to kill. Because effectively that is what we were doing.

But it was the right thing to do. It was humane.

A gathering of neuroscientists, and every worker who was involved in the research project, gathered outside the Lab. Still. Silent. Chins trembling. Tears falling.

I gave Biran a tense nod, and walked over to each of the glass boxes and placed my hand on it, trying to connect to them, and whispered, 'Hi.'

When I finished, I sniffed and wiped my tear, then cleared my throat. 'Hi, Quinn, Emerson, Ardon, Jamie, Alex, Mica, Jordan, Hunter, Charlie and Nic.'

Spikes.

'This memory experiment you consented to take part in has been a resounding success. Thank you.'

Spikes.

'Remember my friend, Yolande, who I told you about after I removed her traumatic memories.'

Spikes.

'I went to her wedding the other day. I was a bridesmaid. It was so beautiful and magical. It couldn't have happened without brave people like you helping out with research.'

Spikes.

I sighed. 'Your EEGs show that you are not happy, and it makes Biran and I sad. It makes all of us sad. You know that we want what is best for you. So … I have a serious question I need to ask you all. Are you up for it?' I wasn't up for their answers. My stomach clenched.

Spikes.

I inhaled deeply, shook my head and covered my mouth. My eyes burned. I hate goodbyes when I knew it was a final goodbye. *The* final goodbye. I took my hand away from my mouth. 'I'm just going to come out with it … do you want to stop this experiment, essentially, resulting in the end of your earth consciousness, so you can rest in peace.'

Spikes. All ten of them.

I closed my eyes. I knew they would agree. But it still hit me right there in the heart like the piercing of an arrow laced with poison, just like the arrow of betrayal released from Tobi. Silent tears poured down my face. I opened my eyes and looked at Biran. His hands were covering his face, his chest moving in and out in time with his sobbing.

'Brave. Thank you. On behalf of Biran and all of the neuroscientists and researchers and staff, I want to say thank you, but this is not goodbye, but, a see you again, one day.'

I hung my head as I stumbled over word shapes and letters in my mouth, trying to find the perfect words to say next. 'You were fearfully and wonderfully made on that day of your conception, when that flash of light sparked at the very moment the sperm cell made contact with the egg … and you are still loved, more than you can ever know.' I breathed out, feeling a peace where I should have felt pain.

This was the right thing to do.

I inhaled fully, and looked about at the brain holograms—the sparkling galactic stars of firing neurons ever present in the living brain. It was like having a universe of stars inside us, like all the colours above in the nightdom.

Shining. Twinkling. Communicating. Sacred.

There is nothing new under the sun. Everything was created in the beginning, as it was meant to be in the future. We only have to discover it as technology allows at the time, and if, only if, we are given permission to discover it, by the Creator. We have been given all the answers. We just have to ask the right questions, at the right time.

And no matter what we discover, no matter how shocking, or mind blowing, or reality-altering, love is what makes us human. It is what binds us. It is what connects us all, as humankind.

Love. An immeasurable force that can only be felt with the heart—the most fragile thing. And with love comes truth, kindness and forgiveness—let us live with this as an internal symphony of pure joy and grace in an endless melody flowing through us to share with others.

I breathed out the depth of my ruminations and walked over to Biran and put my arm around his shoulders. 'Let's do this quickly. I have the injectable medications ready. I'll inject into the female life-sustaining fluids. You do the males.'

Biran nodded, and I commenced my duty of care to my courageous friends, in quick succession, one after the other. At the completion of the last research subject, I stepped away and faced the wall in silence. I didn't want to watch the death of our living brains. I didn't want to watch the flat lines.

After a moment I lifted my head, 'May the Lord bless you and keep you, and make His face shine upon you, and give you peace.'

A single continuous beep sounded, followed by an alarm. *Flat line.* Another continuous beep started, filling the Memory Lab with a signal of death. Biran switched off the alarms. We didn't need them to alert us to a catastrophic event.

A catastrophic event we had caused.

It was finished.

I ran from the room throwing my letter of resignation to my boss, then out through the doors, down the lift and through the foyer, across the road and sat under the 100-year-old sugar maple tree in the middle of the park.

My place of contemplation.

I lifted my face toward all the colours above in the middle of the daydom. The dark clouds parted in that moment and the glorious sun beamed down its happiness, and peace filled me.

The research subjects were free from their clear glass boxes, their coffins for their brains in the state of between worlds. They were no longer in the *neither here nor there* world, but where they were destined to be.

For a moment, I wondered whether the Mind Lab was filled with angels who had come to take them home. Were there soul deliverers, angels, at their time of death, ministering to them, welcoming them, and guiding them as their souls entered the spiritual realm to their spiritual bodies, finally released from the physical restrictions of the human body, their human brain?

I recalled the surreal feeling of pure peace, of love, of deliverance, of victory, like that day my grandmother breathed her last breath. That cognizance of ... *knowing*.

And with my next breath, I knew their chains were gone, and oddly, so were mine.

I closed my eyes and entered that place of deep contemplation. Memories. They shape us. They define us. They impact our personalities. They control our behaviour. And if you let them ... they'll destroy you.

But now there was a choice. Traumatic and debilitating memories could be removed. And stored. *Digitally.* A life lived without fear, a life lived without PTSD resulting from the trauma, could now be achieved.

And justice. It would be served to perpetrators. To those who committed an offense without the consent of their victims. Enough was enough. Their time was coming. The truth would be exposed. And there would be no escape.

Chapter 39

One Year Later …

'I didn't think you'd come,' I said, and looked to beyond *Zero*, to the ocean full of blue. Myrtle Beach. Waves grew tall with hope in a triumphant melody, then crashed in a spectacular fall of shattered white—a melancholic key, effervescent, until all hope was gone. Still. Silent.

He pulled a piece of paper, folded into thirds, from the pocket of his burgundy-coloured chino stretch shorts. 'I found this in my house, and I was curious … *Lucinda*.' His tongue caressed the name, like tasting it, while he held my eyes in his, ocean-blue to greeny-blue. He handed the paper to me.

I opened it. *Dear Finn …*

My handwriting, decorated the home-made paper, filled with the blue ink of panic.

'You look exactly as I remember you that day at the Adventure Park,' he said, eyeing me with caution.

A ripple of anxiety skirted over my skin. Should I stay? I looked up from the letter. 'So do you. Except your face is nearly as hairy as my dog.' I raised an eyebrow at him. He brushed his fingers over his facial hair, and looked down at the sand with a shy smile, tinted with a depth of sadness.

My heart …

Buddy bounded up to me with an orange tennis ball. 'That-a-boy?' I gave him a pat then looked up at Finn, noticing the way his white buttoned cotton shirt accentuated his broad shoulders and strong chest. 'Finn, meet Buddy.' I stroked Buddy's long, golden fur.

Finn reached over, but didn't pat Buddy. Instead, he touched the ring on my fourth finger of my left hand. 'So … *Lucinda* … you're married.'

I shook my head. 'No. It's my reminder about—'

'Love,' he finished. He looked down and frowned, then looked at me. 'I'm so sorry.'

I looked away from him and toward the ocean as my throat constricted. Those were the three words I longed to hear from him a year ago, but didn't. Just three words. *I'm so sorry.* It would have changed everything.

A tear fell from my right eye, out of his view. My mind filled with confusion. Do I listen to what he has to say? Do I let him into my heart again, or do I build a fortified wall as protection?

I stood, and stepped away from my multi-coloured beach towel before I became a sobbing mess, the musical notes of my sadness rupturing in a pool the colour of self-pity. I threw the ball for Buddy, then wiped my tear.

He stood beside me, his scent a mix of woody and cinnamon notes, and pushed his hands into his pockets, then crossed one foot over the other, and my heart hammered. 'You outsmarted me,' he said.

'I got you out of a difficult situation.' I breathed out a knotted ball of panic. I didn't want to remember how he used to make me feel.

'And then you disappeared before I could talk to you again, after that night at the fire pit.'

'It was … I was …' I walked closer to the water and let the waves wash over my feet. I lifted my long, white, flowing, off-the-shoulder bohemian dress a little higher to stop the ocean from touching it … 'I thought I'd never see you again.'

'Unfinished business.' He pulled a hand from his pocket and rubbed the back of his neck.

'Same,' I said.

'I've left the force.'

I turned and faced him. 'Why? You're so good at saving lives.'

'But at my own cost. I lost everything I cared about. The one person I've loved since I was twelve.'

I looked down and brushed my finger over his, and there it was. That current. Exhilarating. Sizzling. Terrifying.

'I'm so sorry. Please forgive me,' he said.

Three words. *Just three words.* He had said them, again. A different combination, but still relevant. I looked up at him. 'For which part? Letting me fall in love with you? Leading me on with the intention of getting inside the research facility I had devoted my adult life to? Or believing I had killed someone with my stupid wish?' I shook my head.

'I was given an assignment. You don't know how torn I was when I found out it involved you. But I figured, it was better that it was me, than someone else. I could protect you, others wouldn't. And I did. Everything I learned about the memory research is unspoken. And will remain unspoken. Your attempt at removing my memories on that day were unsuccessful. And that is the truth from my point of view. And that's why the case was dropped. I did it for you. I did it for innocent victims of violence and crime who your lab and knowledge and technology can help.'

I looked down at the sand and the wishy-washy water that came and went with each wave. 'And your totally implantable hearing technology?' I looked into his eyes, searching for truth, his *essence*. Was he here as himself?

'Removed. I no longer hear voices inside my head that nobody else hears.' He gave a crooked smile, pushed his hand back into his pocket and looked out beyond *Zero*, the ocean full of blue, the afternoon light illuminating his eyes with a colour I wanted to fall into and never climb out of.

He looked back at me. 'I want to begin again. With you.' His watery ocean-blue eyes held mine. The eyes I loved so much. He was hurting. He was offering me his heart. He pulled his right hand out of his pocket and held out some paper to me. 'Here.'

I took it from him. Two letters. My love letter to him, and my wedding vows, written the night he asked me to marry him, twice, on that luminous night of the full moon. I swallowed the cry that wanted to escape from inside, and pushed the letters into my pocket to stop them from exposing painful memories from the mind box of "Do Not Open" in my mind.

'How? When?' I was checking that his story matched up to his memory that I had seen in the lab.

'After you left that night, when Willow fell from the tree. I went back to get her. She had saved them from blowing into the water. I'm pretty sure she would have read them while she was waiting for me to return, otherwise she wouldn't have kept them to give to me.' He looked down. 'I climbed the Jacaranda tree and read them. Willow waited for me in the boat.'

Truth. I started to walk along the shoreline, and Tobi walked in sync, like we had spent a lifetime with our strides matching, our bodies reading each other's.

'Did you realize at any point that there was another layer to our relationship?' His question.

'I started questioning things when you would turn up,

disguised—the old man, the homeless man, the newspaper reading man, the cleaner ...'

'But my disguises were done to perfection by a team at the force … how—'

'Your eyes, your lips, your Adam's apple, the scar on your fourth finger on your left hand … you have no idea how much you were a part of me. How you held my heart in your hands, then—' I sucked in a sharp breath, pulled my eyebrows together, and looked away, '—you shattered it.' I looked back at him, scared to blink in case my tears fell.

His eyes were wide. I watched them redden before a tear rolled down his face. 'I'm so sorry.' His voice was broken.

Those three words I longed to hear, *again.*

'That was never my intention. I had a tight control on the narrative of the operation to protect you, until Willow was thrown into the mix. The force was impatient with my progress.' He ran his hand through his hair. 'I came here hoping …' He looked down, shook his head and dug his foot into the wet sand.

'When I woke this morning,' I said, 'I had two choices. To come to the beach according to the letter I left you, or stay away, ending our story of boy meets girl. I came here hoping …' I sighed. 'And that's all I have. Nothing beyond that.' I connected my eyes to his.

Tobi moved his fingers to touch mine, and my stomach fluttered. His touch was too soft, too comforting, too everything. He lifted my hand to his lips. 'That's all I need,' he whispered, then kissed my skin, sparking that current between us.

Buddy dropped a ball at Tobi's feet. Tobi crouched down to pet Buddy, then picked up the ball and threw it. And Buddy was gone.

I started to stroll along the shoreline again. 'I want to assemble a team. I want to start a program. Will you help me?'

'I miss you.'

His words wove their way inside my mind, and I tried not

to blink. If I did, it would mean I had just heard what he said. 'The program is for people who have been through trauma, and are trapped in a living hell of that moment that changed their lives. People who feel they can't go on because of what happened to them—not just women, but men, teens and children … although, I know many of the clients will be women ... and we need an education program, to stop violence before it happens, to get to the root of the problem—'

'I can't stop thinking about you,' he whispered.

I crossed my arms across my chest. Maybe it was a subconscious attempt to stop his words from serenading my heart. 'We offer counselling before presenting the choice to remove the traumatic memories. And if we remove the memories, we store them for police evidence. The victim will never have to go to trial to prove their innocence, having every word and action and expression analysed, or their appearance, or what they wore at the time of the assault. They won't be humiliated in front of a courtroom of people until what little of their of sense of self is left, after the criminal act, is totally destroyed. They will never be called a liar—'

'I love you.'

I paused, his words making me stumble with my breath. 'It's like a reset. It's like beginning again,' I continued, then looked beyond *Zero*, to the ocean full of blue, and at the rising full moon.

Luminous. Breathtaking.

I was desperately trying to block out his declarations, but they were weaving their way to my broken heart, mending and healing, replacing the darkness with light.

'Be mine again,' he whispered.

I stopped walking and lifted my face to him. He was a good man. He was proof that good men still existed. But I wanted him to stop with his declarations of *us* again. I didn't know if I could let myself be vulnerable to love again. I didn't want to get hurt. Love terrified me. Love … *hurts*.

'Join my team. Help me to help others?' I knotted my fingers together. 'Yolande ... she ... look how she was helped, compared to what she was like when ...'

'You saw Yolande's memory, didn't you?' he said.

'Yes.' My breath shuddered.

'That's what I love about downloaded memories being used in trial. I was there when Yolande gave evidence. I heard the lies the two men gave, their version of the story, telling the court that Yolande and Mia made them do it. "Look what you made me do", words used too often by offenders pushing blame onto the victim, totally refusing to acknowledge their chosen actions. Their accountability.' Tobi tilted his head a little, and shook it from side to side, his eyes filled with a thousand stories of tragedy.

He reached out, pulled me towards him, gently, and folded his arms around me. I wanted to push him away, but decided to give in to my internal war, and sagged against him.

'Thank you for the USB filled with memories of my brother. It must have taken you days to edit everything else out so it was just of him. Happy memories,' he whispered. 'When did you break into my apartment and leave it there?'

I stepped away from his embrace. His protection. His comfort.

'It was difficult for me to watch, knowing how his life ended. But I wanted you to have all the good memories as a masterpiece of his life, to honour him.'

Tobi brushed a lock of hair off my face, his finger leaving a fiery trail.

'I didn't put it in your apartment. I gave it to your mother, and she placed it near the box of Matt Memories that I saw in your house, when I picked you up that day.'

He looked down and pulled his eyebrows together, then looked up and gazed into my eyes. 'You saw that?'

I nodded. 'Yes.'

'On the second visit to Jacaranda Island, you told me you

were chaotic, messy and lost, sometimes. Filled with too many questions and not enough answers. Remember?' he said.

My lips curled up. 'I still am.'

'You forgot to add compassionate. It oozes out of you.'

I looked towards the waves. Gentle. Soothing. 'At times it's painful to be that way, especially when you absorb people's stories and emotions. My debriefer has their work cut out.'

'Lucky debriefer. He or she?'

'It used to be he … *you*.'

Buddy dropped the ball at Tobi's feet. Tobi picked it up and threw it.

'It's a "he" again,' I said.

'How often do you see him?'

'Once a month.'

'On the full moon?' He lifted his chin and gazed into my eyes; his eyebrows furrowed.

'Never on the full moon. He goes a little crazy.'

Tobi grimaced. 'Are you sure you have a good therapist?'

'He could be better. It's a one-sided conversation. But he's a good listener. And he doesn't judge. I pay him in dog treats.'

An enormous smile stretched over Tobi's face. 'I'm kinda feeling a little jealous of your therapist.'

'He doesn't kiss as well as you.' I gave Tobi a shy smile.

Tobi grinned, crookedly. 'I miss you.'

'Will you be on my team? I need someone with a ridiculously high skill set and success rate of helping people. You're the one I want. If you say no, I will have to deny seeing you and having this conversation.'

Tobi looked beyond *Zero*, the ocean full of blue, ran a hand through his hair and closed his eyes for longer than a moment.

'All they need to say is … I choose to forget, or … I want to begin again.' I looked up at him, my eyes welling, willing him to open his eyes again. 'And the traumatic memories are gone.

The PTSD is no more. They can be happy, again. Women. Men. Children.'

Tobi opened his eyes and looked at me. His gaze shifted from my eyes to my mouth, and my insides melted. 'I want to begin again, with you.'

'Is that a wish?'

'It's a need. And you know I don't believe in wishes. You have to act on a plan.'

'You have a plan?'

'I wouldn't be here if I didn't.' His hand covered mine, and the gentleness of it took my breath away.

I led him away from the water and back to my towel, to where the sand was soft, and pulled him down to sit next to me, then reached into my bag.

I pulled out a book with a dark blue, hard cover—the book of endless possibilities, of mind probing, and inner revelations. The book of once upon a time … and of the dark night.

Tobi smiled. 'So, you're the keeper of my book. I thought I'd never see it again.'

I brushed my fingers over the cover. 'I stole it. I wanted to keep a memento of … *us*.'

'It was my prop. I used the story beginnings to see if you would divulge any research information during your storytelling.'

I grimaced. 'Clever, but not clever enough.'

'There was one story you told about being betrayed that freaked me out. A lot. I was close to telling you the truth about my assignment, right then and there.'

I frowned. 'I used to love creating those stories. Yours were my favourite, Tobi, *my magnificent storyteller*.'

His eyes flickered with sadness. He blinked then raised an eyebrow at me. 'And the metal box?'

'Stolen. Guilty as charged. I wanted to keep our heart pieces.'

He lifted his chin and looked at me with hooded eyes.

'Willow's compact?'

'I found it next to her body and picked it up, then panicked because my fingerprints were on it. I kept it on me every day until I accidentally stood on it.' I smiled. 'It broke. Two mirrors. It could equate to fourteen years of bad luck, if I believed in that stuff.'

'And do you?'

'No. There's no such thing as good luck or bad luck. It's your point of view and whether you're an optimist or pessimist.'

'So … are you saying, it could be good luck, or bad luck, that I'm sitting here with you?'

'If I didn't want to see you, it would be bad luck, but because I came in the hope of seeing you, it's good luck.'

Tobi's gaze lingered on mine, a little longer than necessary. I breathed in the euphoric feeling he gave, but then pulled myself out of his spell.

I ran my fingers over the hard cover of the dark blue book. 'Close your eyes,' I said, 'and give the story life, with your mind, then speak it with words.'

Tobi closed his eyes, and I mapped every part of his beautiful face with my vision, settling on his lips. *Just a little taste. Again.*

I extracted my wayward thoughts and focussed on the book of unfinished stories and opened it at the dog-eared page.

Chosen. By me.

I hesitated, seeming to struggle to form the text as words in my mouth, to release them as audible words. But then they followed, in the right order, and with the right tone, 'Once upon a time, a boy met a girl …'

Tobi's chest rose, then relaxed. He opened his ocean-blue eyes and set them on mine. My stomach fluttered as my fingers ached to reach out and touch his face. But I didn't.

'Once upon a time a boy met a girl.'

He paused, then blinked. Twice. Like he was summoning the bravery to tell his story that needed to be told.

> 'He wanted to kiss her in that instant because his light matched perfectly to her light, his goodness to her goodness; his soul yearning to spend earth time with hers.
>
> But he didn't kiss her, because that would be totally awkward and inappropriate, and if her light didn't recognise his yet, because she had met too many false lights, she would run from him. He had to hold back. Their kiss would come when the time was right. And he would wait for it, for as long as it took.'

Tobi's gaze moved to my lips.

> 'But regrettably, this is a tragic love story. It's a story of forced bad choices and betrayal. All his. He wanted to reverse time and start all over again and hold her heart in his hand like it should be, as the most precious thing in his world, to be loved, and cherished, and protected.
>
> He reached into his pocket and pulled out his great, great grandfather's fob watch. It was rough and the colour of grey. He pushed on the button and it flipped open. On one side was a clock, ticking in a soft, calming way, and on the other side was a secret compartment; sealed.
>
> He ran his finger over it, remembering the day he sat on the porch steps with his great, great grandfather.
>
> "Finn. This fob watch is yours." It was all gold

and shiny, like it was new. "It has been passed down the generations. I skipped a couple because I saw you in a vision before you were born and wanted you to have it. I have written a letter and placed it inside, here."

Great, Great Grandfather tapped the metal, and the sound tap danced in his mind.

"In the letter are instructions for *The Undoing*, when you feel that you need to reverse time and start anew. But it's for one event only. It will break your heart to choose. But your heart will mend, over time."

Great, Great Grandfather snapped the shiny gold fob watch shut, and placed it into Finn's hand, then closed his fingers around Finn's. "I know how it ends. You will need courage, and seek forgiveness. It won't be easy, but all things work for good."

Finn slipped Great, Great Grandfather's fob watch into his pocket. And it stayed with him every day and every night. He believed he would know the time to reveal the letter, and he believed he would have no doubt about when to use it when the time arose.

Now Finn sat on the beach alone. He was misery, like the colour of charcoal. He had pushed away the only one, who his soul had searched for, who his heart loved, and who his mind craved.

He had crushed her with betrayal forced upon him by his job. He believed he was doing the right thing in trying to extract information from her about her classified research.

He was the one he thought would save the entire world from research that would get into the wrong hands. He could save everyone from lies and deceit and trauma ...

But he didn't know that the research facility had all things in place to stop it from being corrupted by unscrupulous individuals.

And by continuing to follow orders given to him, he lost the person he loved the most.

How could he forgive himself?

He placed their time together in the "Lucinda Box" in his mind and closed it, and placed it on top of the "Matthew Box". He made a mental note to *never* open either of them.

He ran his finger over the fob watch, rough and the colour of grey, then looked over at the ocean, that should have been the colour of azure, but it too was a shade of grey. The colour in his world had been stolen. Twice.

The first time the colour around him dulled, was after his brother's death.

And the second time was when he had broken the heart of the only woman he had ever loved, and it was then that colour completely vanished.

Finn knew this was the time that his great, great grandfather had spoken of. When there was nothing left for him, and of him. When the last thread of his life was about to snap.

It was time for *The Undoing*.

He pushed the button of the grey, dull fob watch, and it flipped open.

Tick. Tick. Tick. The heartbeat of time echoed throughout the universe.

Finn tapped on the compartment, just like his great, great grandfather had, then pushed it further down until it released the lock, opening with a sigh. The aged letter unfolded like a book, wanting to be read.

He pulled it out and flattened it, and ran his finger over Great, Great Grandfather's handwriting, words like calligraphy painting a story of love, created and shared from his heart to Finn's.

To My Dearest Great, Great Grandson,

Two events in your life have brought you to your knees, and that is why you are reading this letter. Both are catastrophic to your heart.

You seek change. You seek to reset, to begin again, to make things right, as they should be. You want to choose to forget, and no matter how hard you try, these two events are part of you, and cannot be forgotten.

You have a servant heart of gold, of compassion and of love for others. But you can't save the entire world like you wish. Only the Chosen One can do that.

However, I give you a lifeline. This is a special fob watch. It is the fob watch of The Undoing. *But be warned. If you choose to press the button three times, it will change your story.*

Before you choose The Undoing *- and you can only choose one of the events - you must seek forgiveness from others, and of yourself. Once you have done this, you have permission to press the button three times, and* The Undoing *will be put into motion, unable to be stopped.*

With love and fondness,

Eternally your Great, Great Grandfather Edward
x x x

Finn folded the small letter, and placed it back into the compartment. He waited, sitting on the beach until the moonrise of the full moon, reminding him of days of secret rendezvous with his love. His true love.

He looked down and ran a finger through the sand. He knew which event he would undo—it would be his brother's death.'

Tobi paused and his bottom lip quivered, his eyes filling with tears.

'Finn lowered his head more, and his fears fell. Why did he have to choose? Why couldn't he have both?

Finn pushed the button of the rough, grey fob watch. Once. And it opened.

Tick. Tick. Tick.

As the luminous moon rose higher in the nightdom, he left the beach and returned home to his parents. They sat in front of the fireplace, warm mugs of hot coffee in their hands.

'Ma, Pa,' Finn said, and looked down and swallowed. He looked at his mother, then his father. 'I'm sorry I couldn't save Matt. He died because of me.' He placed his hand over his mouth as a sob escaped.

'No, no, no, no, no,' his mother said. 'Matt chose to do it. No matter what you did or didn't do, he still would have succeeded in ending his life, or his cancer would have taken it.'

'What?' Finn said.

'We are the ones who should be sorry, son,' his father said. 'Matt didn't want you to know about his incurable cancer. So we kept it from you after promising Matt that we would.'

'What?'

'He had an inoperable brain tumour,' his mother said. 'Chemo and radiation were ineffective. He was having seizures, headaches, changes in his speech, changes in his hearing, he couldn't see properly and he had no taste left. He was starting to fall over a lot. He hid all of it from you. He wanted you to keep loving him as the big brother you adored. Near the end, as the cancer spread, his personality changed. Completely. He behaved in ways he never would have if he was well. We you arrived that day—'

'He was walking around his room with a gun, stumbling,' Finn cut in. 'I thought he had taken recreational drugs. His speech was slurred and he kept walking into things like he couldn't see. Three times I almost got the gun away from him. The fourth time he was about to hand it to me when he stumbled, his arm rising as he tried to find his balance and—'

'It was accidental, Finn. It wasn't your fault—'

Finn cried loudly. 'I held him until he took his last breath. I loved him. If we could go back in time—'

'There's nothing you could have done. It was the cancer that did this.'

Finn's father stood, and walked over to him.

He pulled him into his arms. Finn felt his mother's arms wrap around them, and they cried together.

Finn's father spoke, 'My great grandfather once told me that life is filled with choices, every moment of every day. Most of the time we get our choices right, but other times with make the wrong choice. And that is how we learn, how we grow. He also told me that you can't control what other people do, and you shouldn't. Their choices are not a reflection of you. It comes from a place that shows their true character. My great grandfather told me that kindness trumped everything in life, that, and love.'

Finn stepped back from his father and mother, and looked into his father's eyes, weary and old.

'Son, forgive yourself. You have a great gift to give to others. Use it. You make us proud, and we love you. Always be kind to yourself. Always.' His father's voice was gentle, imbued with the power of unconditional love—'

'Is this part of your story true?' I cut in.

Tobi nodded, his face painted in the colours of misery, of an unspeakable memory, dripping with a melody of deep distress.

'I'm so sorry,' I whispered. *Three words.*

Tobi closed his eyes for a moment and inhaled slowly. Deeply. Then returned to the story…

'As Finn left his parent's house, he realised the world around him wasn't so grey anymore. Muted colour entered his vision.

Finn returned to the beach.

The light of the full moon touched the sand

> so that it glowed. But this time he wasn't alone. A young woman sat there, her hair the colour of honey, blowing in the cool breeze. A goofball of a dog sat beside her while she watched the waves.
>
> 'I didn't think you'd come,' she said.
>
> Finn pulled out his great, great grandfather's fob watch from his pocket for *The Undoing*, and a folded piece of paper from his pocket. He held out the paper to her. 'I found this in my apartment, and I was curious ... *Lucinda*.' Finn connected his eyes to hers, in the hope that she would remember their eye love.
>
> 'I thought I'd never see you again,' she said.
>
> 'I'm sorry for what I did to you. Please forgive me.'

A tear ran down Tobi's cheek. I wiped it away with my finger. 'I forgive you,' I whispered.

Tobi lifted his chin and looked down into my eyes, lingering, soaking me in.

> 'Finn wanted to dissolve into a puddle of happy tears. He looked at the gold fob watch in his hand, all shiny and new. His full colour vision had returned. All he had to do was push the button three times, and *The Undoing* would begin. Time would reverse and he would meet Lucinda once again at the park around the fire pit. But this time, he wouldn't make any mistakes. This time, he would choose his words carefully, and he would refuse to take part in the undercover cop assignment. He would never risk hurting the love of his life.
>
> Finn pushed the button of the fob watch.

> Again. A second time.
>
> *Tick. Tick. Tick.*
>
> He focussed on the heartbeat of time. Echoing throughout the universe.
>
> He positioned his thumb to push the button a third time, ready for *The Undoing*—'

'Then Lucinda's hand reached out to stop the third time,' I cut into his story. 'I don't want to reverse time. I don't want to lose the memory of our words of discovery, of searching, of falling in love, of our first kiss.'

Tobi sucked in a short, sharp breath, and continued,

> 'Finn looked into Lucinda's eyes, overcome by her words. He snapped the fob watch shut and slipped it into his pocket. He didn't need *The Undoing*. He had done that himself by seeking forgiveness. He lowered his eyes to Lucinda's lips. There was only one thing on his mind, and that was to kiss her in that instant, because his light matched perfectly to her light, his goodness to her goodness; his soul yearning to spend earth time with hers.'

I placed my hand onto Tobi's chest, over his heart. His eyes held mine with a controlled emotion, before he covered my hand with his, the tenderness of his connection seeping into my being.

Tobi's eye caress shifted to my lips, and then back to my eyes. '*May* … I kiss you?' he asked, his voice tender, his pupils large, filled with longing, like he was trying to absorb all of me, but overflowing with a vulnerability like my answer could injure him.

'Yes,' I whispered.

His lips were on mine then, slow and sensual, like he was

balancing on a fine line between an uncontrollable passion, and being careful not to hurt me. And I was falling. Totally. I was ready to begin again. With him.

With our memories intact.

Our lips parted, and I opened my eyes and connected to his, the reflection of the full moon making the colour of his irises impossibly more beautiful. I inhaled gently to disperse his addictive presence, then turned my gaze to the nightdom, to all the colours above.

The moon danced with the earth in a romantic waltz. The earth spinning, and the moon orbiting to the song of the universe.

Luminous. Sacred.

And all the stars above. Scattered. Chaotic, but not chaotic. Our universe was planned and organised, consistently obeying the same rules, and beyond spectacular in the darkness of nightdom. You can't have light without darkness. And the light needs the darkness to sing its triumphant victory over difficulties in a melodic key, highlighting all the colours beyond our wildest dreams, beyond the human limited colour spectrum.

And yet, there was a gift more powerful than all the beauty and majesty of our universe—*love*.

I inhaled deeply, high on the potion that Tobi offered me, again—my heart blooming like a thousand red roses, with the scent of rich citrus, spice, and sweet fruit, surrounded by a meandering, dreamy, exhilarating love melody in my internal consciousness.

I closed my eyes and placed my hand over my heart. I wasn't in the habit of falling in love until, Tobiah had undone me. *Again.*

'Indigo Feather Danube … I need to take you to Jacaranda Island.' Tobi's voice interrupted my ponderings. He raised an eyebrow at me. Was he was hiding something? Was there a problem?

'Should I be worried?'

He looked beyond *Zero*, to the ocean full of blue, and paused before he looked back at me. 'Well … it's possible that I broke Rule Number 4 — you cannot be on the island alone — because of Rule Number 8 — you may only break Rule Number 4, to add an element of surprise for the significant other.'

'And …'

'It took me almost a year to complete the element of surprise.' His eyes were wide.

'Tobiah Lucas Brooks … is this element of surprise legal?' I lifted my hand and trailed my fingers over his facial hair to try to soothe his unease.

He closed his eyes and leaned his cheek into my hand. 'Yes,' he said, lingering on the "s". He opened his eyes. 'I want to take you there, now.'

I inhaled deeply, trying to dissipate the burn of anxiety that skirted over my skin. I wasn't sure I was ready to return to the park of our youth, nor the tree where I fell in love with him, and where I was bitterly betrayed.

'Please,' he whispered. His jaws flexed as he clenched his teeth together.

In a state of internal conflict, I looked at all the colours above. The moon. The stars. The darkness. The darkness within. I had been there before, and I never want to return to that place of depression that sounded like an entire out of tune orchestra piling up in a music jam of discordant, dark, and torturing notes.

Could I trust him again?

Tobi reached over and traced my fingers, one at a time, sending that familiar spark through me. He pulled his hand away and closed his eyes, and frowned, then shook his head. After a moment, he stood and walked towards the ocean, placing his hands behind his head, before sitting on the sand and draping his arms around his bent knees.

My heart sank. Of course he could feel my uncertainty. But

surely, he must have expected that after everything that had happened between us.

Buddy left my side and walked towards Tobi. He sat next to him and rested his head on Tobi's arm. Sadness filled me and I closed my eyes. A dog's intuition.

I stood, gathered my beach towel and followed in Buddy's path, stopping in front of Tobi. He looked up at me. 'I'll meet you there in half an hour,' I said.

It was better to know whether he and I should be a we, an *us*, than keep wondering about it for a lifetime. Live my life with no regrets ...

Tobi closed his eyes, presumably taking in the moment that looked like a silent prayer of thanks.

'Buddy. Come,' I said, turned and left the beach.

He waited by the gentleman's rowboat. I lowered my head as an ache in my heart, and a longing, took me completely off guard. Tobi had arrived before me, even though I left before him. Dropping Buddy off at home took longer than I thought.

As I walked toward him, I noticed a structure on Jacaranda Island that I couldn't bear to focus on. Right now, I was using all my strength just to meet him here, and to be honest, I didn't know if I was ready for him to be mine again ...

I stopped before him.

'By the light of the full moon,' he said, his voice deep and rich in its tones, creating a growing melody of heart-string vines, flourishing and surging through my veins directly to my core in a key full of longing, and of searching. His hands were behind his back, emphasising his broad shoulders, and behind him, impossibly large, the full moon was stealing all the colours above.

I breathed out his allure. 'As planned.' I gave him a shy smile. 'And Rule Number 1,' I whispered, as a wave of anxiety travelled through me. Should I have come here tonight?

He clenched his jaw then pulled a single pink rose from behind. 'I do believe we met at another time,' he said.

My lips curled up with an amused smile, remembering the story he once told me. I took the rose from him and lifted it to my nose, inhaling the fruity, floral, scent, reminding me of warmer days in the Springdom. I gazed up at him. 'Great pickup line.'

He lowered his head and the corners of his mouth turned up, then he lifted his head and held out his hand to me. My heart raced. I placed my hand into his and he kissed it, connecting his eyes to mine. Ocean-blue to greeny-blue. I climbed into the boat as a euphoric warmth blossomed inside me, like watching a flower bud opening to the sun on time-lapse.

I sat, then watched as Tobi pushed the boat off the shore and jumped aboard. He leaned forward to take control of the oars and looked across to beyond *Zero*, to the lake full of dark inky blue at this time of nightdom, as we picked up the pace. Then his gaze settled on me.

'Borrowed or stolen?' I said.

'Owned.' He smirked and looked away from me.

My eyes twinkled and I nodded, approving of his purchase. 'Left a little,' I said, guiding Tobi as he rowed.

He kept the left oar in the water to turn the boat, then started to row again.

After a while I said, 'Left a little more, and glide.' We were getting closer to Jacaranda Island. I tried not to focus on what I could clearly see, but didn't want to acknowledge. What he had done would mean too much. Right there in the heart.

He held my eye connection and stopped rowing. The boat glided in the quietness, filled with expectation.

'Now,' I said.

Tobi reached out to his left and stopped the boat against the jetty. With his right hand he grabbed the rope and secured the boat. He leaned forward then, and offered his hand to me with gentleness, steadying me as I climbed out of the boat and onto the jetty.

I stilled as I stared in awe at what I could no longer deny I was looking at.

'I want to give you a fairy tale,' he said. His whispered words were warm against my neck.

I closed my eyes, totally enamoured by him, but refusing to fall for his charm. I wanted to tell him I didn't believe in fairy tales. I didn't like princes or princesses. And happily-ever-afters were rare. I wanted to tell him that fairy tales started with once upon a time, the prince married a poor girl who was absolutely incapable of helping herself, and his choice was always based on her beauty, and it ended with they lived happily ever after, but then the story stopped, and no one ever knew how the rest of their lives played out, the high and the lows, the storms and the sunshine ...

I calmed my thoughts. Before me sat a stunning lake house, built partially on the land of Jacaranda Island to the right of the tree, and the rest of it built over the water on wooden piers. It was a single storey house with white, timber exterior cladding, walls of windows, a deck, a chimney and a gabled, metal roof. I heard the click of a button, and at once, outdoor festoon lights lit up the deck.

Tobi's hand wrapped around mine, and the gentleness of it made my knees weaken. He led me along the jetty he had built many moons ago, that now extended to the lake house. My insides jittered as we walked, my mind was in a whirl.

Was he backing me into a corner?

Was he trapping me somehow?

Was this a type of emotional blackmail?

We stepped onto the deck of the lake house, and Tobi stopped and faced me. He reached into his pocket and pulled out a golden key and held it out to me. 'For you.'

I shook my head and closed my eyes.

'I built it for you … it's yours, with or without me.' His voice cracked.

I opened my eyes and connected them to his, a sadness shining in the waves of his beautiful ocean-blue eyes, almost undoing me.

'Open your gift. I'll wait here,' he said.

I inhaled a sharp breath, and half blinked in an attempt to stop my tears from falling, then walked to the white timber door, inserted the key, unlocked it and pushed it open.

The moment I stepped inside the lights came on. I was in the mud room, all white, and to the left was a bathroom. I walked forward through a doorway that opened up into a great room on the right, with a wall of windows, and double doors overlooking the lake.

There was a white lounge setting and fireplace, with a pale blue rug on the timber floor. I looked to the left at the island bench and kitchen—all white, except for the bouquet of pink roses, infusing the air with the scent of musk and myrrh, with a hint of citrus.

I looked up. A stunning white cathedral ceiling, scattered with sky windows took my breath away. I could see all the colours above—the luminous moon singing songs of nightdom, and stars that punctuated the heavens with light and goodness and wonder.

I placed my hand over my mouth to catch the cry that threatened to escape, then sucked in a deep breath, and turned on my heel, admiring the chandelier that adorned the centre of the room.

I walked forward through another opening to a large white bedroom, with a vaulted ceiling and sky windows. I stepped towards the king-size bed and ran my fingertips over the bedding and pillows and quilt, all white, except for the throw rug, a shade of ocean-blue. There was a vase filled with white daisies on a bedside table. One wall of the bedroom housed windows with an outlook of the lake, and another wall had windows and a door that led out to the deck, overhanging the lake.

The lake house was stunning. Spectacular.

It was … overwhelming.

I strolled to the corner of the bedroom with no windows, and rested my back against the wall, then slid down and sat on the timber floor. I looked up through the sky windows and all the colours above, covered my face with my hands, and let my tears fall.

Patient. That's what Tobi was.

By the time I pulled myself together, wiped my tears away and walked out the door and onto the festoon lighted deck, he was still there waiting for me.

I stopped beside him, my arm touching his, igniting that spark between us. 'There's an important piece missing from the lake house,' I said.

Tobi turned his head toward me and frowned.

'You.'

He closed his eyes at my words like the weight of the world had been lifted from his shoulders. I leaned in and placed my lips on his, with gentleness.

He opened his eyes and stood, facing me, then placed a finger under my chin, and lowered his lips close to mine, hesitating, magnifying my heartbeat and the fire that burned beneath my skin. He brushed his lips over mine once, twice, waiting, then again, seducing me with a slow, soft kiss. I ran my fingers through his thick hair as I melted into him.

Tobi pulled away from our embrace and dropped his forehead against mine. 'The lake house is yours … with or without me,' he whispered, his voice rough. 'I don't deserve your forgiveness.' He lifted his head from mine and looked into my eyes. 'Just say the word, and I will leave, and never return, happy in the knowledge that I built this for you, and that you might like it.'

'You … built it?'

'Yes,' he said, lingering on the "s". 'I wanted to make you happy again … with or without—'

'With you,' I said, then grabbed his hand and pulled him over to the Jacaranda tree. I stopped before the wide rough grey trunk and looked up at all the colours above. 'Do you see that, Tobi?'

I watched him as he raised his head and smiled. He squinted. 'Yes. I see it.'

'See what?' I said.

'Lavender-coloured blooms creating an umbrella of magic. Each bloom filled with stories, thoughts, whispers, dreams, love, hope … and the unknown.'

I took a deep, enchanted breath. 'Rule Number 2,' I said. 'On the nightdom of the full moon, when dark shadows become a whisper of themselves, the Jacaranda Tree must be climbed.'

'Absolutely,' he said, and kissed me below my ear, sending a fire through my body.

'See you at *Above*,' I said, then disappeared up into the tree and settled on a branch, like I used to.

I heard the ground moan below, and looked down to see Tobi moving from foot to foot, while he plotted his climbing gig. The ground grumbled again, and then there was silence, like all the music of nature on Jacaranda Island was holding its breath. I watched as Tobi hugged the tree while he climbed at the speed of a sloth.

'Tobi, *the Brave*,' I said when he sat beside me. 'My sloth.'

Hi cheeks dimpled and the corners of his eyes wrinkled. 'The sloth that you love?'

'More than you think I do,' I said. I looked down, then back up at him. 'Thank you for building my lake house,' I whispered.

'I would build you a hundred more if you asked me to.' His words were whispered and warm.

'Tobi,' I lifted my chin to stop my tears, 'if you were a melody played on a piano, you would be all the white keys, while I'd be the black keys.'

'Indigo, white keys and black keys make the most beautiful music together,' he whispered. A tear fell from his eye. 'Be mine again … *please* ... I'm giving you my heart.'

And at that moment I knew, this Jacaranda tree was not *my* Jacaranda tree, it was *our* Jacaranda tree, again, and the lake house was not *my* lake house, it was *our* lake house—of moments never to be forgotten. Of moments to be created. Of moments that would be etched upon our hearts and minds. Of moments to be shared, just the two of us. We could never go back. It was too late. It had already begun. And it couldn't be stopped …

Behind the Story

All the Colours Above never existed in my writerly imagination until my friend and fellow Meniere's disease warrior, *Judy McNamara Tripp* (Creator of *The Meniere's Awareness Project)* sent me a gift all the way from New York, USA, as a thank you for *The Colour of Broken,* a novel with a main character with Meniere's disease which became #1 on Amazon in its category a few times.

Readers of *The Colour of Broken* kept asking me to write a sequel because they wanted to know what happens with Yolande and Xander. They wanted the story to continue, pleading with me. I kept saying, *Sorry, I have no other story line for them.* It was true, but also only a half truth. I couldn't continue writing about Yolande and Xander because I needed time to heal from writing *The Colour of Broken.* Tears still come to my eyes when I think about the book, and how many times I stopped typing and just sat and sobbed about what Grandmother Fleur was going through with her Meniere's Disease. Three years later, I still have readers sending me photographs of whenever they see a Cruiser bicycle with a basket of flowers on the front, saying, 'I saw this and thought of your book.' *Powerful.* It blows me away. Every. Single. Time. Thank you.

On that day that Judy's gift arrived in the post, I excitedly opened up the box, and inside was a classic, diamond-studded, gold compact, exactly like the one in this story. I pushed on the button and it flipped open, revealing two mirrors - one magnified, and one normal - and in that split second, I had the beginning of a new novel. *Mirror. Mirror.* Who am I? The me of the past, or the me, now?

As an empath, I have a lot of compassion for people who have suffered trauma. Their stories break my heart and all I want to do is make everything better for them so they can live happily ever after. And that's what I explored in *All the Colours Above*. I always think, *if only they didn't have to go through that* ... which led me to the idea of removing the memory of the trauma, but leaving all other memories intact. And so the research phase of writing began. I sank into vast amounts of neuroscience and memory articles, and the latest technology, neurotechnology and nanotechnology, and created my own form of memory removal technology.

During the research phase of the novel (2018 - 2020), I also became buried under tons of research about Meniere's disease (again), refreshing my knowledge and adding to it, with what happens during an attack, the possible causes and various treatments of Meniere's Disease, as Xander is a medical research doctor who is committed to finding a cure for the disease. In my quest to find something that is even the remotest way possible or legitimate, I racked my brain, trying to find an avenue for curing Meniere's disease that possibly hadn't been investigated yet, and that was with nanobot technology. Is it possible? Maybe. And who knows, as technology evolves in the future it may open doors in medicine that weren't open in the past.

Meanwhile, while I was writing the novel, *in between teaching Secondary Art, Music and Drama, part-time,* I had Cochlear Implant surgery in December 2019, after being deaf in my Meniere's ear for 15 years. It changed my life (besides having my balance cells destroyed with Gentamicin in 2004 to stop the vertigo). It was like I had been freed from Meniere's, taking back what the Meniere's monster had taken from me. And so, I decided to add a character into the novel who had, not only a cochlear implant, but was also trialling regrowing hearing cells - Scarlett.

However, I took the cochlear implant technology one step further with the main character, Tobi. I decided to give him a totally implantable cochlear implant, so no external processor was needed. No one would have any idea he had hearing technology under the skin on his head, even though he could hear perfectly with both of his ears. I found that possibility quite intriguing, and scary, with computer brain interfacing.

There are three other main elements I included in the story just because I love them to bits - Jacaranda trees, the full moon, and looking up at all the colours of above, day or night. They make my heart happy.

Acknowledgements

Firstly, thank you to my friend, and fellow Meniere's disease warrior, *Judy McNamara Tripp* (Creator of *The Meniere's Awareness Project). All the Colours Above* would never have existed without the gift you sent me.

A BIG thank you, again, to *my husband*, for his forever support and understanding that writing is the only place where I can escape from my Meniere's disease - 26 years at the time of printing this novel, since that day changed my life for my earth time. (Dx:1995)

My three beautiful children, thank you for all you do. And thank you for s from the torturous violent vertigo where I would stare at the wall for hours and hours at a time, and as adults, thank you for listening to me rant on about my writing or wacky ideas that pop into my head, and for your compassion as you watched my tears fall as I struggled with life, or was overcome with emotion from readers thanking me for writing *The Colour of Broken*. I am indeed blessed.

A heartfelt thank you to *my dear mum and dad*, who always dropped everything the moment I went into a violent spinning session for at least 4 hours at a time (I used to call it a SPAT – spinning attack), which was often, and they would come to take care of my three kids while I was totally debilitated. I will eternally cherish your love and support.

Thank you to my team of medical doctors, *Dr. Ann Masjakin (GP), Dr. Maurice Stevens (ENT), Dr. Christopher Que Hee (ENT and CI Surgeon), Professor Graeme Clark*, who pioneered the Multi-channel Cochlear Implant for severe-to profound deafness at the University of Melbourne, my Cochlear Audiologist, *Karen Pedley*, who fine-tunes my cochlear hearing at "mapping" sessions by connecting me to a computer, and to the legendary, *Emeritus Prof Bill Gibson AO* aka *The Meniere's Guru* ... 'Look for the helpers!' - you are the helpers! Thank you for your extraordinary care.

Thank you to *Bryde Dodd* & *Ash Stephens*, amazing Secondary Art Teachers, and beautiful friends, who were always supportive when I spoke about my novel in progress.

A huge thanks to my beta readers, especially to the wonderful *Michelle Upton, Shez Kennington* and *Belinda Hind*. Your feedback was gold. *x x x*

And to you, the reader of this novel, and to my friends and family, thank you for choosing to read my fictional story. It means more to me than you can ever know!

Finally, thank you to *my Creator*, for always carrying me through the terrifying storm, for giving me hope when it felt like there was none, and for giving me a Light to hold onto in the darkness so I could find my way back home.

Art is a big part of who I am. It's a place where I can lose myself and find myself at the same time. When writing novels, I like to create artwork that encapsulates the storyline, or a part of the book. In 2020, I created *I Wish* ... which was on display at an art exhibition in the month of August.

I Wish ...

I Wish... 2020
Digital art using Procreate
Printed on textured Aquarelle paper, 303mm x 216mm
Diptych

I Wish ... explores the concept of making a wish – your heart's desire, fanciful thoughts filled with extravagant wants, a bliss-bomb of a dream that can never be achieved, or a wish for a result that you never put in the effort for. The unattainable. *I Wish* ... then explores the reality of a wish – blown on the wind in silence, and destined to return to the earth, unfulfilled.

Perhaps you should have prayed instead?

The Colour of Broken

#1 Amazon multiple times

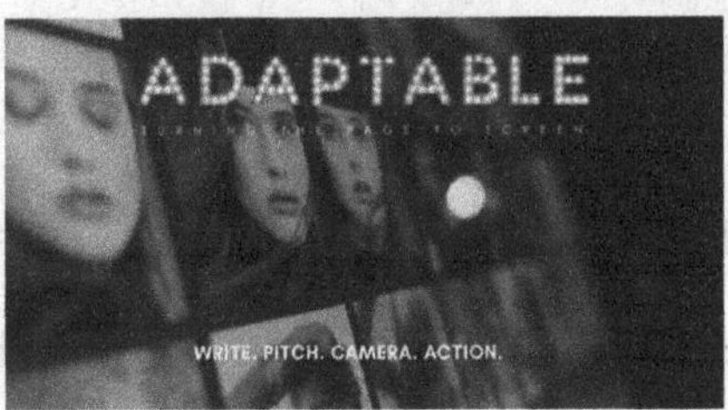

Longlisted for Adaptable - from book to the screen (2021)
Print Book eBook AudioBook
(Online Bookstores including Amazon)

Praise for The Colour of Broken

"I just finished reading The Colour of Broken. I read it in 2 sittings (only stopping the first because of the onset of a migraine). It was beautiful, and powerful. I lost myself in it, and forgot that I was reading, which only happens with the very best of stories. As a fellow MD sufferer I truly appreciated Fleur's depiction of the illness, but it was Yolande and her PTSD which hooked me from beginning to end. I, too, suffer from anxiety and panic disorders, and your portrayal of Yolande's brokenness and fear was masterful. Thank you for this extraordinary experience!"

"Beautiful story... on so many levels there's a connection there for everyone - a must read!"

"I am 3/4 the way thru it and love/hate it. Love the book and all it stands for, hate the book for all of the bad/sad memories it is bringing back when my Meniere's was really awful. Everyone who has or knows someone with Meniere's should read this book!"

"Yolande and her PTSD struggles were compelling and had me hooked from the start."

"I would single this book out as one of my favourite books, ever!"

"My hubby is reading the book now too! I am so pleased. He got to page 50 and remarked he felt like crying."

"I am in process of re-writing my will and looking into bequests and since buying your book have put them on my list. Not formalised yet but at least in my papers for people to find."

"I'm at the very end. I'm going to be sad when its over."

"I finished The Color of Broken. I was crying throughout. Very good."

"I loved my book, I've read it twice! It's now one of my most treasured possessions."

"I just finished The Colour of Broken, and I just want to say congratulations on writing one of the best books I have read in a long time. I'm an avid reader so I've read a lot of books , and I could not put it down. I laughed, cried, loved all of the characters. A wonderful storyline, characters which you fall in love with, truly an incredible book - congratulations, you are very very talented x"

"My mother never believed I had MD. She thought I was faking the symptoms. I gave her your book and she came back to me begging for forgiveness. Thank you from the bottom of my heart!"

"Love my book - will keep it for ever!"

"I've nearly finished it Julieann and it's BLOODY fabulous!! Long time since i enjoyed a book this much. My partner started reading before me the bugger so I had to wait till he had finished(his special way of being supportive). He said (as a non sufferer) that from his outside perspective, the portrayal of MD symptoms was fantastic."

"I loved your book, please do a follow up I'd love to know if Andi & Xander end up together too lol x"

"The story captures you from the first sentence and keeps you entertained with passion and hope for the future. It shares the very real struggles of life with Meniere's and the hope we have for a cure. A must read!"

"Could not put this book down."

"I was hooked from the beginning of this book. I'll be reading it a second time."

"I just finished reading ***The Colour of Broken***.
I read it in 2 sittings (only stopping the first because of the onset of a migraine).

It was beautiful, and powerful.

I lost myself in it, and forgot that I was reading,
which only happens with the very best of stories.
As a fellow MD sufferer I truly appreciated
Fleur's depiction of the illness, but it was Yolande
and her PTSD which hooked me from beginning to end.
I, too, suffer from anxiety and panic disorders, and your
portrayal of Yolande's brokenness and fear was masterful.

Thank you for this extraordinary experience!"

Meniere's Disease

Prosper Menière (18 June 1799 – 7 February 1862) was a French doctor who first identified a medical condition combining vertigo, hearing loss and tinnitus, which is now known as Menière's disease. It's a disorder of the inner ear.

Very briefly, Meniere's disease causes episodes of:

- *vertigo* (episodes of feeling like the world is spinning)
- *tinnitus* - ranging from mild to severe.
- *a feeling of fullness* or pressure in the ear,
- *sudden falls* without loss of consciousness (*drop attacks*) may be experienced by some people, or a sensation of being pushed sharply to the floor from behind.
- *low-frequency hearing loss,* which usually fluctuates in the beginning stages and becomes more permanent in later stages, so that little or no hearing remains.
- a common and important symptom of MD is hypersensitivity to sounds, also known as *hyperacusis.*

Attacks may be characterized by periods of remission and exacerbation. After a severe attack, most people find that they are extremely exhausted and must sleep for several hours. People with Meniere's disease may suffer from psychological distress, high anxiety and depression.

It is important to note that many people suffering from MD lead productive, near-normal lives; others face greater challenges in coping.
There is no cure for Meniere's disease - yet. But with advances in medicine and research, there is always hope for a cure.

Further Information and Support

- *Brain Foundation Australia*

http://brainfoundation.org.au/disorders/menieres-disease

- *Meniere's Society - UK*

www.menieres.org.uk

- *Vestibular Disorders Association - USA*

http://vestibular.org/menieres-disease

MEDICAL DISCLAIMER:
The information provided is designed to support, not replace, the relationship that exists between a patient and his/her existing health care professionals.

The spark of hope can never be extinguished ...

Follow Amelia Grace
Website: *www.julieannwallaceauthor.com*

*www.instagram.com/julieann_wallace_*

www.instagram.com/myshadow_menieres

myshadowmenieres.wordpress.com

All the Colours Above music playlist at *Spotify* created by Jules

Reviews ★★★★★

Reviews are like gold to authors. They can make a huge difference in the success of an author. If there are 50 reviews on Amazon, they list the book in newsletters and other promotions. Reviews are the easiest way to say thank you to an author - it can be as short as "I liked it!"
So, if you can, *please leave a review*. The more books I sell, the more money I can donate to Meniere's research to help find a cure.

Proudly supporting **Meniere's Research**
at the *Macquarie University, Australia,*
with a portion of sales donated to help find
a cure for Meniere's disease.

If you'd like to donate to help find a cure for Meniere's disease, go to:
https://secureau.imodules.com/s/1404/afc/event.aspx-?sid=1404&gid=1&pgid=1762&cid=3651

Printed in the USA
CPSIA information can be obtained
at www.ICGtesting.com
LVHW031446301023
762551LV00025B/1542